The Misadventures of Braxton Hicks

Volume 1

Three Ravens Publishing
Chickamauga, GA USA

Table of Contents

Who is Braxton Hicks? 7
When Vulcans Cry 13
Gimme Some Lovin' 33
Dryad's Dance 57
Send in the Clowns 61
Murphy Madness 85
Key Lime Succubi 113
Shock n' Awe 135
Love and Justice 155
The Velvet Hammer 199
Mooneyed Mandy 221
Dance with a Daemon in the Pale Moonlight 247

Who is Braxton Hicks?

I know, weird name for a character, isn't it? Well, there just happens to be a long, convoluted Trailer Park type story behind the character's name

Braxton and the universe I've created around him is really a tale of my author's journey. Out of all of the other short stories I've written since grade school, writing Braxton feels like coming home. And he should, since I based a lot about him on myself and my past. As they say, write what you know, and I know myself better than anyone else.

I think the major thing that makes writing Braxton so easy is that I don't have to think about what this character will do when I throw them into a situation. I just have to think about how I'd get out of the situation and roll with it from there. It's fun and doesn't feel like work, which helps the words flow even better. As writers, we all know how our writing suffers when we force words onto the page.

So, where did Braxton come from?

Well, once upon a time, a mommy and daddy really loved each other... Oh, wait. No. That's way too far back, and his parents... Let's just say Jerry Springer would be proud.

Actually, let's start back around 2004 when I was getting the boot from the Air Force on a medical discharge, and forced back into civilian life. During this time frame, I'd spent a good bit of time on light duty thanks to an injury I sustained while stationed at Kadena Air Base on Okinawa.

2004 was when the military ramped up downsizing, and those with a medical profile were among the first to go. Because I'd had several flare-ups of my back issue that year, I was on the chopping block, and well, life happened.

That downtime left me with loads of time to think, process, and world-build just to stay busy. I played with several different genres, primarily a fantasy series that I haven't gone back to, but I was also having a blast coming up with ideas for urban fantasy, and a mechanic/biker type of character just sounded fun. Then I started tossing in a bit of X-Files, Unsolved-Mystery-type ideas into it to see what would stick.

The sad thing is that over the years, I lost most of those notes since I'd been concentrating heavily on the fantasy universe, but the ideas still lingered in the back of my noggin, which became the foundation for Braxton.

From there, my writing took another hiatus. I jumped right into college, got my degrees, got divorced, got married, then landed a job in Chattanooga, and we started having babies. Any of the parents out there know exactly how much free time you have with wee ones around and working your ass off to make ends meet.

When I finally started to dig back into writing, I was all over the board. I jumped from science fiction to fantasy, horror, urban fantasy, and even some contemporary fiction just to get an idea of what I really wanted to write.

I struggled.

The only thing I knew for sure was what I'd seen in the books I had read up to that point. I could see form, patterns, and storytelling styles, but I was still missing something.

One of these random scenes I'd started working on just started to flow, and I was having fun. In that particular scene, Proto-Braxton was disposing of a barn full of genetically engineered bunnies because they were a plague about to be set free by this mad scientist granny. He had Granny tied up to her rocking chair on the porch while he took care of the problem. I slid the scene into my first-ever anthology invite, but in the end, it was cut. Though I did use it later as the opening to "Gimme Some Lovin'". That's about the time this Proto-Braxton character was working as a contractor for the US Government, doing the weird crap X-Files type jobs no one else wanted to deal with.

That fed into the character's passion for cruising across America on the back of his Iron Horse with nothing to tie him down, living life in the moment, and getting paid to do it.

Scenes like that one were just that, scenes. But they lead into developing the idea and really start world-building everything about his twisted little life.

Again, life happened, cancer, taking care of elderly family members, the babies were growing, etc., and writing went by the wayside once more.

My wife's oldest son, The Boy, who had stayed in Florida when we moved to Chickamauga, Georgia, landed himself in the ICU. Shortly after that, he moved back in with us and established himself here. A little time later, his Best Friend moved up, and The Boy started dating the Neighbor's Daughter.

Well, that's where we take a slight detour to Jerry Springer land.

It wasn't long before the Neighbor's Daughter was pregnant. Just before she was about to give birth, The Boy packed up and went north, where he married someone else and pretty much abandoned his best friend here with us.

Fast forward a little, and the baby is born, visitations and baby trade-offs are happening back and forth, then the Neighbor's Daughter and the Best Friend start dating. It wasn't long before they married and were having a child of their own.

Some time around 2015, I went with the neighbor's daughter on a baby exchange run to Kentucky. She drove and I jotted down notes, working on story bits as we waited for The Boy to show up. Then the Neighbor's Daughter flinched and started rubbing her swollen belly.

"Oh my God, these Braxton-Hicks contractions are going to kill me."

That was the moment when it clicked in my brainpan that Braxton Hicks could be a pretty cool character name, especially if his mother had named him that after one of the nurses mentioned it in the delivery room.

Yes, stupid Trailer Park humor!

But I still had no idea who this character was. All I had were a handful of scenes and slush pile ideas. A couple more years passed by before I learned about LibertyCon, held here in Chattanooga every summer.

I will preach all day long about the glory of LibertyCon, because it's what really kicked me off. If not for LibertyCon, I wouldn't be where I am now. It is so worth attending for any budding author. Now, where was I?

So, it was 2017, my first convention ever, and I learned so much, made connections, and found my *people*.

The biggest turning point of my writer's journey was meeting author and creative writing teacher, Charity Ayers, who was holding a writing workshop at that LibertyCon.

She talked for a little bit, then had everyone write for fifteen minutes. Nothing major, just a quick scene. The first character to come to mind was

Braxton, so I jotted down a scene with Braxton fighting his way out of a pack of demon spawn and cops responding to all of the gunfire.

When she stopped the clock, Charity had everyone interested in reading their scene to the class stand up and do so. The look on this woman's face after I read my little scene blew me away.

Now, we all understand what a "mom" answer is, or at least I hope you do. For those who don't know the term, it's when someone gives you hollow praise because they love you unconditionally or don't want to hurt your feelings. I despise "mom" answers. There is nothing constructive about them. You can't learn and grow if you don't know where you are failing. Being my own worst critic, I expect my stuff to suck. Unfortunately, I expect mom answers from everyone, including my wife, Meg.

But this woman, who I'd never met until I stepped foot into her workshop, had a reaction I never expected. It was one of those, *Oh my God, holy shit* type of looks.

That's when the switch flipped for me. I thought, maybe there is something to this. Maybe I can do this.

At that first LibertyCon, I also walked away with an invite to the Sha'Daa: Toys anthology by Moondream Press. I took that character and that scene and wrote it into "When Vulcans Cry" for the Sha'Daa: Toys anthology. It was my first invite, my first sell, and the cleaned-up/expanded scene from the workshop was worked in toward the end of the story.

I was over-the-moon excited and beside myself with joy. It was like, all right, cool, something's happening. I'm doing it. I *can* do it.

From there, Braxton grew. I continued writing him into shorts for my It Came From the Trailer Park series or any other anthology I could shoehorn him into. The more I wrote, the more he grew on me. It was so easy to put this character into a situation, share his love of riding, enjoying life for the moments, and kicking cryptid ass in the process.

At this point, Braxton has encountered all sorts of cryptids: aliens, demon-possessed toys, elementals, ghouls, zombies, and the list just keeps growing. I will say that there will be an encounter with vampires in the near future, just because I haven't played with them yet, and I have a really fun idea to toy with.

This collection is every Braxton Hicks short story I have produced by this point at the end of 2025. I was surprised when I started putting it together and discovered I had over 100,000 words in short stories for this character.

Luckily, that will change next year. I'm working on the first Braxton Hicks novel, and I feel like I'm truly finding my stride when it comes to putting down good words and writing a fun story.

For reference sake, all of these stories take place after the novel series which will kick off in 2026 and has let me expand on Braxton and his universe, which will hopefully translate into one hell of a novel for the series.

As an extra side note, while building this world that Braxton inhabits, I've come up with several spin-offs in the process. Granted, some are loosely tied in, but why world-build twice, right? Even my first novel, fLUX Runners, takes place 200 years in Braxton's future, where one of the main characters is Braxton's great-great-grandson or something like that. I never sat down to figure out exactly how many greats were in there, but he's wearing Braxton's threadbare gray Corduroy Kutte, which had been passed down through a family of bikers who loved to cruise and enjoy those little moments of life.

The stories in this collection have been placed sequentially as published, except for the last two, "Mooneyed Mandy" and "Dance with a Daemon in the Pale Moonlight", so that from start to finish you can see my progression in writing style and voice as I've grown in the craft while working with this character.

Also, nothing has been edited. Each story is as it was originally published, so hopefully the growth is apparent as you read through.

Now, with the last story, "Dance with the Daemon in the Pale Moonlight", I seriously think I found my groove for Braxton. It just felt right and flowed so well as I wrote the scenes.

I hope you enjoy this collection and look forward to the first Misadventures of Braxton Hicks novel. I'd love to hear what you think of the characters and world that I've fallen in love with while riding along with them on their adventures.

William   Joseph   Roberts

When Vulcans Cry

By: William Joseph Roberts

First published in Sha'daa: Toys – MoonDream Press May 2018

As I stated in the opening, this piece started with a scene written in Charity Ayres writing workshop at LibertyCon XXX 2017. That scene and the invite to the Sha'Daa: Toys anthology launched me and Braxton forward in a universe I love.

Braxton cruised along the empty country road. The early morning air was warm and smelled like summer dew. Thin wisps of moonlit fog hung lazily in the air. The open exhaust of Valerie, his twenty year old Vulcan 800 reverberated among the trees along the roadway. Ragged strings of his gray corduroy cut; what was once a jacket, now a roughly cut sleeveless vest, fluttered in the breeze. Braxton found his Zen. The rhythmic pounding hum of the bike chanted a mantra to his soul. The wind felt as if it wanted to lift him away. The numb bliss of nothingness beckoned to him. In that brief moment his soul transcended time, space, and deer.

"Shit! DEER!" Instinct possessed Braxton in that moment. He squeezed the clutch, stood on the rear brake lever and leaned the bike hard to the right as he turned the front wheel to the left. The bike skidded with a belched cacophony of rubber against pavement. The doe leapt away into the darkness just as Braxton braced himself for the impact. He downshifted then released the clutch with a slight roll of the throttle to right the bike and brought it to a stop.

"WOO! Shit! That was close!" Braxton shifted the bike into neutral and removed his helmet. "Dammit man, that'll wake you up for sure." He rubbed his face vigorously and shook off the tension. "Nearly back to the house and I almost get splattered by a deer. DAMN! You did good, Val," Braxton lovingly stroked the bike's fuel tank. "That's my dirty girl. You'll never let me down will you?"

Beyond the idle of the motorcycle, Braxton heard a yip from the darkness to his right. Then another followed by two or three, then a dozen or more. "Oh what the hell now," he turned the handlebars to the right and shined his headlight on a pack of coyotes. "Hell no, go on now GIT!" He rolled the throttle to the full extent. Valerie roared to life. Flames leapt from the downturned exhaust pipes onto the pavement in a blinding pyrotechnic display. The coyote pack exploded into motion and melded back into the darkness.

Blop blop blop …

"Are you fucking serious?" Braxton hit the starter button over and over but the engine refused to turn over. *Maybe I just flooded her.* "At least the sun is coming up," he muttered as he stared at the reddening sky. He pushed the bike to the side of the road then leaned back on the seat and propped his feet on the handlebars.

"He must rise early, the one who wants to have another's wealth or life. Seldom does a lying wolf get a ham or a sleeping man victory," warned an unseen voice. A chill ran down Braxton's spine at the sound of a tight lipped giggle that subsided with a deep nasally breath. He leapt to his feet.

"Well this just turned into a B-rate horror flick. Who's there? Show yourself."

"Should you sleep your day away, then mayhaps you sleep your life away as well? If that be the case my friend, I will wait for the crows to pick your bones to conduct my business." A chorus of caws and flapping wings filled the air. The odd voice blurted out a maniacal giggle, then suppressed it. "Be leery and tend to yourself before all others guardian," warned the strange voice.

Braxton focused his gaze in the direction of the voice. Perched on the upper branch of a nearby oak he spotted a tall, slender figure silhouetted against the morning sky. The dark apparition was oddly dressed for this time of year. He wore a full suit, long coat and a wide brimmed hat all in black. The figure grinned. One golden tooth shone bright in the shark like smile of his sunken face.

"I am Johnny, Johnny the salesman." He pulled a pocket watch from his vest, glanced at the time then returned the watch. "I trade, I barter, I wheel and deal. This for that, thing for thing, but all of importance and tied to the wheel."

Johnny leapt from the branch as the sky erupted with life. Hundreds of crows took to the air and began to circle as he floated the last few feet to the ground.

"What the fuck? How..."

"How is not important now that the Sha'Daa has begun."

"Bullshit, you just floated to the ground man. How is that not something important?"

"We all have our gifts," Johnny grinned.

"Well yours are a tad bit on the weird side, wouldn't you say?"

"Perhaps, perhaps not," Johnny produced a scroll from his jacket and briefly examined it as he walked toward Braxton. He then bent at the waist and stared at the underside of the bike. "A guardian bell for a true guardian," he sang.

"Gremlin bell man, not guardian bell. It knocks those pesky gremlins off the bike every time it rings."

"This bell is much more special than that. It has an ancient power to protect that few can comprehend. Another is in need of it before the night is over and I offer a trade."

"How about hell no man, I'm not about to trade you my bell."

"All things have a price my friend; the greater the need, the higher the price." Johnny flung open his long coat like a flasher in a nunnery. An assortment of strange objects dangled on the inside of his coat. "Name your price my friend."

Braxton scratched at his scruffy face in thought. "Tell ya what buddy. You show me a wallet that never goes empty then we might have a trade."

Johnny smiled wide, then reached into a pocket and produced an ordinary looking wallet on a chain. He tossed it to Braxton.

Braxton checked the wallet and pulled out five, twenty dollar bills. "Well hell man, if you're just giving it away I'll not argue." He tucked the bills into his pocket and tossed the wallet back to Johnny.

"You may wish to look again," he said as he returned the wallet to Braxton.

"Okay, sure, I'll play your game for another minute." Braxton opened the wallet and removed five more twenty dollar bills. "Oh what the hell man. Are you serious or shitting me?"

"Open it one last time," Johnny chortled.

Bewildered, Braxton dug inside the wallet once more, then froze. He stared at Johnny for a silent moment. "You aren't shitting me. You got a deal," he said with excited reluctance.

"A deal is a deal, a trade has been made," Johnny chortled with a snort. He waved his right hand and rolled his wrist. Out of thin air, Braxton's bell dangled between Johnny's thumb and forefinger. With another quick flourish of his hand, Johnny dissolved and soaked into the surface of the paved country road.

Bells chimed as Braxton opened the door of the Phantom Horse pub. The scent of fresh baked biscuits and bacon filled the air. A group of twenty somethings mingled around the pool tables and juke box in the side room. A few sang along with a classic rock tune. Two individuals danced apart from the rest of the group. A young man in what could qualify as rags and a graceful young woman. She was petite and covered head to toe in sweat streaked body paint.

Braxton pulled his attention away from the dancers. "Oy, James," he shouted toward the kitchen as he leaned against the bar. "I'll take my regular with a stout."

A middle aged man with a massive pot belly and baker's apron appeared from the kitchen door. "Brax, you ugly son of a bitch. Biscuits are almost done. Let me get back to the kitchen and I'll send Suzi out with your order. Good to see you again. You're looking good Brax." James smiled, then disappeared through the kitchen door. Braxton took a seat in a nearby booth and stretched out on the bench.

The door bells rang again and a familiar figure in black entered. Johnny flashed his toothy grin as he approached Braxton. "I must apologize for my outburst earlier," Johnny said as he slid into the booth across the table from Braxton. "My work has taken its toll on me as of late."

A waitress appeared with Braxton's order. "Here you go hun, can I get you anything else?

"No, that'll be it Suzi. Thank you."

The rumble of motorcycles rattled the windows of the pub. Braxton sat up to look out the large front windows and saw a dozen bikes roll into the parking lot. As the bikers turned and backed into the parking spots, Braxton caught sight of their colors. A grinning skull over a Confederate flag. "Damned Confederate Reaver ass holes," he mumbled to Johnny. "Just don't look at them and they might not cause us any trouble."

"James! Beers and house specials pronto," the lead biker shouted as he entered the pub. "Well would you look at what we got here. Ain't you just a pretty little thing darlin." The lead biker sucked on his teeth in a lusty smile as he admired the young woman in body paint.

Johnny turned in the booth and glanced at the biker for moment. His head tilted at a slightly odd angle. He scanned his scroll then stared at the biker.

"You got a problem preacher? There ain't no souls around here to be saving."

"Get him Hound," a massive biker urged as he sauntered up to the young girl near the juke box.

"A cross of silver, a cross of blood, the one to possess, a compulsion will come," Johnny fitfully chortled. "A deal to be made, a cross to trade," Johnny stood and moved toward the biker. A gaunt finger pointed to an iron cross pinned to Hound's leather vest.

Hound looked down at the pin on his chest then back to Johnny. "Hey buddy, you can fuck off. My great grandfather pried that from the corpse of a Nazi General he'd killed."

"Johnny, sit back down," Braxton urged as he shoveled down his breakfast.

"Listen to my counsel and you will fare well. It will help you much to heed my words. Pain of one to profit another, the Valkyries frown upon such things. The Sha'Daa will prove a man's worth, be he fodder for the crows?" Johnny flashed a grin at Hound.

"What the fuck? Did ya hear that Moose?"

"Is he speakin' in tongues or something," the massive biker at the jukebox replied.

Hound shoved Johnny. As if a choreographed move, Moose shoved the girl toward a rat faced biker and pinned Johnny's arms behind his back. Hound gut punched Johnny over and over again.

The room burst into motion. The group of hippies scattered and ran for the side door, followed by six of the road worn bikers.

"Shit!" Braxton leapt from the booth and shoulder charged into Hound. The pair collapsed to the ground. In one swift move Braxton kneed Hound in the groin and head butted the biker into a dazed stupor.

"Let go of me," the young girl screamed. Braxton jumped to his feet and sprinted toward the girl. He leapt into the air with his arm outstretched and hooked Rat Face around the neck. Braxton perched himself on the man's back and locked the choke hold in place.

Another biker whose name patch read Bubba, picked up a nearby chair and swung it at the Salesman. Johnny melded backwards through the man called Moose and rematerialized behind the massive biker. The chair impacted Moose across the jaw and he collapsed to the floor. Bubba pulled a spiked trench knife from his boot and lunged at Johnny. Johnny caught the man's wrist and snapped the joint backwards with a sick crack of bones. Bubba screamed and dropped to his knees.

"Be leery of yourself Braxton. These men be enforcers. They answer to the one who be the true master of none. The Piper plays and the sheep obey," Johnny sang.

"You gonna die preacher man!" Hound pulled a revolver from his waistband as he sat up and aimed it at Johnny.

Johnny opened his longcoat wide. Inky black tendrils of oily smoke expanded from the depths of his coat like a living vine. The tendrils sprouted new offshoots that pursued and engulfed each of the bikers.

Braxton gaped as the group of bikers fell unconscious. He stared in shocked disbelief, then walked back to his table and sat down. Unnerved, he took a quiet sip of his now warm stout and grimaced.

"Are they dead?"

"Only the one," Johnny restrained a giggle with a giddy smile. "He was taken by the hand of his associate, not by I, nor you."

The young painted woman appeared from behind Johnny. Visibly shaken, she stepped cautiously around the salesman and approached Braxton. "You came to the aid of a stranger when you didn't have to. I invite you to our circle tonight and offer you a gift of the heart."

"No worries. It's all good Miss." Braxton sipped at his beer.

"My name is Laura. The memories that this gift represents are precious and dear to me," she continued. "It was a gift from a dear friend who helped me when no others would. I was stranded in Chicago and by chance met Willy in Oz Park a few days after being abandoned. He offered me a safe place and a job if I wanted it. So for six months I worked at his toy store, Whirligigs. When it was time to move on, he gave me this to remember our time together." She slid a thin metal armlet off of her paint streaked arm and lightly tossed it into the air above her palm. It exploded and formed a torus of thin metal strips. "I now pass it and all the warm kindness that it embodies to you." She collapsed it back into an armlet and gently slid the ring onto Braxton's forearm.

Laura leaned forward over Braxton and placed her forehead to his for a brief moment. "Bless you brother."

"The name is Braxton. Thank you."

"Bless you, brother Braxton." Laura smiled. "We will be celebrating the summer solstice at Four Quarters Farm this evening. Please join us to call in the ancestors." A horn honked from the parking lot. She turned and ran out the door.

The sound of metal on metal drew Braxton's attention. "What the hell now," he growled. Braxton ran out the door, to find Valerie lying on top of a line of fallen bikes. The door bells chimed as Johnny exited the pub.

"What the hell Val, you decide to take a nap all of a sudden or some shit?" Braxton turned to Johnny. "Ya see what you caused? I want my bell back."

"A deal is a deal, a trade has been made," Johnny replied in a plain tone.

"Then what's the cost? You can have the wallet back."

"The bell is intended for use by another."

"If I've learned anything, it's that everything has a price tag. I thought it was a good deal at the time. A chance to change my life a little. You see how my luck has gone to shit? I need my bell back. I should have never traded it in the first place. There has to be something worth trading," Braxton begged.

Johnny pulled out the scroll and glanced over it, then he looked back toward the building.

"Oh what the hell? I can't ride without my bell and you're worried about a pin?"

"You have nothing else that interests me, though I do need that cross." Johnny looked back to the building. "He must willingly offer it. I cannot merely take it."

Braxton stood his bike back up and set the kickstand. "Oh fucking hell man!" He stomped off inside the pub and quickly returned. He handed Johnny the iron cross with a forceful clasp of the Salesman's hand. "Possession is nine tenths of the law. Now how about my bell?"

"You are the persistent interesting sort aren't you my friend? That has sweetened the pot to be sure." Johnny forced a deep breath to restrain another fit of laughter.

"I tell you what," Braxton started. He stared at the ground in contemplation for a few moments then looked back to Johnny. "I don't have anything worth an ounce of what you traded me to start with. But any real man's word is as good as gold, and I live by my word. If I say I'll do something, then by fucking God I'll do it come hell or high water. I don't know what kind of business you're really in, but I've learned to not ask too many questions in my line of work. I do what needs done and that's that. A contract is a contract, an oath an oath.

Johnny stared at Braxton with a curious grin. "We are somewhat similar in that manner Mister Hicks."

Braxton unsheathed his belt knife and sliced his palm then held out his hand to shake. "I give you my word stranger. If you call, I'll answer. I can find nearly anything if I dig deep enough. If I can't then I know folks that can. Day or night, my services are yours." Braxton gave Johnny the thousand yard stare. "Karma is a bitch and right now she's dry humping the hell out of me. With this shit ass luck I can't ride another mile without my bell."

Johnny doubled over into another spasmodic fit of laughter. He fought to hold it back. His jaw clenched and his cheeks puffed as he regained control of himself. Johnny marked the scroll, then tucked both scroll and cross into his coat.

"I have another matter that I must attend to immediately or all will be for naught. This is an absolute rarity that has never before happened, but the Sha'Daa is fully upon us. Your offer is both enticing and absurd, but nonetheless may be critical to our success. Payment in full for services to be rendered in the near, present and future time as I see fit on your promise of blood oath. The aforementioned payment; the bell, will be available for my use in the minutes prior to its intended utilization and returned afterwards in the event that the Sha'Daa has been overcome."

Braxton stared at Johnny in dismayed confusion. His bloody hand hung slack by his side. "Sha'Daa? What the hell is that? You keep saying it like I'm supposed to know what it means."

"Tonight the veil between worlds will be at its weakest. Portals will begin to open and many lives lost. Tonight is the Sha'Daa. Armageddon. By midnight tonight it will literally be Hell on earth," Johnny quirked. "I have need of your services while I…" Johnny forced a deep breath, "while I attend to a personal matter." Johnny held out his right hand to shake. The bell dangled from his left.

"Ooookay. You are certified bat shit crazy aren't you? But after seeing what you can do there's got to be some kinda truth to it. I've worked for the government and seen all kinds of weird shit plenty of times in the past. This can't be any worse." Braxton enthusiastically grasped Johnny's hand and shook. "Son of a…" he leapt away from Johnny. Smoke lingered around the cauterized wound.

"A contract is a contract and you agreed by blood." Johnny tossed the bell to Braxton. "The armlet that you now wear, placed there by a maiden's hand. Another has need of it and you of another. A trade for a trade, a tit for tat." The salesman chortled then produced a small leather pouch from his long coat.

"Sure boss man," Braxton slid the armlet off and tossed it at Johnny. It spun and expanded to form a whirling torus as it soared through the air. Johnny caught and examined the torus with childlike wonderment.

"Yes yes, this will do nicely. So we have a deal?"

"Sure man," Braxton said in a firm, but unsure tone.

"A sale! A trade! A deal is done!" Johnny collapsed the torus, then slid it out of sight within the sleeve of his coat. Johnny opened the small leather pouch and poured six dark jack-like objects into his hand. Braxton watched as Johnny sniffed at the objects. He prodded each of them with tip of his tongue. "Yes this is exactly what you need my friend," he gleefully sang. He returned the jacks to the pouch and tossed it to Braxton.

"You must seek out the maiden that gave you this treasure. In her possession is an enameled bronze censer that once hung in the temple of Athena. Your first assignment is to retrieve the censer."

"Censer? What the hell is that?"

"It is a decorated bronze pot that hangs from a chain."

"Ok gotcha, but how do I get it to you?"

"I won't be far, you need only call….hee hee… Out...tsss ha….. My name." Johnny took a deep breath, then doubled over in a fit of laughter. He straightened to his full height with a conniving grin and glowered at Braxton. "To the south and to the west they journeyed during the night. The Piper called and the children followed." Johnny chortled and vanished as a shadow fades in the morning light.

"Oh what the hell? The devil did come down to Georgia and I just sold him my soul."

Braxton spotted the sign for the Four Quarters Farm. He turned off the main road onto hard packed clay. He eased the throttle and crept along the rough dirt road. The road meandered through the thick Georgia forest. A few hundred yards from the highway the road opened up to a small clearing. At the far end of the clearing stood what looked like an old church.

Why do I get a bad feeling about this? Random church in the middle of nothing. Naw, can't be anything wrong with that set up. Just your average every day snake handlers or something way out in the woods. Oh sweet, bikes…

Four highly polished motorcycles came into view as Braxton neared the building.

A little heavy on the chrome and polish but…wait, those look like…

"You son of a bitch! My brother is dead because of you and that preacher friend of yours!"

Braxton spotted Hound on the small side porch that jutted out from the far side of the building.

"Aw hell, fucking Reavers!" Braxton squeezed the front brake handle and rolled the throttle hard as he turned the bike on the spot then released the brake. He exploded from a massive cloud of dust and raced down the dirt road as fast as he could.

"Shit shit shit. There's the pavement Val! Bite hard and let's get out of here," Braxton shouted as he skidded in a hard lean on the blacktop. He could hear the heavy rumble of a large v-twin close behind him.

"You're a dead man," Hound shouted and slid into formation to Braxton's right. Another large fully dressed bike rolled up along his left.

Braxton downshifted and throttled hard. His eight hundred cubic centimeters were no match for the two large bore motorcycles. Hound pulled a pistol from his waist band and pointed it at Braxton.

"Pull it over and I'll make it quick." Hound chuckled as he nodded to the other biker.

Braxton looked to his left just as the other biker swung a long weighted whip at him. The opposite end of the whip was attached to the bike's right hand grip. In that instant instinct overtook him; Braxton snatched the end of the whip out of the air with his left hand and grabbed his handlebar grip. He cut the throttle and sparks flew from his foot peg as he leaned hard right, throttled hard and swung in behind and to the right of Hound. The other biker and bike were unceremoniously yanked off balance.

"Fuck you asshole," Braxton shouted as he straightened the bike and released the whip. He tapped the brake, leaned hard left and rolled the throttle hard. The two large motorcycles collided with a loud sheet metal crunch. The second bike flipped and threw the biker ahead of the pack. The second biker landed flat on his back on the pavement. Braxton glanced to his right. He watched as Hound became the soft gooey center of a Harley crunch. The mangled mess tumbled and sparked on the roadway as it skidded past two parked police cars.

"Fucking hell, can my day get any worse?" He dropped a gear and rolled full throttle.

"It won't be too much longer before the sun fully sets. Are you sure that you want to go wandering over there in the dark after what happened with the Reavers?"

"No choice in the matter Doll," Braxton replied as he stretched. "I got a job to do. Though I do appreciate you letting me lay low till dark. I know it's been awhile since I came around. It's just lucky for me that your place is just over the ridge from Four Quarters Farm." He smiled with a cheesy wide mouthed grin.

"Those guys are egotistical psychopaths," Amy said. "Why don't you stay here and wait till daybreak? I'm sure we can find something to keep ourselves busy."

Damn fine sight, Braxton thought to himself. Amy was a cute little redhead with big doe eyes and braided pigtails. "As tempting as that is, I can't. I have to find the girl and the package before midnight," Braxton replied. He stretched again and shifted on the couch.

"Why? Is she going to turn into a pumpkin," she snickered.

"No. Nothing like that. Or at least I don't think so. Trust me. If what Johnny said has an ounce of truth to it, we're all screwed if I can't pull this off."

"What if the Reavers catch you snooping around?"

"Don't know. Hell I'm just winging it. Just gotta hope that my luck gets better before the night is over."

Amy sat on the edge of the couch and hugged Braxton close. "Don't do anything stupid. This evening has been the best I've had since Dad died. I haven't had much time for anything but running the farm. It isn't much, but it's all that I have left of him. But it can get lonely after a while."

"No worries. I don't plan on getting myself killed…" Braxton sat up with a jerk at the sound of something outside.

"That sounded like it came from my Dad's shop. Think it could be a thief," she asked.

"Probably just a critter, you stay here and I'll go check it out. Time for me to get off this couch anyways.," He kissed her temple then stood.

"Wait," Amy ran into the bedroom and returned with a shotgun in one hand and a box of ammo in the other. "Here, it's my Dad's old gun. It's already loaded."

"Alright. If it'll make you feel better." He took the shotgun from her and admired the carved walnut stock. "Nice looking piece. Don't worry. I'll take good care of it." Braxton put a handful of shells into his vest pocket and headed for the shop.

A loud *pop, pop, groan* came from the rusted hinges of the shop door. Braxton reached in and fumbled for a light switch. With a loud *click*, the hum of electrical current flowed through the overhead shop lights with a warm orange glow.

"Come out with your paws up and no one gets hurt." He looked around in the dim light. A thick layer of dust covered old car parts, tools and assorted other mechanical bits. *She wasn't lying. It doesn't look like anyone has been in here for years. I don't see anything. Time to get my lazy ass to work.* He turned to leave and felt an odd vibration against his side. His lower vest pocket began to heat up. "What the hell?"

Braxton started to reach into his pocket when something launched him into a set of shelves. The shotgun flew from his hand as the shelving and all of its contents toppled over him. Braxton blinked to clear away the fog of unconsciousness.

"That's going to hurt in the morning." He blinked again. An oily black figure emerged from the shadows on the other side of the shop. It took on the shape of a man. It was almost as if it absorbed all of the light around it.

"Holy fucking hell! I did sell my soul to the devil and now he's come to collect!" Braxton searched around him for anything that could become a weapon. His hand grasped something long, cold, and, metallic. "My debt hasn't been paid yet salesman," he shouted. Spittle flew from his mouth. He charged the figure and swung with all of his might. The camshaft connected with the side of the thing's head. The creature clutched both of Braxton's wrists; its mouth agape with what looked like a scream, but there was no sound. A high pitched siren shrieked inside of Braxton's head.

"Get out of my head! **ARRRRRRR**," Braxton screamed, then slammed his forehead into the thing's face. He tore his wrists away from the creature and swung again. Bits of inky black ooze splashed to the floor with each strike of the camshaft. Over and over again he struck until it fell to the floor. He straddled the thing and struck until what might have once been a head, rolled away from the body of the thing. "AHHHHHHHHH!" His lungs gasped for air as he paced. He glared at the inky black mass.

What in the hell is that thing? Did I really sell my soul?

"I didn't send that creature to collect your soul, Braxton."

Braxton spun around to see Johnny leaned against the doorframe of the shop. "What in the hell was that thing?"

"That is merely one of millions of creatures that are about to engulf the Earth. That is what we are trying to stop. Time is ticking away and the gates have begun to open."

"Feeling a bit better I take it," Braxton asked.

"Yes, indeed."

Braxton took a deep breath. "I can't say that I've ever seen anything stranger or worse, but it is what it is. I made a deal, and I keep my word."

"Retrieve the censer while I deliver the bell as we contracted," Johnny rolled his wrist and the bell once again dangled between his thumb and forefinger.

"Will do Boss man, I'm on it."

Johnny faded away as if a shadow himself. Braxton dropped the camshaft and picked up the shotgun. ***BOOM! BOOM!*** Two rounds ripped through the thing. Braxton turned and walked out of the door.

Three steps outside of the shop and twilight ignited into the blinding surface of the sun.

"Drop the gun and put your hands above your head!" A metallic male voice shouted. "Hey, isn't that the guy that wrecked those bikers earlier," another voice insisted inadvertently over the loudspeaker.

"I think you're right Grady," the first voice said amidst the sound of shuffled papers. "That sure as hell looks like him. What's the name on there?"

"Braxton Hicks," the second voice replied.

"Braxton Hicks, you are under arrest."

"What in the world is going on out here," Amy shouted as she ran out onto the porch.

"Back inside!" Braxton sprinted for the porch and pulled Amy inside with him.

"What the hell happened out there?"

"It's hard to explain. Just trust me. You don't want to go out there." The front windows of the small farmhouse exploded with white light. "These guys need to go away. Too many people are counting on me now."

"Braxton Hicks; drop the gun and let the girl go," the voice echoed over the loudspeaker.

"Run out the back through the field to the county road and just go," Amy pleaded.

He stared into her glistening eyes. "I can't Doll; a job is a job. I'm sorry that you got wrapped up in all of this." Amy nuzzled into the hollow of his chest as he pulled her close. The faint smell of her vanilla perfume mingled with sweat tingled in his nose. He kissed her slowly on the forehead then turned her face upward. He leaned down and kissed her tenderly on the lips. "I'm sorry," he whispered then took a step back and struck her in the head with the butt of the shotgun. "It'll hurt in the morning, but at least you'll be alive." He pumped the shotgun, reloaded and opened the front door of the small farmhouse.

"Lay down your…"

BOOM!

The shotgun slug plunged through the cruiser door and the deputy that hid behind it. Blood splattered the interior of the cruiser.

"Oh my God! Grady," the Sheriff screamed.

BOOM!

Another slug demolished the cruiser's roof lights.

The sheriff dove into the car and pulled the deputy in. "Grady! Talk to me! Grady!" The police cruiser plowed through the yard, leapt the roadside ditch and sped away down the dark country road.

"It can't get much worse at this point." Braxton sighed as he reloaded then set off at a jog. He turned the corner of the house and skidded to a stop. Tiny red eyes glared at him from a moon-lit gator-like face of another beast. It grunted and sniffed at the air.

"Well hell, you're just big and ugly, aren't you?"

A thunderous growl rumbled from the thing's throat as it charged. It barreled into Braxton's motorcycle and became entangled. It roared and pounced on the downed machine. Claws and teeth alike ripped through leather and steel.

"Valerie! No!" Braxton ran toward the creature. The creature crouched on the bike like a wolf defending a kill. It roared again. Braxton heaved as the stench of week old sun baked fish engulfed him. "Die you son of a bitch." Point blank he leveled the shotgun at the thing's face.

BOOM! It fell on top of the bike with a solid thud.

BOOM! BOOM! BOOM! BOOM! BOOM! *Click.* A loud ear piercing squeal came from beneath the creature as air escaped a tire. Braxton sniffed at the heavy scent of gasoline.

"Shit, see what you made me do!" Braxton smashed the butt of the gun into the thing. "I'll do what I can later Val. I've got more important things to tend to at the moment." He sprinted off into the moonlit night.

From his hillside perch Braxton could see the full length of the valley. Groups of people mingled about the numerous bonfires below. Some danced, some sang, while others laughed or made love.

"Damn that looks like a good time," Braxton mumbled to himself.

Other shit to do, time for that later.

At the far end of the valley, dozens of torches illuminated the entrance to a cave. Two men in what looked like loincloths guarded the entrance. A man in black robes with a large curved ram's horn exited the cavern.

BRUUUUUEEEEE! The horn reverberated through the valley below. All activity came to a momentary halt. Individuals hugged one another, some laughed, others cried. A portion of the gathering made their way to the cave entrance. Braxton waited and watched. The celebration continued below as the chosen group entered the cave.

A flash of light caught his attention. Braxton's eyes locked onto a single dancer. Laura danced around a large bonfire in all of her painted nude glory. The intricate body paint that covered her petite frame enhanced her well defined curves. Like a master martial artist she spun and twirled around the fire as she swung a pair of firepots in wide arcs. Her cat-like grace entangled within the swirl of flame mesmerized Braxton. He shook his head and rubbed his face. "Time enough to daydream after this is over with." He set off for the valley below at a quick but quiet pace.

"Laura. Pssst. Hey Laura." She turned with a start. She scanned the darkness for the voice. Braxton took a step into the firelight from behind one of the many tents.

"Brother Braxton!" She ran over and gave him a tight hug. "Oh no, your vest. I've gotten paint all over it. Let me fix it. Hold this." She handed off the fire pots to Braxton and sprinted over to a stack of bags near the fire.

"Well shit, that was easy. Now where the hell is Johnny?"

"Right where I am supposed to be." Johnny replied from the shadows as he edged into the light.

"How the hell do you do that? One day you'll have to teach me that trick." Braxton held out the firepots in Johnny's direction. "As promised boss man."

"Thank you," he replied and tucked the censer into his coat.

"What's next boss?"

"A delivery," Johnny grinned. "You already possess the key to close off the gate deep within that cavern. You'll know what to do when you get there," Johnny reassured as he melded back into the shadows.

Laura returned with a wet towel and began to wipe down Braxton's cut.

"No, wait. It's all good; you just gave me an idea," he exclaimed as he took the leather pouch from his vest and put it into his pants pocket. He removed his vest and shirt and laid them to the ground with the shotgun. "I need you," he said as he pulled Laura close and kissed her deeply. Braxton double clutched her butt cheeks and lifted her to him. She wrapped her legs around his waist as he kissed and bit her neck.

"Ohhhhh God," she leaned back and moaned as she began to grind herself into him.

Braxton lowered her back to the ground with a gentle kiss.

"Wait, what," she asked, confused.

"Keep that thought for later and get yourself out of here. There's a house on the other side of that hill," he pointed behind him with his thumb. "Go there and wait for me. You'll see what's left of my bike out back. There's a girl there named Amy. She may still be unconscious. Stay there with her till I get back. No time to explain, just do it."

"Okay," she whimpered before Braxton picked up the shotgun and sprinted through the darkness for the cavern.

Dark silence greeted Braxton at the cave entrance.

Well that's not suspicious at all. No guards, no priest, no nothing. This seems too easy.

"Now or never I guess," he mumbled to himself as he stepped toward the opening. Braxton followed the line of torches that flickered in the damp corridors of the old mine. Broken, rusted and otherwise discarded equipment littered the floor of the mine.

I've gotta be halfway to China by now.

The torches branched away from the main tunnel and sloped upward toward a narrow passage. The rhythm of a low, guttural chant echoed from the confined space. Careful of his step, Braxton made the short climb up the slimy slope to a small landing. The passage turned sharply then opened into a large chamber.

He tiptoed to the edge of the opening. Torches mounted high on the rough cut walls dimly lit the large chamber. At the far end of the room two large stone doors stood in drastic contrast to the darker surrounding stone. Their surfaces polished smooth. A small balding man in black robes knelt before the doors. His head tilted back and arms outstretched, he chanted.

A hum resonated within the chamber in rhythm to the chant. Dust fell from the edges of the doors as they shuddered.

Braxton gasped. "That can't be a good sign." An odd reflection from the floor caught his attention. He crouched low and crept slowly into the chamber. Braxton groped about in the dim darkness.

What the hell?

A wet sticky mass blocked his path. He felt along its length and locked fingers with an unknown hand.

Did this bastard kill all of those kids that came in here earlier?

The man's chant grew louder, more forceful. The hum of the doors grew louder in time with the priest. Braxton felt the heat and vibration in his pocket again.

What the hell?

He reached into his pocket and pulled out the leather pouch of jacks. It droned along with the sound that resonated from the doors. The heavy grinding of stone on stone drew his attention.

The chant grew louder, its rhythm faster. Dark forms writhed and slithered from the opening as it widened.

"Oh fuck me. This is gonna hurt for sure." Braxton took aim with the shotgun and stepped forward.

BOOM! Black ooze splattered from one of the man like forms.

BOOM! The head of another exploded.

BOOM! The slug severed a thick tentacle that extended from the opening and left a crater in the face of a door.

BOOM! A gator headed thing slumped to the floor.

BOOM! Two more of the inky shadow creatures collapsed.

BOOM! The slug ricocheted off of the far wall and whizzed by Braxton's ear.

BOOM! Another shadow thing exploded with a shower of inky black ooze.

Click.

"Your blood will complete the opening. Bring him to me," the priest shouted.

"Oh shit." Braxton fumbled in his vest pocket for more ammo.

A pair of the shadow creatures charged at Braxton. He took the shotgun by the barrel and wielded it like a club. The first shadow creature to reach Braxton summersaulted from the impact of the gun stock.

Braxton dropped the gun and pouch as he clutched his head. His brain erupted in pain from the second shadow creature's unheard scream.

"Shut the hell up," he shouted as he drew his belt knife and heaved it at the shadow creature. The blade of the knife disappeared into the thing's head.

Sudden waves of warm pain washed over Braxton. He shook his head and cleared the fog. The large scaled snout of a gator thing pressed down on his left shoulder. He collapsed to his knees under the weight of the thing as it bit deep into his flesh. It shook him like a rag doll and flung him to the ground.

Braxton could feel the sticky cold of the mine floor seep into him. A soothing silence engulfed him. It held him close in this cold womb of the earth.

A distant reverberating hum broke into the dark silence.

"Will someone please shut that off," he mumbled as he rolled over onto his back and opened his eyes.

"Dammit man, not a dream." Braxton forced himself upright. He fumbled for the small leather pouch and poured the jacks into his hand. The smell of burnt flesh filled the air. The odd little objects glowed red hot and scorched his palm. Instinct screamed at him.

Throw them!

He slung the jacks toward the doorway as the gator thing approached. The scattered red specks formed a grid-like pattern as they soared through the air. They doubled and then tripled in size. Their points elongated and connected to one another. Sparks flew from the white hot points as they welded themselves together. The jacks formed what looked like a large iron castle gate that collected and impaled priest and beast alike. It slammed into the stone doors with a solid metal *twunk*. Tentacles and other appendages projected from between the dark iron slats like a festive Thanks-Hallo-Mas display.

"Don't let the door hit you in the ass on the way out," Braxton said with a chuckle and a wince of pain. "Ungh," he poked at his left shoulder. Blood seeped from the deep puncture wounds of the gator thing's teeth.

Braxton slumped to the cold sticky ground. He smacked his dry lips together. "You owe me a beer Salesm…"

Gimme Some Lovin'

By: William Joseph Roberts

First published in It Came From the Trailer Park: Volume 1 – Three Ravens Publishing, October 2021

I struggled to come up with an idea to kick off this anthology series, wanting to hit it just right. Braxton was already my character of choice, but what he was going to be dealing with was the problem. While on a fishing trip with my dad and brothers, we stopped at the marina to pick up our boat rental and the idea hit like a ton of bricks. Several of the characters in this story I met on that trip, helping to fuel the chaos by ramping up their personalities to 11 and letting Braxton tell me what was going to happen next.

"Oh, no you don't! Get your little ass back here. You aren't squirming away that easily. Hey now! No biting!"

My earpiece crackled to life and Mandy's voice came through crystal clear, "Everything OK, Brax?"

"Yeah. These little bastards are biters, especially the red ones."

Mandy let out a muffled giggle. "Redheads always were your downfall."

"Oh, ha, ha, ha," I laughed. Red hair was probably the only thing my business partner didn't have going for her. God she was beautiful. Part African American, part Korean, five two with this big pair of golden almond shaped eyes.

"Just hurry up and be careful," she said with a tone of caring annoyance. "The sooner you get the crazy lady dropped off with the feds, the sooner we can get paid, and you can get back home."

"Will do, Mandy," I mumbled before returning to the task at hand. I held the large reddish-gray rabbit by the ears against the blood splattered wall of the weather aged barn. "Hold still for one more second and I promise it'll be over with quick."

The machete cut through easily in one swing and embedded into the blood-soaked wooden wall. I picked up the rabbit's thrashing carcass and tossed both it and the severed head onto the pile just inside the barn doors.

"You, sick sadistic son of a bitch!" the old woman shouted. "Those were my babies! You killed them! Murderer! Murderer!"

I glanced back over my shoulder at the front porch of the rustic farmhouse. "You call me sadistic? You seriously think that I'm sadistic?! You were going to release your mutant Veloci-bunnies of doom to destroy the entire Midwest! People like you are the sadistic sickos of the world," I shouted as I jabbed a bloody finger at her. "People like you cause regular folks to suffer!"

That's when I noticed my blood caked arm. The thick layer of dried blood nearly hid the dragon tattoo on my right forearm. The thought of what I had just done, job or not turned my stomach. I struggled to gulp down a breath then I swallowed hard and forced my lunch back down.

"No one would take my organic soy sprout research seriously! They wouldn't have had a choice after my babies ate their way across the country!"

"Brax," Mandy shouted through his earpiece, "Just gag the crazy lady and let's go!"

"I hear ya, Mandy," I said and let out a long sigh as I looked at the ground around me. Scooping the remainder of rabbit parts into a bucket I walked into the barn and stared with dismay at the heap of bodies.

"Sometimes I really hate my job."

I tossed the contents of the bucket onto the pile then doused it with two large cans of gasoline. "I'm sorry about this, fuzzy buddies." The thought of my cats in a similar situation left a lump in my throat. I poured a trail of gasoline out of the barn and shut the doors behind me.

"You'll burn in hell for this," the woman shrieked.

"Shut UP!" I exploded, glaring at the woman. My ears rang from the rage that began to build deep inside as I stomped toward the farmhouse. A deep growl escaped from between my clenched teeth. "Because YOU created them, I was called! Because of YOU, the government men called me! Because of your insane plan I was sent here! Because of you, they had to die!"

"Noooo," she moaned as I stepped onto the porch. "No, no, no!"

"Because of you, my hands are covered in innocent blood!" I leaned down and forcefully grasped the arms of the wooden rocking chair. Spittle flew from between my clenched teeth as I fought to control the rage building in me. I brought myself nose to nose with the terrified woman.

The arms of the rocking chair creaked and groaned under the strain of my grip.

"*You* created them, and I had to destroy them!"

The woman suddenly went limp and slumped in the chair, her head falling to her chest.

I closed my eyes and straightened, taking slow, deep breaths.

"One....two....three....four....." I mouthed quietly then stared at the unconscious woman for a long moment, questioning why I was even here.

"I really need a vacation."

A vacation was exactly what I needed. Even Mandy thought I could use a break after the last couple of weird jobs I'd taken on. Since I was in the neighborhood of Watts Bar Lake, I decided to take up an offer from my buddy, Leo Daniels. He always said to drop in anytime if I wanted to do some fishing and drinking. More drinking than fishing I'm willing to bet, but that still counts, doesn't it?

I'd met Leo shortly after being stationed at Seymour Johnson Air Force Base. He had originally been a Crew Dawg on the F-4 Phantoms and one of the best damned mechanics on the airframe from what I'd been told. Once the Air Force had begun phasing out the F-4's in favor of the sleek new F-15 Eagles, Leo had been transferred over and landed in the 335th fighter squadron. I'd gotten to know him on swing shift while turning wrenches till the wee hours of the morning. He retired shortly after I'd arrived on base, but we stayed in contact over the years. I had stopped in once or twice before, but it had been a few years since my last visit.

The summer evening was more than comfortable when I rolled into the Bayside Marina and Resort RV Park. Fireflies flashed and danced about as the sweet smell of barbeque lazily hung in the air. The place was just like I remembered it. Dirty, run down, and overly decorated with pink flamingos.

I rolled up and parked outside one of the newest looking RV's in the park. A twenty-eight foot long dark brown and grey number with several slide out sections. Careful not to rev Valerie, my Kawasaki Vulcan 800, I shut off the engine and dismounted. No sooner had I knocked on the door of the RV than a low growl came from inside. RV rocked side to side with heavy footed steps as someone made their way from one end to the other. After a few long moments of fiddling with the locks the door flung open, and a massive red-faced beast emerged. Her look of anger quickly shifted to a glowing smile. She leaned against the door frame and shifted as to show off some naked thigh from beneath her pizza sauce-stained nightgown.

"Hey big boy, looking for some fun?"

"No, I was looking for Leo Daniels."

The anger returned to her overly plump cherubic face. "Leo don't live here no more. He's down at the docks. Slip sixteen in Henry Danielson's old houseboat," she said with a snarl. The camper shifted as she leaned out of the door pointing a chubby finger in my direction. "And if Bobby is down there with him, you tell him he still owes me a bottle of Mad Dog. An if he don't bring it like he promised, you tell him me and him's gonna have words the next time I see him."

I started to back away slowly, half afraid that she was about to pounce on me from her doorway perch.

After moving Valerie to the marina parking area, I made my way to the docks. On one side was the main marina area, complete with bar, grill, bait, tackle, gas and fishing licenses. Someone was setting up to play live music at the far end of the dock near to where a guy was mixing drinks in a small dockside tiki hut. What looked like a small river barge sat half beached and sunken on the marina's boat ramp. I continued along the shoreline another fifty feet to the gangplank that led to the marina's docking slips. The metal awning structure that covered the docking area creaked and groaned with my every step. Several of the support posts looked as if they had collapsed and broken multiple times in the past before being repaired in the cheapest manner possible without the use of duct tape. The underside of the dock looked like a veritable forest. Weeds and small trees had taken root in every available crack and cranny possible across the structure.

I found slip sixteen at the far end of the dock, occupied by a houseboat that looked like a left over from the fifties, miraculously still afloat. I picked up a piece of metal tubing I'd found lying on the walkway and tapped at the awning frame. "Leo! Hey Leo, you in there?"

Mumbled curses accompanied the sound of someone stumbling and fumbling with the door. The cabin door at the front of the boat opened and Leo popped his head out of the half-opened door.

"Who the hell is beating…"

I dropped the tubing and smiled wide. "Permission to come aboard?"

Leo rubbed his eyes and blinked to clear his vision and just stared at me for a long moment. "Well, I'll be damned, you dirty son of a bitch. What the hell brings you out to slum with the likes of me?" He motioned for me to come aboard, then stepped back into the cabin and returned with a pair of beers in hand. He twisted off the top of one, flicked the bottle cap into the water with a snap of his fingers, then offered the bottle to me.

"My pleasure." I took the beer and took a long swig. After a long day on the road, the ice-cold barley goodness was soothing to my parched throat.

Leo grabbed a cooler from inside then led the way to the sun deck of the houseboat. He promptly twisted off the top of his beer and snapped the cap off the side. Kicking off his flip flops Leo propped his feet up onto the side rail, relaxing back into one of the dry rotted deck chairs.

I gently sat back in one of the other chairs and stretched. "So, what's with your lady friend up on the hill? You lose the camper in a divorce or something? You must have had your hands full with her cause she sure is a whole lotta woman."

Leo choked on the swig of amber goodness, shooting a golden stream out of both nostrils. "Who? Deloris? Oh, good lord no! We just traded up. Between the boat being on the water and the waterbed on board it was enough to make her seasick. Otherwise, she's mostly harmless as long as you stay out of reach of those sausage fingers of hers."

"Alright," I conceded. "Then who's Bobby? Cause she was sure interested in knowing where he was."

Leo leaned up and pointed toward the marina bar. "She should know where he is. He runs Rum and Rednecks, the marina bar and grill." He took another swig then chin nodded at me. "So, what brings you around these parts?"

"Been doing some contract work for the government and I just happened to be passing through."

"Good pay?"

"Yup."

"I probably can't ask what it is, can I?"

"Nope," I said, then took another long drink from the beer, finishing it.

Leo finished his then tossed the empty bottle overboard and reached into the cooler for another. "Dammit, man."

"What's wrong?"

"If you want another beer, we'll have to go over to the marina. Got nothing but ice left in here."

"Fine by me." I stood carefully, not wanting to fall through the dry rotted fabric of the chair.

We strolled over to the main pier just as one of the musicians strummed the chords for Margaritaville. I took a dark Maduro cigar from my vest pocket as we took a seat at one of the outside tables after placing our order at the bar. I struck a match and puffed, enjoying the smooth sweet flavor of the mature tobacco.

"I didn't expect to see you this evening, Leo," a short pudgy man said as he approached. "You don't get out and socialize much."

Leo laughed. "It happens from time to time. This time it's because I have company and we ran out of beer."

I stood and offered my hand. "Braxton Hicks."

The pudgy man looked me over for a long minute, then took my hand and shook. "Bobby Raker."

I looked to Leo who gave a slow nod. "One and the same." Bobby flashed a look of confused concern from me to Leo and back again.

"Deloris expects that bottle of Mad Dog that you promised her," I said as I took my seat.

Bobby sat, propping his elbows on the table as he leaned forward. He took off his hat and rubbed vigorously at his face. He slicked back his long greasy looking, dirty blond hair then pulled the hat back on.

"I swear to God that woman is about to get on my last nerve." He pulled a crumpled pack of menthol cigarettes from his pocket and lit up.

A waitress dropped a beer and shot of whiskey in front of Leo and me before Bobby snatched one of the other bottles from her tray meant for another table. He took a long drink then hotboxed most of his cigarette.

Leo laughed then slammed back his shot and took a swig of beer. "What's wrong?"

Bobby glanced from me to Leo like a paranoid ferret on crack. He turned up his beer then let out a long sigh of resignation. "There's just no pleasing that woman. You'd think she'd be appreciative of an affectionate man such as myself. Especially when I'm all the time bringing her little gifts and something specials, like picking up a plate of her favorite barbeque or those twice deep-fried pork rinds that she loves so much. You'd think the least she could do when I come over to give her some sweet lovin' is to keep her kids put up and out of my way. And ya know what? I'm an adult. I can be the bigger man and keep my mouth shut about how rude and unchristian she's being. But the one time she catches wind that I went hoggin out of town she just won't let it go. Enough's enough ya know." Bobby lit a new smoke from the stub of the last one and sucked down half of the menthol stick in one draw.

Trying my best to hold in my laughter, I dipped the unlit end of my cigar into the shot of whiskey and took several long puffs. I glanced over at Leo who wasn't much help. He just shrugged and looked away as he nursed his own beer.

"You ever thought about maybe apologizing to her?" I asked.

Bobby stared at me with that unmistakenly angry look of *are you crazy* painted across his face. "Why the hell would I ever do that? It's not like I'm married to her or anything. We just have a fun rough and tumble whenever I'm in the mood for some meaty pork chops. I swear to God," he fumed then took another slug from his beer.

I could tell that no matter what I said, nothing would ever change Bobby's mind on the subject. I waved at the waitress and held up two fingers, then downed the rest of my beer. Doing my best to ignore Bobby's trailer park nonsense, I focused my attention on a small group of dancers gathering near the stage. They started a line dance to the tune of some country song I didn't recognize. It was an enjoyable enough show. Ample cleavage and ass cheeks peaked out from low-cut shirts and shorty shorts of the dancers as they bobbed and jiggled in time with the song. Lake princesses every one of them. The best mix of that dirty country girl you could never have and a leathery tanned bleach blonde beach bunny.

A blood curdling scream from the RV park broke my focus from this particularly fine pair of legs I'd just been watching. The music stopped just as suddenly as the next scream resounded across the still surface of the lake and reverberated off the opposite shore of the cove.

A gunshot broke the eerie silence that had settled over the marina. Frightened screams arose from the gathered crowd on the dock.

"What in the hell is going on over there," Bobby muttered as the three of us stood and gawked in the direction of the RV park.

"Die spawn of Satan!" a gruff male voice shouted followed by the pop and flash of two more gunshots.

"That sounded like Mason," Leo said.

"It sure as hell did. And he just signed his eviction order. He knows better than to discharge a weapon in the RV park. I swear to God," he said with an exasperated sigh. "Some people's kids."

Another scream followed by a pair of muzzle flashes that erupted from behind Deloris's RV just as a young woman appeared from the left of the trailer. She stumbled and nearly rolled her ankle several times as she sprinted across the dusty gravel road and onto the pier. The messenger bag slung over her shoulder slapped heavily against her thigh as she ran to the heavy clomp of her military style boots across the weathered wood planks of the dock.

"Isn't that Lucy Mae?" Leo asked, squinting to get his eyes to focus.

"Lucinda," Bobby corrected. "Remember? She identifies as Lucinda the ancient succubi now."

I looked over at Bobby with what must have been a contorted look of confusion because he shook his head and shrugged.

"Don't look at me. I don't get it either, dude. Kids these days, I swear to God."

Lucy collided with Leo and buried her face into his chest. "Those things!"

"What things? What's going on, Lucy?"

Motion drew my attention back to the RV park. An older man with a cane in one hand and a pistol in the other hobbled around from behind Deloris's camper.

Bobby cupped his hands and shouted at the man. "I swear to God, you know better than to fire that thing off in the trailer park, Mason!"

There was a sudden mix of confused gasps and frightened screams from the crowd gathered on the dock as we all spotted the things chasing Mason. More of the things suddenly appeared, clamoring their way from the water and onto the dock.

The things looked like something right out of a bad horror movie. They were humanoid but bloated in that way a body does after it's been in the river for a few days before the state troopers fish them out. They were a slime greenish color with bits of lake grass and twigs clinging to their matted mops of hair. Some of them were missing sections of flesh, as if something had been chewing at them or maybe it had sloughed away off of the bone.

One of the lake princesses standing near me fainted and her old man caught her, then unceremoniously dropped her, and sprinted for an expensive looking speedboat tied off to the far end of the dock. Screams of absolute terror overshadowed the gurgling roar of the creatures as they swarmed over the dock. People scattered in all directions. Most ran for their docked boats while some sprinted across the ramp to shore or lept into the water to what they thought was safety.

One of the creatures quickly snatched up the lake princess that had just fainted and dove back into the water, taking her to the depths with it.

Bobby snapped out of his stupor and did one of the most awkward fat man shuffles I'd ever seen as he sprinted for the door to the bar. "Everyone! Get inside," he yelled then disappeared into the building.

Leo shoved Lucy in the direction of the door then drew a blacked out 1911 from the pit of his back under his baggy shirt and fired at the creature nearest to him. I picked up the plastic patio chair I had been sitting in and threw it at the next nearest creature then drew my Taurus Judge revolver and fired. The one quarter ounce rifled .410-gauge slug easily penetrated the creature's head and blew out a sizable chunk from the opposite side.

Leo fired at two more of the creatures then kicked one of the patio tables into the path of another. "What the hell are these things?"

"A pain in the ass is what!" I stepped forward and put the muzzle of my revolver against the side of another creature's head as it climbed out of the water and pulled the trigger. It fell back with a hard belly-flop slap against the water. "All I wanted to do was relax and maybe fish a little bit, but nooo. I get to deal with blob things from radiation lake instead."

"There isn't any radiation in this lake," Leo argued.

I laughed. "Really? Then what the hell are these things?"

"Okay, that's fair."

A dozen more of the creatures swarmed onto the dock and ambled our way. I fired the last of the shotgun slugs and reholstered my revolver.

Leo let out a roar. "Dammit!"

I glanced over to see Leo fumbling in his pockets and the slide of his 1911 locked back.

I grabbed a long-handled gaff hook that hung from the side of the bar as a decoration and charged at the creature nearest to Leo. The spiked tip of the gaff sunk into the creature's torso with a sloppy wet pop.

It opened its mouth and let out a gurgling hiss, then pulled itself toward me, further onto the gaff and over the hook. Using the pole as leverage I pulled the creature toward me then swung it into two more of the things.

"Banzai!"

A small Asian man in a chef's hat suddenly charged from the entrance of the bar and decapitated one of the creatures with a comically oversized meat cleaver.

"Koichi-San! Don't let them things bite you," Bobby shouted as he reappeared from the entrance. "I don't want to have to find another sushi chef on short notice before the summer rush, I swear to God."

Bobby charged from the bar's entrance and swung one of the most back yard engineering abominations I have ever witnessed. It was a battery powered side grinder that had been heavily modified. Fitted with what looked like a three-foot-long chainsaw bar and chain crossed with the hilt of a great sword. He depressed the trigger a split second before the blade contacted the creature. The chain sword chewed its way through the thing's torso like a hot knife through butter.

"Yea, freaking haw!" Bobby shouted. "Didn't I tell you this thing would come in handy one day, Koichi-San?"

The sushi chef gave Bobby a baleful glance then hacked another of the things in two with his meat cleaver.

I stomped on the thing's chest after forcing it to the dock, then twisted and pried the gaff loose. It clawed at my steel-toed boots, trying to squirm from underfoot. I brought the tip of the gaff down with all my might through the creature's left eye, pinning its head to the dock.

Between the four of us, we made short work of the remaining creatures. Body parts littered the dock and several of the dismembered chunks continued to quiver and squirm.

I slammed down a shot of whiskey from a nearby table then drew my revolver. Opening the cylinder, I tipped the revolver up letting the five spent shotgun shells slide out and clatter to the dock. "So, when did y'all start having these pest problems around here?" I asked as I reloaded then holstered the Judge.

"Chū ni ikou. Anzen." Koichi-San said, then hurried back into the bar.

Bobby flicked at a piece of flesh that clung to the chain sword. "Come on y'all, Koichi-San has a good point."

Leo managed to fish his spare magazine out of his pocket and reloaded the 1911. "I didn't know you could speak Japanese, Bobby."

"I can't."

"Then how did you know what he just said?"

"I didn't. But he's heading inside and that sounds like a good enough plan to me for now," Bobby said then slipped into the bar.

Leo shrugged. "At least this is better than listening to Deloris bitch at the neighbors," he said as he followed Bobby into the bar.

I followed behind Leo and we both made a beeline for the bar. Bobby was already behind the taps pouring a fresh round for everyone.

"So, anyone going to tell me what the hell is going on around here?"

"Well, bless your heart," Bobby said with a hissing laugh. "Do you think we know what that was?

Leo sucked the froth from the top of the beer. "You've got me. I'm just glad the rest of you could see them. That's when I knew it wasn't a flashback."

I looked at Leo and shook my head in confusion. "You've seen those things before?"

"No. Just had a few bad acid trips before that come back to haunt me every now and then."

Koichi-San reappeared from the kitchen area and placed a platter of sushi on the bar top. "Eat." He nodded with a grunt then disappeared back into the kitchen.

"Well, hello there, darlin's." Bobby snagged a handful of sushi rolls from the platter and popped one in his mouth. He let out giggled moans I'd only heard come from a lady in the heat of passion. "I swear to God, you don't get any better than this."

Leo picked up one of the rolls and stared at it. "What is it?"

"Koichi-San's special curried catfish roll." Bobby's eyes rolled into the back of his head after popping another roll into his mouth.

"So, what the hell are we supposed to do about all of those bodies out there?" Leo asked.

Bobby just continued his mouth breather chewing as he swayed side to side, drunk on the trailer park goodness of Koichi-San's catfish sushi.

I raked my hand across my face from frustration. "You know this isn't anything natural, right?"

Leo laughed then took another sip of his beer. "I kinda figured as much."

"Well, I've dealt with a lot of strange stuff in my line of work. Just not mutant lake monsters."

"Well, I will tell y'all this. Ain't no one at the Sheriff's office going to believe any of this. If anyone mentions that Mason shot first, they'll just run him in for all of the bodies and the dead tourists so they can go and sit on their fat asses back at the jailhouse."

That's when I heard a sobbing wince come from the bathroom. Leo must have heard it too, because he looked at me at the same time I looked at him.

I quietly stood and drew my revolver. Leo slid from his seat and stepped ahead of me.

"I swear to God, ya'll."

Both me and Leo glared back at Bobby, motioning for him to be quiet. We continued toward the bathrooms. Leo stopped and listened at the women's restroom door for a moment then nodded. He drew his pistol and grabbed the door handle then mouthed the word one. Leo yanked open the door on the count of three and Lucy let out an ear-piercing scream. She had crouched and tucked herself into the corner of the room between the sink and the wall.

"I'm sorry! I didn't mean to do it!" she said between breathy sobs.

Me and Leo looked at each other again with that *what the fuck* look.

"Dammit Lucy! I almost shot you full of holes," Leo grumped as he made his way back to the bar.

I holstered the Judge and held out my hand to her. She was a cute little thing. Thick hair, the shade of midnight that hung down past her shoulders in little spiral curls framed a face as pale as the dead with heavy mascara and black lipstick. Black leather pants, spiked leather collar with pentacle, combat boots and her Marilyn Manson t-shirt tied in a knot just under her ample breasts rounded out the overall goth chick look.

"Come on. Let's get you a drink or something." I said as she took my hand and pulled herself upright. Clutching her messenger bag to her chest, she avoided eye contact and headed straight for the bar.

I closed the restroom door and followed behind her. "Bobby, pour her a drink."

"I don't know who you think you are, mister stranger," Bobby said with a sideways bob of his head, "but I would like to keep my liquor license." He leaned up on the bar and cupped his hand away from Lucy then whispered, "she ain't legal."

I turned to Lucy, and she just gave me that shrugging smirk look. She sure could have fooled me.

"Legal to drink," she said. "I'll be twenty next month."

Leo slammed his empty beer bottle onto the bar. "Just give her a drink and put it on my tab, Bobby! After what she just went through, she deserves it. And give me another one. I ain't seen shit that weird since Vietnam."

He threw up his hands and backed away from the bar. "No sir I will not. I cannot legally serve a minor in my establishment."

Leo walked around the end of the bar then grabbed three shot glasses and the first bourbon on the shelf. "And just because some bureaucrat in Washington says it's alright, she can fight and die for her country at the age of seventeen," Leo said with a growl. "Piss on them and piss on you, Bobby Raker." He poured the three shots then picked up one for himself and saluted us. "Cheers."

I took my shot and leaned against the bar, facing Lucy. "So, what did you mean earlier when you said that you didn't mean to do it?"

She pulled her messenger bag tighter against her chest and stared at the bar top.

Leo grabbed Lucy's shot glass and set it behind the bar. "That's the exact look my daughter used to get when I'd catch her red handed in something she knew she wasn't supposed to be doing."

Tears began to darken the canvas bag that she cradled.

"Lucy, honey," Bobby said in a caring tone. "It's alright. You can tell us whatever it is."

She sobbed for a moment longer before sucking in a shaky breath and looking up at the rest of us. "I just wanted to change my fate and get out of this trashy trailer park."

"Hey, now!" Bobby threw a bar towel at her. "There ain't nothing trashy about this place." He hummed in thought, shifting his weight from one foot to the other. "Eccentric maybe, but definitely not trashy."

Leo laughed and took another shot of whiskey. "She's right, Bobby. It's trashy." He leaned toward her and then spoke in a soft, fatherly voice. "Go ahead, Lucy. Tell us what happened?"

Chewing on her lower lip, she let out a reluctant sigh. "I might have raised a powerful necromancer from the dead."

That's just perfect, I thought. "I step away from the weird shit for a little break, and it just happens to hunt me down like a crazy ex-girlfriend." I poured myself another shot and slammed back the dark amber liquid.

"Alright, are we talking about an ancient necromantic practitioner or some man bun wearing dead dabbler?"

Bobby slapped the bar top, so flustered to find the words as he stumbled over himself to get anything coherent out. "I swear to God, you people are crazy."

Leo nodded at me with a grumble. "This the weird government contract work?"

"Yup."

"Fair enough," Leo said with an unsure nod then poured another round for each of us.

I turned back to Lucy. "Alright, Lucy. Give me all of the details of what happened and exactly what you think you did to cause all of this."

"I just wanted to change my fate." Her voice was as soft as a kitten's purr. She glanced at each of us and continued. "Necromancy had interested me for a while and while doing some research online I came across a story about the rise and fall of America's most powerful necromancer. Her name was Annette McCallie, the wife of Colonel Gerald McCallie, a wealthy landowner and businessman from Rhea Springs during the early 1800's.

Just after his death in 1840, Miles, Gerald McCallie's right-hand man on the plantation, found Annette McCallie in the family mausoleum, speaking in tongues over the disinterred body of her dead husband while under the guard of her manservant, Claudius, who was said to be a mountain of a man.

Supposedly Miles convinced the other slaves on the plantation that she had become the devil's concubine and that she was doing his evil work. They overwhelmed Claudius after the loss of dozens of men. When they entered the mausoleum, they found Annette in the necrotic embrace of her late husband, chanting and screaming in an unknown language as the undead fiend writhed atop her in the throes of passion.

The slaves decapitated both the fiend and the witch, then placed them in their respective vaults. A silver stake was driven through each of their hearts, and their bodies covered in wreaths of garlic and bathed in holy water.

The slaves attempted to burn Annette McCallie's book of spells, but nothing would so much as smudge the pages, so they placed her book of evil in the vault with her corpse and sealed the vault lids in place."

"Honey," Bobby interrupted, "did you hit your head on something, because that's one hell of a tall tell. Rhea Springs has been at the bottom of this lake since the early '40s."

"I'm not lying!" Lucy opened her messenger bag and produced a leather-bound book. The faded black dye of the cracked leather showed years of wear and weathering. She gently caressed the lines of the embossed Celtic knot that decorated the face of the book before jerking her hands away.

I turned the book around and opened the two brass latches that held the cover closed. "What's this?"

"Annette McCallie's spellbook," she said sheepishly.

Leo let out a hearty laugh and turned up the whiskey bottle. "I thought you said her book was buried with her."

"It…was." Lucy glanced up at each of us with sad doe eyes.

I flipped through the pages. Beautifully flowing handwritten script danced across the yellowed rough-cut sheets of paper. The opening line read:

Maireann an chraobh ar an bhfál ach ní mhaireann an lámh do chuir

I couldn't understand a word of it, but page after page was the same sort of script meshed with sketches of plants and archaic symbols.

Leo slid the book away from me and leaned back to get his eyes to focus. "That's Gaelic," he said, then shoved the book back to me.

"Irish Gaelic to be specific," Lucy added. "It really isn't that hard to learn once you understand the basis of the language."

I leafed through more of the pages then latched it closed. "If this was buried with Annette McCallie, and Rhea Springs has been under water since the '40s, then how did you manage to get your hands on it?"

"The McCallie family graveyard was located on the top of a hill, which has since become known as Cemetery Island near the south end of the lake."

I wiped my hand over my face out of frustration. "Okay, so you stole the dead witch's book. Was it cursed or something? Is that what caused the bodies from the black lagoon to come after everyone?"

"Um…," she trailed off for a moment in thought. "Everything was fine until I read a particular passage out loud." She opened the book and flipped to a page near the back then turned the book so we could see it.

"Alright, but what does it say? I can't read any of it."

"I thought it was a channeling spell, but I must have translated it wrong." Lucy looked away and started to mumble. "I think it's actually a…resurrection spell."

I snatched the bottle from Leo and downed a mighty gulp. "And let me guess. You meant to channel the witch's powers but instead you managed to resurrect the evil witch of the east, who's pissed and wants her book back."

"That's…yeah, that's pretty much it."

"Dear, God, Lucy," Bobby huffed. "Have you lost your ever-lovin' mind? How did you even get out there in the first place?"

"I kinda stole one of the boats from the marina when you were out of town." She shrugged innocently.

Leo stole the bottle back from me. "We're about to do something stupid, aren't we?"

I shrugged. "Maybe."

He took another swig from the bottle then passed it off to Bobby. "Does that book of yours say anything about how to kill the witch?"

"No, but I did see a binding spell that might slow her down. And if I had to guess, we can stop her by putting this back into her chest," Lucy said as she produced a tarnished silver spike from her bag.

I took the spike and bounced it in my hand. "I'll be damned if it isn't solid."

"I bet it's worth a small fortune," Bobby said, licking his lips.

Leo laughed. "No shit."

I placed the spike and spellbook back into the bag and slung it over Lucy's shoulder. "If this is what will put that witchy bitch back in her grave, then I'm gonna shove this thing where the sun don't shine."

We scrounged around Leo's and geared up before climbing into one of Bobby's rental boats. I snatched Bobby's brand-new Mossberg 590, complete with red dot sight and mounted tactical flashlight from behind the bar. Leo strapped on a pair of .45 Long Colt six shooters that looked like they were right out of an old spaghetti western while Bobby looked like a military surplus store. He'd gotten decked out in flak vest and Kevlar helmet with two shotguns crossed in holsters on his back, dual Desert Eagles in hip holsters and his great chain sword, fully charged with a backup battery in each cargo pocket of his Bermuda shorts.

It was sometime after midnight with the moon full and high in the sky when Bobby idled the massive pontoon boat up to the rocky beach of

Cemetery Island. I grabbed the mooring rope tied to the bow of the boat and jumped to the rocky beach. A hiss like the sound of steam escaping met me on the ground.

"Someone shine a light down here."

Leo appeared at the front of the boat, shining a Maglite down at me. "Whatever you do, Brax, don't move."

Following the light to the ground I found three massive orange and black water moccasins. Their coiled bodies looked as thick as a baseball bat.

"Don't you hurt those beauties," Bobby shouted. He fumbled in a side compartment under one of the seats.

Lucy quietly shushed him. "Do you want to let the witch know that we're here?"

"Honey, if you only knew what Koichi-San could do with water moccasin meat, you wouldn't be complaining."

No sooner had Bobby reached over the bow of the boat with a pair of mechanical grippers than a bloated figure charged out of the water toward me. Leo drew and fired both of his revolvers, shooting from the hip before the ghoul could even clear the water.

I was at a complete loss for words. I'd never seen anyone move that fast in my life, let alone with a pair of six shooters that splattered the creature's brains across this side of the lake.

Leo shrugged and holstered his guns. "Retirement left me with a lot of free time."

Remembering the snakes, I looked down to find they had slithered away at some point amid the commotion. I took Leo's Maglite and tied the boat off to one of the many scrub trees that covered the island.

Bobby lept to the shore in an amazing three-point superhero landing with his chain sword in hand. He knelt and held the monstrosity out like it was some legendary sword of power. "Oh, holy trinity of the trailer park and Mason's bathtub Madonna! I call upon y'all to bless this here weapon of purity and vengeance! And to protect us from the evil we are about to kill."

Leo dropped from the front of the boat to the shore. "You've been playing Dungeons and Dragons with Donnie and Earl again, haven't you?"

Bobby shrugged. "Maybe."

"Let's get this over with…" I had started to say before Lucy cut me off, screaming. I spun, scanning the overgrowth of the island behind me.

Between the trees and brush, malformed figures had appeared from the darkness of the undergrowth.

"Brax, get back!" Leo's six shooters rang out again amid the buzz of Bobby's chain sword.

I unslung the Mossberg and with the soul satisfying sound of the shotgun's pump action, I chambered a round.

Six of the watery ghouls charged onto the beach at us from the underbrush. Bobby charged forward to meet them head on. The chain sword chewed into the bloated corpses with ease. I fired, cycled the pump action and slam fired the next three rounds, shredding the torsos of things charging at me. Leo fired round after round into the creatures, dropping three more by the time I put a final round into the back of a ghoul's head.

"Alright," I said, turning to face Lucy. "Where's the crypt?"

"Mausoleum," Lucy corrected.

"Doesn't matter," Leo grumbled. "Let's just take care of this thing."

She pointed directly ahead. "It's just a few hundred feet ahead through those trees."

I slung the shotgun and fished an aluminum baseball bat from the boat that I had brought along just in case ammo got scarce. I held out my hand to help Lucy down from the boat. "Let's get this over with."

She let out a whimpering sob. "I don't know that I can do this. I've never killed anything before. I don't even know for sure how I brought the witch back to life."

"You're the only one that can read the spells in that book," I reminded her. "Anything you can do to slow those things down so we can put that stake back through the witch's black heart will be helpful. It doesn't matter if you know how you did it before or not. The fact is, you're a natural magician whether you want to admit it or not, and you've already done it once."

"But you're a wizard, Lucy…," Bobby whispered in a cryptic voice.

She glared down at Bobby and sucked in a composing breath before taking my hand to steady herself as she slid down from the bow of the boat. "Yeah…maybe, but I'm not a very good one."

"That's beside the point."

"Just stay close and be ready to cast that binding spell that you found. I've got no doubt that you can do it," I reassured her. "We're going to need all the help we can get."

Bobby took point as we pressed forward into the underbrush. The light of the full moon filtered through fog enshrouded branches of scrub oaks and privets that covered the island. The McCallie family cemetery which was the namesake of the island quickly came into view. Wrought iron barriers embedded in stacked stone pillars encircled the site. Simple headstones and intricately carved stone monuments seemed to glow beneath the light of the full moon. The beautifully forged gate hung open, one side slumped to the ground, its hinges relenting to time and corrosion. The other was swung inwardly enough for a person to easily pass between the two.

Lucy hunkered up against me, clinging to the back of my arm. "That's the mausoleum," Lucy said, pointing at a large marble structure that stood out at the back of the clearing. It looked like a miniature gothic temple of sorts. Ornately carved white marble that towered over the other monuments of the small graveyard.

Bobby whimpered. "I swear to God this place gives me the heebie-jeebies." Bobby turned to Lucy with a contemplative glare. "Bless your heart, girl. You were either really desperate or stupidly brave to come out here on your own like that. I sure couldn't have done it," he admitted as he continued forward.

Lucy slapped a hand over her own mouth and let out a muffled scream. Her panic-flooded eyes bulged as she pointed ahead of us into the graveyard. Following her stare, I easily spotted the cause of her distress. A petite figure emerged from behind one of the many monuments. She danced to a silent song as she crossed the clearing. Her long blond locks floated softly about her face like a glowing halo. The flowing white silks of her gown hovered around her and drifted slowly like heavy smoke.

Bobby crossed himself as he muttered quietly. "Blessed mother of the great trinity."

"Let's get this shindig on the road already," Leo said in a low cautious tone then stepped through the open gate.

The night had gone eerily silent after our beach landing. It was so quiet that I could hear the beating of my own heart. That was, until Leo passed through the gate, crossing the threshold of the graveyard. No sooner had he entered that every shadow seemed to come to life. Bloated, misshapen forms skulked out from the foggy darkness throughout the graveyard.

Muzzle flashes accompanied the cacophony of Leo's six shooters. In a split second he had dropped two of the charging ghouls.

I brushed Lucy away from my arm and charged into the fray. "Keep her safe, Bobby!"

"But who's going to keep me safe?"

Baseball bat reared back at the ready I charged for the closest creature, connecting with a solid thunk with the thing's skull. One more solid whack crushed in the side of its face as it slumped to the ground.

The unmistakably strange buzz of the chain sword meeting flesh resonated throughout the clearing amid the discharge of Leo's .45 Long Colt rounds.

"Braxton!" Lucy shouted. "She's getting away!"

I put my full body weight into an uppercut swing that connected with a sicky snap of bone under the chin of the next creature. Its neck snapped back awkwardly as it spun in a reverse somersault. Continuing, I skull checked one after another of the advancing ghouls. It was like shooting fish in a barrel. If the zombie apocalypse were to ever actually happen, the shambling type like these guys would hands-down be more preferable to the freaky fast sprinting type.

I stole a glance in the direction of the witchy apparition and caught a glimpse of her as she disappeared through the entrance of the mausoleum. "Get ready to cast that spell!" I looked back over my shoulder to see Lucy heading my way, fumbling in her bag for the book. Ribs cracked and broke as I struck another creature across the chest. Swinging my bat in a wide, overhead arc, I crushed in the back of the creature's head.

This just seems way too easy, I thought as I took down the next ghoul to charge at me.

"I swear to God!" Bobby shouted.

That's what I get for thinking. The gods of dumbassery must have been watching with riveted amusement or I just jinxed the hell out of myself, because a swarm of the things overran Bobby as he swapped out battery packs. Skidding to a halt I fought for traction in the damp grass.

Leo charged in, shouldering his way through the pack of ghouls surrounding Bobby. "Chase down the bitch and put this shit to rest! I've got Bobby!"

I got my feet back under myself and grabbed Lucy by the wrist. "Stay close." Lucy fought to keep up with me as we sprinted for the mausoleum. Three of the creatures appeared from behind the building just as I reached the opening. The first one snatched the bat right out of my hand and backhanded me, knocking me to the ground. The thing fell on top of me and let out a gurgling roar that bathed me in the stink of fetid flesh and rotten fish. The ghoul lunged, latching itself to my chest. Its black teeth gnashed down on my left pectoral. I couldn't get a grip around the creatures' neck no matter how hard I tried. Its bloated skin was as slick and slimy as it looked. I punched and clawed, pounding my elbow into the side of the thing's head. It was like it didn't feel pain, which made sense if it was undead. Arching my back, I rolled to one side and drew my revolver then sent a four-ounce slug soaring through the ghoul's rotten skull. Pushing the corpse off of me, I fired three rounds into the other creatures that loomed over me, poised to pounce on their prey.

I pulled up my shirt to check the wound. It was mostly superficial. No worse than a few bite marks I'd willingly earned with much better looking wrestling partners, except for the single tooth that had been left embedded in my skin. I gripped the slime covered enamel and wiggled it loose. Squeezing the wound caused blood to run freely, flushing the wound of any other debris.

Lucy rushed to my side. "We have to hurry, Braxton. I have no idea what she is capable of right now. But the longer she has, the more chance she'll have to build her power up."

Getting back to my feet, I dusted myself off and holstered the empty revolver. A quick glance around didn't reveal where the baseball bat had been dropped, but I couldn't waste any more time. I adjusted the straps on the shotgun, flipped on the mounted tactical flashlight and brought it up to the ready position before stepping over the threshold of the mausoleum.

Aged marble steps led down into the musty darkness of the crypt. Mischievous giggles echoed up from the underground chamber on an icy cold breeze. Fog formed in front of me from my next exhaled breath. Gooseflesh suddenly rose with the hairs on the back of my neck. Lucy moved in so close that she should have easily melded with me if that were possible. If Lucy could have gripped my arm any harder, I'd swear she would tear the flesh from the back of my arm with little effort.

"I welcome thee, valiant warrior," the sweetly sinister voice said. Rusted hinges creaked as the iron doors of the mausoleum clanged shut behind us. I suddenly felt like a fly in a spider's web, being politely welcomed to the dinner table.

"I reward those who serve me well."

Reaching the bottom of the stairwell we entered the burial chamber. Two large, ornately carved marble vaults took up most of the available space in the room. An alcove, complete with stone altar and braziers that burned an ethereal blue flame were set in the opposite wall.

"Don't be afraid, warrior," the voice said in a soothingly smooth tone.

Without pulling my eyes away from the altar, I blindly reached into Lucy's bag and retrieved the silver spike. Leaning close to her ear I whispered, "Get your spell ready."

"I promise," the voice said with a sultry hiss. "Return my book and I will reward you with an eternity of whatever your heart desires."

The apparition reappeared, laying nude across the marble altar. Smokey white tendrils formed from the discarded gown beneath her. The ghostly appendages cupped her ample bosom while writhing about. The witch let out a soothing moan as the other worldly tentacles caressed and undulated across her body.

"Come to me, my brave warrior."

Everything around me blurred. Blues became reds and greys shifted to greens as the world distorted around me. The witch arched her back and let out another low moan before spinning where she sat my direction.

She softly cooed with a sly smile then opened herself to me. "You can have all that I am and all that I will be."

I stepped forward, unable to stop myself.

"Be mine." She motioned slowly with a slender finger. "Become one with me."

The witch's pale flesh glowed with golden radiance. I could feel the pulsating warmth of her building the closer I got. She was peace; she was warmth; she was happiness; she was pleasure.

"Cluinn mi, o spioradan Uisge, Talamh, Teine, agus Adhair. Aoighean nèamhaidh, Deamhain nan rìoghachdan ìochdaranach Agus spioradan nan sinnsirean. Tha mi a 'gairm ort, Gus a cheangal…"

The words that floated into the warmth that surrounded me sound so familiar. Like something I had heard before. Like Scot's Gaelic…Lucy…That sounded like Lucy reciting the spell.

I blinked then shook my head to clear the fog of whatever the she bitch had done to me. I looked back, finding Lucy reciting from the open spell book. Her black hair floated about her head like an evil spider about to pounce. She suddenly flew backward, smacking against the stone wall of the crypt then limply fell to the floor.

"Time to finish this," I growled and turned to face the witch. Something with the grip of a steel vice pinned my arms against my sides, forcing the breath from me.

"A pity," the witch sighed. "You could have had it all."

I flexed my arms, gasping for the slightest breath I could get.

"I could let Claudius crush you like the husk that you are..." She slinked down from the altar and began prowling across the stone floor like a hunting cat. A loud laughing grunt filled my ears. Looking down I found two massive ebony arms the size of my thighs wrapped around my chest. My ribs felt like they were about to shatter every time the muscles flexed in the slightest.

"Or perhaps I could have some fun of my own..." she leaned back, kneeling before me. A self-satisfied grin stretched across her pallid face. Claudius loosened his grip just enough that I was able to take a quick breath and laugh. The witch jerked her head back in an unsure glower.

I fumbled for the grip of the shotgun with my right hand. "Gimme some lovin', baby," I growled, then raised the shotgun and forced the tip down her gaping maw and pulled the trigger.

Her head snapped back and limply fell backward to the stone floor. Pulses of ethereal flames erupted from the gaping hole in her head. Claudius convulsed with each pulse of energy, then released his grip and fell backwards. I collapsed to the floor and sucked in a gasping breath.

The witch's body wriggled and squirmed with each pulse, wrapped and encircled by the smokey tendrils of her gown. A sudden motion caught my eye. Chunks of the witch's skull vibrated and moved like an amoeba in search of its next meal, making their way back to the body.

"Shit!"

Pain shot through my left side when I tried to stand. Her muscle-bound servant must have cracked a few of my ribs after all. Holding my elbow close, I let the shotgun drop to the sling and swapped the spike to my right hand. The silver spike plunged easily into her soft flesh. Blue flames licked out from the spike, transmogrifying the soft pale skin to the desiccated husk of a long dead corpse.

"Yup. This was the perfect getaway from all the weird shit." I forced myself to my feet and stumbled over to where Claudius's remains lay. I'm not sure that I could ever eat another piece of jerky after a night like this. His skin had drawn and sunken in, pulling tight over his massive frame.

Lucy let out a low moan and started to stir.

"Don't try to get up too quick. You hit the wall pretty hard."

She jerked upright, looking around for the witch.

"She's dead…," I started, "again."

I slid down against the wall next to Lucy and picked up the book. "Let me catch my breath and we'll get out of here."

Lucy brushed the hair out of her face and stared over at me in the dim glow of the flashlight. "What do we do about the book? The legend says that it can't be destroyed. And what about the witch? That silver spike is the only thing containing her."

"Nothing to worry about. I happen to know a guy that will help me put both her and the book in a safe place where no one will bother them."

"I sure hope so."

I grunted, pushing myself upright. "It's O'beer thirty somewhere, and I think we earned a few drinks tonight."

Lucy helped me to straighten myself, and we limped our way out of the McCallie family mausoleum.

Dryad's Dance

By: William Joseph Roberts

First published in Tales From the Street: A Corner Scribblers Urban Fantasy Collection – Three Ravens Publishing, December 2021

This little flash fiction piece was a spin off idea that spawned from "When Vulcans Cry", tying back to Braxton encountering a group of hippies celebrating the Solstice.

Wispy tendrils of fog hung in the warm summer twilight and glowed with an ethereal power that only a full strawberry moon could imbue. Shadows seemed to dance and sway as I cruised along the empty country road. I had found my Zen once again.

I was one with the universe. One with all that surrounded me. Embraced in the warm air that felt as if it would lift me away into a numb bliss of nothingness as the rhythmic pounding hum of my motorcycle threatened to push me over the edge of transcendence.

Shapes seemed to coalesce between shadow and mist. Faces of long-dead friends merged and melded into the ghostly forms of bear, wolf, and a great horned stag that stood in the middle of the road.

"Shit! DEER!"

I squeezed the clutch, stood on the rear brake lever, and leaned the bike hard, throwing it into a power slide. Skidding to a stop amid the belched cacophony of rubber against pavement, the engine shut off as I stood the bike upright.

"Every freaking time I get into the zone, something totally blows it out."

I patted the side of the tank and hit the ignition. A heavy scent of gasoline overpowered the fragrant scents of summer. The *drip drip drip* of fuel on pavement gave way to the eerie silence of the moonlit night.

"Really, Val? You're just going to flood out like that on me?"

A scream, followed by the faint sound of drums, echoed across a nearby field. I froze and stared in the direction of the noise. "I must be hearing things…" I said to myself, when another scream raced across the distance of the field.

"…Or maybe not."

Dancing light glimmering through the trees on the other side of the field to my right caught my attention.

"It'll be a bit before you'll start again, so I'm gonna go check this out, Val. Be a good girl and don't go anywhere. I'll be back shortly," I said with another pat on the tank.

Navigating my way through the underbrush, I emerged on the edge of a small encampment surrounding a massive bonfire. Men and women alike dressed in little to nothing danced in a clockwise circle around the blazing fire. Torches mounted to posts bearing colorful strips of cloth encircled the fire on the outskirts of the encampment. Harmonized chants in time to the drums set the pace of the dance.

A small group of drummers occupied a space near a large pile of pallets and split logs. Others lazed about around the fire on bedding or blankets spread out on the ground. They sang, they drank, they loved.

One dancer in particular caught my attention. Her petite frame was covered in intricate body paint that accentuated her already well-defined curves. Like a master martial artist, she spun and swayed about the fire while swinging flaming pots on chains in wide arcs around her. Her cat-like grace entangled my senses within the swirl of flame and the sway of her bare hips. Within the flashing shadows of light, her features seemed to shift and change. Her visage transformed into something more feral. Pointed tips of her ears protruded from beneath her unkempt hair. Thick fangs accentuated her smile and her cat-like eyes glowed with a primal desire.

The drums continued a slow beat as the chanting subsided. The dancer walked a slow, tiptoed pace around the bonfire. Her firepots rocked in slow steady arcs counter to each other like the ticking of slow pendulums.

Her hips swayed and bumped to the rising beat of the drums, the motion of the pots smooth and fluid. Mindlessly, she leapt and spun. Faster and faster before leaping through the roaring flames of the bonfire to the sudden BOOM of the drums. Unscathed, she landed on the other side, the firepots slack at her sides. With a soft paw trot, she strolled over in my direction.

"I welcome you, brother," she said as she paced slowly around, as if examining me. The sweet scent of lemongrass hung heavy about her. "I am Aria." A playful giggle escaped her lips as she set down the pots.

"The veil between this world and the next is the thinnest on the Solstice night. As the light reaches its peak, the darkness begins its return to the world once again."

I stared blankly as she knelt before me in all of her painted nude glory. I could almost feel the glowing warmth of her personality radiating off of her. "I welcome you to our circle and offer you a gift of the heart."

My knees suddenly felt weak, as if compelled to kneel. I dropped to the ground.

Aria raised up on her knees over me and leaned forward, placing her forehead to mine for a brief moment. "Bless you," she whispered, then sat back on her heels and plucked a small rose-colored crystal from between her breasts. "I give you, my gift of the heart."

Suddenly, I could see all the colors of her aura radiating out as her visage blurred.

The chill of morning dew nipped at my skin. Shifting, something hard poked me in the side of the head. Removing the offending something. I glanced at it. It was small, pink, and faceted. Bleary-eyed, I sat up and rubbed the sleep away. It was the rose-colored crystal Aria had handed me.

"Aria…"

I glanced around at the surrounding field and found… Nothing. No sign of the encampment. No evidence of a fire. No sign of Aria… My hand suddenly tingled.

I could hear Aria's giggle float in on the wind as the crystal glowed with a warm pulse of life.

Send in the Clowns

By: William Joseph Roberts

First published in It Came From the Trailer Park: Volume 2 – Three Ravens Publishing, October 2022

Who doesn't love a clown, right? After outlining the first Braxton novel, I had lots of material to play with, so I figured, why not revisit some of the folks he met years ago.

Five days! Five freaking days, completely wasted, tromping around the Everglades because a couple of kids wanted to have a little fun and mess with their neighbors. As trigger-happy as folks are, you'd think that natural selection would have taken place and eliminated the problem before I got involved.

But I can't argue too much. It was a paid trip to South Florida for some fresh seafood, cash in my pocket, and the wind in my hair all on the government dime. And on top of it all, I didn't have to be anywhere anytime soon. Life doesn't get much better than that.

Now, the only good thing about working for the Feds is that they have notoriously deep pockets. The KCG, (Krypto, Cults, and Gangs) wasn't much different from the other alphabet agencies, but as a subcontractor, I had a bit more flexibility than the bona fide government men. It was a nice little arrangement. Situations were rectified and the suits had plausible deniability on their end if anything went sideways on a job.

Having almost no operating expenses gave me a flexibility that the other contractors couldn't match. I could bid stupid low, have my choice of gig, make a bit of spending cash, and experience America in the wind on the back of a steel horse, the way the Gods intended.

It was a nice arrangement. No real deadlines to speak of, just results. I could swing by to visit old friends while enroute from point A to point B. There were days I really needed it to unwind, and today was one of them.

The aforementioned idiot kids nearly got me eaten by a territorial pack of gators in the middle of mating season while trying to save them from their own stupidity. Other than a few pairs of stained drawers, and the loss of their swamp monster costumes, the lot of them came out of it unscathed. Rich kids with nothing else better to do.

After dealing with a pack of HOA Karens, I needed a beer and some serious downtime. For the life of me, I can't understand why anyone would sell their soul to a Homeowner's Association.

That's why I found myself on a slight detour, cutting across State Road 780 through central Florida on my way back north. I decided to pop in and see my buddy, James O'Connel, the Ring Master Extraordinaire!

He'd been exiled from Gibsonton, aka Carnietown, for some dirty dealings he'd been involved in a few years ago. A portion of the community split and followed him like a disgruntled church congregation to strike out and establish Carnival Hills, their own community dedicated to the carnival lifestyle, where folks lived the life all day, every day. Their dedication to the craft seemed a bit extreme but to each their own.

James even established a call center corporation so his people could live and work in peace without otherwise dealing with the outside world.

Every time we'd chat on the phone, he'd remind me that I was always welcome and had a bunk at his place. So before leaving South Florida, I called him up to let him know I was on my way.

Around mid-evening I rolled into Carnival Hills. It was located in the middle of nothing swamp country off of State Road 780. They established a planned community along the banks of the Myakka River that fed into Cason Lake.

Colorful canvas tents, ancient carnival equipment, and other sorts of circus paraphernalia peppered the landscape alongside all ages and styles of mobile homes. Kids in full clown makeup waved and ran along beside me as I cruised through the delightfully quiet and cheerful neighborhood.

James must have heard me rumbling down the street because he was waiting for me on his screened-in porch. He saluted with an open beer in one hand while turning something that sizzled on the grill with the other.

"I know it's been a few years, but I swear you've gotten uglier," James yelled over the rumble of my bike as I pulled up and dropped the kickstand. He closed the lid of the grill and made his way down the steps. Even in this heat, he was dressed in full makeup and his ringmaster's outfit complete with a top hat, minus the tuxedo jacket.

I laughed and killed the engine. "At least I don't hide the ugly behind layers of paint."

He smiled and rocked casually on his heels, hands in his pockets. "That's to save the public a visual image that no one needs the mental scars from. Come on. Burgers are almost ready."

He pressed a cold beer into my hand and leaned in, slapping me on the back. "Good to see you again, Brax. Been way too long."

"Agreed," I said, then turned up the beer, taking two good gulps. "The government gig has me running from one place to another. It's just been a while since I had an assignment down this way. Where's your old lady, Freida?"

He raised a questioning eyebrow, then raising the grill lid he flipped the burgers once again. "She's out in the swamp, living up to her Frog Charmer title. She'll be back in before it's too late." He pressed each meat patty and dripping grease sizzled over the hot charcoal. Not much better meal than beer and burgers after a long day on the road. We ate, drank, and shot the shit for a good long while.

"You are not going to believe this, James," a voice uttered from inside the double-wide followed by a giggling squeal.

James looked at me and smiled. "Weren't you single, Brax?"

A creepy feeling of dread that I expected was similar to what brides of arranged marriages felt washed over me. I turned up the beer in my hand, finishing it before I responded. "I might be for the right price." I let out a foamy burp, then pulled a cigar from the breast pocket of my kutte.

"Leah! Come out here and meet someone!" James shouted then finished off his own beer. He reached into the cooler and popped the top on two more ice-cold bottles of suds, handing me one of them.

The front door opened, and the trailer shifted as she stepped out onto the porch. She had to be all of six foot six and four hundred pounds, before adding in the weight of what had to be literally thousands of piercings covering her body. There were even metal studs peeking out from under the terrycloth daisy dukes flossing her ass crack and the threadbare strip of cloth that barely passed as a tube top. Three rows of implanted ridges stood out on top of her head beneath a few days worth of stubble.

"That's why there ain't any beer in the fridge, you've got it out here," she said, stomping her way toward the cooler.

James laughed. "You'll have to go get your own. These are the last two in the house," he chuckled then downed his beer in two long gulps. "Get a job and buy your own."

She placed her fists on her hips and huffed. "That's just rude."

"Nope," James said, shaking his head. "That's life. What do you think, Braxton? Keeper material?"

I wasn't sure how to respond.

"If you'd just hire me back on over at the call center, I would have a job."

"If you hadn't lost us two major contracts, you'd still have a job there. You just aren't cut out for customer service, sis."

"Sis?"

"Oh, yeah. Where are my manners," James said. "Leah, this is my friend, Braxton. Braxton, my sister Leah. She used to be part of the freakshow in Gibsonton, but when they exiled me, they booted any family I had as well."

"Pleased to meet you," I said, saluting with my beer. She rounded on me and licked her lips like I'd seen some people do when a slab of meat was placed in front of them. She smiled wide, and surprisingly still had all of her teeth.

Leaning against the side of the trailer she struck a pose, jutting out her right hip. "What sorta things you into, hun? I bet I could show you a new thing or two that you'd never forget."

"Because you're freaky enough that you scare the regular freaks," James laughed.

She smiled and nodded with a self-satisfied look of knowing. "Rule thirty-four, baby. If you can think of it, there's a porn for it out there somewhere." She lifted up her left breast and retrieved a smartphone from between the layers and immediately started tapping away at the screen.

"It's just like this one guy on my OnlyFans page. He's got some sort of foot fetish going on, but he wants to see my toes covered in green Jell-O and sprinkles. He was offering a hundred bucks, but that's just too strange, even for me."

I finished my beer and tossed James the empty. "Where's the closest place to get more beer?"

"Actually, just down at the mouth of the park on the main road is the Red Velvet Lounge."

"Sounds perfect," I said before slipping past Leah, down the stairs, and on my way down the road toward the Carnival Hills entrance. I turned and yelled while walking backward. "You coming, James?"

I'd never say that I was a prude or that I was a pervert even. I'd been in my fair share of establishments ranging from gentlemen's clubs to skanky backwoods strip clubs over the years and witnessed some very strange and very local flavors.

The Red Velvet Lounge was an entirely new experience that I really wasn't ready for. At least not after a long day on the road.

But here I was, right up against the stage, sipping on one hell of a tasty microbrew, while Danielle the Dog Girl and Jasmine the Bearded Lady stripped and teased to the beat of a dubstepped circus song, following the lead of Mira the Mystical Midget Madam.

It would take something hellacious to get the image of the three of them wriggling and writhing about out of my mind after Gini the Lobster Girl joined the group on stage, adding a special flavor to the number with her pincer-like hands that turned the entire number into an interpretive dance routine of good versus evil.

I held out a five that signaled Mira to eagerly thrust a hip in my direction. I tucked the bill neatly in her G-string, smiled, and nodded then quietly sipped on my beer while trying to not stare.

"Come on Brax, you in on this hand or not?" James asked over the music. I turned back to the table and ante'd in so James's buddy Darrel the Strong Man could deal the hand. Another friend of theirs, Harry the Hobo, a clown that immediately reminded me of a down-and-out Harpo Marx tossed in his ante.

While Darrel dealt the hand, I took in the room around us. The club absolutely lived up to its name as the Red Velvet Lounge. Every wall was framed in dark stained hardwood, accented with a rich textured blood red wallpaper and elaborate, if not gaudy decorations of thick velvets with bronze and brass highlights like you'd expect to see in any respectable brothel. All forms of carnival geek, circus clown, and freakshow oddity mingled about in the dimly lit gentlemen's club.

"Brax, your turn," James yelled. I glanced at my cards and folded on the spot. A pair of deuces and a mix of other crap cards was no kind of hand to bet on.

"It'd be nice if I was dealt something worth having. I'm starting to wonder if you're just trying to nickel and dime me to death with the ante."

Darrel's chair went flying behind him as he stood, then placed both fists, knuckles down on the table. "You calling me a cheater?"

Harry squeezed the bulb of a bicycle horn in response then pantomimed laughing.

"He didn't say anything of the sort, Darrel," James added.

I stood and held my hand out to Darrel. "Just making casual conversation is all, man. I didn't mean anything by it. Can we sit down and play?"

Darrel grunted and blew out his nose like an agitated bull before he nodded and sat back down in his seat. Harry folded and the hand continued around to James.

Other than the overlying carnie theme, it wasn't much different than hanging out and shooting the shit with any other folks I'd hung out with. They had families, bills to pay, doctor's visits, birthday parties, and fishing trips just like anyone else, except they did it with a carnival flair and owned every moment of it.

The waitress was one of the better ones I'd had in recent memory. She was a cute thing with a Creep show zombie look. I'd lost track of time and the number of beers drank since she kept the table cleared and fresh rounds coming. It had to have been a while by this point. At least three other acts had been on stage and gone, and I really needed to hit the head. No sooner had I stood to excuse myself than this large balding fellow sauntered up to our table behind James.

He was a larger guy wearing sweatpants and a nearly threadbare, stained, off-white t-shirt advertising some barbecue joint called ODBQ up in Ambridge Pennsylvania.

"The guy at the bar said that one of you fine gentlemen would be James," the guy continued in a soft-spoken lisp. James turned in his seat and glanced up at the guy before Darrel butted in.

"Who's asking?"

"A, concerned citizen," the guy hissed.

"What's your business, friend," I added to keep the conversation moving.

He wriggled his head and folded his hands across his overly large potbelly.

"The honor of a damsel is at stake, friend," he replied with a pompous air.

"I think you might be in the wrong place, pal," James said, turning fully to the side in his seat to address the man. "You aren't likely to find a damsel in this establishment." He let out a deep-seated gut chuckle before slapping Darrel across the shoulder.

"Indeed." The man let out an amused chuckle of his own then daintily picked up James' beer with the tips of his thumb and forefinger and took a quick sip. He smacked his lips together, like an aristocratic taste tester. "Interesting yet unpleasantly disagreeable." He dropped the bottle back onto the table and wiped his fingers on his shirt. Complete revulsion played out across his contorted face.

Harry squeezed his horn with a slow, disappointing wa wa wa honk.

"Get to the point already," Darrel growled. "You're interrupting our game."

The man stared down his pudgy nose at Darrel and scowled, "indeed…"

I took another swig from my beer and decided to toss in my two cents. "I'm in firm agreement with my larger-than-life associate here," I said pointing at Darrel. "We were just in the middle of a very enjoyable and high stakes game of chance when you so rudely interjected yourself into our company and conversation, not to mention, ruined my companion's recently opened beverage. A timely explanation and acceptable compensation are in order, friend."

The man grinned, blinking and shaking his head in what looked like sporadic confusion. "I dare say, I did not suppose to cross paths with such an articulate, and I would assume, educated individual as yourself in an establishment such as this." He smiled and motioned as if tipping his hat. "'Tis an honor, my good man.

"Yup, Braxton uses his mouth as pretty as any back alley hooker," James interjected. "So you two gonna go out back for a spell or are you going to get to the fucking point?"

"Very well." The man shifted, shuffling a step closer to James before smacking him across the face with a leather welders glove that he suddenly produced from his pocket.

"You do not deserve the rapturous attentions of an angel as beautiful and pure as Leah," he said in a tone that was nothing if not calm, collected, and sincere.

I choked, nearly spurting the swig I had just taken through my nostrils. Foam poured over the lip of the bottle after I slammed it back down onto the table.

"Leah?" James shook his head. "What the hell kinda trouble has she gotten into now?"

"I am here to fight you for her hand, you disgusting, degenerate ogre!"

James collapsed onto the table in laughter. The rest of us grabbed the unfinished bottles of beer as soon as he started beating his fist against the table. "You want to fight me for her hand? Are you stupid or something? She's my sister, dumb ass."

"And a dependapotamus," Darrel said into his drink.

"Still fair game in Alabama," I added.

Harry honked out a duck laugh on his bicycle horn.

The guy snatched a drink from the tray of a passing waitress and tossed its contents across the table in my direction then struck a superhero fighting pose. "No matter! Her honor is at stake and must be avenged!"

I didn't even have a chance to react before Harry leapt onto the table and bounded onto the man's shoulders. He locked his legs around the rubbery tree trunk the guy called a neck and started beating him in the head with his horn. A painful goose honk followed every well-placed strike.

The guy stumbled back from the added weight of Harry perched on his shoulders, and into two heavily muscled carnies seated at the bar, spilling their drinks. Harry toppled over backward, falling behind the stained and worn bar top.

One of the carnies at the bar turned and shoved the guy across the room, sending him sprawling across a table of patrons and their drinks.

The other carnie, shaking beer from his arms, turned in our direction.

"We don't want any trouble, Hank," James said as he stood and put the chair between him and Hank, the muscle-bound carnival worker.

"Bit late for that, ain't it?"

The carnie lunged for James, kicking the chair out of the way.

Darrel was on his feet before I could blink with the carnie locked in a full nelson hold. As big as Darrel was, the carnie forced himself free of the hold, turned, and hammered Darrel across the jaw with a fist the size of a large ham.

"You shouldn't bring trouble makers in here if you can't handle the shit they stir up," the carnie said, punching a fist into his other open palm. He flung the table across the room in one quick swipe, then lifted me from my chair by the collar of my kutte.

"I'm going to have fun breaking you in half," he said, before launching me like a rag doll over top of the bar. I tumbled, scattering beer bottles as I fell behind the bar and impacted the shelves along the wall behind it.

Before I could get back to my feet, the sound of breaking glass and half-drunken battle cries filled the air. The entire joint had come to life in an old-school roadhouse rumble.

Darrel was knocked out cold, sprawled across the floor in the middle of the bar. Harry was once again perched on top of our original assailant, legs wrapped around the man's neck, strangling him. James on the other hand had the first carnie he'd called Hank, distracted in a bare-knuckle fist fight.

The carnie that tossed me had already forgotten about me and turned on another patron.

Dumb mistake.

I leapt across the bar and planted my size eleven boot in the crook of the carnie's knee, dropping him to the ground. He moved like any other big guy I'd ever known. He might have been barrel chested and muscle-bound with the strength of a grizzly, but guys like that were slow, stiff, and vulnerable once they were on the ground.

I just needed to stay out of his reach, because if he managed to get those thick dick beaters of his on me, I'd be royally fucked.

Go figure, it's just my luck that I happened to cross paths with the one big guy that looked like he'd destroy the center of any NFL team, who just happened to know kung-fu.

Fuck my life.

The carnie spun in his kneeling stance, sweeping my legs out from under me. Landing with a thud on the sticky, beer soaked floor, I could have sworn I heard a few ribs crack. Everything hurt and my head swam from the impact.

Hank loomed over me and smiled, sucking in an exhausted big guy breath. "Told you I was going to have fun breaking you in half."

He grabbed my left boot and twisted, pulling me clear of the floor. He spun like an Olympic athlete competing in the hammer throw, carrying me around with the momentum of his turn.

It's a funny feeling when you have absolutely no control over your limbs because of the sudden and excruciating use of physics forced upon you before the sensation of zero-G apogee and free fall washed over you.

That in itself wouldn't be so bad of an experience, if not for the blunt force trauma of impacting a laminated safety glass window at the front of the building afterward.

Tumbling to a stop against the windshield of an older car, shattered glass covered me and the hood of the crappy old dodge sedan I'd landed on.

Everything seriously hurt. Careful not to move too much too quickly, I systematically flexed muscle groups starting with my toes and working my way up to stretch and pop my neck, just in case I happened to have a serious injury.

Grunting, I leaned over and rolled off the hood of the car. I froze where I landed, crouched between vehicles, face to face with probably the most disturbing thing I had ever encountered in the backwoods of Florida.

It looked like a full-grown flamingo, but like something had dragged it through the ditches across three state lines and left the dumpster fire of a creature for dead in the scorching Florida sun. Festering sores stood out amid bare patches of missing feathers that sporadically covered the bird's body. Its eyes glowed with an ethereal purple haze.

The smell of the thing was something else entirely and my eyes began to water from the stink of it, like the worst combination of a fast food dumpster mixed with a nine-day-old rotting calf. It was a scent that slapped you across the face and demanded immediate action by one's innards that I wouldn't soon forget.

Glaring at me with that one beady eye it flicked its head sideways and drunkenly swayed. It let out a barking call, like the demonic crossing of a Canadian goose and a baboon, then struck.

Flicking its snake-like head in my direction it smacked me across the chest with the tip of its hardened beak. It had ripped my shirt and left a gouge across my chest where it struck me.

Sounding like a mini machine gun, it clacked its beak together then let out another barking call before taking a step toward me.

More of the barking calls answered my stinky little buddy from the tree line at the far side of the parking lot. They stalked forward at a hurried pace, their heads drunkenly snaking up and down, like a flock of zombie flamingos.

"Hey, James! Y'all been having critter problems lately?"

I backpedaled and stood, rounding the end of the old car. More of the flock were filing in from my left around the end of the building.

The brawl still raged on inside the building. Breaking glass and grunted screams emanated from the broken window.

The bird struck at me again, leaving a gash across the back of my forearm. It clacked its beak and barked like some twisted demonic laughter.

"Why the hell can't I ever catch a break?" I shouted. "I just wanted to stop for beers and relax a bit, but NOOooo… Braxton isn't ever allowed to relax. That would just go against everything the universe has against me."

About the time I reached the door, two more of the birds dropped in next to me and struck, flicking their heads in my direction.

I snatched one by the neck and flung it to my left. The other two advanced, opening new gashes across my arms.

I reached for the Smith and Wesson model 649 revolver holstered in the pit of my back and fired. Point blank with .357 magnum against a ragged zombie bird did some serious damage. Feathers exploded everywhere. The other birds scattered in all directions, lingering a short distance away. They barked and clacked their beaks like angry threats directed toward me.

"What the hell are you doing, Brax?" James yelled from the broken window. Others joined him at the opening, a few of them armed, including the bartender who held a pump shotgun in the crook of his arm.

On the other side of the parking lot, the driver's door of a white sedan opened and the occupant of the vehicle, a red-nosed circus clown, stepped out. He swayed, barely able to stand on his own.

"Hey!" he slurred. "Can't a guy get a little rest around here?"

Barks and clacks from the zombie flock responded to the yelling. They turned their attention to the drunken clown and advanced. In the blink of an eye, they swarmed over the clown like a nest of fire ants over a dead rat. The eerie barking grunts quickly drowned out the drunken clown's blood-curdling screams.

High-pitched tribal screeches like some sort of war chant bellowed out from the tree line at the far side of the parking lot. From the dark shadows of moss-covered live oaks, emerged what could only be described as

Florida man's Amazonian warrior wife, or some bath salts infected Cajun Red Sonja.

Armed with a five-pronged frog gig the size of a pitchfork, she charged the flock of flamingos. I blinked, trying to comprehend what I was seeing. Her fire engine red hair contrasted her chalky white skin and glowed like the flame of a ghostly candlestick. Bound together with what looked like bailing twine, she'd strategically positioned five bullfrogs to form the strangest bikini I'd ever seen.

She let out another screech, diving into the flock gig first. Spearing one of the zombie flamingos, she leveraged the weapon like the arm of a catapult, flinging the zombified bird over her head. Other birds rushed over to their fallen comrade, attacking it like a pack of starving cannibals.

"Freida!" James shouted, leaping through the broken window.

The wild woman swung the frog gig in a low arc, knocking over dozens of birds in one swipe. James charged into the gathered flock, broken beer bottle in hand, and stood back to back with the swamp warrior. The pair chanted a shrill battle cry, fighting back the oncoming hoard.

I jumped into action, firing another round into the amassed avians. Other patrons from the lounge followed my lead and charged into the melee with chairs, pool cues, or anything that happened to be in easy reach.

By the time I reached James and Frieda the jungle bunny, the flock had begun to disperse, retreating into the tree line to the strange barking call of the birds.

"What in the short bus hell just happened?" someone shouted through exhausted breaths.

I couldn't have said it much better, because that's exactly what I was thinking.

We carried a number of the dead flamingos inside the lounge to examine them in a better light, then realized that maybe they weren't undead after all. Festering sores covered their bodies, some so deep that exposed bone protruded above the flesh in featherless patches.

James introduced me to his better half, Mrs. James O'Connel, better known in these parts as Freida, the Frog Charmer after she'd mentioned how most critters in the area had been acting really weird the last few weeks.

Her specialty was a flea circus-style sideshow using trained bullfrogs to jump through hoops, tightrope walk, and other oddity type tricks. When not performing, she spent her spare time in the nearby swamps and bayous fishing, hunting, and trapping anything she could make a fast buck with. Normally Frieda was the go to fountain of knowledge on creatures great and small for the community, but she was totally out of ideas about what might be affecting the swamp critters.

About the time we were ready to pack it in and go back to drinking, someone mentioned Mother Bluebird. James seconded the suggestion, kicking himself for not coming up with the idea first.

He explained that Mother Bluebird was probably one of the most educated people in these parts. As far as he knew she had a multitude of college degrees, was a professor for Florida State down on the big campus, and was a bona fide doctor, even though she hated being called a doctor.

So we finished our drinks, disposed of the dead birds, and headed down the way to pay Mother Bluebird a visit.

On the outside, the doctor's house looked like a quaint little Florida farmhouse, complete with a beautiful and orderly flower garden. On the inside, the house could be best described as an immaculate library beyond the scope of any civic organization.

We were greeted at the door by the doctor's partner, Karen, whose smile could brighten the sun. At first glance through the doorway, my mind reeled trying to comprehend the enormity of the house on the inside. I slid the thought to the side and chalked up the mental brain fart to a coincidental optical illusion.

Inside the house, shelves of hand worked teak housed thousands of books that covered every possible square inch of wall space within view, some of which were decorated with this or that odd trinket, animal skull, feather, fossil, mineral specimen, and more.

Karen led us to the study, just off to the left of the entrance, and encouraged us to sit and relax while she let Mother Bluebird know that we were there.

The study was a place out of time. Like it had been pulled from the private collection of a Smithsonian elite from the turn of the nineteenth century. The place had that vibe of look with your eyes, not your fingers, with museum-quality pieces and volumes of books that were probably rare, one-of-a-kind leatherbound editions.

I had been examining a set of Roman coins in a small display stand at the far side of the room when the double doors opened and in strode the most confident waif of a woman I had ever had the pleasure to meet. Filthy, save for her hands after removing her leather gloves, she reeked of something foul mixed with chemicals of an unknown origin. Short and thin, she looked like a strong wind might carry her away on a whim.

"Please excuse my tardiness." She removed her gardening hat and placed it with her gloves on a side table by the door. "I was in the middle of cleaning several new display specimens."

Freida tapped the end of her frog gig onto the hardwood floors and popped to attention.

Mother Bluebird let out a frightened screech and glowered at the Frog Charmer. She looked from Frieda to me to James and back to Frieda. "Oh darn. I am so sorry dear. I spoke with one of your cult mates the other day and informed them that I just wasn't interested."

Freida tilted her head with that look of confusion when the brain refuses to process the information presented to it.

Mother Bluebird continued into the room. She made her way past all of us and took a seat in a leather-covered high-backed chair, then motioned us toward the couches circled around a beautifully carved coffee table in the center of the study.

Several other seats with lamps and side tables that occupied dark alcoves were the only other furniture in the room aside from a large boardroom-style table at the far end of the room covered in books and unrolled maps.

She crossed her legs and laced her fingers over her knee. "What can I do for you fine folks?"

James sat on the end of the couch nearest to her left, I sat to her right, Harry and Darrel sat on the opposite ends of the couches while Frieda stood stoically like an Amazonian warrior on guard duty.

Karen returned with an ornate wooden tray and Asian themed tea set, complete with a brilliant emerald dragon encircling the teapot and each of the small tea glasses. She placed the tray on the table and served each person before seating herself on the arm of Mother Bluebird's chair.

"It isn't anything fancy, just a simple blend that I find soothing," Mother Bluebird said, then sipped her hot tea.

James whipped out his phone and showed Mother Bluebird the images he'd taken of the zombie flamingos we'd encountered at the lounge.

"Oh, my…," Mother Bluebird gasped. "And they just attacked without provocation?"

"Yes ma'am," I answered. "They swarmed out of the tree line by the Red Velvet Lounge and started attacking anyone nearby before Freida charged in and scared them away."

Mother Bluebird tapped at the phone screen. "Do you know where those wounds came from?" she asked as she stood. "Were they possibly inflicted by other flamingos"

"Possibly," I said. "But they stank like something dead."

"And looked like something undead," James added.

Hank squeezed the bulb of his horn, so it let out a long sad honk.

Mother Bluebird took a long sip from her tea, then sat it on the table before searching through the shelves of books. "Necromancy, possession, undead, zombie, hoodoo, voodoo, zoodoo," she mumbled as she grabbed one title after the next from the shelves and returned to her seat. "Which one of you is the fastest reader?"

We all looked around at one another, unsure how to answer. She handed me a thick, leather-bound book. "You look intelligent enough to understand what is in this selection. Do be very careful with it though, it is one of a kind and quite old," she said, then continued passing out books to the others.

"I don't mean to sound rude, ma'am. But what fields do you hold your degrees in?" I asked.

"Literature and English, of course."

I let out an uncontrollable laugh and leaned back on the couch, preemptively rubbing at my temples to head off the headache that I was sure was coming. "Alright then, let's go back to basics. Who, what, when, where, why."

Mother Bluebird brightened up and smiled. "Alright, the first four are the easiest to start out with. Zombie flamingos attacked the patrons of the Red Velvet Lounge this evening."

"That just leaves the why," Darrel added then slurped a sip of tea.

"Maybe they're hungry," I said.

"Or sick," James added.

"Or zombies," Karen said with a dreadful sigh, accentuated by a slow honk of Harry's horn.

"And this was the first sighting?" Mother Bluebird asked. "The attack was completely unprovoked, and you haven't seen anything else out of the ordinary?"

I snapped my fingers, remembering what Freida had said. "You mentioned before that the critters have all been acting strange lately."

Freida shifted uncomfortably, like she didn't like being the center of attention. "Yeah, more than strange. Some of the critters have even started changing colors. They have been overly aggressive, even for the grumpy old gators, and they seem slower if that makes any sense."

"Where have you noticed this happening?"

Freida started rambling off locations in the swamp based on landmarks and I stopped her in mid-description of the old swamp hag's shack. I turned back to Mother Bluebird. "Do you have any good maps of the local area, not just highway maps?"

"Would a topographic relief map be sufficient?" she asked.

"That would be perfect, ma'am."

She hurried to the back of the room and opened a floor-to-ceiling cabinet that concealed cubbies for rolled maps. Searching through the cabinet she let out a quick ah ha, before pulling a map that had to be all of four feet tall from the cabinet and stretching it out on the large table at the back of the room. I stood and turned. She'd spread out a map of the surrounding marshes and wildlife areas.

"Freida," I said, motioning for her. "Could you come show us where you've seen issues with the animals?" She nodded and hurried over to the side of the table.

"Here's Carnival Hills," I said, pointing to a space along the main road, "and the Red Velvet Lounge should be around here." I tapped at the map with an index finger.

Mother Bluebird retrieved a small leatherbound journal from a side table and began scribbling notes so fast I thought the paper was going to ignite.

"Big Tom, the biggest gator in these parts, has been acting really weird lately. Even saw him trying to climb a tree after a squirrel the other day back over here north of Sparrow Island."

"What about the flamingos?" Mother Bluebird asked.

"Oh, they are all over the place. But there's this one bunch that start dive bombing my boat any time I go through their area."

I looked to James then back to Freida. "Where would their area be?"

"Oh…," she said, leaning over the map she pointed. "Right about here."

I turned back to James. "Just north of Sparrow Island."

"There used to be a family of rum runners cooking off homemade hooch that lived out there," Darrel added. "They got caught by the law a few years back."

Karen held up her hand and cleared her throat. "Could someone be back there practicing voodoo, or summoning demonic spirits?"

I shrugged. "Considering the weird shit I've seen, anything is possible."

"Seems like someone should pay a visit to the island," Mother Bluebird chimed in.

"Can we even get back there?" I asked.

"Harry's truck should be able to get back there without too much trouble," James added. "It's been a bit dry this season."

I slapped the table and started for the door. "Alright, then. Let's roll!"

Harry honked an excited quack on his horn.

The road leading up to Sparrow Island was worn, rutted, and not the easiest thing to navigate in the dark. Lucky for us, Harry's Suburban was lifted and on forty-four-inch mud boggers. It was easily one of the funniest sights I'd ever seen. A scrawny little white-faced clown driving what was essentially a monster truck, decorated out like a circus clown and complete with a big red nose through the back road swamps of Florida.

Ancient piles of trash and junk cars littered the sides of the path and had become more frequent the further we traveled. A short time later we spotted the flickering torchlight ahead of us. The path ended at a waterside clearing and a rickety suspension bridge that led to an island with a dilapidated cabin built at the peak of its rise. The wrap around porch looked like the only thing holding it to the cabin was the heavy layer of moss growing on it. Torches burned slowly, glowing a dull orange and spaced every twenty or so feet around the perimeter of the island. It reminded me of a scene straight out of one of those cheesy B-rate horror movies.

A chill ran down my spine. What was it about swamps and evil shit? Was one a prerequisite to the other or was it just a complete coincidence that I kept finding trouble in?

We came to a stop and Frieda climbed out through the window onto the top of the Suburban. She slid down the windshield to the hood and crouched, sniffing the air. "Something smells off. Like heavy chemicals or something."

She was right. I could smell something hanging in the humid air that made me think of mixed cleaning chemicals. I pulled a flashlight from the glovebox and shined it around. Piles of discharged batteries, brake fluid bottles, gas cans, and tins of acetone littered the waterline at the edges of the clearing.

"Well, that would explain where my gas cans kept going," Darrel said.

Harry honked his agreement.

James let out a low whistle. "You aren't lying. This would explain the last three years of thefts from people's sheds in and around Carnival Hills.

I scratched my head then turned in my seat to look back at James. "Have you guys had any problems with drugs in the trailer park?"

James shook his head. "No, not really. At least nothing out of the ordinary that I know of. A little marijuana or ecstasy here and there, but that's really about it. Why?"

Before I could answer, the report and flash of a rifle from the cabin grabbed all of our attention. One of the headlights flicked out with the impact.

"Are there flood lights on this thing?" I asked.

Harry honked a quick yes, or what I assumed was a yes, because everything ahead of us lit up brighter than the noonday sun. A scrawny individual in bib-overalls and muck boots buried their face in the crook of their left arm from the blinding light generated by the Suburban's over-compensated light bars.

I opened the passenger door of the Suburban and slid from the seat.

"Tuck and roll! Every man for themselves!"

I sprinted for the bridge. No sooner had my boots clopped the first step on the wooden planks of the suspension bridge than the individual let out a warbling whistle, then ran back inside the cabin.

The swamp exploded with motion. Flamingos swarmed the cabin out of nowhere. The water beneath the bridge churned with activity. I skidded to a stop, feet from one hell of a massive gator that launched itself from the water and onto the bridge. Sections of flesh were missing in places along the reptile's head and back.

Another gunshot and the sizzling zip of a round buzzed me as it flew by my head. I kicked the gator's snout, sending it back into the water then sprinted the distance to the island. The guy fired another round, knocking out one of the multitudes of lights mounted across the Suburban.

"Go, go, go!" Darrel shouted from behind. The big guy barreled into me, pushing me to the side as he charged for the house.

"Aiyeee!"

I regained my footing and turned back toward the scream. Freida charged headlong into the flock of flamingos that had gathered behind me. She leapt, pushing off from the side cable of the bridge, then parkoured against the support post, somersaulting in mid-air. Like some blood-thirsty shield maiden, she soared into the fray, pinning several of the demented flamingos to the ground with her frog gig.

Harry honked with every strike against a massive python that had wrapped itself around the Suburban.

More gunshots rang out from the swamp cabin. Bullets whizzed by in my general direction, peppering the ground around me. About the time Darrel disappeared into the structure, something tore across the back of my leg.

I turned, not sure what to expect, but it couldn't be worse than some redneck zombie gunmen. Reared up behind me was the largest snapping turtle I'd ever seen. Its head alone had to be all of three feet wide of bone-crushing maw and muscle.

I jumped, stumbling backward in the nick of time. It snapped its massive jaws closed on the space I had just occupied. Not to be denied, it charged toward me. I backpedaled, running into the porch railing.

"Stand still you son of a bitch," Darrel shouted. Three small caliber rounds popped off from inside the cabin. "Guys! I could use some help in here!"

"Gladly!" I shouted. Turning I sprinted around and up the steps to the front door. Just inside the doorway, Darrel leaned against a large bookcase, clutching at his blood-soaked arm. Two burning candles lit the small sitting room.

"You gonna live?"

Darrel nodded. "The dirty swamp rat shot blindly around the corner and got lucky as hell. Plugged two into my arm then ran upstairs." He nodded toward the stairs through the doorway straight ahead.

"Just keep pressure on it and stay put. Trust me. You don't want to go outside just yet." Shifting the flashlight to my left hand I drew the revolver from the holster at the pit of my back. Aiming with my right, I crossed my left wrist beneath my right with the flashlight in hand to both steady my aim and illuminate my target. Proceeding carefully, I checked the other two rooms on this level before heading for the stairs. The kitchen was packed full of copper tubing, glass jars, and gas cook stoves. It looked like one of the fanciest redneck chemical labs I'd ever seen. Kinda surprising there hadn't been any issues in Carnival Hills with backwoods chemical nirvana.

The sound of rifle fire reverberated down the small stairwell from the second story.

"That the best you got," James shouted from outside before a cacophony of gunfire riddled the upper story.

"Dammit, James!" I shouted. "Hold your fire!"

No sooner had the gunfire stopped than I charged up the stairs and spun to the right to find my target. The raggedy man had ducked behind a heavy-looking wooden desk a few feet away from the window.

"Hands in the air, buddy!"

He spun, bringing the rifle up as he did. I fired, aiming low for his left leg, trying to hobble the guy. The round grazed the top of his thigh just enough that he reflexively spun back the other way in defense. Rushing forward I held my weapon on him at center mass.

"I said hands in the air! Drop the rifle!"

An explosion erupted out front of the cabin, turning the humid Florida night into day. The guy took advantage of the distraction, knocking my weapon off target with the barrel of his rifle, then butt-checking me in the face.

Shoulder charging into me, we tumbled through the ramshackle window frame, over the cedar shake porch roof into the dark oblivion of night. I landed unceremoniously on top of the guy, butting heads in the impact.

I fell back, clutching at my face. The guy must have been kin to Wolverine or something because it felt like my face had just gone ten rounds with a cast iron skillet. The dude gasped, coughed, and rolled to his side trying to catch his breath.

Shaking off the haze in my head, I crawled back over to the guy and rolled him onto his stomach, sitting on his legs. Before I could pin his arms behind him, the snapping turtle from hell rushed up and snapped at my face. I leaned back and landed a left hook on the side of its head.

The guy struggled to get out from under me when Godzilla's little brother let out a gurgling hiss and struck at him. He twisted and wrenched his right arm loose from my grip then reached into the chest pocket of his bib overalls. Pulling a red handkerchief from the pocket he snapped it, letting it unroll, and dislodged a large purple-brown something that landed nearby.

That something looked like a large chunk of amethyst that you'd find in any rock and mineral shops, only brown and dingy looking.

Mega turtle lunged for the crystal, panting like an excited pup. One of the zombified flamingos swooped in and pounced on the crystal. Gripping its prize it flapped, pushing off from the ground. Before it could fully launch itself into the air, more than a dozen other crazed flamingos swarmed the first, attacking it, plucking feathers from the already pitiful-looking bird.

"Get me away from them!"

The guy bucked and kicked, forcing me off of him before he backpedaled away from the melee in the nick of time. Jumbo the ninja turtle struck as quick as lightning, crushing two of the sickly birds in a single bite. Other birds dove into the fray joined by the alligator I'd kicked off of the bridge. It lunged for the stone and was sideswiped by the massive alligator-snapping turtle. Jumbo bit deep into the side of the gator's snout and thrashed about.

I drew my backup pistol, an old Army surplus Beretta M9 that I kept holstered in my shoulder rig and cocked the hammer back. I spun, leveling the gun at the swamp rat's face.

"Not so fast buddy!"

Shaking like a terrified chihuahua, the guy froze. A single finger scratched compulsively at one of the many open sores on his neck.

I did a quick check around me for the others and any new threats. James and Darrel exited the cabin heading in our direction. It looked like James had used a curtain to field dress Darrel's arm. Freida reappeared from behind the cabin with a smug look on her face and a stride in her step. She carried a bundle of flamingos and a few small gators strung together by the feet and hung from the end of her frog gig like a hobo's bindle bag.

Looking back I spotted Harry sitting on the hood of his Suburban, smoking a cigarette. At the edge of the clearing a dozen or so feet away from the Suburban was the fiery remains of the gas can mound. Trees and underbrush all around the pile burned bright as thick black smoke roiled into the sky from the burning plastic cans.

"Is that what exploded?" I shouted back at him.

Harry calmly nodded, honked a slow honk, and took another drag from his smoke.

I turned back to the guy just as James and Darrel walked up.

James nudged the guy with the tip of the barrel of an AR. "Hey, shit head."

The guy stared up at James with wide frightened eyes.

"Where'd you get that from?" I asked. "I know you've had your head up your ass on many occasions, but that doesn't mean it's big enough to hide a rifle."

"Harry keeps a few special toys on hand in the back of his truck for those just-in-case moments," James said with a wink then turned back to the guy. "What the hell kinda weird shit have you been doing out here with the animals, you freak?"

The guy shrunk back away from the rifle. I motioned James away and holstered my nine.

"I don't know about the animals, but I know he's been cooking up something in the kitchen. Probably meth from the mix of materials laying around here."

Kneeling next to the guy, I tapped him on the arm to get his attention. "Hey, man. What's with the critters? And what the hell was that rock you dropped?" I asked, nodding in the direction of the critter pile and the stone.

He nervously smiled at me and took a deep breath. "I…I think they started getting into the slag."

"Slag?" Darrel asked.

"Yeah, man. The slag. You know, the bad stuff, the stuff I dumped out back."

I looked over to Darrel and James, both of which shrugged.

"Hey man," I said, getting the guy's attention back on me. "The bad what? What was it that you dumped out back?"

"The bad I…I…Ice man. It keeps coming out ugly and nasty looking. No respecting buyer is gonna go for something that looks like it was shit out by an amateur."

"And you aren't an amateur?"

"Hell n…n…no man! I take pride in my product. It's an art form of the perfect process and ingredient selection. There's a science of art to the entire thing, man. And I wanted to make something special like that guy on television did. I wanted to call it purple haze," he said, panning his hands out in front of himself like he was pitching a movie idea. "You just wait. I get the formula tweaked just right and it'll be the thing with the movers and the shakers. Then everyone will want to try Megaamp's purple haze, man. I'll be fucking famous!" He started to push himself up to his feet, and I drew my M9 on the guy again.

"Woah, there buddy. Calm down. Take a deep breath."

"So what you're saying," James interrupted, "is that we have a swamp full of meth head animals?"

"That were just fighting over one hell of a rock," I added.

The guy just shrugged and went back to picking at the sores on his neck.

"Someone call the sheriff to pick this guy up so we can get back to what we were doing." I holstered my pistol again and rubbed at my face in frustration. I stepped away and took a seat on the porch steps of the cabin, then pulled a partially flattened cigar from my pocket and lit it, enjoying the sweet capped tobacco.

"Why the hell can't I relax and take a break without the weird shit following me?"

I puffed slowly, focusing in on the mesmerizing sounds of the swamp on a warm Florida evening.

The End

Murphy Madness

By: William Joseph Roberts

First published in It Came From the Trailer Park: Volume 3.5 – Three Ravens Publishing, April 2024

After a visit to Buck Bald Brewing in Murphy, North Carolina the idea for this story struck me, and I couldn't help but drop a few of the locals into the mix while I was at it.

You'd think that after two weeks of being on a lake, I would have had the opportunity to drop a line, catch a few fish, have a few beers, and just relax. But oh no. I've come to the conclusion that it's never going to happen. I must have managed to piss off the universe somehow and now I was paying some sort of karmic debt. I've all but given up on ever getting the chance to relax because the jobs just keep getting even weirder and downtime never seems to work out.

What the hell is it with when you tell them *'sure, I'll take the weird jobs',* but the weird jobs turned out to be over-the-top super-duper freaky weird jobs that no one would ever expect. I'm talking about the kind of stuff that would send your mama crying to the corner because of the evil things you had to do to finish the job off right

I'd just wrapped up a gig up in Ashville investigating a Loch Ness monster-style creature that the locals lovingly named Sammy several decades ago. And since I happened to be investigating a lake creature, you'd think I would have been able to catch something. Not one single time in those two weeks did I have a chance to toss in a line, have a beer, and relax for a few.

It might have happened if word hadn't gotten out about what I was doing. Let slip one mention of finding Sammy to this cute little waitress at a local mom-and-pop dinner, and the bat-shit-crazy locals come pouring out of the woodwork. They were seriously upset that the government had sent anyone to prove or disprove that Sammy existed. They liked things just the way they were in their little rural town, and they preferred it if Sammy was left alone. The locals didn't want the world to know about

Sammy. They loved Sammy for who she was, and they were perfectly fine with leaving it like that. Then on top of it all, there wasn't one of them that wanted anything to do with the Government.

It got so bad near the end of the investigation that some of the seriously bat-shit-crazy locals started to get aggressive and tried their damnedest to sink my rental boat.

Then the next thing I knew, the shoreline of Lake Julian, south of Asheville was lined by bleeding-heart hippie protesters. They claimed that Sammy was a mutation caused by the chemical pollution from the power plant while others swore that she was an ancient and elegant beast that had to be protected since she was one of a kind. Those animal rights types had jumped on the bandwagon with the stories the old timers told of gigantic hellbender salamanders that stalked the rivers and streams of the surrounding mountains since ancient times.

That's where they seemed to toss out any iota of common sense when you presented facts that didn't align with their preconceived narrative.

Even though I had the records of construction in hand proving that Carolina Light and Power, who eventually became Duke Power, had constructed Lake Julian in 1964, they refused to accept it as anything other than fabricated lies.

Needless to say, I *really* needed a break after dealing with the previous level of stupidity.

After wrapping up my investigation that didn't turn up any evidence one way or the other, I decided to take the scenic route back to Chickamauga, swinging by Murphy, North Carolina. Or more specifically, Buck Bald Brewing for something dark, chewy, and in liquid form.

The brews they kept on tap ranged from hard seltzers and IPAs to heavy-weight stouts that were so dark and thick I couldn't turn them down.

Besides being a good time to pull off and stretch my legs, it just happened to be the day before the Murphy Music and Brews Festival. Considering I didn't have another contract lined up, I figured it wouldn't hurt to get a hotel room and hang around for a few days to enjoy the *scenery*.

I'd initially heard about Buck Bald Brewing from Marissa Stevens, better known as Rissa to most in our line of work. She'd first stopped in after her uncle and handler Benji sent her up this way on a job for the church. So on one of my runs out his way, I stopped in, checked it out, and fell in love with the joint. It's one of those places that just feels like home when you walk in the door. Good people, great drinks, and amazing memories.

That's also when I learned about the Shepherd's Men, a great veterans program that Buck Bald and, well the whole town supported when you got down to it.

The Murphy Music and Brews festival was a one-of-a-kind charity event that brings amazing live music, delicious craft beer and wine, and unique food trucks together to support the Shepherd's Men. One hundred percent of the proceeds from the event are donated to the organization. The funds assist with their mission to advocate and raise resources for the Share Military Initiative. As a bonus to the cash collected through ticket sales, all vendors tend to donate a percentage of their revenue from the event to the charity as well.

Not a bad way to conduct business in my opinion, but since I was a veteran, I might be a bit biased. I'd never had a great experience when working with the Veterans Affairs office. But at least my experiences were better than some of the horror stories I'd heard from other veterans.

When I rolled into town on the back of Valerie, my badass Iron Horse, I was kinda surprised at the lack of people in town considering the Music and Brews Festival was supposed to be tomorrow. I pulled off the main road and rode along the side drive to the back of the building where Buck Bald Brewing was tucked in nice and tight.

Even with the lack of people in town, there seemed to be a decent little crowd at the taphouse. Several older dudes were out back tossing horseshoes to the tunes of Drivin' N Cryin' playing over the outdoor speakers.

Backing the bike into a spot near the back of the lot, I shut off the engine, dropped the kickstand, and sat there for a long minute just watching the other patrons while I stashed my gloves and helmet. I was hoping Patrick, the owner and head brewer of Buck Bald had something dark and chewy on tap. He usually did, but that would be just my luck.

Strolling my way inside, I couldn't help but admire the eye candy playing a round of cornhole. Probably college kids that had come up from Georgia Tech in Atlanta or something. In my experience music festivals or anything involving music and beer brought out the college crowd in droves.

Matt was behind the bar pouring drinks when I walked into the tap house. A small group of patrons were in the back corner playing what looked like a game of Munchkin.

"Long time no see, Matt."

Matt glanced up from his pour and smiled. "Braxton! What the hell brings you to the backwoods?"

"Just passing through after a gig up in Ashville. Figured I'd catch the music festival and sample the wares for the weekend. Seems kinda thin on folks the day before an event."

Matt shook his head as if he were unsure about something. "That's if we're still having the festival. It's one of our biggest events of the year, but there's been some strange sightings going on lately."

That little bit of hope I had that I could get some quality downtime and relax suddenly started to feel like it was fading away.

"Give me one sec," Matt said. "I need to deliver these drinks." He gathered up a tray loaded with drinks and headed for the gaming group in the back.

"Where's Patrick?" I asked.

Matt nodded toward the back where the brewing gear was located. "He's been back there preparing the tanks for the next batches." I glanced over and spotted Patrick carrying a grain sack on each shoulder, heading to the rear of the brew room. If he wasn't working, I'd holler at him, but better to not distract a man who's in the middle of making *artistic creations* we could all enjoy. He'd eventually get done with what he was doing and come out to the front to visit with everyone. Even though it was his taphouse, he was just that kinda person that always checked on folks and made sure they were having a good time. We could catch up later, but in the meantime, I was looking forward to seeing what new tasty treats they had on tap.

I turned, leaning back against the bar, and took in the room. It sounded like the gamers were having a good time. You couldn't miss the laughter and good-humored jeering coming from their table. Several other people sat scattered around the room at the bar and the tables of the room, but one in particular caught my eye.

I could hear Piotr Mierzejewski at the far end of the room complaining about his electric wheelchair being broken and that it was going to take weeks to get the replacement parts. For the time being he was stuck in a manual wheelchair that made things that much harder on him, but that didn't stop him from following his passion.

I'd met him once before when visiting Buck Bald. Social services work by day, science fiction author by night. The man could talk your ear off when it came down to the works of David Drake, David Weber, or Robert Heinlen. His first series was an alien invasion story that took place in New Zealand called *Dragoon*. It even hit it off well enough that he'd gotten comments and reviews along the line of Heinlein-esque for his work.

Then, low and behold, sitting alone at the end of the bar was someone I hadn't seen in a long minute. I must have missed her when I first walked in because her back would have been to me when I walked in the door.

I met Charli Cox a few years ago down in Key West Florida while sorta working a job for the feds. That was before I got hired on as an independent contractor for the KCG, Krypto, Cults, and Gangs, a special detachment of the U.S. Marshals that deals with the weird shit.

Charli had been working at the Green Parrot as a waitress at that time and was a fountain of knowledge that helped me hunt down Lenny Raynard, one of my veteran buddies from my Air Force days. She seemed to be the type that just happened to be in the right place at the right time, because of the random useless information she had packed away in her brain pan happened to be pertinent at the time. I'd tried several times to score her phone number, but none of my debonair charms had worked on her, yet.

She hadn't seen me yet. While she scrolled through her phone, I slid out of my seat and made my way to the other end of the bar.

"Charli Cox," I said, drawing out her name. "What exactly brings a pretty lady like you up to the mountains and away from the white sandy beaches you love so much?"

She turned to look in the direction of my voice and smiled wide. Those golden amber eyes of hers seemed to light up the room. She had her dark brunette hair pulled back into a braided ponytail that draped over her right shoulder and dangled low enough to cover most of the visibly ample cleavage not already covered by the low-cut tank top. She bore the distinctive features of Italian or Eastern European descent. She wasn't drop-dead baby doll gorgeous, but she also wasn't *handsome* as some might put it. Her features were strong and almost regal, which matched her personality. On her looks alone, I could picture her in a fancy gown as an upper-class lady running an estate while the Lord was away on business. Then mix in her no-bullshit eyes-on-the-target attitude, I had no doubt she'd have been the one working her way up the social power structure of the royal European courts.

"Well I'll be damned if it isn't Braxton Hicks," she said with a surprise. A sly smile crossed her face. "What old dog dragged your sorry ass into this place?"

"I could just about ask you the same." I flashed one of my best smiles and slid into the empty seat next to her. "Just passing through and thought I'd stop in for a few beers and visit with a few old friends in the process. What brings you this far away from the beach?"

"Doing a little vacation of my own." She smiled. "You know the kind, a little shopping here, some sightseeing there, and then I heard about the Music and Brews Festival. But it seems unlikely that it's going to happen now."

I shook my head, not sure what she meant by that. "Do you know something that I don't?"

"The locals are getting scared of this thing that keeps popping up around town. Word is getting out that there's something strange going on up here, so the tourist numbers have dropped significantly. The hotels and rentals around here should be packed to the gills, but they aren't, or at least that's what folks here at the bar are saying."

I shook my head, more from amazed frustration than anything. Could a guy just not get a break for a change? I mean, what did I do to the universe that it refuses to let me relax just a little bit?

"They're calling it the Murphy Madness," she continued. "People keep seeing what they claim is some kind of alien or a weird new beast. Hell, half of the younger crowd keep calling it a cryptid or an *SCP. It's become enough of a problem that they're not even sure if the music festival is going to happen. The rumors have scared away a lot of tourists."

"Hey Brax," Matt shouted as he returned to the bar. He thrust out his right hand. I took the offered hand in mine and shook. "What can I get you?"

I looked back at the tap, unsure what any of the interesting names were when it came to beer types. That's one thing that I found out about these craft breweries. Unless the type of beer was directly in the name, you couldn't be sure what you were getting. So I'd learned to ask one simple and direct question.

"What do you have on tap that's dark and chewy?"

Matt flashed a smile then took a quick glance at the taps. "How about our Moonlight mocha milk stout? Sweet, chocolatey, caffeinated, and all with a respectable percentage of alcohol for a beer."

"That sounds wonderfully perfect to me," I replied. "I'll take a pint." Matt returned to the taps and poured a tall glass of the thick dark liquid.

"Here you go Brax," he said as he scraped away a little excess foam before setting the glass on the bar in front of me.

I picked up the glass and was immediately blown away. That first taste was sweet and chocolatey with a hint of coffee flavor at the back end that mingled with the bitters. The best part was that it was thick-thick, just the way I like my beers and my women. The kind that you can really sink your teeth into that leaves you feeling full and satisfied afterward.

"This is something akin to heavenly bliss right here, Matt."

"That's appreciated," Matt said, "but I just sell them. Patrick's the genius behind the scenes."

I spotted Patrick, empty-handed this time and stood, holding my glass high. "Hey, Patrick!" He looked up from what he was doing, saw me, and nodded, acknowledging me. It was interesting to watch Patrick at work. There was this entire science behind it that he would ramble on about that I didn't understand at all, but I could sure appreciate the end product of his labors. You could tell he was passionate about what he made because of the way he talked about it. He could talk for days about each and every flavor and then some. Down to the fine flavor notes in each brew and what inspired each one of the recipes.

"You've outdone yourself this time, brother man!"

"Thanks, Brax," he shouted back with a thumbs-up thrust in my direction.

"So what's going to happen with the music festival," I asked, turning back to Matt.

He just Shrugged. "Dunno yet, but I wouldn't expect them to just cancel it out of the blue considering how much promotion they've already done for it."

I nudged Charli's arm with my elbow. "I guess we have a music festival to attend this weekend."

"I guess so," she replied before taking another sup from her drink. Her glass was looking a little low, so I flagged Matt.

"Another one for the lady please, on me."

"You don't have to do that."

"Are you kidding?" I said, turning in my seat to face her. "It's the least I can do for all the times I harassed you for your phone number."

"Fair enough."

"What did you have," Matt asked, trying to remember.

"The Pixie Punch, please."

"Try to help and just get screwed over for it," someone yelled from the back table. Several of the patrons gaming in the back started to disburse, saying their goodbyes before leaving the building.

I turned back to Charli. "You up for a game?"

She shrugged. "Sure, why not." We grabbed our drinks and headed for the back table to join the others in a round of Munchkin, which ended up turning into several hours and multiple rounds of Munchkin with nearly a dozen different people. It was a great game and an easy way to kill time. You didn't have to think too much, but it could get competitive as hell in a heartbeat.

One of the big tricks of the game was to work with the other players and then at the very last minute before everyone made it to the last level you pull any dirty trick or move in your hand that will let you win the game. Now granted, a good portion of this has to do with the luck of the draw with the cards that you get on the initial deal or as you Kicked in the Door. You could end up with a crap hand that gets you nowhere from the get-go or you can end up with several level-up cards that put you way ahead of the other players. And that's exactly what happened with Charli in the first game. She kicked everyone's ass in short order and made sure to rub it in so we remembered who won.

We even went so far as to toss in minor bets on each game with the lowest level loser buying the next round of drinks for everyone at the table.

"I'm done," Piotr announced, backing his wheelchair away from the table, he turned and wheeled himself toward the bar. "Tap me out for the night, chief."

Several of the patrons shouted their *good night's* and *be safe* to him as he rolled out through the large roll up garage door at the back of the building.

"Good night, man." I shot back at him with a wave. "Better luck next time, buddy."

Charli slapped me on the side of the shoulder. "What are you talking about? You lost your ass off."

I shrugged, then finished off the beer in my glass. "I still beat him, and we had fun. Or at least I did. Didn't you have fun?"

Charli rolled her eyes. "I don't know. Dealing with you and your immaturity most of the time isn't exactly fun in my book. It's more of a chore than anything else."

"I can be mature."

"Really? You're really going to say that with a straight face?"

"Hell yeah, I am. Just watch this." I walked back up to the bar and waited for Matt to have a moment from the other patrons. "Good sir," I said in my best English butler accent. "Would you be so kind as to refill mine and the lady's drinks?" Matt blinked and stared back at me, a look washed over his face like you'd see on a confused puppy.

"He said he could be serious and not immature," Charli said, filling Matt in on the joke. Matt turned back to me and smiled with one of those huge shit-eating grins.

"You did, did you?"

"Indubitably, my good man. Now, would you be so kind as to fetch our drinks like a good lad? The night is still young, and we'd like to enjoy every possible moment of it."

"Coming right up, sir," Matt replied in his own fancy accent that sounded more French than British, almost like the French Kanigits from Monty Python's Quest for the Holy Grail.

I'd barely returned to my seat before a commotion of cussing and hollering from the parking lot caught my attention. Someone was pretty pissed off by the sounds of it. I listened for another moment before Charli spoke up.

"That sounds a lot like Piotr."

"Yeah... it does, doesn't it?" I agreed.

I hurried over to the large open garage door and peeked around the corner. The parking lot ran along the side of the building and sloped downward slightly, heading toward the main road that ran perpendicular to the front of the building. Piotr had somehow gotten himself jammed in between a small sedan and a large diesel pickup truck.

"Hey man, you okay?" I hurried over to see what the hell he had done to get into this situation.

"Yeah, I'll be fine," he huffed in frustration. "My regular wheelchair is in the shop because they couldn't get a replacement motor. I had to use this one and the brakes are just, shit. I got rolling a little too fast and then couldn't stop in time before I ran into this car, bounced, and managed to get jammed between the two of them." He struggled to turn and free the wheelchair. They *were* parked a bit close to each other. Hell, I'm not a big boy but, I'm not some scrawny little skeleton either; they were parked so close together it would have been hard for me to slip into the driver's door of the truck.

"Hang on, man. You're going to scratch the hell out of their paint jobs," I said. Grabbing the wheelchair by the sides of the frame, I jerked, pulling the wheelchair free. One more good yank and I shifted the angle, making it easier to roll him out from between the vehicles.

Slapping him on the back, I stepped around to face him. Piotr had gone sheet white. His face was frozen in a wide-eyed stare of confused horror. Goose pimples stood out across his neck, like he'd just seen a ghost of something.

Following his gaze towards the woods at the back of the property, I spotted the thing that held his attention.

Several others must have caught a glimpse of the thing as well because I heard sharp gasps and excited comments about getting inside coming from the back of the taphouse.

It was hard to explain *what* it was that I was seeing at the end of the parking lot. It honestly hurt my eyes to focus on the creature and made my brain ache trying to comprehend exactly what the hell I was looking at.

The thing was small but muscular and bulky with a strange triangular head that featured a stubby snout. It was almost like one of those little green men from classic science fiction or what they call a gray alien now had crossbred with a big dog or gotten bitten by a werewolf or something. The damned thing just looked wrong on so many levels. Like some bastard love child from a furry convention gone wrong and so unnatural that even Mother Nature would have shunned it.

"That ain't something normal," I mumbled.

"That looks like what the locals have been describing," Charli said.

A snarl escaped the thing's snout and then it was gone. It was the strangest thing. One minute it was there, the next it had completely disappeared. It could have been supernatural speed like a werewolf or vampire. The gods know I didn't want to deal with any kind of shenanigans like that right now. Maybe it was some kind of time dilation where it could sneak away before we realized it was even there. Or maybe it just ducked down behind the trees surrounding the back of the lot. That would be a hell of a lot better than a *were* or a *vamp*.

"Well, that sure as hell wasn't nothing," I said, turning to Charli, then I noticed the crowd of folks still standing around. "Show's over folks. How about we all get inside for right now just in case that thing might have rabies or something," I said, thumbing over my shoulder as I urged everybody back inside.

I grabbed Piotr and pushed him back inside. It just wasn't right to leave him out there to fend for himself. But it was seriously tempting after he started cussing me for dragging him back into the taphouse.

Patrick had come out from the brew area and started lowering the garage door. Closing it up tight behind us he latched it down while Matt went around locking the man doors.

"Who's up for another round?" Matt shouted, shifting the crowd's attention as he returned to the bar and poured himself a drink. Patrick had stepped off to the side back into the brewing area and was already on the phone. I assumed he was calling the sighting into the police since it had become such an issue.

By the time Patrick had come back out to the main area, several of the patrons had made their way over to the bar placing new drink orders. He came over to where me and Charli were standing and showed us the picture he'd gotten of the thing on his phone.

"I let the cops know we had another sighting and sent this to them."

"Send it to me too, if you don't mind."

Patrick nodded "Easy enough, buddy."

"Is that the thing that everybody's been talking about?"

"Yeah," he confirmed. "I'd say either we've all got a touch of the Murphy Madness, or that thing is real."

"I haven't been here more than a few hours," I said. "If this was some kind of mass hallucination induced by bacteria, virus, or even a mold spore, I wouldn't think that I'd been in the area long enough to have been affected."

"So, the thing had to be real," Charli said, chiming in.

"Yeah..." Patrick agreed, half laughing.

"What's back there in that area of the woods?"

Patrick looked up from his phone and cocked his head in thought for a moment. "The Murphy Walking Track and the Murphy Riverwalk are back that way. It's a public area with a pretty good bit of acreage."

I started thinking back to the kids in Florida who had been tormenting the locals with a Sasquatch outfit. "What are the odds that it's just a couple of kids playing pranks on everyone?"

"It's possible," Patrick said with a shrug. "But if that's the case, they are some top-level pranksters. Nobody's had any luck finding out anything about them. And this is the first time anyone has seen anything this deep into town. The sightings have always been out on the outskirts of town or around private residences up in the hills, mostly to the north of Murphy."

"Okay," I started. "First off, we need to know what the hell this thing is. If it's a critter, and I'm assuming predator since its eyes were in the front of its head. During times of drought or lack of food predators will come out in areas they wouldn't normally go to because they are desperate."

"That's possible," Patrick said, "but we haven't had either. It's been an exceptional year for rain, and there haven't been any issues with crops or livestock around the area."

"Alright, that's out then. So, what's north of town?" I asked.

Patrick walked over to the far wall where a large map of the area had been placed, framed in what looked like aged barn wood and backed with corkboard.

"A lot of locals and tourists use this map to plan out their trips," Patrick explained. "It doesn't matter if they are rafting, kayaking, or hiking. It's an easy way for folks to keep track of each other, with pins assigned to individuals or groups. They'll mark where they are putting in or starting from and their planned path. When they get done, they come back or call to have their pins removed. It's especially helpful if someone decides to set out alone. It gives us a heads-up to contact the local authorities when they don't check back in after a day or two. Beyond that, we also mark sightings of bears, mountain lions, and bobcats," he said, pointing at several special pins.

"Then one of our crafty locals made these to represent sightings of that thing out there." He pointed to several alien-shaped pins pressed in the map. Several locals who had encounters with it have started calling it Fred the Fuzzy One, so we ran with it. One of our regulars even made hand-crafted plushies and I started a special IPA named after Fred."

I couldn't help but shake my head in disbelief at his last comment. What the hell was it with this newer generation that they keep giving things cute, innocent-sounding names when it could be something deadly as hell that would devour your soul in two seconds flat?

Sometimes I wondered if the next generation were going to make it or not. Murphy's Law was real, that I knew for a fact.

I focused back on the map as Patrick continued to talk, pointing out this trail or that one. It would be easy to get lost in these mountains if you didn't know your way around.

I could just as easily jump on my bike and head out of town. Hell, I was only a few hours from home. I could be back in Chickamauga before it got too late. Everyone deserves a little break every now and then, don't they?

I swear, sometimes it felt like life, the universe, and everything was never going to give me that break. All I wanted to do after working a gig was to have a cold beer with a good cigar, throw in a line, and just relax. But noooo… I can't even get one of those things to line out without some bullshit happening to screw it up. I'd love to know what curse I picked up so I could get it removed like the plague it was on me.

Just is what it is, I guess.

I turned to Patrick and held up my finger. "Give me a minute. I… I need to make a phone call." He nodded and I stepped to the side looking out the back door towards the tree line. Darkness had started to fall as the sun crept lower and lower to the ridgeline of the Appalachian Mountains surrounding Murphy, North Carolina.

I pulled out my phone and dialed Mandy's number. Mandy was the proprietor and sole owner of Karatech, a multi-disciplined business model housed in what used to be one of the old school Pizza Hut's in an outdated shopping center that had long since been abandoned by the franchise back in Lafayette Georgia, the county seat for Walker County.

And by multi-disciplined, I mean multiple businesses under one roof. But her's was a little more fancier than the once large department store turned into an indoor flea market. Or the once state-of-the-art arcade and ice cream shop that had morphed into Krystal's corner; bait, notary services, taxes, and dog grooming all under one roof. The remaining section of the complex had been converted some years ago into "A Wheel and a Prayer", Delbert Johnson's Bible and Tire Center. That was the glory of Walker County, right there.

Mandy's place was a bit fancier than that, though. Karate studio, video rental, and computer services and solutions all under one roof, and besides being best friends since junior high, she was my electronic wizard guru and partner in crime when it came to researching anything on the interwebs.

The phone rang and rang and rang and finally went to Mandy's voicemail, so I left a message.

"Mandy, Braxton. Got a situation in Murphy and need some intel. Call me back."

I had barely hung up the phone before she was returning my call.

"What the hell do you want Braxton? I'm about to go pick up Amy and head to Chattanooga."

"Wait? Chattanooga? Why are you guys going to Chattanooga at this time of the night?"

"So we can go out," she said, nervously.

"Wait, what?" I scratched at my chin, trying to wrap my head around what she'd just said. "But you don't go out. The last time *I* asked you out, your excuse was because there were new updates for some server or something or another that you had to do."

"And besides, that's not the case right now."

"Well then how the hell does one get you out for the night? Cause I'd sure as hell like to know the answer to that little riddle of life."

"You had your chance in high school, Brax, and you blew that when you signed up for the Air Force and disappeared for six years."

"Ouch. That hurt."

"Well, good. It should."

"So why are you *going out*?"

"If you must know, Amy's going on a blind date and I'm playing wing girl for her. She didn't want to go out and meet some stranger by herself, so I've got her back."

"So it's just going to be you, Amy, and her date?" I asked, curiosity lacing my words.

"Not exactly…" she said reluctantly. "Her blind date is also bringing a blind date for me."

"Wait, so there's hope for the male persuasion?"

"Only in your wildest dreams, Brax. If Amy didn't insist on being the social butterfly that she is, I'd still be sitting at the office knocking out updates on the county servers so, ya know, I can get paid."

"Uh huh…"

"Don't you take that tone of voice with me, Braxton Hicks."

"I don't know what you're talking about. I'm innocent."

"Bullshit! Can we just get on with this already? I've got someplace to be, no matter how much I don't want to go."

"How up to date are you on Cryptids and strange new creatures?"

"Fair to middlin' I suppose. Why?" I could hear her tapping away at the keyboard already. I'd put serious money on the fact that she was probably looking up the best Cryptid database there was or hacking some government computer to access it.

"What sort of thing are you looking for? Does it have a name or what?"

I cringed at the cute name the locals had given the creature already and decided against letting that leech its way into the interwebs. "No name, other than the symptom that everyone is calling the Murphy Madness."

"Okay… But you did see something?"

"Yeah," I said, drawing out the word. "Something was an understatement."

"Then what did it look like?"

"Short. Three to four foot tall at most. Scrawny. The shape of the head, face, and eyes really made me think of a gray alien, but it was covered head to toe in patchy white fur. Its face was deformed, too. Almost like it had a canine snout."

Silence answered me from the other end of the line.

"You still there Mandy?"

"Yeah, just trying to think," she said, then I could hear the flurry of fingers clacking away across the keyboard again.

The keystrokes stopped again and we're silent for a long moment before another short flurry of typing followed by several heavy strikes on what I assumed was the enter key.

Then more silence.

"Is something wrong?" I asked. "I'm here if you want to talk about it."

"Yeah… noooo thank you. The problem is that I'm not finding anything that comes even close to that description."

"Nothing?"

"Yeah, nothing." She laughed. "Absolutely freaking nothing at all. This might be a new creature, if it is a creature."

"Okay…," I said, drawing out the word as I thought for a moment. I really didn't want to stay here and deal with this. I just wanted to relax and enjoy life a little bit. But if there was a finder's fee on a new creature that hadn't really caused a lot of trouble yet and I could snag it before anybody else, it might be worth the time spent dealing with it.

Cash had never really been one of my driving forces in this job. I enjoyed the hell out of just traveling around the country on the back of my bike, doing odd government contract jobs here and there to make ends meet. It's not like I had a lot of overhead, either. I didn't have any family to take care of, well, minus my cats. It was just me, the road, and Valerie, my old Vulcan motorcycle.

But, if a new discovery had one hell of a finder's fee, I might could afford to go on a real vacation and get away from everything. Maybe even take a cruise to somewhere nice. But hell, if I took a cruise, I'd probably have to take my mom with me. She's always bugging me about taking her on a cruise like her friends' kids take them on. But that's another problem for another day.

"What's the KCG's rules on newly discovered creatures?" I asked.

"Hang on," she said, followed by another flurry of keyboard clacks. It was almost music to my ears that all but guaranteed she would find an answer. And if she couldn't find an answer, there wasn't one to find. She was just that good.

"All right, so the good news is that yes, the KCG does payout for newly discovered creatures. The bad news is that you have to have some sort of physical evidence to turn in. Something that can be lab tested and dissected. Otherwise, it's no bueno. Audio, pictures, video, none of that counts to log a claim.

"Well, damn." That could be promising if I could track it down. My reluctance to take on this gig was starting to waiver just a little bit. I could see myself now, deep sea fishing with one of those long poles, fishing off the back of a cruise ship, being served up drinks by bikini clad beauties.

"So what's the price tag if I can snag real evidence or bag one of these things?"

Mandy grunted a laugh. "Do I still get my standard ten percent on this, like all the other contracts you tap me for?" She sounded extremely excited about the prospect.

"Yeah, I guess so. I don't know why we would do anything different than normal."

"Good, cause I'm going to need you to go and get that thing and bring it in. I don't care if you have to strap it to the back of your bike. You can make a detour to the lab in Atlanta before you head home."

"Why would I carry it all the way to Atlanta? Why wouldn't we call Freeman and have him send his clean-up crew like always?"

"I just want you to make sure that *you* get it turned in. No subcontractors or anything else involved that could screw it up."

"Okay? Why are you being all kinda weird all of a sudden?"

"Because I believe in you, Braxton. I believe in everything you do. You've got this. Go get 'em tiger!"

There was something seriously up. Mandy has never in my life said anything like that to me before. The only time she truly got excited was a computer wizardry challenge, or one hell of a paycheck, which meant she could get even cooler hardware.

"Alright, Mandy. Spill it. What's the payout?"

"You're going to shit yourself."

"Really? You get all loving and supportive, then you give me an answer like that? *You're going to shit yourself*," I said in my snarkiest imitation of her. "Come on, Mandy. Give me a number. I'm either going after this thing or going home. It isn't hurting anyone, and only being a minor annoyance."

"If you can bring back physical evidence that they can confirm, it pays out up to one million cold hard United States bills, depending on the amount of evidence collected. So start taking notes, big boy."

"Holy fucking shit, Batman," I muttered to myself. She was right. I almost shit myself. With that much I could completely overhaul Valerie, go on a month-long fishing trip up in the mountains, or I could get one of those fancy mega cat condos for the kerfuffle waiting on me back at the house.

"You weren't lying. That is a serious chunk of cash."

"Yeah," she chuckled. "Tell me about it."

I rubbed my face out of frustration and seriously thought about it. That was a real serious bit of money. On the flip side, I'd be going into this blind with no information whatsoever other than the word of mouth rumors from the locals and what little bit that I'd seen myself.

For all I knew this thing could have some kind of psychic powers, or it could be poisonous with deadly spikes that it throws like a porcupine or some weird shit I'd never seen before. There was no telling. But that was if it wasn't some asshat kids playing a prank. Been there, done that.

But a nice vacation sounded really good.

Dammit to hell. I must be batshit crazy, 'cause by the grace of the gods that watch over dumbass redneck bikers, I set my sights on catching the thing.

"Okay, yeah. I'm going to do it," I said. "Keep digging and see what else you can find. There's bound to be some other mention somewhere about this thing or something similar. It can't be the only one."

"But what about Amy?" Mandy asked. "I'm supposed to be going out with her and her blind date."

"Which is more important? Going out with Amy and her booty call, or more than twenty-five grand in your pocket once this is over?"

"Yeah," she said. "I think I'd rather go after the money. Let me call Amy and let her know that I might be coming down with something." She forced a cough into the phone. "I'll see what I can find out."

"Have I ever mentioned how beautiful you are when you get excited?"

"Shove it, playboy, and get your ass to work. We got rent money to make."

"There's the Mandy I know and love."

"I'll let you know if I find out anything"

"Roger that," I said, and she hung up.

Now that I had the research on this thing into full swing, the big question was how was I going to find this thing again? I walked back over to the map and stared at it for a few moments. There didn't seem to be any kind of pattern to the sightings other than the majority of them were concentrated to the north of downtown Murphy.

The side door suddenly shook, like someone tried to jerk it open from the other side, followed by a heavy handed knock. I stepped around the corner and saw a man standing in the doorway holding a rifle in his left hand.

"I got that dirty son of a bitch. No damned bastard critter can get the best of me," he shouted.

I stood there for a long moment, perplexed. The guy looked like he could have been either a hunter, ex-military, or one of those oorah military wannabe types that never went in but tended to spout everything in mil-spec.

"The hell are you doing JR?" Patrick shouted, pushing me to the side so he could unlock the door.

"Being his paranoid batshit crazy self as normal?" someone shouted from the other side of the bar.

"I could say the same thing about y'all," JR shouted back as he entered, then turned to Patrick. "Why the hell is a door locked? You're still open, aren't you?"

"It's 'cause the creature was here," Patrick waved him on, hurrying him away from the door and toward the bar.

"It was?" JR stopped in his tracks and turned back to Patrick. "Maybe that's why I managed to catch up to it this time."

"What do you mean, catch up to it?" I asked.

"I've been tracking this thing for weeks. In all of my attempts to nab it, I haven't been able to so much as catch up to the thing. Then it just so happens a little while ago I crossed paths with the damn thing in the middle of the woods coming off of the Riverwalk. I think I scared it as much as it scared me, but I still managed to get a shot off."

"Wait," I said interrupting. When you came to the door, you said you got it?"

JR smiled wide. "Yup, I tagged that son of a bitch something good, too."

"At least that's something we can actually believe," someone else from the peanut gallery shouted, adding insult to the conversation.

"What's that supposed to mean?" JR bowed up, puffing out his chest. I could see the anger welling up in him as the color crept up his neck.

"At least more than just you saw this one," Patrick said, reassuringly. "This one you can prove, unlike the fairies that were harassing you back in the fall."

"Fairies are some of the most ferocious forest creatures there are and they're almost like a plague once they get established. You can barely get rid of them, short of a good old fashioned forest fire."

"Let's not get wound up about that again," Patrick said, patting JR on the shoulder. "You said you tagged the thing?"

"Yeah," he said, beaming with excitement. A huge shit-eating grin crossed his face. "I hit that sumbitch with a tracker tag. The way I figured, no one was ever going to get up close and personal to it. So if I could get close enough to hit it with the tracker, I could locate its lair and hunt it down later. That's why I came running out here. Buck Bald was the closest place open, so I come running back up this way to see if somebody could give me a ride to track the thing down."

Holy shit! I thought. The gods of aircraft maintainers and dumbass redneck bikers must have been looking down and smiling on me today. If this guy could track it and lead me to the creature, it would make my job ten times easier. But that was also assuming that dude could track it and he wasn't just blowing smoke. But then, he was right about the fairies, so maybe he wasn't off his rocker like they thought.

"You can track it?" I asked, grabbing JR by the shoulder. I turned him back to face me. "How do you track the thing?"

He dug into his pocket and pulled out a phone that he waggled at me. "With this. I've got an app on my phone that ties into the locator beacon built into the tag I hit him with. It gives me a GPS location that gets me within three feet of where it's at. I just need a ride to get there."

It was a seriously rare moment that I ever considered pulling out my badge. I honestly hated the thing, but it had gotten me out of more than a few tight spots when I really needed it. If my grandpa knew I was working for the government outside of the military, he'd probably roll over in his grave.

And granted, for most people it didn't matter jack shit. It was a tin star connected to just another one of those government alphabet agencies that they'd probably never heard of and really couldn't give two shits about. But it was a legal government agency badge, and I was a duly appointed special deputy marshal of the KCG, working under the jurisdiction of the United States Marshals office.

But then again, by the looks of this guy and the comments floating around the tap house, this guy might high tail it out the door just as soon as he smells anything resembling feds or the government.

I really needed this guy to lead me to the thing, so I could bag and tag it. I still needed to find a ride though. I sure as hell wasn't going to be cruising around the North Carolina countryside with this guy riding bitch behind me.

Reluctantly, I pulled out my wallet and flashed my badge at JR and Patrick. "By the power vested in me as a duly appointed special deputy marshal with the KCG and the United States Marshals office, I need to commandeer you, your tracker, and a vehicle."

Patrick immediately took a step back. "You never told me you were a fed."

"I never really saw the need to, honestly," I replied

"You never told me that either," Charli added with a slap across the back of the head. "The last time I saw you, you were running with a motorcycle club down Key West."

"Well, that was before I started working for the KCG."

"And what the hell is the KCG?" Charli asked. Her fists had almost immediately went to her hips as she started to talk.

"A special branch of the Federal Marshals office. We deal with the weird shit that pops up, just like this creature."

"So…" JR started. "You're the one who has to deal with Bigfoot, fairies, or anything else that people call in."

I turned back to JR. "Yeah, more or less. The upside is, I get to pick which jobs I want to take on."

"JR grinned ear to ear and started laughing. "See! I told you guys I wasn't crazy! I know what I saw!"

"Is this tracker live," I asked, interrupting JR's gloating. "Or is it the kind that updates every couple of minutes?"

JR looked down at his phone, then to me for a long minute before he looked up at Patrick. Patrick nodded. "Go ahead JR. I trust him, even though we need to have ourselves a nice *long* chat after this is all over. For now, this thing is more important. If there's anything I can do to help capture this thing, then let's do it."

"All right," JR said, a nervous stutter slipped into his speech as he spoke. He turned the phone to face me after he gave it a good once over. "It's moving north, heading back into the mountains. And damn if it ain't moving fast. It's already across the river and hauling ass."

"What kind of terrain are we talking about?" I asked. "Can we get up that way with a regular car, or do we need something with four-wheel drive?"

"All the roads up that way are good. Small businesses and some residential areas once you get out of downtown, then you get into the rural properties up in the hills. The only other thing north of here before you get into the full-blown wilderness is Tanglewood Dam and the reservoir, but that's over two and a half miles north of here."

I tapped the screen of the phone and dragged the map down. JR wasn't lying. The thing was moving at one hell of a good clip for it being on foot, which to me meant a four-wheeler, dirt bike, or it wasn't a bunch of kids playing dress up.

"How long would it take us to get up that way?"

"Five, ten minutes tops," Patrick answered. "It's just a matter of what route we take."

"Then let's get gone and catch ourselves a critter."

Patrick volunteered to drive his truck, so I jumped into his King Cab pickup truck along with JR and Charli.

Once we were on the road, I gave Ronald Freeman, my boss at the KCG, a call to let him know I was actively pursuing a new case that just kind of happened. That way he could call the local district office and let them know that there was an active agent and now an open case file in the area.

The last thing I wanted to do was deal with extra paperwork and possibly a reprimand for not following procedure.

Freeman said he'd take care of all the legal crap as long as I kept him updated on what was going on and to not cause any serious damage that the agency would have to pay for.

That was generally easy to do, unless whatever I was chasing tended to destroy shit. But so far, this thing just popped up, scared folks, and disappeared. It hadn't actually damaged, destroyed, or harmed anyone. Even so, I was still leaning towards a bunch of kids playing pranks, but that didn't explain how fast they were moving on foot, unless they had transportation.

Patrick was right about the drive time. It only took us about ten minutes to get up to the area where the reservoir was, which was exactly the direction the thing went.

The area itself was a bit of a strange mix, where rustic and ritzy were smashed together with little lake houses lining the edge of the lake. Some of the places were fancy stone and brick, while others looked more like ancient log cabins. The one driveway that we pulled up to looked like an old fishing shanty. Luckily, tonight the moon was full so there was a good chance that if we did run into the thing, we'd be able to see it even if we didn't have any flashlights. Patrick had that covered in his little emergency kit under the rear seat of his pickup.

"The thing's real close now," Jr said. "I can only zoom in so far, but I can tell you that it's within a hundred yards of us at this point." He pointed straight ahead up the driveway and along the edge of the water line past the shanty house.

I tested the flashlight that Charli had handed me from under the seat then flicked it back off quickly so as not to blind everyone.

"Considering this is now a federal case," I started, "and I have no idea what this thing is going to do if we corner it, how about y'all stay here?"

"And what are *you* going to do if you actually do corner the thing?" Charli asked. I could swear that snark had to be her first language as heavy as she laid it on in that sentence.

"If push comes to shove," I replied before reaching behind my back and producing my trusty Little J-frame Smith & Wesson revolver. You couldn't ever go wrong with .357 Magnum hollow point rounds. They'd put one hell of a hurting on anything not armored.

"I can handle myself with a gun," JR said, drawing his own semi-automatic pistol that looked like some sort of Glock knockoff.

"It is a free country," Patrick added, butting into the conversation. "But do you really think you could handle it yourself if you came face to face with the thing? What would you do if its first order of business was to try to eat you? Tagging it's one thing. Going toe to toe is something else completely."

"That would probably be pretty bad," JR agreed.

"Yeah… That would be pretty damn bad," I said, agreeing. Thinking back to exactly what the fuck was I doing. Oh… right. I was trying to earn enough to go on a stupid vacation. Maybe I should use the money to get my head examined or something if I survived this gig.

I looked back to Patrick. "What about you big man? Staying or going?"

"Staying. I got you up here. I'll hang out till you're ready to go, but, yeah… no. I'm good. Beer is my thing, not running through the dark forest at night chasing some unknown critter.

"Fair enough," I agreed. "Stay here. I'll be back soon as I can," I said and slid out the door. Charli, sitting across from me in the backseat, opened her door and slid down as well.

"What the hell do you think you're doing?"

"Helping you."

"Are you sure about that? You might want to think long and hard about that before we go tromping off into the woods."

"I'm sure," she shrugged and flashed me one of those nervous but resigned smiles. "I've got nothing else better to do."

There was something about her demeanor that just all of a sudden shifted. It went from calm and collected to determined, and now she wore one of those *I will cut you in your sleep* looks as she glared at me. Mandy got that same look from time to time when I was getting really annoying. It was important to learn when you had absolutely zero chance of changing the mind of someone. Because ignoring a look like that could land you in hot water at minimum, or get your balls cut off while you slept.

"All right," I said, agreeing with her, "but I don't want to hear you blaming me later after the thing eats your face off."

"Wait? Are you kidding?"

I shrugged. "Maybe, maybe not. We won't know 'til it happens."

Charli laughed and pulled her own pistol from an appendix holster hidden beneath her loose blouse. It looked like it could have been a Sig or maybe a little 9mm Hellcat. Either way, she held it like she knew how to use it. I just hoped that she actually did know how to use it, because that would at least be something that could be considered backup.

"Sorry, but I've got to ask. Do you know how to use that thing?"

She holstered her piece, put her hands on her hips, and glared at me again. "I can finish the Bill Drill in four seconds," she said. It wasn't perfect but she could probably give me a run for my money with that kind of time.

"Good to know. In that case, by the power vested in me, I duly appoint you as a special deputy marshal to the US Marshal Service assisting me in the service and execution of the responsibilities of the KCG."

"That seems a bit fancy. Do I get a tin star too?" She smirked knowing how full of herself she was.

"No, but if you're a good girl, I'll buy you an ice cream later." She perked up at that.

"Oh yes, chocolate please, with sprinkles and hot fudge."

"Deal, now let's go get this done," I said, and closed the truck door. I walked around to the front passenger door where JR was seated and knocked on the window. He rolled down the window and I held out my hand.

"Yes?"

"I'm going to need your phone if I'm going to use the tracker."

"Oh," Jr said, and looked away nervously to Patrick.

"Just give him the damned phone," Patrick ordered. "He'll give it back when he's done." JR looked hurt but handed the phone over anyway.

"Don't worry. You'll get it back. I promise."

"But what if it eats your face?" JR asked, a whimper threatened at the edge of his voice.

"Well, I guess if things go that direction, you'll have to pull it off my dead corpse." I turned my attention back to the phone. "How do you unlock it?"

JR showed me the screen swipe pattern, opened it, and there was the tracker flashing on the overlaid map. It placed the creature just ahead of us by about maybe one hundred yards, just like JR had said.

"Thank you," I said and nodded to JR. "We'll be back as quick as we can."

"Good luck," Patrick added, leaning forward on the steering wheel to look around JR.

I turned back to Charli and showed her the screen. "Are you ready?"

"Hell yeah. Let's do this thing."

"Just stay behind me and don't do anything stupid," I warned her then began walking down the driveway towards the shoreline. What looked like a small shack that sat maybe fifteen to twenty feet up the hillside from the water line came into view. The closer we got to it, the better I could see that it was in the same kind of condition as the house we'd passed.

If I was reading the tracker right, the thing was hiding either in the shed or behind it. There wasn't much else to hide behind on the shallow slope of the hillside. I thought that maybe it was just an old garden shed or storage for fishing rods until we got a little closer and I could see the front clearly in the moonlight.

It was a dilapidated outhouse complete with a crescent moon cut out in the upper part of the door to let air flow pass through.

"Well, shit," I whispered.

"Literally," Charli added.

I glared back at her, and she gave me a nonchalant shrug before I turned my attention back to the outhouse. Tucking away the phone into my pocket I slid my revolver from its holster and readied my weapon.

"US Marshals! Come out of the outhouse with your hands up. This will go a whole lot easier if you cooperate with us."

We stood there for a long moment and heard nothing other than the creak of tree branches swaying in the wind. Charli let out frustrated huff after nothing happened for several minutes, then proceeded to throw a rock striking the side of the outhouse.

The low growling croon that came from within the shithouse made the hairs on the back of my head stand on end. The sound shifted to a low guttural bark of sorts, like those raptors from the Jurassic Park movie, but softer and not quite as harsh.

"That really doesn't sound good," I whispered over my shoulder to Charli.

"No, it doesn't," she agreed, quavering fear lacing her words. She'd barely gotten out the last word when the pop of rusty hinges snapped our attention back to the outhouse.

I pulled my revolver up, aiming for the crack that started to widen in the outhouse door. Charli followed my lead, aiming her weapon in the same direction. I doubt she'd ever done anything like this in her life. Her nervousness showed outright, rocking side to side while trying to get her footing on the loose leaf litter covering the path.

A three fingered, green gray hand covered in a light gray fur crept out from behind the door and reached for the corner of the shitter. That's when the light breeze slapped me in the face with the sickly sweet scent of rotting citrus, like a bag of rotten lemons or oranges. I swallowed back the bile that had suddenly risen up in my throat.

"Brax," Charli forcefully whispered, "what in the fucking hell is that?"

"I… don't… know." I adjusted my grip and centered my aim on where I thought the things head might be.

"Come out with your," I paused, taken aback by the lack of extra fingers on the creature's hand… "Come out with your hands up, now," shouting forcefully enough that it echoed off the trees on the opposite side of the lake across the water.

The door of the outhouse exploded outward with such force that the rotten aged wood planks splintered from the force. The creature rushed us, and I fired.

Two rounds struck home center mass, stalling the thing's forward movement for a split second. Charli followed suit, squeezing off several rounds before the thing closed in, striking her in the side of the head as it rushed past us then continued up the hillside.

"Charli!" I dove to her side, kneeling next to her on the ground. The thing hit her hard enough that I could already see where a very nasty bruise was going to be prominent on the side of her face by tomorrow morning. There wasn't any other damage that I could make out. No puncture marks, cuts, or anything, but she was out stone cold for the moment.

Picking up her pistol, I tucked it into my pocket then quickly checked JR's tracker, before I hurried uphill after the thing. Why the hell did the thing have to run uphill, deeper into the dark in the forest? This was the perfect setup for any of the horrible horror flicks I'd ever seen. If I were a blonde with big tits, I probably would have been dead by this point of the movie.

"Yep… I'm just a brilliant mother-fucker, ain't I?" I mumbled to myself between panted breaths. "If I'm going to keep doing this kind of stupid shit I need to start going to the gym or something."

By the time I reached the top of the rise, I could hear a high-pitched crooning that wavered back and forth in tone. It almost sounded like a whale song and probably would have resonated like it if this thing were in the water.

Topping the rise I started downhill on the opposite side and found myself in a small forest glen. If I wasn't chasing some unknown thing the scene might have been picturesque, but I didn't have time to enjoy the scenery.

Large oak boughs arched over a small babbling brook fed by a small pool of crystal clear water that formed from what looked like a natural spring in the hillside. It honestly reminded me of the scenes in some video games where fairies would pop out and heal you because you were at their magic wellspring of power. I quickly glanced around in search of the annoying little devils just in case I had stepped into their glen. Fairies were the last thing I wanted to see right now. They wouldn't do anything but cause trouble and distract me from the creature. Or if I'd really pissed them off, there was always the chance of death by a thousand cuts with those little buggers.

Crouched in the middle of the pool was the creature. It knelt in the waist deep water, arms outstretched to the sky as if it were praying to the full moon above. Its crooning song grew louder and louder, resonating off the nearby trees and hillside. The frequency of its song wavered and struck like a sonic attack, disrupting my eardrums like the buffering of a pressure wave.

My flashlight beam started to flicker, then cut out completely. My entire body began to tingle. The hairs on the back of my neck and my arms rose up like goose flesh, but it wasn't. It was more like that feeling you get when you've built up too much static electricity and you're ready to zap the shit out of someone.

The stainless steel of my revolver felt red hot in my hand, as did Charli's pistol in my pocket, my belt buckle, and even the rings on my fingers.

Everything metal that I had on me felt so hot to the touch that I could barely stand it. Then the world erupted in a cacophony of noise and white hot light. My skin tingled to the point of burning. It honestly felt as if I had started to float above the ground. I couldn't feel the pressure of the earth beneath my feet any longer. The universe hummed with a numbness that penetrated to the core of my being, then vanished.

Nothing.

It was gone like it had never existed.

The light, the vibration, the distorted cacophony of sound were all gone in the split second of a moment.

Once my eyes adjusted back to the darkness of the moonlit forest, I noticed the thing was gone as well. Where it had been kneeling in the pool of spring water, something light gray floated aimlessly, riding along small ripples that ran across the surface of the pool toward the water's edge.

Grabbing a nearby stick, I fished the thing out, dragging it over to the shoreline and lifted it out of the water.

It was a light gray mass of fur, but not like it was part of a costume or furry suit. The fur was connected to a membranous material that sort of resembled latex, but the way that it was ripped along one side brought thoughts of shed snakeskin to mind. I untangled the mass and stretched it out on the ground among the leaf litter. Sure enough, two legs, two arms, and all four appendages had three digits each while the head was only partially intact because it looked like it had been ripped away. A sickly gray-blue color tinged area around where several holes penetrated the base material.

"Well shit on a biscuit and fuck me sideways," I muttered, staring at what I could only assume were the holes left behind from the several rounds that both me and Charli had hit the creature with.

"It may not be the creature itself," I said to no one in particular, trying to calm the nervousness that started welling up in my gut. "But it is evidence. And if that blue gray stuff is blood, and this is a shed skin then there's going to be DNA for the eggheads to study.

I folded the suit like you would a child's onesie to make it easier to carry out. The less damage it, the better. I wanted to keep it as intact as I possibly could for headquarters to examine. The main upside is no one got hurt. There was still a slight chance I might get a good payday out of it, but right now the only thing I wanted was a cold beer, because I wasn't looking forward to that call to Freeman to debrief him on what had happened.

"One thing I know for sure, life never gets dull in this line of work," I muttered, and began my trudge up the hill heading back to where I'd left Charli.

*Special thanks to the SCP foundation for letting me give them a mention and all the work they do to document new and unusual cryptids.

Key Lime Succubi

By William Joseph Roberts

First published in It Came From the Trailer Park: Volume 4— Three Ravens Publishing, October 2024

This was another story I had a hard time coming up with the idea for. I wanted to do something out of the ordinary for Braxton since the sub-theme on It Came From the Trailer Park: Volume 4 was vacations. So why not toss him into his own little slice of hell while on vacation with his mother?

"Braxton Eugene Hicks!"

I stopped dead in my tracks. My mother's shrill, grating tone told me I was about to get another one of her *talking to's* before we could even board the ship.

I'd been wrapping up a job in West Palm Beach when I happened to mention to her where I was over the phone. Before we'd hung up, she booked a cruise aboard the Opulent Odyssey for the two of us, using the *just-in-case of emergency* credit card I'd given her to pay for it, and told me to meet her in Fort Lauderdale in two days. Considering she'd been hounding me for the last few years to take her on a cruise like all of her friends' kids had taken them on, I just bit my tongue and let it go.

Sure, there was bound to be a whole lotta skin and tiny bikinis, but it wasn't exactly my ideal vacation… sand and sun never was, especially after a few deployments to the Middle East. At least there would be beer… well, considering I had no idea what kind of cruise she'd booked for us, I hoped there'd be beer. It was still better to burn some cash than to hear my mom bitching about how horrible a son I was compared to my brother Judd or her friends' kids.

I stared up at the ship from the dock and thought to myself, *It's only a week. I can spend a week with my mother on a cruise ship.*

Slowly, I turned to find her glaring up at me with one of those perturbed matronly scowls, arms crossed in front of her with the gaudy gold sequined canvas beach bag my brother had gotten her hanging from her right shoulder. I'd expected to see her matching six-piece luggage set stacked next to her on its little cart, but no. It was just her.

"Where's your luggage?"

"Checked with the porters." She cocked her head to the side and let out a long sigh. "Son… What in the world are you wearing?"

I did a quick glance, looking myself over but didn't find anything torn or out of place. "Clothes?" I answered, looking back at her.

Her frown sagged even deeper. "Don't be a smartass. Why can't you dress like you're on vacation?"

"I am dressed like I'm on vacation."

"What makes you think that when you're still in jeans, steel-toed boots, and that nasty motorcycle vest of yours?"

"Kutte…", I said, grabbing the edges of my grey corduroy vest and tugging at it.

"Whatever," she said, waiving the term away.

She immediately began to rub her temples. "Please don't embarrass me, Braxton. This is the first vacation you've ever taken me on. Don't make it be the last."

The only thing I could think of at that moment was the fact that she'd forced me into the situation in the first place. But it was what it was.

"My preferred vacation usually involves beer and a fishing rod. I don't even know what you're supposed to do on a cruise ship."

"You're supposed to relax."

"But fishing and drinking are relaxing."

"Braxton," she said with a low growl. I'd have been willing to bet my mother's cold scowl could have frozen a nun in her tracks. "Please act like you have some sense. There will be beer. I made sure to get the premium drink package for both of us, so all of the food and drink on the cruise is included."

"Alright, alright," I said, holding up my hands defensively. I really hoped the *premium drink package* didn't include the cost of an arm and a leg or signing over my eternal soul. I've seen how those last-minute add-ons stack up quickly before you pull the trigger and sign on the dotted line.

Mom continued past me heading for the gangway. I lifted my duffle over my shoulder and fell in line behind her. She stopped and glared back at me.

"You can check that bag so you don't have to carry it around all morning. It may be a while before our cabin is ready."

I shrugged. "It's all good. I'd rather not trust someone else to look after my stuff if I don't have to."

"Well, suit yourself. I'm off to find Ethel. She's excited to meet this televangelist she's seen on television so she can give him a piece of her mind. He's supposedly holding several sermons during the cruise. You keep yourself busy and out of trouble. We are in cabin 241, so keep an ear open." She hurried away up the ramp.

"Wait, you're just taking off without me? I thought this was supposed to be our vacation."

She stopped and quickly turned back toward me. "It is. We're here together aren't we? And besides, I promised Ethel that I would be her wing girl this trip."

"Wing girl? What the hell kind of cruise are we on?"

"The kind with rich old timers and Ethel's in the market…"

"Well, what am I supposed to do in the meantime?"

She shrugged. "I don't know. Go hang out at the bar or something. Mingle… make a few friends. You never know who you might meet on one of these cruises," she said with a smile and a knowing wink, nudging me in the side with her elbow. "Remember cabin 241. Listen for it, then you can drop your bag. Otherwise, I'll see you sometime before the end of the cruise." She rushed up the gangway, chuckling to herself as she shuffled away.

"Yup," I mumbled to myself. "This is going to turn out to be a great trip." Adjusting my duffle on my shoulder, I hoofed it up the gangway.

After what seemed like an eternity of wandering, I found myself outside the Caribbean Sunrise lounge on the Lido deck. Even though we were just boarding the ship the place was already packed. Gray and balding fifty-somethings dressed in their beach best crowded around the bar and poolside area.

"I am seriously out of my element here," I mumbled. I was undoubtedly the proverbial sore thumb sticking out for all to see, and I sure as hell felt like it when nearly everyone turned and stared in my direction, dropping their sunglasses to look at the weirdo who just walked in. So, I did the one thing I did know how to do on a cruise ship. I wandered through the sea of swimsuits and made my way to the bar. Sliding into the first seat I found empty, I dropped my duffle at my feet and waved at the bartender.

It didn't take him long to wrap up the drinks he was working on before he made his way toward me at the end of the bar.

"What can I do you for, pal?" he asked, wiping his hands on a damp bar cloth.

What I could really go for right then was one of Patrick's Peanut Butter Paws from Buck Bald Brewing, but I seriously doubted they'd have any microbrews on tap, let alone a peanut butter chocolate stout. It was probably the standard commercial fair, but I was hopeful.

"Do you have anything dark and chewy?" I asked. He cocked his head to the side in one of those curious dog sort of ways and squinted like he didn't understand my answer. He flicked the toothpick in his mouth over and over like some greaser creep plotting his next move.

"We have Miller Lite, Bud Light, Modelo, Heineken, Amber Bock, and Corona on tap."

"Let me get an Amber Bock," I said. He pulled a glass out of the cleaning rack and began filling it like a pro, leaving just the right amount of foam before dropping the glass in front of me moments later.

"Eight bucks, buddy."

"For an Amber Bock? Holy shit, that's highway robbery."

"That's cruise line prices, my friend."

"What if I have the premium drink package?'

"Easy, it goes against your room. Cabin number?"

"241."

He plugged it into the computer and looked back smiling at me. "Done and done, buddy. You're good to go. Just let me know if you need anything else, and I hope you have a great cruise."

"Thanks," I said, raising my glass to him before taking a sip. Might not have been exactly what I wanted but it was the darkest thing on the menu, so I'd have to make do. I turned to watch the crowds and the surprising thing was there were very few young bikini-clad ladies. Most of the patrons were probably in that fifty to sixty-something age range and nearly everyone clad in ill-fitting swimsuits, fanny packs, and sun visors. The number of literal *blue hairs* and purple-headed ladies was astonishing.

At least the beer was free, or at some point it would become free because I could drink my weight in beer and still be good to go on most days.

"Well hey there, sailor," a smooth, seductive southern belle voice said from behind me. I turned in my seat to find a very buxom, and minimally clad woman with wisps of grey coloring her otherwise raven black hair. It felt like her ice-blue eyes were boring into my soul. She definitely had the look of a cougar on the prowl. Not my normal go-to because she was probably twenty years older than I was, but she had sure as hell aged well. MILF, maybe. GMILF, possible even if highly unlikely, but you really never knew when it came to the Deep South.

"I'm Maria. What brings you into port, big boy?" She asked, her right hand making a beeline for my left inner thigh, kneading the muscles beneath my denim jeans. Her smile stretched from serious to excited in a split second.

"I'm not sure, yet," I said, returning the smile before I took a long drink from my beer. "Most folks call me Braxton. What brings you here?" I asked, trying to play it off like I didn't already know what her vacation plans were.

"Oh, just trying to relax and *center* myself before going back to the rat race," she said, slowly twirling a finger in one of my many natural curls.

I wasn't sure if I should run or have a little fun of my own, but I couldn't fight the immediate feeling that I really needed an adult at that moment. Meh, what could it really hurt, right? I was pretty sure she knew exactly what she wanted and hurt feelings were not even close to the menu. "Uh, huh. And what exactly does it take to help you with *centering* yourself?"

"Oh, a little of this and a little of that," she caressed my jawline with a manicured finger. Leaning in close she whispered several of her preferred methods when being *centered.*

"Who's your new friend, Maria?" A graying redhead of similar age said, sashaying her way up to the bar behind Maria. Maria rolled her eyes before putting on one of the most forced chipper smiles I'd ever seen before she turned to face the newcomer.

"No one important, Cybill."

"I disagree, Maria. He must be important if you're trying to climb into his lap." Cybill smiled and held out her hand to shake, shouldering her way in front of the first woman. "I hope Maria isn't being too troublesome. Ignorance isn't always bliss." She flashed a predatory smile at Maria then quickly turned back to me. "I'm Cybill."

I took her hand and shook it gently. "A pleasure to meet you, Cybill."

"Oh, my. What do we have here?" A small Asian woman suddenly appeared, wedging herself between Cybill and me. "You definitely aren't one of the average over-the-hill middle managers that we constantly see on these cruises. Ooo, let me guess. Bouncer? Bounty hunter? Hmmm. Oh, who cares? My name is Faith, and the pleasure is about to be all mine." She purred then slid a tiny hand across the outside of my bicep. That's when she noticed the patches on my kutte. "Oh, no, no, no. Soldier of fortune on a secret undercover mission." She let out what sounded like a feral growl mixed with an excited giggle. "I have dibs on this one."

Maria let out an exacerbated gasp.

Cybill shoved Faith aside. "We were here first, slut."

Faith let out a roar and returned the shove, pushing Cybill back a step.

"Ladies, ladies, please." A dashing man in an off-white suit rushed ahead, putting himself between the prowling cougars and me. He leaned against the bar and adjusted the hunter green handkerchief in his right jacket pocket then looked me over with an appraising glance before he turned back to the woman. "Could you please give us a moment, ladies," he said with a venomous lisping hiss.

Amid grumbled sighs, Maria stepped ahead of the other two and shoved the back of the dashing man's shoulder. "You'd better not ruin this one like you did with Armondo." She glanced at me and then back to the guy before storming away in a huff followed by the other two.

The guy's leer and creepy smile beneath the thin pencil mustache sent chills up my spine setting off every stranger danger alert that had been beaten into my young brain in grade school. I was pretty sure this was another one of those *I need an adult* moments, considering the way he looked me over when he turned back. I had that distinct feeling that I was being mentally weighed and measured like a hunk of butcher house prime beef, but at least he ran off the cougars for me.

He drew in a long breath, then let it out in a huff before looking at me with pleading eyes.

"I need you..." he began.

"Whoa, there buddy. You ain't at least going to buy me a beer first?"

His pleading look shifted to annoyed exasperation in the blink of an eye. He clicked his tongue, counting through several long calming breaths before he began again.

"My name is Aubrey. Aubrey Harris" He extended a hand to shake. I took the offered hand, finding it very soft and delicate to the touch. He cringed at first from my grip then smiled.

"Braxton Hicks."

Aubrey cocked his head to the side with a curious, unsure look. He twirled the tips of his thin mustache. "Alright, then." His creepy smile returned, and I pulled my hand back.

"I appreciate you shooing away the barflies, but if your plan was to clear the field for yourself, I'm afraid you're barking up the wrong tree. Don't get me wrong, I'm flattered. I just don't swing that way, man."

He flashed what looked like a condescending smile. "I'm sorry that you got the wrong impression, Mr. Hicks. But to be explicitly honest, you aren't my type. My introduction and inquisition are reluctantly of the business persuasion and not that of a personal one, unfortunately."

I ran a hand down my face, let out a long sigh, and rubbed at my temples. What was it that the universe had against me taking a vacation? Even if this isn't the vacation I wanted, it's still a vacation. This bullshit was really starting to get annoying.

"No offense, but if you don't mind could you please cut through the bullshit and get to the point? I'm supposed to be on vacation. Remember? Exactly what do you want?"

"You see, Mr Hicks, I am the head host of this ship. It is my job to ensure that the passengers enjoy themselves thoroughly, be that through conversation, dancing, shows, or other scheduled entertainment and events."

Well, not exactly what I expected him to say, but at least there wasn't something weird going on that I had to deal with. I had a feeling this was going to be something long and drawn out, so I adjusted in my seat, leaning against the bar and turning toward him to get comfortable. "Alright, but what does that have to do with me?" I asked.

"Four of our hosts have been put off the ship for contracting some sort of contagious illness which has inevitably left me struggling to fulfill the needs of the passengers for the remainder of this cruise. Of course, I see the captain's point. It is for the betterment of the crew and the passengers that any contagious staff members not be present. But regardless, it has left me in quite a predicament."

I took a slow drink of my beer, trying to figure out what this guy was getting at. "So, what exactly does this have to do with me?" I asked.

Aubrey flashed a toothy grin at me. "Considering the number of heads you turned when you walked into the bar and the attention you received within moments of arriving, I'd like to offer you an opportunity of employment."

I nearly choked on the sip of beer I'd just taken. I stared at him trying to figure out if he was screwing with me or if he was serious. The man really didn't have any tells. He had one of the most stoic poker faces I'd ever seen.

"You want to do what?"

He flashed another brief annoyed smile. " I said I'd like to offer you an opportunity of employment."

I glanced around looking for the cameras because this had to be some kind of setup for one of those reality TV shows and they were waiting to catch my reaction.

Aubrey continued to stare at me, waiting for my answer.

"You're serious, aren't you?"

"Very."

I wasn't sure how to take that. On one hand, I was supposed to be on vacation but on the other, I had no idea what the hell I was supposed to do while on this vacation. There wasn't any fishing to be had, but there was beer and a few hot ladies roaming about, but other than that I was completely out of my element.

I turned up my beer, finished it, then flagged the bartender for another.

"Put that on my tab Jimmy," Aubrey said to the bartender, "and if you wouldn't mind, I'd like my regular, please."

"You got it, Mr. Harris," the bartender answered and poured me another glass.

"That is overly kind of you and very much appreciated," I said, raising the beer in salute toward Aubrey.

"Consider it a small sample of what I'm offering."

This guy was either serious or it was the oddest roundabout way I'd ever been hit on. But, it might be just the thing to keep me occupied during the cruise.

"Alright, I'll bite," I said. "What exactly did you have in mind?"

Aubrey smiled with excitement and leaned forward. "As I previously stated, Mr. Hicks. Four of our hosts have contracted a contagion, leaving me to fulfill the needs of the passengers alone. While the additional bonus and tips would be a small boon in itself, it is too much for one man. I am unfortunately left in a predicament, and I require your assistance."

I tried not to laugh, but a low chuckled grunt managed to escape. "What makes you think I could do the job of a host? This is my first time stepping foot on a cruise ship."

"You fail to see your own potential, Mr. Hicks. When you emerged on deck, you were surrounded whether you knew it or not." He flashed his creepy smile once again. "True, only three individuals approached you. From my observation, there were at least a dozen more ladies circling their *prey.*"

My Captain Obvious must have been in full force. I took a quick glance around and sure enough, there were more than several older ladies looking in my direction; each of them smiled or winked when I made eye contact with them.

Yup, I needed an adult…

"Even though it's a little unnerving, I see your point," I said, turning back to Aubrey. It could be fun, or it could end up being a complete pain in the ass to deal with. But you only live once, right?

"What say you, Mr. Hicks?"

"What does the gig pay?"

Aubrey shifted excitedly. The look on his face flashed to that of a crooked used car salesman about to land the deal. "I can guarantee you reimbursement for your passage, a cash stipend for off-ship excursions as well as free drinks, dining, and entertainment anywhere onboard ship."

Huh, that wasn't a half-bad offer, especially considering my mom unwillingly wrangled me into this trip in the first place. I could wait to see what else he might toss into the offer to sweeten the deal, but the guy sounded super desperate. His look of excitement had already started to slip away to a forlorn look of hope, bordering on a sad puppy dog face.

"Deal," I said, holding my hand out to shake. "So, where do you want me to start?"

"Let's go get the administrative bits out of the way, then I need you back here poolside until five working your magic, followed by dinner at seven in the grand ballroom." Aubrey leaned back, looked me over once again, and quirked his lips. "You don't happen to have anything resembling *formal*, do you?" he asked matter-of-factly.

"I have a nice dress shirt in my duffle," I said, giving the bag a kick.

He twitched his head, something that looked like a nervous tick, and let out a long sigh. "Guess that'll have to do."

Now, you would think that wining and dining a group of ladies in their late forties to early fifties would be an easy enough task. But it wasn't. It was a constant effort to keep them distracted, entertained, and happy. Not to mention I had to be constantly on my toes with comebacks and reasons I couldn't come in when I'd walk one of them back to their cabins. One, it was completely against the rules for a host to engage in any kind of relationship with a single passenger. Secondly, several of them scared the ever-living shit out of me with the things they said they wanted to do to me if they had the opportunity.

Now don't get me wrong. I love a good wrestling match and romp in the sheets, but these ladies were downright freaky bordering on sadistic.

After three days of keeping them entertained, occupied, and otherwise happy, I was worn out. It was a fun experience in itself, but I don't know that I would ever willingly sign up for it again. Too much drama, not to mention the attention whores that constantly wanted you focused on them and the energy vampires draining the life out of everyone around them.

The worst one of all wasn't one of my Roving Cougar Squad, as Faith had named us, but a male passenger, Chris Christianson of Christianson Ministries and the CCM Broadcast Church of the Evangelical Spirit.

This guy honestly reminded me of the singer and stage performer Meatloaf, average height, thinning wispy hair, barrel-chested, and wide of girth with a vampiric look about him. His eyes seemed to glow a dark red when his little group of parishioners would diminish as they wandered over and joined the ranks of the RC Squad.

On the second night, we easily took over five of the large banquet tables, and I bounced from one table to the next, almost never setting down. I worked the room from one lady to the next so everyone had at least a small amount of time and attention given to them.

Returning from the restroom, Pastor Christianson confronted me, blocking my path to the dining room.

"Son," he began in one of those lazy Louisiana drawls. "I want you to listen closely and take my words to heart. A dog separated from its bone can become a mighty feral beast." Looking away, he fidgeted with a large gold ring on his right hand, then directed his gaze back toward me. His steel blue eyes flashed, then glowed a deep bloody red. "You will find another way to occupy yourself during this cruise. I declare the ladies off limits and out of your league." A victorious smile crept across his face.

My head suddenly spun and my stomach lurched as the inside of my left forearm burned like someone had stabbed me with a white-hot poker. I turned my arm over and found the tattoo of my grandmother's protection sigil I'd had inked there years ago glowing the same bloody red as the pastor's eyes.

The pastor's gloating look of victory quickly shifted to utter surprise.

"Well now, what do we have here? You don't carry the air of magic about you, boy, but you damned sure have a powerful protection over you. Who are you?"

Whatever this guy was, he sure wasn't happy. He let out a frustrated huff, his look of surprise replaced by amused anger. His eyes began to glow once again, and my arm felt like it was going to melt away. He grabbed me by the wrist but immediately grunted in pain and yanked his hand back.

"What the fuck are you, you son of a bitch?" I pulled my arm back, expecting a bloody nub, but found no physical damage.

The pastor glanced about like he was making sure we hadn't been seen. "I am something much older and more powerful than you can imagine, son. I'll tell you what. Let's let bygones be bygones. You keep to yourself and mind your own damned business, and no harm will come to you." He cocked his head with a click of the tongue then straightened his tie and jacket. "You're one and only choice. Don't make it your last," he said then hurried back to the dining room.

"I think I might be above my pay grade this time," I mumbled to myself.

My immediate response was to contact Mandy, my research counterpart and business partner back home in Georgia, but somehow the pastor fried my phone in the process of trying to attack me.

After finding the closest onboard internet cafe, I shot Mandy an email with the situation and hoped I'd hear back from her soon. My guess was I was dealing with some sort of shade or demon possession. It wasn't like I hadn't dealt with my fair share of those over the years while working the weird side gigs for the government through the KCG, (Krypto, Cults, and Gangs), an offshoot of the Federal Marshal's Office, but seeing as we were in international waters, I wasn't sure what sort of official power I had as a special deputy marshal.

In the meantime, I returned to the dining room and continued to entertain the passengers who gathered around my table, all while under the pastor's discontented observation. He might have threatened me and used some sort of magic on me, but I figured it would almost certainly be a death sentence to take him on without an idea of what I was up against. Hopefully, Mandy would get back to me sooner than later. Until then, all I could do was observe and be ready for anything.

The next day we put in at the Grand Turk Cruise Port. Cybill, Faith, and Maria dressed in their finest swimsuits and sunhats, collectively abducted me moments after the announcement of debarkation and whisked me away for a shopping spree along their favorite beachside strip. Maria led the charge when it was time to relax after a morning of browsing and trinket shopping to what they claimed was the best hangout in the Caribbean, the Key lime Breeze Tiki Bar.

It looked like something you'd see in a romantic comedy movie, complete with bamboo and palm frond decor, a little Jimmy Buffett from the speakers on the outside of the bar, and kettle drums playing somewhere in the distance. The smell of fresh jerked chicken wafted out from food trucks parked along the street. The only oddity was the two dozen Elvis impersonators mingling about the bar area, taking their turn singing karaoke versions of Elvis's top ten song list.

Maria and the others were quick to snag the beach chairs closest to the bar, marking their territory by spreading beach towels, magazines, paperback novels, and other miscellaneous items on the sand around them.

"Braxton, be a dear and order us a round of margaritas, please," Faith requested. She wiggled herself into a comfortable position on the beach chair.

"Sure thing."

"And how about some of those little fruit slices, too," Cybill added.

"Oh, don't forget the little umbrellas either. They aren't festive enough without the little umbrellas," Maria said.

I tucked my thumbs into my pocket and turned toward the three of them, letting out a frustrated huff. "Anything else?"

"Do get something for yourself as well, Braxton," Faith said with a lazy roll of her wrist. Two more days and this cruise would be over. At first, this wasn't so bad, the benefits were good, and the tips had been great, but the longer it goes on the more pain in the ass and snooty they'd become.

I strolled up to the bar that looked like something Cletus Miller back in Chickamauga would have built in his backyard to be all fancy-like. Someone had used a rough piece of plywood for the bar top and decorated it with dried strips of bamboo. Either whoever built the place was cheap or they were going for that authentic South Pacific military look.

The open sign was out, but I didn't see a soul working the joint, just the gaggle of Elvis impersonators that took up the far side of the establishment. Rapping my knuckles on the bar top I let out a little whoop, hoping to get someone's attention. Of all the people I expected to emerge from the storage room behind the bar, Luder was not anywhere in the same zip code of choices. But sure enough, there was the scrawny ex-aircraft mechanic I'd served with and a previous member of the Bilge Rats Motorcycle club out of Key West Florida. It had been years since I'd seen him. He must have been as surprised as I was because he froze in place and dropped a bottle of clear liquor he'd been carrying. Luckily the floor of the tiki bar was made of sand and the bottle landed with a muffled thud.

"Braxton?" Luder said. He nervously glanced around, shaking almost as bad as a scared chihuahua.

"In the flesh."

"Am I in some kind of trouble?"

I shook my head. "Not that I know of. Did you do something that might get you in trouble?"

"No, but the last time I saw you, the feds were involved."

"Oh, yeah. That…"

Several years ago I'd worked undercover to track down Lenny Raynard who I'd served with at my first duty station. Others had been disappearing, and it was rumored he'd gotten into some pretty heavy trafficking of all sorts, which turned out to be true.

"The feds offered me a full-time job after all that went down."

"Alright. But this visit has nothing to do with me?"

"Nope. I'm on vacation, sorta. I just wanted to order three margaritas for the ladies over there ," I said, pointing in the trio's direction, "and let me get a beer for myself."

"Well, that's easy. I can do that." Luder looked over at the three cougars relaxing on the beach. "Still a man whore?"

"Naw, more like man servant, but I don't mind it too much. They were short handed and the lead host offered me a job shortly after boarding."

Luder looked at the ladies again then turned back to me. "Lucky."

I laughed. "I wouldn't be too hasty to say that."

"You said three margaritas?"

"Yup."

"Coming right up."

For the most part, I spent the next few hours at the bar catching up with Luder, delivering drinks on demand as the ladies requested them. It had been good seeing him again. He seemed happy in what he was doing; he was the sole owner and operator of the Key lime Breeze Tiki Bar. Shortly after things fell apart in Key West, he moved out here to get away from the circumstances surrounding the Bilge Rats MC and just lucked into the place, really. From the sounds of it, a guy really couldn't ask for more. He was his own boss, he set his own hours, and for the most part, the *scenery* was choice. Pretty sweet deal if you ask me.

"Son," a familiar voice said from right behind me. "You sir, did not heed my warning."

I was about to deliver the sixth round of margaritas to the ladies and did not expect to see hide nor hair of the televangelist, but I'll be damned if he didn't hunt me down. I don't know if it was a stupid coincidence or the universe's fucked up sense of humor, but the Elvis impersonators were on at least their tenth karaoke rendition of "Devil in Disguise" at that point.

I grunted a laugh and turned in my seat. Sure enough, there he was in the flesh, sliding into the seat next to me.

He tapped the bar to get Luder's attention. "Old fashioned, please." Luder looked at me with those scared chihuahua eyes as if waiting for me to give him permission. I gave him a quick nod, and he set to work making the pastor's drink.

"I'm a little surprised you left the ship, Pastor," I said, turning so my full attention was on him. Luder served up the pastor's drink and took it upon himself to deliver the tray of margaritas.

"Now, son," he began. His genteel drawl seemed to suddenly deepen. "I want you to know, not one single person has defied me in over three hundred years. While this has been a refreshing change of pace, I'm at a point in my life where I'm not interested in competing. Once upon a time, I would have gladly welcomed it. The thrill and excitement of the challenge was something to live for. But any more, I'm happy to just keep these sheep enthralled long enough to feed a little here, a little there, and no one is the wiser. Then, with the donations they happily supply to my ministry, I manage to live worry-free."

He took a long sip from his drink, a smile forming amid his otherwise perturbed countenance. "Damn, that is good." He looked down at the glass and admired the drink. "I'm sorry, that brings back some memories. Where was I?"

"Donations to your ministry?"

"Ahh, yes. Malachi chapter three, verse ten says; Bring the whole tithe into the storehouse, that there may be food in my house. Test me in this, says the Lord Almighty, and see if I will not throw open the floodgates of heaven and pour out so much blessing that there will not be room enough to store it," he finished in one of the best evangelical flourishes I'd seen in a long while.

"And? Your point?"

"The little people are happy to give away their earthly possessions for even the tiniest inkling of hope that they will receive a blessing from upon high. They hope to one day cross through the heavenly gates and partake of the bounty that *God* has to offer the faithful once they shed this mortal shell."

He took another sip and grunted his appreciation. "Flesh… is weak, son. Faith…on the other hand…" He let out a low chuckle. "Faith, boy, is powerful. Faith is all-reaching. Faith is forever if you play your cards right," he said, jabbing me in the shoulder with a withered, bony finger. "They willingly give their all for me; they volunteer for my causes, no matter what the cause, and they *believe*. Faith, son. Faith. It is one of the most powerful tools available to anyone. And if you know how to manipulate that faith to your advantage, you can live like a god on earth. Haha!"

"Well, that's all fine and dandy, bud, but that doesn't explain why you're here bearing witness to me instead of basking in the glory your parishioners fawn upon you," I replied in my best southern Baptist flair.

"Because you have disrupted the status quo, boy. My followers on this cruise have been more concerned about where you went with those three lovely ladies than anything I could offer them. You are an anomaly, son. And the only way to right what is wrong is to remove that which offends." He cleared his throat and took another sip of his drink. "Matthew chapter five verse thirty; if your right hand causes you to sin, cut it off and throw it away. For it is better that you lose one of your members than that your whole body go into hell. And in this instance, son. You are equal to that offending appendage."

The pastor's eyes flashed then glowed a deep red once again. I looked down at my forearm, it glowed dimly, but there wasn't any pain this time.

"Oh, don't you worry none, son. I already learned that my tricks won't work on you. But they will on others." His voice suddenly sounded deep and demonic.

I took a quick look around to assess the situation, and sure enough the entire contingent of Elvis impersonators and their audience members were on their feet and speed shuffling toward us. Their eyes glowed that same deep red as the pastor's.

"Fuck me. I don't remember zombie Elvis's on the bingo card for this cruise."

"Well, son. What can I say? I aim to please." The pastor let out a deep laugh and sipped at his drink.

I hopped over the bar as the horde of zombie Elvis's closed in around me. Luder returned, reaching for me. His eyes glowed the same red as the others. "That's not good." Deflecting his grasping hands, I backhanded Luder and viciously shook him. "Dude, wake up! Don't be one of this asshat's beta-cucks. Luder! Snap out of it!" I slapped him once more for good measure.

"Ow! Dude! What the fuck was that for?"

"You were one of them. I'll explain the rest later," I said, pointing at the small army of thralls closing in. "We gotta go, now."

"Um…. shit… Follow me," he said, and sprinted through the doorway. I followed right behind him.

"Braxton, where are you going?" I heard Maria shout.

"Sorry, something came up that I have to take care of. I'll be right back!" I shouted over my shoulder.

Luder ran into a small garage behind the tiki hut, slamming the door and locking it behind me. It was a cinder block structure with enough room for maybe one vehicle. Miscellaneous car parts and equipment littered most of the areas along the walls. A cot and wooden wire spool took up a small space in the center of the room amid a clutter of clothes and personal items.

"You living in here?"

"Yeah, it came with the lot where the bar is. Used to be a used car dealership and repair shop. It's cheaper than buying another place."

He wasn't wrong there. But it looked worse than his room in the barracks ever had.

What sounded like fists pounding on the metal door reverberated in the small space.

"What are we going to do, Braxton?"

"I need to take down that pastor. You don't have any weapons stashed away in here, do you?"

"Um…I've got some pipes over in the corner, and there's some chain over here on the back wall."

"Redneck Engineering 101 it is then." I hurried to look at what was available, sorting through the random piles of parts and equipment scattered through the garage. Most of it was junk that should have been hauled off to the scrap yard.

"Huh," Luder laughed. "Too bad you can't use these."

I turned to find him holding up a literal set of brass cajónes. "Give me those, I've got an idea. Do you have a set of bolt cutters?"

"Yeah, actually." Luder rummaged around for a moment while I gathered a length of stout chain and one of the pipes from the corner that looked like it had been used as a cheater pipe to break torque and already had a set of holes drilled through one end.

"So, remember when I told you I was offered a job after all that stuff in Key West?"

"Yeah." Luder held the chain while I cut the length that I wanted.

"Well, that job happens to be dealing with weird stuff, which never seems to let me catch a break and relax."

"Okay, so this is one of those times?"

"Exactly." In moments we'd scavenged two bolts and nuts that fit well enough to secure the chain to the pipe and the cast brass balls.

"Braxton's brass balls of bashing plus one."

I couldn't help but let out a laugh at that. "Hold that thought. Got a hammer and flathead screwdriver?"

"Yeah," Luder responded. Digging into his small toolbox he produced a small claw hammer and a screwdriver that was in decent shape. I took them and began carving the protection sigil down the center of the brass nut sack.

"What are you doing?"

"Upgrading it."

"Okay?" Luder looked at me, confused.

"I tried to contact my research partner back home, but my cell got fried when the pastor back there grabbed my arm the other day. He's some kind of demon or daemon, I'm not sure which. And I never could keep the differences between the two straight. The main thing right now is that he's enthralled those Elvis impersonators to eliminate me." Once finished, I held up the flail for him to see.

"If I did it right, now it's Braxton's Holy Brass Balls of Bashing plus five."

Luder laughed hard enough that he snot shot out of his nose.

"This protection sigil on my arm blocked whatever he tried to cast on me and actually hurt him when he grabbed me. Fingers crossed it'll work the same on this flail. I looked around for another way out of the garage. Two small windows mounted high on the wall, the man door on the side, and the roll-up garage door on the end were the only exits.

"Does the garage door work?"

"Sorta." He shrugged. "It starts to hang up almost immediately most of the time. Since I don't have a car I don't worry about it."

I stared at the main door, knowing what was on the other side of it. I could still hear them pounding against the metal door. "We might have to fight our way through the pastor's thralls."

"Whoa, hold on, Brax." Luder stepped in front of the door, blocking my path. "If Ralph and his buddies are thralls like you say, then what they're doing isn't their fault. They are doing his bidding against their will, right?"

"As far as I can tell, yes."

"Then you can't hurt them."

I shook my head, not sure where he was going. To get to the pastor we'd have to fight our way through the sea of zombie Elvis's. "What if we don't have a choice?"

"As much as Ralph and his buddies annoy me with their cosplay karaoke sessions, they're still people, and well, paying customers. Really good paying customers. When I say these guys can drink, they easily keep me in business during the off-season."

Luder was right. No matter how ready I was to bash my way through the crowd, they were unwilling participants of the pastor's control.

"I'm open to suggestions because every solution I can come up with involves hurting them."

"Well, hurting them might not be bad. You slapped me back to consciousness. My face still hurts where you slapped me, but it wasn't like you left permanent damage." Luder snapped his fingers together and dashed toward the back corner of the garage.

"What is it?"

"I think I have an idea that will work. Hold on, one second." He rummaged around in the corner, tossing things haphazardly around. "Ah ha! I didn't think I'd gotten rid of these yet."

Luder turned around, producing a mesh sports bag that contained a set of shoulder pads and a football helmet. "See if this fits you."

"Do I want to know why you have football gear?"

"It was from the guy who owned the lot before me. He'd started a little league football team for the kids on the island to help keep them out of trouble. The only problem was that none of them wanted to play football. So the gear has sat here for years."

I pulled the helmet out and stared at it, knowing it was maybe four or five sizes too small for my head. But Luder was small and wiry.

"This won't ever fit me. How about you try it?"

"Okay, but I'd be lucky to fight my way out of a blanket."

I chuckled under my breath. "Don't worry. I think I have a plan."

A few minutes later Luder was decked out in full gear, shoulder pads, helmet, plus shin and forearm guards. "Alright, done. So what's your plan?"

I tucked the flail handle into the back of my shirt then without warning, I picked him up, holding him at the collar and waistband. "When we get close to the door fling it open, then I'll charge through using you like a battering ram to push our way through.

"That's your plan?"

"You got a better one?"

"Not really," Luder admitted.

"Then tuck in and let's go."

Luder reached for the doorknob as we got closer and flung open the door. Before the thralls could flood into the garage I charged forward, using Luder to bash a path through the horde. For as small and scrawny as Luder was, he sure made an effective battering ram.

In a few steps we were easily through the crowd and back to the doorway of the bar.

"My, my, my," the pastor said, gleefully. "You are proving to be as tenacious as a cockroach, son."

"Can you lock those doors?" I asked, setting Luder back on his feet.

"Yeah, but they're more for looks than anything."

"As long as it slows them down, that's all that matters. Do it, then get out of the way." Stumbling slightly, Luder lashed the door, and then rushed to the other side of the bar, securing the other entrance.

"I hope you've made your peace with whatever god you pray to, *son*." A deep demonic laugh escaped the pastor's lips. "Because your end is nigh."

I charged forward, drawing the handle of the flail from behind me and swung in a wide arc, aiming for the side of the pastor's head. He turned, sliding from the chair so fast that he was a blur. It was almost like the way movies depicted vampire speed. The force of the swing drove the brass balls deep into the soft wood of the bartop.

"Hahaha," the pastor laughed then struck me first in the cheek, followed by a double shot to the midsection. I doubled over and slumped to the floor.

"Whew," he shouted, shaking his hands in front of him. "That stings just a bit, doesn't it, son?" He took in a slow deliberate breath. "This is exhilarating." Stepping back, he paced for a moment, stretching his arms.

"I haven't felt this alive in centuries. Come on, boy. Pull yourself together. You have a fight to finish."

Slowly I pulled myself up, getting my breath back. Before I could brace myself, he rushed forward in a burst of speed striking me square in the chest with his open palm like some kung fu master. The punch sent me sprawling backward into the bar. Besides feeling like I'd just been run over by a Mack truck, searing pain shot up my left arm adding insult to injury.

Fighting for breath, I used the broken bar to pull myself back to my feet.

"Dammit, you little shit!" The pastor cradled his hand, rubbing at it like he'd smacked it hard against a wall. "I'd forgotten about that little trick of yours. No, bother. You'll be mine soon enough." Lunging forward he gripped me around the throat, doubling me backward over the broken bar causing me to drop the flail.

"I'm going to enjoy feeding on your worthless soul, son." His eyes flashed and glowed red again.

A spherical concussion wave radiated out, sending the pastor soaring through the air he crashed through several tables and tumbled to a stop.

Fighting for breath, I pounded myself in the chest trying to force my lungs to work. I'd been in my fair share of bar fights and back alley brawls over the years, but this was probably one of the worst ass beatings I'd ever gotten.

I stumbled forward, gasping and coughing. I picked up the flail. "I don't know what you are. But it's about time you go back to what ever hell you came from." The sigil I'd carved down the center of the scrotum sack glowed, getting brighter the closer I got to the pastor until it was as bright as the white-hot of a blast furnace.

Groaning, he rolled over, revealing his true demonic self. Blood-red eyes glowed beneath protruding brow ridges and horns sprouted across the top of his head, replacing the clean-cut visage of Evangelical Pastor Chris Christianson that the world knew so well.

"You'd better say your prayers, 'cause I'm about to tea bag you so hard your great grandma demon is gonna feel your pain, you sumbitch!"

I brought the flail around in a wide arching swing before drawing it down to strike squarely on the demon's forehead. He let out a bestial roar. The pastors body glowed the same white hot as the brass ball sack. Heat radiated from him as the intensity of the light grew to blinding. Even turned away from the source with my eyes closed, the blinding light seeped through my eyelids. As suddenly as the light had began, it shut off, leaving the inside of the bar as dark as a cave at that moment.

It took several minutes for my eyes to readjust. I could hear Luder stumbling around somewhere behind the bar.

"What the hell happened?"

"I'm not sure," I responded. Blinking away the blur that persisted, I inspected the area where the pastor had been. Several rings and an ancient-looking pendant that reminded me of a Spanish piece of eight stood out among a very large pile of ash that covered the sandy floor of the bar.

"You got any buckets or jars or anything back there?"

"Um, yeah. Hang on." Luder rummaged around under the bar for a few moments, eventually producing an old coffee can.

"Ha! Perfect."

"What are you doing?" Luder asked.

"I need to collect as much evidence as possible. I don't know if this counts since I'm outside of the continental United States, but it sure won't hurt to try. I'm sure they'll find it interesting that the pastor was enthralling his followers."

"What about the damages to my bar?"

"If the KCG doesn't cover the damages, I will. I did cause most of it. Only right that I fix it."

Starting where the pastor's head was, I began scooping ashes into the can, making sure to collect the rings and pendant.

"You know, they probably won't let you take that back with you. They have strict rules on those ships."

"How else would I get it back?"

"I could ship it for you. I have a buddy that flies in from Miami every few weeks. He mails things for me at better than half the price it would cost if I mailed anything from the post office here."

"Could you do that for me?"

"Yeah, man. No problem."

I sealed the can and handed it to Luder. "I'd wrap that in duct tape just to make sure it doesn't pop open."

"Easy enough." He handed me a note pad and pen, and I jotted down my address.

"Braxton Eugene Hicks!" The sound of my mother yelling my name like that sent chills running down my spine. Luder just stared at me.

"Yup, this is turning out to be an awesome vacation…"

Shock n' Awe

By: William Joseph Roberts

First published in A Touch of Aether – Three Ravens Publishing, March 2025

Oh, my. Have you ever ate a low country boil cooked up by a true Cajun chef from New Orleans? I hadn't either until a trip to Colorado Springs for the Superstars Writing Seminar in 2024. As we sat there eating our way through bowls of crawdads, crab legs, sausage, etc. I could just see Braxton swinging by on his way from one assignment to the next for some good food and a friendly face.

I'd gotten lucky so far on this run out west. It was the middle of February in Colorado and the weather really wasn't all that bad. I had to go all the way up into Wyoming to take care of a skinwalker sighting that turned out to be nothing more than a false alarm.

And since I was already kinda in the area, I didn't see any point in wasting the trip, so I decided to swing south and head toward Colorado Springs. I'd heard from a few folks back east that an old friend of mine from the deep south was running her own restaurant out here now, and I wanted to stop in to pay her a visit, and hopefully get a belly full of her cooking.

A few years back, Mandy wanted to go to New Orleans for Mardi Gras, so we did. As usual, things went sideways, and we ended up chasing down a small coven of witches who'd tried to re-establish their name and position in the city's dark-side hierarchy.

While there, we met Bernadette Boudreaux. She was one of the best damn Cajun chefs I have ever had the pleasure of knowing. And her food was so good we'd eaten at Bernadette's restaurant every night while in town, even though some of that trip was still a tad bit fuzzy. When we weren't chasing witches and vamps, we were having fun and drinking way too much.

Well, just before heading out on this trip, I'd found out that Bernadette had taken up a job in Colorado Springs as the head chef for Spring

Orleans. And a great big bowl of her gumbo was screaming my name after the long cold hours on the back of my bike.

Even though I'd gotten lucky on this run and the temperatures hadn't been stupid-cold, it was still a little chilly at interstate speeds. There had been a bit of snow here and there, but if you bundled up well enough, that wasn't a problem.

I pulled up and parked along the street in front of the restaurant. The joint had that quaint little bistro look on the outside, with wrought-iron tables and chairs. I could see a six-man band through the front window that played a Dixieland tune for patrons.

I shut off Jonie, my newer Harley-Davidson Road King, dropped the kickstand, and stretched, popping things back into place. After being in the saddle for the last hundred miles or so, things had gotten a little numb.

Riding through these mountains was a beautiful experience like nothing we had back east. Maybe if I'd gone to Europe, I could find something close. Wouldn't that be a hell of a trip?

I tucked my gloves into my pocket, strapped my helmet to the bike, and made my way inside. A number of heads turned, looking in my direction. It might have had something to do with the kutte and full riding leathers.

The rush of heat from the room on my cold chest when I opened my jacket was something amazing. I hadn't realized how deep the cold had gotten until that moment.

"Well, I'll be, if it isn't Braxton Hicks," I heard shouted from the kitchen area in the back. I stepped past the hostess, who stuttered an unsure *sir* and headed toward the voice. Sure enough, there was Bernadette, a big bright smile on her face that seemed to gleam as bright as the large diamonds she wore in each ear.

"I thought that was you," Bernadette said as I approached the back counter. "Heard you pull in on that bike of yours. What in the world brings you this far west?"

I shrugged. "Heard you were out here working your magic. Figured I'd swing in for some of your finest while I was in the area."

"Well, you just in time, Boo. You pull you up a seat there and take a listen to the band while I get you some grub. I know exactly what you want." She smiled, laughed, and slapped me on the arm.

"You sure about that?" I asked. "There are an awful lot of things in this world that I want," I said with a wink.

She let out a hysterical chuckle. "It is good to see you again, Braxton. You sit'n I'll bring something right out."

Two pints of a dark beer arrived moments later. I wasn't sure what they were, but beer was beer, and the darker, the better, in my opinion. The first sip was a wonderful thing after a long haul on the back of the sled in the middle of the cold Rocky Mountains of Colorado.

I took a sip of what I guessed was a nutty brown ale, then pulled off my jacket and stretched again, trying to get the blood flowing to my extremities. I'd barely taken a good long draw of the beer before Bernadette returned with a bowl full of crawdads, crab legs, andouille sausage, shrimp, potatoes, corn on the cob, and a small bowl of her amazing gumbo.

It smelled wonderful.

From behind her back she produced a small bowl of hot garlic butter, and from her pocket came a bottle of hot sauce labeled *Worst Nightmare* that she placed on the table in front of me.

I looked up at her and smiled. "Yeah, you might happen to know a little about what I want."

"I know your taste buds, Boo. But this one will light you up. It'd light fire to Satan's asshole if'n he ain't careful."

I looked at the innocent-looking bottle and nodded. "So, what you're saying is that this might actually be a challenge for me?"

"Might be," she said, then chuckled.

"Then I graciously accept."

"Thought you might." She slapped me on the back and headed back toward the kitchen. "You just let me know if you need anything else."

I didn't hesitate and dug into the meal. I'd be damned if it wasn't good. There wasn't anything like properly done crawdads, even if I knew they were frozen and shipped in. The middle of Colorado in the dead of winter was not the easiest place to get fresh mud bugs, not to mention the shrimp and crab legs. But you can get away with that, as long as you season them right.

I was in hog heaven. I had no idea where I was going to be laying my head for the night yet, but wherever it was, a food coma would follow close behind because the grub was just that damned good.

I sat there and ate until I'd gotten more than my fill. Hell, I didn't even bother to ask what the cost was going to be. Bernadette knew how I'd grown up, and there's one thing about growing up poor. Once poor, you're always thinking poor. Just one of those things that becomes a habit, so I knew Bernadette wouldn't rip me off too bad.

By the time I'd finished my third bowl and 3rd beer, I was done and throwing in the towel. I sat there for a while just watching the other customers and listening to the band play several ragtime tunes I hadn't heard in a while.

"So what do you think, Braxton?" Bernadette asked, returning from the kitchen with another beer in her hand. "Do you reckon these Rocky Mountain folk even know what good Cajun is?"

I smiled, picking my teeth with a crawdad claw, then let out a long, drawn out "nope." She laughed. "But anyone exposed to your grub is in for one heavenly treat."

"That just makes my heart happy to hear you say that. I've been out here for nearly a year and it's hard to tell if they know what they are talking about or if they're just blowing smoke up my ass because they'd eat at the Big Easy Grille once before and they consider themselves *experts*."

"Well, I'm glad I could be of service." I held up what was left of my beer in toast, then drained the glass.

"So what else has been going on besides keeping the populous of Colorado Springs supplied with fine Cajun cuisine?"

"Oh, not much. Basic stuff really. Trouble from the Air Force Academy brats on occasion, and of course we have the Space Force here now."

I let out a chuckle. "Guess we're going to finally get some space Marines."

"Just maybe," she said with a giggle snort.

"I'm telling you, it's gotta be," someone across the room insisted. We both turned to see a larger guy, animatedly talking to two men sitting in one of the booths along the far wall.

"And then there's that," Bernadette said.

I shook my head in confusion and turned back to her. "And that is?"

"There's been some happenings around town. Most folks think it's all insurance scams and the like. There's been several unexplained fires and electrocutions around the Knob Hill area. And him right there, mister bigshot, thinks he knows everything about everything when it comes down to dat there Tesla fella."

"You mean like Tesla the cars?"

"No dummy. Tesla. As in the engineer and inventor. The one who came out here way back when to do his research."

"Really? Well, now that's something," I said, then tried to listen in over the noise of the restaurant. Sure enough, Bernadette was right. The guy was going on about this fire and that fire, then about one of the strange electrocutions where the victims looked like someone had grabbed onto a live high-voltage wire and been burnt to a crisp.

I chuckled and looked back to Bernadette. "Is he sure it wasn't just spontaneous combustion from all of the…" Bernadette slapped the back of my shoulder and laughed.

"Don't go giving him any new ideas. You finish up your drinks. I have a kitchen to run. Just let me know before you leave."

"Well, I can go ahead and get my tab now."

"No, no, no," she said, placing her hand back onto my shoulder. "I'll have none of that. You're a good, honest man and you give me a good honest opinion. I think that's worth at least one meal."

"You aren't going to let me argue about it, are you?"

She smiled wide, shaking her head. "Damned right."

I nodded. "I'm much obliged, Bernadette."

She smiled and went on back to the kitchen while I sat sipping on the beer, enjoying the music from the small band. It was getting harder and harder to ignore the conversation on the other side of the room, though. The guy kept getting louder and more animated the longer the conversation went on.

I didn't know a whole lot about Nikola Tesla, but I did know of the name. The animated guy kept on about the fires and how there was nothing to cause ignition in those areas, or how surveillance video was nonexistent for over three blocks surrounding each site because something had fried the nearby security cameras.

He concluded there must be something else unexplained going on, but he just couldn't pinpoint the cause or the source and that he was going to get to the bottom of it whether the two men helped him out or not.

This guy must have been desperate. You'd have to be completely clueless to miss the passive-aggressive BS he was forcing into the conversation.

I thought about it for a long minute while I sipped at the beer. I didn't have anything else better to do at the moment, and there could always be something to this thing, so I dialed up Mandy, my research assistant, IT department, and best friend, all wrapped into one.

"Hey hot stuff," I said when I heard her pick up on the other end. "What trouble are you getting into tonight?"

"Upgrades to the county server and a pint of rocky road." I could hear her licking the spoon after another bite. "You didn't call me just to chitchat, Brax. So spit it out. What do you want?"

I could already tell she was in the kinda mood that I really didn't want to test my luck with, so I just hurried and got to the point. "I'm in Colorado Springs and have possibly come across an incident. You ever heard something causing random fires and unexplained electrocutions? And there isn't any video evidence because the cameras have apparently been fried."

"So, some sort of EMP?"

"What's that?"

"Electromagnetic pulse, but generally those are only generated with a nuclear blast."

"Well, there are several military bases nearby," I said. "Could something have come from there?"

"Doubtful. There's too much danger to the civilian population. But then again, that hasn't stopped the government before."

"Okay, well, is there anything in the database that fits the description?" I could already hear her fingers clacking away at the keyboard.

"Huh," she mumbled.

"Got something?"

"Not really. The best I'm coming up with is a fire elemental, but that doesn't explain the electrocutions." I could still hear her fingers clacking away at the keys. She hadn't given up yet. "There is a chance that it could be a Jinn, or well, any other creature that can cast or control lightning."

"Well, that makes for a fun day, doesn't it? Would something like this have a finder's fee?"

"Possibly, but you know how this works. You must have some kind of physical, testable proof if not a specimen."

"Let me see what I can come up with. I can probably find some kind of shiny lamp to stuff a genie into and get it back to the labs."

"I don't think that's how it works, Braxton."

"Well, why not? It works in the movies."

"It's a movie…" she started to say, then let out a frustrated huff.

"Don't worry. I'll figure something out," I said, then hung up and continued listening in on the guy across the room as he talked.

The guy was starting to sound frustrated the more that he talked to the men at the table. They didn't look like they wanted to hear anything he had to say. And by the way that they watched the room, they were probably detectives or plain clothes cops if not part of the government element here in town.

The guy let out a huff and turned to leave, making his way around the tables as he headed for the door.

"Hey, buddy," I said as he passed by. He stopped and did a double take, unsure if I was talking to him or not. "Sit down. Have a beer with me."

Suspicious, he glared at me. "And exactly why do I want to sit and have a beer with you?"

"I overheard a little of your conversation and I'm interested in hearing more." In a split second, I knew I'd probably made a big mistake. The guy's eyes were as big as saucers. I pushed the chair on the other side of the table out with my foot, and he excitedly sat down across the table from me.

"You ain't from some government agency or something, are you?"

"Not really…" He looked taken aback and about ready to leave. "Let's just say I'm an independent contractor. The government hires me to take care of the weird things that pop up. You're going on about weird stuff. So what's the skinny? I overheard you talking about fires, electrocutions, and burned-out electronics."

"See, that's just it." This guy went into a full-out shamwow stance. You could tell he was all-in on whatever it was he was getting ready to spill to me. "These random fires have been happening around downtown, where Nikola Tesla's old lab used to be. I swear it has to be connected somehow, because there's nothing else connecting any of the fires or electrocutions. They keep happening, but there isn't any video evidence or witnesses to any of the deaths."

"How many have there been?"

"Three deaths from electrocution, and about a dozen injuries from the fires and smoke inhalation. One firefighter was burned pretty badly, but he'll make a full recovery."

"How do you know the deaths were from electrocution?"

"From the coroner's reports," he answered. "Burn marks across their bodies that only correlate to being in contact with high voltage power."

"You saw the coroner's reports?"

He suddenly sat bolt upright and stared back at the men he'd been talking to earlier. "Um… Why would you ask something like that?"

"Considering this sounds like an ongoing case, those files wouldn't be available to the general public yet."

He looked nervous and started to stand.

"Whoa, man. Where you going?"

"I'm not sure this is a good idea."

"Why's that? Cause I'm asking questions? I'm curious, and want to know what I'm getting myself into before I jump in feet first."

He let out a calming breath. "I just know some people, okay?"

"Okay. Cool. I feel ya, man. That's how I manage to get most of the info I get on jobs. I either know someone, or I know someone who knows someone. Was there any other evidence of foul play of any kind?"

He shook his head. "Nothing."

"Sounds like it might be a fun little mystery. Can you show me where the incidents took place?"

"Yeah. We can do that."

"You eat yet?" I asked.

"No, I was just about to go get something."

I waved down one of the waitresses. "Get him whatever he wants and bring me the check."

The guy smiled real big and cocked his head to the side. "You sure about that?"

"Absolutely," I said and extended my hand across the table. "The name's Braxton. Braxton Hicks."

He took my hand and gave it a hearty squeeze. "Connor O'Tool," he replied.

"It's a pleasure to meet you, Connor."

We sat for a while longer as he ate and I had myself another of those nutty brown ales. While he ate, he regaled me with the glory and knowledge of all things Nikola Tesla, the scientist's experiments, and everything that happened here in Colorado Springs. I never in my life thought that anybody could have as much information in their head as Mandy, but this guy could easily give her a run for her money.

He was the proverbial bible on everything Tesla. From his early beginnings to his death in poverty, and you could tell he wasn't just one of these batshit crazies. He was passionate to the point of obsessive about the way that man had been treated and how his designs had been confiscated, stolen, or destroyed.

A lot of it screamed conspiracy theory, but after some of the stuff I'd seen over the years working for the government, you never know what might actually be true.

Connor continued on during the meal, telling me about the first reported fire in a warehouse that had been abandoned since the 70s, and the property had been in an airship status all these years, so nothing had been touched on the site for decades.

"Two of the most recent electrocutions," he continued, "happened in the park on top of Knob Hill, where Tesla's lab once stood. The victims, a young couple, had been out for a picnic in the park according to their friends and family. Their hearts stopped with no explanation other than a few scorch marks similar to electrical burns. There had been no storms to speak of, no lightning, and no power lines even remotely nearby."

He leaned onto the table and lowered his voice. "Unless, of course, the military had some kind of secret weapons testing going on that no one knew about, there wasn't any other explanation."

If I could get a look at the sites, I might spot a clue that normal law enforcement would miss and think nothing of. Then maybe I could get an idea of what I might be dealing with.

"Do you think we could get a look at that warehouse that burned first?" I asked.

Connor's eyes went wide with excitement, and he stuffed the remainder of his sandwich in his mouth. He nodded and mumbled a *yes* through the mouthful of food.

"We can maybe do that. I know a guy who could probably get us in."

"What about the other sites?"

I started plugging the addresses into the map app on my phone just to see if there was any sort of pattern as he listed them off from memory.

Once I typed in the last entry, I zoomed it out, but it just looked like random points surrounding the initial site at the warehouse. I turned the phone around and showed it to Connor.

"Oh, holy shit!" He yanked the phone out of my hand and stared at the screen, mumbling to himself.

"Okay? So I'm guessing that's supposed to mean something?" I asked.

"You don't see that?"

"See what?"

He took a screenshot of the map, then brought up the photo and drew a curved line starting at the warehouse that connected each of those points.

"Do you see that curve?"

"Yeah. It's a spiral."

Connor let out what sounded like a slightly maniacal laugh. "It is, but it's so much more than that. It's the golden ratio, known by most as the Fibonacci Sequence. Tesla based almost all his developments on the golden ratio or the numbers three, six, and nine."

"Okay? So what does that mean?"

"That there is a damned good chance all of this weird shit is connected back to Tesla in some way. I just don't know how, yet."

"How can we prove it?" I asked.

"I wish I knew," he said, staring off in thought.

I downed my beer and then dropped some cash on the table for the waitress. "You ready? Let's go take a look at this warehouse."

A quick word with Bernadette scored me parking out back of the restaurant for the bike so no one would mess with it and I jumped in the truck with Connor.

Connor called his buddy that worked security in the warehouse district while we drove and got the combination to the building.

"They got really lucky that fire didn't burn up anything important. My buddy said this place has been untouched for decades. It must have become a catch-all for someone at one point, because of all the extra junk stored there. Luckily, the fire only damaged a small section at the back of the building, and mostly just burned up some empty boxes and crates."

Pulling up to a dilapidated, metal-sided building, Connor reached into the back seat and retrieved two large Maglite flashlights.

"There hasn't been power in this building in decades, so we'll probably need these," he said, testing each of them with a click of a button.

The place was absolutely massive—lots of old industrial equipment scattered here and there in several states of disarray. Nothing seemed to be assembled. It just looked like piles of junk, for the most part. The deeper we went into the building, the older the equipment and items seemed to get. It was like the building was a time capsule of the Industrial Revolution, and we were traveling back in time the further we went.

As we continued, we began to see small boilers, stacks of locomotive parts, and what looked like mining equipment shoved into a corner and left to rot for eternity.

"Oh, hey, look at this," Connor said, pointing at one particular piece of equipment.

"It looks like the bucket off of an old steam shovel," I replied.

"It must have been used in the mines back in the day. And that over there," he said, pointing across the bay. "That looks like an old military transport from the 30s."

He was like a kid in a candy store, and I couldn't blame him. I mean, I loved old equipment. Just part of being a mechanic, I guess. I could spend days in here poking about and exploring if left to my own curiosities, but we had an investigation to take care of. The thought of getting caught here in a snowstorm before I could get out of Colorado Springs really didn't appeal to me, either.

As Connor dug around in another bin of miscellaneous parts, I took a left turn through a doorway into the next bay. In the far back corner, stacked in over a dozen rows of five deep, were these strange metallic cylinders made of copper or bronze, that resembled a copper-top battery like you'd find at the store, but large and more steampunk looking. Several of them had recent scorch marks, like the marks left by high voltage arcing.

I worked my way back to the stack to get a better look, and found one of the cylinders cracked wide open. It looked like it had swollen and ripped along the weld seam of the cylinder. Whatever happened had managed to melt a section out of a stack of train wheels sitting next to the cylinder, as well as the wall at the end of the building. Shattered glass and melted metal slag littered the floor next to the wall.

I'd seen a lot of equipment in my days, but I'd never seen anything like this before. Granted, it was old tech, and old tech was a forgotten knowledge. As technology advanced, we forgot the old ways. Hell, with all of today's advanced computer technology, you'd think it would be easy to work out how things were done before. Then because the know-how from the 60s got lost somehow, the eggheads have forgotten how to put a man on the moon.

"Hey, Connor. Do these things look familiar to you?"

Connor scuttled through some other industrial gear stacked on the other side of the bay and stopped dead in his tracks. "Holy shit!"

He scrambled, getting past all the other stuff, and pushed past me to get a better look at them, laughing a happy little laugh like a maniacal madman.

"Do you know what these are?"

"Nope. Not a clue," I replied. "Kegs for a steampunk frat party?"

Conner turned and glared at me with a serious, *don't fuck with me* look.

"Not even close," he said.

"These look like the descriptions of the original capacitors that Tesla had designed and used at his testing facility for his wireless transmission of power. They were designed to retain energy gathered from the aether and used to boost the transmission signal."

"Okay, I could see where the cylinders resembled a capacitor off of a circuit board."

"Yeah, exactly," Conner said excitedly. "Only these would be about a million times stronger, though. Like if one of these babies were to blow, the amount of power that would go out would be insane."

"Enough power to melt hardened steel and shatter glass?" I asked, pointing at the train wheels and the hole burned in the warehouse wall.

"Without a doubt," Conner replied, nodding as he examined one of the steel wheels.

"Could these really still be holding a charge after all of these years?"

"I wouldn't think so. I mean, they shut down the lab in 1904, and dismantled it to pay off his debts."

"Do you think one of these things rupturing could do the kinda damage you're looking at there?"

Conner nodded. "Oh, without a doubt. Tesla was playing with voltages so high that it could easily vaporize anything that got in the way."

He stood up and looked around, confusion danced across his face.

"What's wrong?"

"This could have easily caused the fire, but the fire wasn't in this part of the building. It was on the west side of the warehouse. It also doesn't explain the electrocutions," he added.

I pointed up to the hole in the wall. "What if whatever it was that was in there escaped?"

Conner grabbed a metal rod laying nearby and tapped at the cylinder that had ruptured.

"Are you sure that's a good idea?"

"I don't know," he said. He shined his light between two of the cylinders and knelt down to get closer.

"What is it?" I asked.

"It's some of Tesla's old equipment. See right here," he said, pointing at a small plate on the side of one of the cylinders with his flashlight. He read the markings. "Manufactured for the Tesla Experimental Station, by Hensley Station Manufacturing, Richmond Virginia, 1900."

Connor stood and set the rod across the top of several cylinders, causing a big, beautiful blue arc of electricity to shoot out, knocking him backward. He slid several feet before crashing into a stack of crates at the end of the narrow path.

"Conner," I shouted, rushing over to him. The arching blast had left black scorch marks across his heavy brown leather jacket, burning through in several places. I shook him and he moaned.

"Perfect, you're still alive. I really didn't want to dig a hole this late at night."

He coughed and shook his head, trying to get up and get his bearings.

"Hold on, dude. Don't get up yet. Give your senses a second to come back. That thing zapped the shit out of you."

Connor's eyes suddenly went wide. That's when I noticed the flickering electric blue glow that seemed to be coming from behind me. Still kneeling, I pivoted on my heel to find a small humanoid-shaped thing that flashed and arced. It looked like one of those lightning balls that you find in a Science Museum, but humanoid-shaped and small.

"What the hell is that?" I asked Connor. He shook his head slowly, at a complete loss for words. He mumbled, trying to get something out resembling a coherent sentence, but it only sounded like gibberish. Connor worked his mouth, trying to form words around what sounded like a swollen tongue.

"I'll take it, that wasn't part of Tesla's experiments and isn't a good thing," I asked, turning to look back at him. "We should go." He nodded emphatically.

I grabbed him by the front of his jacket and yanked him to his feet. "Alright then, we gotta go." Pushing him ahead of me, we headed toward the direction we'd come from.

Glancing back, I saw the creature was following us. Small arcs of electricity lanced out, striking at the building's girders and other bits of equipment as it passed by.

The electrical tendrils sparked and scorched surfaces where it touched like when striking a welding arc.

"Is there any chance that your buddy Tesla trapped that thing in one of his capacitors?" I asked, pushing Connor faster and faster toward the door.

"I… I don't know. Maybe? I don't remember hearing of anything like this in Tesla's experiments, either."

"Well, sometimes things don't get documented 'cause they're too fucking weird."

We rounded a corner into the next bay and stopped for a moment to catch our breath.

"It's possible," Connor gasped. "The government confiscated a lot of Tesla's work early on when they shut the project down. And there was this huge rivalry between Tesla and Thomas Edison, to the point that Edison sent his goons out to bust the place up and steal whatever research they could."

Connor froze, his face going ghostly white. "If I just let that one out, then that means there are two of them things on the loose."

"Okay, Mister Wizard, how do we stop something like that?"

Connor looked at me in disbelief and slowly shook his head. "I have no idea."

"Okay, stay here." Rushing back to the doorway we'd passed through, I peeked around the corner and spotted the creature slowly making its way toward the opening. It seemed to be examining everything as it moved. I took out my phone, snapped several pictures that I immediately sent to Mandy, and hurried back to where Connor rested.

"Okay, so how would Tesla have dissipated a massive amount of energy quickly?"

"He'd have grounded it," Connor answered. "Or you'd place it into a container designed to handle that much voltage."

"You mean like the one that you just broke open?"

"Yeah," he said, letting out a reluctant sigh.

My phone dinged. Mandy replied on it, and I followed with another quick message, to contact the US Marshal's office for Colorado Springs to activate me and show me on a case.

"What are you doing?" Connor asked.

"Agent things."

I didn't even bother to look for a reply. I just shoved the phone back in my pocket and moved further down the bay and away from the arcing electrical strikes.

"If the other one started here and followed that spiral to the park, do you think this one will do the same?"

"Possibly if they follow the same kind of pattern, but I don't know. I've never seen anything like this before."

"Neither have I," I replied. "So, if that's the case, where would the next spot be?"

Connor rattled off an address from memory, followed by several others.

"Okay, cool," I said. "That means we might have time to prep and figure out what we're doing with this thing. What would be the easiest way to send this much power to ground? Or could we quickly get hold of something to contain it?"

"No idea," Connor said, shaking his head as he turned to face me.

"Don't look at me, dude. I am not an electrical engineer. I'm just a grease monkey."

"What if we can't stop it?"

"Don't start that 'woe is me' bullshit. We can't let this thing get out of here and harm the populous. Did you see any other Tesla stuff in the building?"

"Maybe. There were a few pieces of old equipment that could have come from the lab, but it didn't really amount to much."

"Think we could use any of it to trap this thing?"

"Maybe? It would be nice if we had a Faraday cage. That might trap it."

"Faraday cage? What's that?"

"It's a cage that only allows certain wavelengths through the gaps in the cage. It's one way to shield yourself from EMP strikes."

"What would something like that look like?"

"About maybe that big," Connor said, pointing at something covered in tarps at the far end of the bay.

We rushed over, fumbling with the dry, rotten canvas straps that held the tarp in place.

"Oh my God," he gasped, revealing a large wire mesh cylinder a few feet in diameter and maybe eight feet tall. "I can't believe this has been hiding here this whole time."

"So, this is what you were talking about?"

"Oh, yeah, absolutely."

"Okay, so how do we use it to catch that thing?"

"We could use waveguides or grounding rods to guide it into place."

I turned and glared at him. "Do you have either of those things?"

"No."

If I didn't think fast, we were about to end up extra crispy. I glanced around, but it all just seemed like useless junk to me. Then a thought struck me when I looked up.

"You said they cut the power in the warehouse. What about the water?"

"Doubtful. I wouldn't think they'd be allowed to shut off the water because of fire codes and all."

"Well, what if we flushed it?" I asked, examining the sprinkler system stretching across the bay.

"Maybe," he said. "But it could just as easily electrify everything in this building that the water touches if you did that."

"Okay, so we don't want to be in here when we set it off. But do you think it might work?"

Connor thought for a moment. "It's possible. Water and electricity don't mix."

"Well, I don't have any better ideas, do you?"

He shook his head. "Not really."

"Alright, now we need a game plan." I hurried to the next doorway, looking for a way to manually activate the sprinkler system—some kind of valve, or a pull handle. There was no guarantee that the water was even on, but it was all I had to work with at the moment.

The thing continued its slow march through the building, arcing its way through the stacks of materials still heading our way.

I continued through to the next bay. This section of the warehouse was two to three stories tall, with large overhead cranes and an upper-level office box that overlooked the entire bay.

"Let's see if we can't drive that thing into here," I said to Connor. "We might be able to hide up there in that office. See if you can find any rubber matting lying around and carry it up there."

I hurried to circle around through another opening to the section of the warehouse we'd found the capacitors in and found the emergency release valve for the sprinklers. With a quick crank of the handle, a downpour rained down from above. I continued to the next bay, opening the valve there, before cutting back through to the larger bay where I'd left Connor searching for rubber mats. I found him waiting at the top of the stairs to the dock office when I returned.

"Okay, sprinklers are working. Hopefully, that'll keep the thing from retreating. Any luck finding something to insulate us?"

"Yeah, the office is already lined with rubber flooring, and I found these, he said, holding out a set of rubber cleaning gloves that I guessed could easily reach my elbows when I pulled them on."

"That'll have to work." I took the stairs two steps at a time, then took the gloves offered by Conner after reaching the surrounding catwalk. "Did you find the emergency sprinkler release?"

"Yeah, just on the other side of the dock box," Connor said, pointing toward the door on the other side of the small office.

Sizzling electrical pops of blue arcing tendrils preceded the creature as it entered the far end of the bay through the doorway we'd originally passed through.

"Alright, get ready. We're gonna short out this little son of a bitch before it can do any more damage. Just don't touch anything metal when I kick over the sprinklers."

Searching, I looked for something to tie around the valve, so I could open it from the relative safety of the office. It was a long shot, but I was counting on the rubber matting inside the office to be enough insulation to keep us from frying like a chicken in a microwave.

Finding an extension cord, I wrapped it around the valve handle and stepped back into the office, standing roughly in the middle of the room.

"Ready?"

"Ready as I'll ever be," Connor answered.

I pulled, but nothing happened.

Tugging first, I pulled again with the same result, but then it suddenly broke free and the cord went slack.

"Okay? What happened?"

I stepped back to the door and examined the valve from a distance. The release handle had moved, but the thin steel cable that ran from the wall to the ancient valve overhead had snapped halfway up.

"Dammit."

"What?"

"The cable snapped," I replied.

"Can you fix it?"

It looked like the cable had just snapped where it had corroded through over the years. Quickly I found an old barrel that I rolled over to the wall and climbed up on it so that I could reach the valve.

"Stay where you're at," I shouted back over my shoulder. Grabbing the release handle of the valve, I dropped, letting all of my weight pull on the release handle.

It popped and creaked at first, then stopped. Still hanging, I kicked and jerked at the handle. Finally, my efforts were answered by the rush of water passing through the valve into the sprinkler pipes overhead.

Bright electrical arcs flickered, lighting up the warehouse. The hairs on the back of my neck stood up straight. Tendrils of lightning struck all around the far end of the bay where the creature had entered.

"That can't be good," I mumbled to myself. Letting go of the handle, I dropped to the barrel and leapt. Electric tentacles arced around me as I soared through the air, falling toward the steel grading of the catwalk. If it wasn't for the fact I was probably about to die, I'd say it was the coolest *superhero* like scene I could ever hope for. But then I realized I was going to fall a few feet short of the office door.

The world around me exploded in a cacophony of light and smoke when my boots struck the grating. An awkward numbness, like when you stick your finger in a light socket, or accidentally touch the prongs when blindly plugging something in, hit me. I continued forward, rolling headlong into the open office door, where I tucked in my knees and rolled up into the fetal position.

A sudden explosion, like a bomb exploding nearby, rocked the foreman's office. In the distance, car alarms screeched and warbled. Connor let out a laughing scream as blue and purple lights strobed, lighting up the warehouse like some sort of techno rave party.

Slowly, the popping arcs of flashing lights died down. Cautiously, we rose up and glanced out over the bay through the office windows. Moments passed without another sound beyond the shower of sprinklers flooding the building.

Connor broke the silence. "You think it's safe?"

"I don't know, but there's only one way to find out." I looked around the room for anything metal that I could toss out onto the catwalk and test it for current. Leaned in the corner behind the door was a short section of threaded pipe that I chucked out the door. It bounced end first on the grating and tumbled its way down the wet metal stairs.

"Nothing arced," Connor shouted. "It might be safe after all."

"Maybe." There was no telling how long it would take before somebody would come along and find us. Only Connor's security friend even knew we were out here. So either we waited or someone had to give it a shot.

Reluctantly, I took a step out onto the catwalk, testing my luck.

Nothing happened. "I think we're good," I said, turning back to Connor, then hurried out onto the catwalk. Looking in the direction of where the creature should have been, there were scorch marks all around on the concrete and equipment along the aisle down the center of the bay.

The creature wasn't anywhere in sight. Then a tiny glimmer of light winked to life where it should have been. It was like a speckle of stardust floating there, struggling to hold itself together. It flickered and glowed once more. Weak arcs of electricity licked out like the creature was the core of one of those novelty lightning balls. It flashed again, then faded away, dissolving into the darkness to a tiny pinprick that vanished without a trace.

"You don't see that every day," Conner said then slapped me on the back of the shoulder.

"Nope," I agreed. "The worst part is going to be writing the report for my superiors. But if I'm lucky, I'll score a little pay out of it. I did get picture evidence that it existed. One down, one to go."

"I don't know that we'd have to worry about the other one."

"Why's that?"

"Because of the massive snowstorm we had a few days ago. There haven't been any other incidents since then. The storm wasn't anything out of the ordinary for around here, but if the creature was caught outside in the storm, I bet that would have been enough to short it out, just like we did with the sprinklers."

"Sounds as feasible as anything else to me," I said.

Connor hurried down the stairs to the warehouse floor. "Let's get out of here before the cops show up."

"Right behind you." We made a beeline for the door and hauled ass for his truck. "I'm wet and cold, but I could really go for a good beer right now."

"I know the perfect place. Do you like fish and chips?"

"Who doesn't? Do they have stout on tap?" I jumped into the truck.

"They do, and it's a great local brew."

"Sounds like a plan to me."

He chuckled, then started up the truck and shifted into gear. "Jack Quinn's it is then. The best Irish pub in Colorado Springs."

Love and Justice

By William Joseph Roberts

First published in It Came From the Trailer Park: Double Wide
Volume 1– Three Ravens Publishing, May 2025

I had this story idea laying in the slush pile for a long while before I realized it could easily be a Braxton story. And seeing as the Trailer Park: Double Wide edition was meant for novellas, it was a perfect way to take Braxton back to the small town I grew up in during Junior High and High School, and to tuckerize my brothers and several other people we grew up with. I even managed to tuckerize myself, but I'll let you guess which character it was.

I'd gotten a call two days ago from Travis Blankenship, an old military buddy of mine from back in the day. We'd served together overseas, did lots of stupid shit, and had one hell of a great time doing it.

When he called, I'd been working just south of Wheeling, West Virginia. He was a complete wreck, like rock bottom dumps, and had had so much to drink that I could barely understand any of his slurred, pig Latin.

I managed to understand enough of his drunken babble to put two and two together and figure out his wife Janice had left him.

I wasn't too surprised by that. She was one of those high-maintenance trailer park divas that needed nearly constant attention. And Travis, well… he liked to hunt, fish, and drink, none of which she thought a *proper* man should partake in. How in the hell she thought she could find someone in Southern West Virginia who didn't like any of those things was beyond me.

It didn't hurt my feelings whatsoever that I'd have to cruise through the twisty Appalachian roads to reach Travis's place. He'd set himself up a sweet little spot along the banks of the Guyandotte River in the unincorporated town of Justice. Where the fishing was choice and the scenery picturesque.

I made quick work of interviewing the locals and collecting evidence so I could close out the case. It turned out to be nothing more than another bogus run-of-the-mill Mothman sighting.

I figured that the *supposed* incident was most likely induced by the use of some sort of redneck chemical cocktail in an attempt to find that blissful nirvana where they could ignore the world and all of their problems one hit at a time. That sort of thing had become a serious problem in the area and wasn't within my jurisdiction or any of my damned business to start with. So I wrapped up the case, packed my gear on Jonie, my Harley-Davidson Road King, and headed south.

In my opinion, one of the best things in life is an easy, relaxing ride, and this ride ranked up there with some of the best I'd been on. The sun was out, and the temps were perfect, letting the wind wash away the cares and worries of the day as the engine pounded away. Not much else in this world even came close to matching the relaxation a little wind therapy provided.

The miles rolled along effortlessly as the sun slowly edged its way closer toward the ridgeline, casting long shadows in the valley by the time I pulled off of old State Route 52 and into the parking lot of the Justice Church of God.

The first time Travis had given me the directions, I must have made some sort of stupid noise, because he laughed into the phone and asked if he was wrong to have gotten some religion. He let me fumble with that for a few minutes before he told me the preacher was his fourth cousin twice removed on his mamma's side. Travis had won a houseboat in a poker game and talked his cousin, Brother John D. Browning, into letting him park the boat along the riverbank behind the church.

In exchange, Travis donated a hefty tithe to the church each paycheck and did a little work around the place. In order to put the boat into the river, he clear-cut the river bank and built a small launch ramp to the river that the church used to collect a little extra in charitable donations. With the influx of tourists and promotion for the Hatfield & McCoy riding trails, there were plenty of city folks coming into the area who wanted to kayak, paddleboard, or canoe down the now *"historic"* Guyandotte River.

I pulled in and parked next to Travis's old Ford Bronco. It was beautifully quiet. Nothing but the sound of the slow-flowing river down the hillside and songbirds filled the air.

"Can't say I blame him one bit for setting up shop back here," I mumbled to myself. "It's absolutely peaceful." I took my time along the steep path down the river bank to the water's edge. Travis had built a small dock of sorts and had several lines tied back to the larger trees along the riverbank to secure his houseboat.

On a covered upper deck of the dock that overhung a deeper section of the river, he'd built a smoker and a large grill from fifty-five-gallon drums and bricks. Several camping chairs surrounded an old wooden wire spool, a full sized fridge, and along the deck's railing were about a half dozen fishing rod holders made from PVC pipe and in the corner was a stack of rods.

"Almost heaven, West Virginia," I said, looking over Travis's setup. "Can't say I ain't a little bit jealous." I popped open the fridge and found it partially stocked with a mix of Miller Light, and Coors, the standard watered-down horse piss that passed for beer in these parts.

"Beggers can't be choosers." I shrugged and snagged a pair of beers from the fridge. Being the nosey sort I checked the drawers, and sure enough, found a small cup of nightcrawlers in the back of the cheese drawer. I baited a few lines and tossed them in before kicking back, lighting up a long overdue cigar, and making myself comfortable.

"Yup…" I said, popping the *p* extra sharp. "Travis has to be the richest man I know. This is nearly my perfect idea of heaven." I let out a sigh, took a long drink, kicked my feet up, and closed my eyes.

Of all the times I've tried to relax and visit folks, something always goes wrong. Maybe this will be the one time that the universe lets me take a break.

Taking my time I finished both the beer and the smoke, then lit several of the Tiki torches mounted around the deck before I grabbed an extra beer and headed down to the boat.

Stepping from the dock to the deck of the boat left my legs feeling a bit shaky, but it didn't take long to get used to the odd motion. Most of my childhood fishing was spent along river banks or wading along and fishing the hard-to-get-to pockets along small rivers and creeks of Northwest Georgia. It was a rare occasion that I'd fished from a boat.

I made my way to the rear and started to open the door into the cabin when Butch, Travis's bluetick hound let out one hell of a braying howl. I let the door clack closed and heard claws scratching at the inside of the aluminum door. With the way the sound carried down here, it wouldn't surprise me if half of the town of Justice heard Butch carrying on.

"Travis! Hey Travis! You in there buddy? Come on Trav, if you're in there say something. Butch won't let me in."

Something shifted inside the cabin. I could hear what sounded like empty cans being tossed about.

"Butch come," Travis said from inside.

"Well, at least you're on the right side of the green. I was starting to worry that you'd gotten drunk and fell over the side or something."

"Braxton?"

"Yeah, man."

"What the hell are you doing here?" I could hear him fumbling to stand, as he waded through what I expected to be a sea of empty beer cans. The door to the cabin opened and there stood Travis, eyes bloodshot, his features worn and ragged.

"You don't remember calling me, do you?"

He opened his mouth and started to say something, then just shook his head. "Nope, I don't. Come on in, man. Excuse the mess," he said, waving at the disaster surrounding him as he waded his way back through the flood of beer cans then flopped on the bed. He pressed the heels of his palms into his eyes and let out a slow groan. The small horse of a dog followed suit and flopped onto the rug next to the bed after kicking several cans out of his way.

Travis let out a long sigh, looking around at the mess surrounding the small bunk. "Ah, there you are," he said, grabbing a can from the shelf behind the bed. A small amount of liquid sloshed around the nearly empty can when he shook it. Travis shrugged and grimaced as he downed the remainder of what had to be lukewarm piss beer by this point.

"Hair of the dog," I asked, tossing him one of the beers as I stepped into the cabin.

"Mighty kind of you, Braxton. Free beer is good beer." He popped the pull tab and took a long drink from the fresh can before laying back on the bed.

"You wouldn't say that if you knew where I got the beer?"

He looked up at me with a confused curiosity, then shrugged and laid his head back. "At this point, I really don't care. Beer is beer."

I popped the top on my beer and cleared a space to sit at the small corner table to the right of the door. "So what's up, Trav? You sounded pretty torn up on the phone."

"Go home, Brax. It isn't your problem."

"It kinda is, man," I said, chuckling. "You called me, and I'm not the kinda guy that will ignore a brother when they need him the most."

Travis downed the rest of his beer, crumpled the can and tossed it against the far wall. "Well, maybe I need some time to think things over."

"You've had two days since you called me, Trav. You're alive, so I'll give you that much credit for not going skinny dipping with your toaster, but that don't make it any easier once you sober up."

Travis chuckled and held up his index finger, motioning me to wait. "Hold that thought." With great effort, he rolled over onto his side and reached for something amid the cans and other trash littering the cabin. He lifted a small hatch from the floor, then reached deep into the opening, retrieving a dripping can of beer.

"What's that?"

"Live well. It's great for keeping beer cold, too." He popped the top and downed the beer in a few gulps. "See," he started to say, then let out a rumbling burp. "Problem solved. I don't have to think about it if I'm not sober." Travis flashed a cheesy grin, then fished out another beer from the live well.

"That ain't exactly healthy either, Trav."

"Who cares." He shrugged.

"Do you really think that's a good idea? I mean, ain't you gotta go to work at some point?"

"Nope." The crack, pop, fizz of the beer can opening almost chimed within the confines of the small cabin. "Besides, like you said earlier. It's just a little hair of the dog to knock the cobwebs out of my head, is all."

"So what the hell is going on, Trav? You look like a complete trainwreck."

He let out a grunted laugh. "Life."

I stood, downed the beer, then crumpled and tossed the can at Travis. "Guess I wasted a trip all the way out here then." I turned and opened the door.

"Dammit, Brax…" An empty beer can hit me square in the back. "Sit your ass back down."

I turned and glared at him. "You sure? I have no problem jumping on the bike and scooting on down the road. I wanted to make a run over the twisty roads across Horsepen while I was up this way."

Travis stared back at me with baleful eyes. "Please, Brax."

I reached into the live well. The water was nice and cold. Probably something to do with natural springs in the area that fed into the river. Grabbing the last two beers from the makeshift cooler I tossed one to Travis, who fumbled the can several times before it landed on the bed.

I took up my previous seat and lit up the last cigar I had on me. "Alright, spill it."

"Hell, man. I'm not even sure where to start."

I shrugged, and leaned back, getting comfortable for story time. "Start at the beginning."

Travis sat quietly for a few moments, nursing the beer while he thought. "More than a few of the boys have seen Janice schmoozin' round town with that big banker from up north."

I shrugged. "Okay? Didn't you say she worked at the bank?"

"Yeah, she does. She's the head associate."

"Then maybe it's nothing, and you're worried for no reason. Did you confront her about it?"

"Nope," he said, then took another drink.

"Trav…"

"Don't," he said, cutting me off. "Janice pulled a fast one on me, Brax. She left a few days ago in a tizzy. She was going on about how I was worthless, lazy, and never going to amount to anything, not to mention how much of a mistake it was to have married me in the first place. She said that if she stuck around any longer, it would undoubtedly ruin the rest of her life. She's gone and gotten so spiteful about it all she even had that uppity Yankee banker repo my Peterbilt."

"What? You gotta be shitting me, man."

"Nope," Travis said, shaking his head slowly. He placed the cold beer can against his temple.

"Damn, man. That's a whole new level of petty." I let out a long hissing gasp then took a long draw from the cigar. "That just ain't right. You don't mess with a man's truck. She oughta know that."

"Hell, Brax, she even tried to take Butch."

I looked from him to Butch and back again. "I mean, he is a big loud stinky nuisance. But what in the ever-loving hell has gotten into her? She's always hated that dog. Is she trying to write the perfect country western song?"

"I don't know, Brax. But the funny thing was that Butch wouldn't budge an inch for her. I think he likes me more because I let him have a beer every now and then. Oh, and she filed for divorce and had me served. She couldn't bother to hand the papers to me herself." He chugged the rest of the beer, crushed the can, and tossed it over his shoulder.

"What the hell, man? You treated that woman like a queen." I grunted a laugh and slapped my knee. "If her daddy knew she was runnin' round with a yank, not to mention a banker, he'd roll over in his grave. A banker ain't much better than a lawyer or revenuer."

Travis let out a long sigh and let his shoulders slump. "Guess she just got tired of livin' on this old boat. I got the letter here someplace. The postman delivered it yesterday."

He craned his neck, glancing at the tiny kitchenette countertop, then shrugged. "Tell me this Brax, what does that banker fella have that I don't?" Tears glistened in his eyes. "It's incomprehensible how she could want to be with the likes of him. I'd be willing to bet he couldn't do a hard day's work to save his life."

"Want me to round up the boys and we'll teach him a thing or two about southern hospitality?"

"NO! I don't want you or any of the boys to do nothing." He started to stand, then unsteadily collapsed back onto the bed.

"We can't just sit by and watch you suffer, Trav. Not to mention, I only got a few days to kill before I need to head for the next gig."

"Your Mamma would shoot me if I let you get into trouble on account of me. Just go away and let me sleep it off."

"If that's what you really want I'll head out first thing in the morning. Otherwise, I'll go pick up some supper and another case of beer for tonight."

"That sounds like a plan." Travis laid back on his bunk and almost immediately began to snore, wrapped in the warm numbness of alcoholic slumber.

I stepped out of the small cabin and stopped at the end of the dock to relieve myself of a few of those beers before jumping back onto the bike. The darkness of night had fallen over the valley, letting the Milky Way shine bright overhead. It was amazing what the sky looked like without the light pollution of a big city nearby.

A low rumble grew in the distance, slowly vibrating the boards under my feet as I stood at the end of the dock. Downstream on the opposite side of the river, a bright white light came into view. The rumble grew more pronounced the closer the light got, approaching at a pretty good clip.

By the time I finished my business the head of the coal train had passed by, crossing the trestle bridge that crossed overhead of the river and road at the end of town. Quietly, I stood there for a few moments finishing my cigar as I watched the train chug on by and out of sight.

Taking one last puff, I tossed the cigar into the river and started to turn when I realized the low vibrating hum continued to drone on. I could have even sworn it was getting louder.

Strange lights appeared in the sky above the mountain range on the opposite side of the river to the south. It looked like something straight out of Star Trek. I couldn't say that I was a mega fan of any sort but I'd watched enough to know what was going on and recognize most characters and such.

The thing had to be the size of an aircraft carrier and looked wrong the way it just hung there motionless in the sky. The incessant hum perforated everything. What looked like search lights panned across the small mountain town and surrounding hillsides.

I rubbed my eyes to make sure I wasn't seeing things, but sure enough, it was still there when I looked back up.

"Hey, Travis," I shouted over my shoulder, not taking my eyes off the object. "Travis!"

He replied with a wincing shout. I could hear him grumbling under his breath, shuffling his feet among the beer cans littering the floor. Travis stepped out onto the dock and stopped. I could hear him behind me, struggling for the breath to make words. All he managed to get out was a strangled "Huh…" as he made his way down the dock to stand beside me.

"I'm guessing this isn't something normal around here, is it?"

"Nope." Reaching over the side of the dock Travis pulled on a rope, retrieving what looked like a minnow bucket from the water. After a moment of fighting with the top, he pulled a can of beer out and handed it to me, pocketed one, and took the last beer for himself. He dropped the bucket, popped the top of the beer in his hand, and finished it in a few gulps. Crushing the can, he tossed it overboard then retrieved a crumpled pack of smokes from his pocket. He looked down at Butch, who had followed him out of the cabin as he lit the smoke.

"Whatcha think, Butch?"

The dog let out one hell of a braying howl.

"Reckon we should head up the hill and see what that's about? Or should we stay here and throw an end-of-the-world party?"

Butch licked his nose, grumbled, then turned and hurried back onto the boat.

"Yeah, that's true. We are about out of beer." He took a long drag on the cheap generic cigarette. "I suppose I should toss on a clean shirt before we take off."

The unmistakable sound of a CB crackling to life broke through the eerie hum from above. "Breaker breaker one nine. This is Shag Nasty. Anyone out there got their ears on? Come on back. We be in a mess of hurt."

"Who the hell is that?"

"Shag." Travis rushed to the helm on the upper deck of the houseboat. I hurried behind, hanging back on the ladder. Travis picked up the mic and keyed it.

"Break one nine, this is T-dog, I gotcha loud and clear, Shag. What's up?"

"Did you not see the fucking mothership hanging up there in the sky?"

The voice on the radio sounded overly excited and flustered at the same time.

"It's exactly what I've warned everyone about all these years. It's finally happened! The aliens are here to invade! I've been making shielding for as many people as I can, but I'm out of foil. Can you bring some to me? I'm up on the hill at Mom and Dad's place."

Travis let out a long sigh. Rubbing at his temples, he slowly smacked the mic handset against the side of his head before he keyed it again. "You just sit tight, Shag. Is anyone else up there?"

"No, it's just me right now. Mom and Dad are in Charleston for a bowling tournament. Al is probably at the office still and there ain't no telling about Glen. He's probably back down there with Tammy all over again. I tell you what Travis, it wouldn't hurt my feelings none if them there aliens just up and took that woman. She ain't nothing but a no good cock teasing devil woman, I tell you what."

Travis looked at the radio and shook his head. "Will you shut up already you damned crazy ass." He retrieved the last beer from his pocket, popped the top, and stopped himself just as the edge of the can touched his lips.

Butch grumbled.

"Where are my manners? I'm sorry, buddy." Travis poured half of the can into the dog bowl sitting nearby then held the can up in salute.

"Cheers, bud."

He chugged the rest of the beer and tossed the crushed can over his shoulder. "Guess we should go save the world, hu?" He smiled back at me with that half-lit look of invincibility then headed below.

For the most part, I'd always been the law-abiding type, except in those moments where being law-abiding tended to be… inconvenient. After signing on with the KCG, Krypto, Cults, and Gangs, an offshoot department of the Federal Marshals, I had to make sure to follow the rules…more or less…because the bean counters really didn't like explaining to their superiors why one of their agents needed bail money.

But, hell, we're all guilty of bending the rules every now and then in some way. From speeding, to double parking, to selling a little moon shine on the side. It's just one of those things, ya know. So, I really didn't see where it would be much of an issue when Travis came back on deck toating an M4 carbine with extended capacity magazines, targeting laser, and an underslung 40mm grenade launcher. Considering there were what looked to be honest-to-goodness aliens invading the backwoods of southern West Virginia, I took it as one of those times it was okay to bend the rules.

We hopped into Travis's old Ford Bronco and headed north along Route 52 toward Gilbert.

It seemed like a lot of other folks had seen the ship as well because the road was clogged with hastily loaded vehicles leaving the area as fast as they could.

The alien vessel hung in the air, twenty or thirty feet above the overgrown gravel field that took up a rare acre of flat land between the river and the only road leading out of Justice.

Travis pulled off the road, put it in park, and climbed halfway out the driver's window.

"Don't you deal with weird shit for the government," he asked, sliding back into his seat.

"Yup."

"So what do we do about this?"

I shrugged and shook my head then leaned out the window to take in the enormity of the craft. "I honestly don't have the faintest clue, Trav. This is way above my pay grade."

Travis shifted the old Bronco into gear and spun her around, kickup up a cloud of dust and gravel as he pulled back onto the highway.

"Where we going?"

"Let's go pay Shag a visit. Maybe his crazy ass will have some sort of bright idea."

I looked over to Travis and laughed. "What sort of crazy are we talking about exactly? Conspiracy theorist? Paranoid schizophrenic? Psychopathic megalomaniac?"

Travis's face twisted like he was thinking really hard about my question as we turned off the main road and continued up the hill onto Plum Street.

"I'd say he falls somewhere between conspiracy theorists and paranoid schizophrenic with prepper tendencies if that gives you any idea."

"Okay," I said, nodding. "Good to know he isn't the type that'll cut out my liver and wear my face."

"Naw, not even close. Shag is more or less harmless even if he is a little eccentric. But he knows lots of off-the-wall things that normal folks wouldn't even think about."

Travis gunned the engine and raced uphill like we had a load of homemade hooch in the back and a government man was hot on our ass.

We pulled off into the driveway of a three-story split level that looked like it had been built in the 80s. Travis slid out of the truck, slung his M4, and followed a sidewalk around the front side of the house that faced the hillside. A very large canvas yurt came into view just down the hillside on a weathered wooden deck as we rounded the corner of the house.

"What's the deal with that," I asked, motioning at the yurt.

"Shag never really left home, but did at the same time. He talked his folks into letting him build that down there after nobody cared about having a pool anymore.

"G…g…god, is p…p…punishing us!" came a stuttered shout from inside the yurt.

"Thought you said he wasn't the certifiable kinda crazy?"

Travis spun on his heel and poked a finger into my chest "I did not say that. I said he was mostly harmless, And besides, that ain't Shag, that's Red."

"Who the hell is Red?"

"He went to school with all of us and lives a few houses down the hill. He found Jesus a few years ago and turned into a bit of a bible thumper since."

Travis continued down the weathered wooden stairs toward the yurt. "Hey Shag!"

"Travis? That you?" The canvas flap of the yurt flew open and there stood a ragged bum of a guy. Shaggy beard, long shaggy matted hair topped with a tin foil hat in the shape of a pirate's tricorn.

Travis fought to hold back a laugh but just couldn't help himself. "What the hell is up with that, Shag? Did you all of a sudden turn pirate on us?"

Another figure appeared in the doorway behind Shag. "His b…b…belief in false gods, will be his failing. The end is nigh brothers!"

"Dude!" Shag turned in the doorway and glared at Red. "Will you please, give your biblical doomsday bullshit a rest already. It ain't demons. It ain't Angels. It ain't even some kind of burning bush or some other fancy fantasy nonsense," he said counting off with his fingers. "It's an alien spaceship, plain and simple."

Shag turned his attention back to me and Travis. "And to answer your question, no I have not turned pirate. But there's nothing says you can't also be fashionable when protecting oneself from alien brain wave control." He flicked the brim of the tricorn and smiled wide.

"T..t..tin foil will not save you from God's wrath and fury."

Red stumbled forward with a little nudge from Shag assisting him out of the yurt's door. "Get out and don't come back unless you have a suggestion to save us from the alien invasion!" Red stormed past us, shouldering his way past me and up the hill.

I tapped Travis on the back of the shoulder and leaned forward to whisper to him. "Are you really sure about this, Trav? Tweedle Dee and Tweedle Dum don't exactly seem sane enough to be giving advice."

"Red, maybe not so much. But Shag…" Travis cocked his head and smiled. "Even if his hobbies are making tin foil hats and creative taxidermy on roadkill, he's the real freaking deal. If there's any truth to any of the conspiracy theories out there, I do not doubt that Shag will know something useful."

Shag snapped his fingers in our direction. "Hey, you two! Don't you know it's rude to be whispering around other folks?"

I nodded to Travis. "Alright, I trust ya, Trav. If you say he's a good source, I'll follow your lead."

"Good." Travis nodded then turned his attention back to Shag. "So what have you got? Bring us up to speed."

Shag let out an honest-to-goodness squee like some happy little feral gnome and then stepped aside, holding the flap open for us to enter. "Come on in and get comfy. It isn't often I get visitors down here, so look over the mess." The heavy flap slapped close behind him as he made his way to an old folding table with a stack of tin foil hats piled at least five deep. "Oh! Would either of you like a drink? I might have a few beers or cokes stashed away in the fridge."

"I'm good," I said, then noticed a low-toned beep that seemed to warble and fade in and out amid the sound of three dot matrix printers set up at the back of the yurt. "What is that?"

Shag flashed one of those excited lunatic smiles at me. "Caught your ear too, didn't it? I don't exactly know, but it started shortly before the mothership came over the ridgeline. It's on a repeating loop that lasts exactly four minutes, and twenty-two point two five five seconds with a point two two nine-second segment of silence before the next cycle begins."

I looked at Travis. "Automated message?"

Shag clapped and let out a triumphant shout. "That's exactly what I thought!"

Travis shrugged. "Possible. But the question is, what's the message."

"Ah," Shag proudly gushed. "I've already started translating it… Or, well…" he paused for a moment staring off into nothing as his eyes ticked back and forth. He licked his lips and turned back to us with a dead serious glare. "At least I'm pretty sure that's what I was doing before Red burst in preaching his hellfire and brimstone."

Shag picked up several large pieces of poster board with patterned grids of symbols placed on several folding tables in the middle of the room. "If I'm right, the key to the transmission is contained within the first three minutes of the signal, but it's hidden on a subsonic track buried within the message below the infrasonic frequency threshold. Similar to when the CIA slides subliminal messages into radio and television commercials. The main difference is whoever created this audio wanted it to be found."

"Why do you think they wanted it to be found?"

"Because the layering is as plain as day. They, whoever *they* are, wouldn't have made it so easy to find if they didn't want it found. It's also possible that there's some sort of data stream attached to that audio. The compression packets are tighter than anything I've ever seen before."

"Huh," I grunted, looking up at Travis. "You weren't shitting me, were you?"

Travis grinned. "Nope."

"Shitting him about what?" Shag looked up at us.

Travis waved off the question. "Nothing, Shag. Inside joke. Do we know anything else?"

"Not really…" Shag shuffled through several stacks of printouts that were still running on old dot matrix printers.

I stepped around Travis and scanned over the poster boards which were marked with different frequencies and instances showing the pattern. "Well, what do you think they want?"

"Oh, that's easy," Shag said matter of factly. "They're here for our women. They mean to breed us into submission and take over the planet for the resources and the breeding stock."

I chuckled. "There it is. That's exactly what I was expecting." I straightened and took a step back from the table.

"Well, maybe they're depraved explorers, and they see us as sheep on the galactic scale."

"Yeah, Trav. Galactic sheep," I prodded. "You know, all warm, soft, fuzzy, and if you catch one with its head stuck through the fence…"

Travis threw his hands up and rubbed his face in frustration. "Okay, I don't need that mental image."

Automatic gunfire erupted from somewhere in the distance.

Knowing how the people in this part of the country were, automatic gunfire at any hour of the day was not a surprise. But knowing that there was an alien ship hovering over the little mountain town, it could only mean two things. Either somebody snapped and they're killing everything in sight or some dumbass is shooting at the ship.

"That can't be good," I said to Travis.

"Nope."

A handheld radio on the end of the table with tinfoil hats suddenly came to life, crackling with static. "Break one nine. Shag, you got your ears on up there?"

The voice was almost as annoying as the sound of grinding brake pads on a second gen Chevy Silverado. It was nasally, high pitched, heavy with a backwoods West Virginia drawl, and I was pretty sure it was female.

"Dammit to hell, devil woman." Shag picked up the radio and keyed the mic. "The hell do you want now, Tammy?"

"Listen, Shag. Josh and his daddy are trying to start world war three or something."

Shag muttered something under his breath, then keyed the mic again. "Yeah. What you want me to do about it?"

"I want you to tell the damned green men to go away before Josh does something really stupid."

An explosion reverberated through the valley.

"Too late," Travis added as he hurried out of the yurt.

I turned and followed Travis. Sprinting up the steps two at a time we hurried across the driveway to the road just in time to see a rocket or RPG streak through the sky and impact on the nose of the alien vessel. Black smoke and flames roiled around the front of the ship, reaching high into the darkening sky.

What sounded like a crew-served heavy machine gun rattled away, flinging tracer rounds skyward from what I guessed was Josh's daddy's place. The rounds ricocheted in all directions off of the ship's hull.

Several rebel yells screeched above the noise of the machine guns then the night sky lit up from another rocket that raced skyward and exploded on the ship's lower hull.

"God dammit," Travis said through gritted teeth. "Those idiots are going to get us all killed."

I turned and laughed at him. "What are you gonna do? You gonna go down there and ask them to stop or something?"

Travis sighed. "Yeah, no. Josh and his daddy start something they see it through to the end."

A blinding flash of green light from the ship bathed the valley in an eerie glow. A green beam shot out from a point on the bottom of the spacecraft and passed over everything within sight of the ship.

"That can't be good," Shag said, puffing as he came up behind us.

"Nope, that can't be good at all," I replied.

Travis punched me in the arm. "You're the Star Trek nerd. What do you think that was?"

"Dude! What the fuck?"

"Well?"

I rubbed at the knot starting to form on my arm. "If I had to guess, I'd say they just scanned the area."

"Scanned for what?"

"How the hell should I know?"

"Aren't you the one that works for some semi-secret alphabet agency?"

"You do what?" Shag shuffled backwards. "You're a fucking spook?"

Travis turned and slapped Shag across the chest. "Hush. He's a good kinda spook," he said then turned back to me.

"Honestly I have no idea. I'm way over my head with this one. They could be doing some sort of terrain mapping… Maybe some sort of life form or weapons scan?"

There was a slight pause in the automatic gunfire. If I were a betting man, I'd say they'd run out of ammo and had to reload considering the rate they'd been flinging rounds at the alien vessel. In literal seconds the all too familiar rat-a-tat-tat began again.

Short-lived as it was…

Three points of green laser light flashed from the lower hull of the ship. Each beam tracked about separately for a moment before coming together, focusing on the source of the gunfire like the Death Star focusing its planet-killing death ray.

A pulsing ray of light discharged from the underside of the craft, bathing the valley in a blinding pinkish glow while the sudden discharge of energy sounded like a dragon's roar that reverberated off the mountainsides. The targeted area ignited, trees flashed to flickering flames, then the whole area burned white hot. Scorched earth and burnt ozone filled the air following the burning winds that rushed over the hillside to meet us.

I turned away, shielding my eyes from the blast. Silhouettes of trees, cars, and Travis who stood a few feet away shone through my closed eyelids. Even from this distance, the heat of the blast felt ten times hotter than an F-15 in full afterburner on a pad run. I could only imagine that the area was glassed as close to what a nuclear blast would cause without the radiation.

A sobbing murmur caught my ears as the howling wind died down. I blinked, trying to clear my vision. "Travis! Shag! Y'all still alive?"

"Here, I think," Travis responded.

Shag coughed, gasping for breath. His voice came out like a shaky hoarse wheeze. "Here, I think."

Shag's radio crackled then a faint voice came through amid the static.

"Shag! Where are you, you crazy sumbitch? You ain't gonna believe this shit." I recognized the voice. It was Tammy, the woman who'd called earlier. "You ain't gonna believe what Mama found when she was taking out the trash."

Travis laughed from somewhere beside me. "Did she find some sanity? Her mamma is as crazy as she is."

I blinked harder, still trying to get my eyes to clear. A white haze like a thick fog seemed to cover everything.

"Can anyone else see?"

"Just give it a sec, Brax," Travis replied. "Mine is getting there; it's just slow about it." I heard the beep as Shag keyed the mic.

"What the hell do you want, devil woman?"

"Trust me, Shag. You're gonna wanna see this," she said through the static. "I'm bringing it to you. Be there in a few minutes."

The mic keyed again. "Come up the back way. Pretty sure Pos's place and the whole west end are gone.

"Copy that. See you in a few."

My eyes were finally starting to clear, like the fog of war on a battlefield dissipating. The area downhill to the west of us was nothing but charred devastation. It looked like something out of a war movie. Nothing within a quarter mile of the strike point was left standing. Dozens of structures had been decimated to burning piles of slag as fires raced up the hillside in several places.

Motion caught my attention. A small craft separated from the larger craft and cruised up river, toward Towbar's gaming house and Ellis's Restaurant, the heart of Justice. Bracing myself against my knees I pushed myself upright and attempted to balance while my eyes finished adjusting. "That can't be good."

Shag tossed each of us a beer as he went over the translations again when Tammy stepped into the yurt, laughed, and let out a excited squeal. "Oh, damn, Travis. I didn't know you were up here. I heard tell that Janice ran off with that banker from up North. How you just going to let her go and do that?"

"Cause it's the least of my worries right now. Have you not noticed the alien ship floating over the Gravel Pit?"

Tammy shrugged. "Eh. I figured they wouldn't bother us too much if we didn't mess with them. And I figure if they were just here for a little light probing, that might not be so bad either."

All three of us turned and looked at her.

Travis chuckled. "You know, Tammy. Sometimes I wonder if you're crazier than Shag.

"We sort of have a situation here," I reminded them, taking control of the conversation. "What did you find?"

"I'll tell you what. It wasn't easy to get here. Those aliens look like something right out of one of those alien movies. Body armor, ray guns, the works. They're going door to door searching for something. We had to hide behind the log trucks parked over by Miranda's mommy's house. They started with the hotel, gas station, Ellis's, and the Justonian diner. I don't think they've started going through trailers yet. We ducked out as soon as they weren't looking and cut up the little walking trail."

Shag let out a frustrated grunt and started toward Tammy. "So help me, woman…"

"So help you what, you crazy old coot?"

Travis stepped between the two of them, blocking Shag's advance. "Can we stop the bickering and get on with it already? What did you find, Tammy?"

She let out a cackling laugh, put her hands behind her back, and started rocking like an innocent schoolgirl. "I might know what they're after."

"Come on, now," I shouted. "If you're just going to keep leading us on, go on ahead and leave. We have things to figure out before anyone else gets hurt."

An angry glare twisted Tammy's face. She crossed her arms and tapped her foot for a moment before she turned her glare on Travis then looked back over her shoulder toward the entrance of the yurt. "Hey, Hairy. Come on in. It's safe."

The door flaps swung to the side and a massive mound of fur and flesh stepped through the opening. He was all of eight feet tall if not more, covered head to toe in thick brown fur, and easily recognized as what most would call a Sasquatch or Bigfoot, but dressed in some sort of high-tech jumpsuit.

Tammy crossed her arms and bowed up at us. "Mommy found him out back when she took the trash out. It didn't take me long to coax him inside. No man or beast can resist a good scratch and a stroke."

I shook my head, unsure of what I just heard her say. "Do what now?" I blurted out without thinking.

"Oh, don't go gettin' your hopes up, buddy." She flashed a wide, gap-toothed smile at me and waggled her eyebrows. I wiped my hand down my face in disbelief.

"We…are…friends," Shag began as he stepped closer to the hairy alien, sounding like an idiot talking to a native in an old-school western.

I slapped Shag across the back of the head. "Will you stop?"

"Hey! What was that for?"

"He's a space-faring alien, not an idiot. Where do you suppose he comes from? Nebraska?"

Travis shrugged, then leaned back on the table. "No telling. I've heard them egghead scientists have found hundreds of possible worlds out there that could sustain life."

"Well, all I know for sure is there ain't nothing *little* or green about this man," Tammy added as she snuggled up against the creature's side and ran her fingers across its chest.

Travis shook his head and laughed again before mumbling something and rubbing at his temples. "I'm sure that whatever you're talking about was inappropriate, even on a galactic scale. But don't you think molesting alien visitors would give them the wrong impression of us as a species?"

"Well, for your information Mister Wizard, he didn't complain one little bit while I…"

"Okay! Let's slow up a bit," I shouted, hoping that the visuals coming to mind were wrong, but I suspected every bit of rule 34 was in effect when it came to Tammy. "I think that's about enough for the moment. How about we get back to the problem at hand?"

"Oh, there's no problem at all from where I'm standing, Shug." She gazed up into the alien's eyes and squeezed him even harder. An odd, uncomfortable look suddenly washed over him, like the look of guilt and disgust a new troop shows the morning after spending a night in Bangkok, Thailand.

The creature peeled Tammy away from him then retrieved a small device about the size of a smartphone from a pocket and held it out. He pointed to his mouth and motioned like he wanted us to continue talking.

Tammy gasped at the creature's rejection. "Well, I never."

"Probably won't ever again according to the look on his face," Travis said, fighting back a laugh.

The creature motioned more excitedly. I stepped closer and looked at the object in the alien's massive palm. "What do you suppose that is?"

"Maybe it's one of those hidden camera prank things like you see on TV," Shag added. He flinched at the sideways glance I gave him. Travis took a step forward, joining me in examining the object. It was a small, black, and squarish with all edges rounded, almost giving it the look of a flattened egg. The creature touched the edge gently with a large bulbous fingertip and it emitted a cheerful beep. It opened its mouth and uttered a series of grunted growling barks.

"Hello," the device said in a robotic English that immediately brought Stephen Hawking to mind. *"My name is Larrs'Neytee. I am a RohBandī."* The last word rolled off the creature's tongue with a long sighing gasp.

Shag let out a shrill cry and collapsed to the floor, curling into the fetal position beneath the table.

"Freaking Nonner," Travis said over his shoulder then looked up at the large creature. "Sorry about that. Numbnuts down there has issues." Travis whistled and made the twirling motion of crazy along the side of his head.

"I, see."

I cleared my throat and broke into the conversation. "So… I'm no rocket scientist or anything, but I'm guessing those guys out there torching the place are hunting for you?"

The creature let out a cooing chortle and nodded. *"Indeed, they are,"* the device translated. *"They are known as the V'ril. They are ravenous and bloodthirsty. Their race is renowned throughout the galaxy for their vicious, indiscriminate methods, and as such are hired by most other races to fight their conflicts for them."*

"Nothing against you, man," Travis said, taking a step back. "But what kinda trouble have you brought down on us? I'm all about helping folks, but that generosity does have a limit."

"I am a political refugee," Larrs said. *"The Salorians and my people have been in conflict for several generations. Recently the V'ril were enlisted to overthrow my home world. Being one of the most outspoken dissidents to survive the invasion, they see my*

existence and message as a threat to their invasion. Upon entering this system, my ship was irreparably damaged. I landed in the valley just beyond the ridgeline to the southwest across the river."

"Probably Lost Branch if I had to guess," Travis interjected to me as a side note.

"So, what's to keep us from turning you over to the… V'ril?"

Larrs flinched as the device translated my words back to him. He immediately took a step back in retreat. I put my hands up defensively, palms open. "I didn't say we *were* going to turn you over, I just asked what *keeps* us from turning you over?"

"Because now that they know that your people are here, and pose little threat, they will come back to enslave your race and conquer your planet for the available resources."

I turned to Travis. "Sounds like a pretty damn good reason to me. What do you think?"

"See, what did I tell you?" Shag shouted.

Travis mule kicked the table behind him. "Will you shut the hell up."

I turned back to the Rohʙandī. "So what happens if we help you?"

"If we succeed, freedom." He paused for a moment in thought. *"The V'ril have no way of alerting their people without connecting to the galactic network. We are light years beyond any consortium relay arrays. They would have to jump to a system with a relay in order to upload any data or messages."*

"And what happens if we fail," Travis asked.

"Pain…suffering, and death." Larrs drifted off in thought and shuddered. His eyes looked hollow and sad like a man who had seen too much suffering. *"So much death…"*

I turned and faced our alien visitor. "How many V'ril are aboard that ship?" The big guy waited patiently as the device translated for him and he began to speak back to it.

"Up to ten warriors at their maximum, with possibly three of them deployed to the ground with the drop shuttle."

I turned back to Travis. "What sort of armament do we have available?"

Travis shook his head. "I don't have anything but the M4 and a shotgun in the truck. If it hadn't all gotten blown up I'd say let's go down to Pos's and see what he's got, but that sorta got fragged quick. What all you got stashed away, Shag?"

Shag nervously tapped out of rhythm on the table. "Come on, Shag," Travis said. "Braxton is an old buddy of mine, and I trust him with my life. He's good people. I can vouch for him."

Shag hemmed and hawed for a moment before he looked back up at us. "If you say so Travis. I trust you, and I'll take your word on it."

"So what do we have?"

"A few boxes of flash bangs, several dozen home-brewed frag bombs, a few M4s, several shotguns, 9mm pistols, and plenty of ammo for each. Nothing really fancy but it'll get the job done in most cases."

"It'll be hours before we see the National Guard or any sort of reinforcements." I drew my .45 from its shoulder rig and pulled the magazine to double-check my rounds then slammed it back in the hole. "I guess that's settled then. We go on the attack and stop them here and now."

"Whoa," Travis said with a nervous laugh. "Hold your horses, Lone Ranger. What's this *we* shit? You got a mouse in your pocket or something?"

"You'd really let me take on an alien invasion by myself?"

"You got Shag, the big guy, and Tammy to work with."

I chuckled and wiped a hand down my face. "A crackhead, a crackpot, and Sasquatch walks into a bar…"

"Hey," Shag and Tammy both groused.

"See!" Travis punched me in the shoulder again. "It might not be the A-team, but it might be enough to get something done."

"Yeah… How about hell no, Trav. If we do this, I need you by my side."

"Then what's in it for me?"

I thought for a second, scratching at the scruff on my face. "Being the hero and saving the planet ain't enough?"

Travis tucked his hands in his pockets and shrugged. "Meh."

"Okay, then how about a chance to make a shitload of extra beer money?"

"Oh, hey. Now you're talking my language. But how you gonna guarantee that, mister fancy pants?"

I looked over at Shag. "You got a bible or anything like it in here?"

Shag drifted off in thought for a moment before his eyes lit up with excitement. "I might have the perfect thing." He scuttled away to a dark corner of the yurt and rummaged around in a pile of boxes, returning moments later with a small picture frame.

"How about this? Do you think it would work?" I was kind of surprised at the document he held out in front of me. It was a replica copy of the Constitution of the United States of America.

"All enemies foreign and domestic," Shag said with a wide, beaming smile.

"That'll do pretty well," I said, then took the document and turned back to Travis. "Hold up your right hand and place your left on the Constitution."

"What the hell you doing?"

"Swearing you in."

"How the hell you going to swear me in?"

"Remember that government agency I work for? Technically I'm a federal Marshal because we fall under their jurisdiction. Therefore I have the power to swear in deputies to aid me in my mission, which does come with pay and benefits."

Shag let out a worried squeal. Tammy turned on her heel, heading for the door. "Nope, ain't gonna have nothing to do with no government spooks," she said before disappearing out the door.

Travis tilted his head with a curious look. "Are you sure about this Braxton? It ain't like I really have anything left to live for. I could be that wild card that causes the mission to fail."

"Trust you with my life, brother. Then and now."

Travis placed his hand on the Constitution. "Alright, then. Let's do this. Come on, Shag. Get over here." Reluctantly the conspiracy theorist shuffled his way around the table and put a shaky hand on the Constitution.

"Alright, y'all. Repeat after me..."

Larrs might have looked like an eight-foot-tall hairy monster, but the more we chatted as we geared up, the more he sounded like my kinda people. Down to earth, level-headed, and enjoyed long rides on his people's equivalent to a motorcycle, even if it was a hoverbike. He'd just been caught up in some sketchy political shit of galactic proportions and ended up on the wrong people's shit list.

While we prepped for the op the small frigate, as Larrs had identified it, had moved upriver towards the dam. The drop shuttle on the other hand wasn't hard to find. It lit up the area around Towbars and the motel like a freaking Christmas tree with searchlights and drones running search patterns, scouring the area around it for our new fuzzy friend.

Larrs warned us that the search lasers coming from the drones were searching for his biological signs, which would be easy to pick out from all the human life signs in the area. The trick was that it was a line-of-sight system. As long as the beams couldn't touch him, they couldn't pick him up. Most metals blocked the scans, but then they relied on thermals to search within structures.

I didn't think that was such a bad plan. We could easily avoid those if we timed their movements. It wasn't any different than any good video game level, really.

The trick was going to be dealing with any of the V'ril warriors on the ground if we ran into them.

The way that Larrs described them, they sounded a lot like the Klingons from Star Trek, only they were ten times nastier. Raised from birth as warriors, they lived it every waking moment of their lives. He said the one thing that set them apart from the other warrior races in the galaxies, was that they thrived on keeping their prey alive. To let prey expire too swiftly was heretical. A talley was kept to record the duration a particular prey was kept in captivity and the number of procedures they'd managed to survive. The V'ril did this for two reasons. Experience of skill and technique, but mostly for the pure enjoyment of inflicting pain and suffering.

The V'ril were essentially evil incarnate on a galactic scale, and we had to stop them at all costs. We couldn't let the word of Earth and mankind reach the rest of their people.

Once we were ready, we cut down the back side of the hill and down the holler till it met with the old service road heading towards the dam before dropping down among the trailers behind Ellis's restaurant. Larrs ran point, even though he stuck out like a big hairy sore thumb.

From our position we could see several of the drones slowly hovering along Dolly Atkins Street just ahead of us, and along Old Route 52 on the other side of Ellis's Restaurant.

Larrs started forward then suddenly stopped, backpedaling into the shadows alongside the trailer. For a big dude, he moved super fast and slammed into me before I could come to a complete stop with Travis stumbling into me.

Larrs held up his hand, then turned and motioned for us to be quiet before pointing at something hiding in the shadows between Ellis's and The Justonian, the *other* diner in town.

It couldn't have been more than a few minutes that we remained motionless, but it felt like an eternity while I stared into the darkness, expecting to see some horrific xenomorph ready to pounce.

Larrs tapped at the device then quietly spoke into it. *"The warrior is moving away."*

"Moving away?" Travis stepped ahead, standing next to Larrs' elbow. "I didn't see anything at all besides shadows."

"That's because my people's eyes are better adapted to seeing in the dark."

Before I could ask him anything about the V'ril he sprinted ahead, quickly putting his back against the back of Ellis's restaurant.

"Let's go," I whispered over my shoulder before following Larrs across the street, Travis and Shag close on my heels. While Larrs made his way to the left side of the building, I hustled to the opposite corner and slowly peeked around the edge.

Further down the highway, I could see another drone scanning the area, heading our way from the west. I froze when I spotted the shuttle taking up several parking spots between other vehicles across the street at the motel. It was like something out of a movie. An eerie purple under light reflected off the pavement and the ship's dark, mirror-like surface.

"I'll be damned…"

A forceful release of breath and a sickly crack drew me out of my stupor. I turned to find Larrs restraining an individual by the neck, its head lolled limply to the side as it kicked and writhed.

The individual was short, even shorter than I was, but broad-shouldered and barrel chested like one of the heaviest football linemen alive, and sported some of the most impressive-looking combat armor I'd ever seen.

That didn't necessarily mean it worked well, but it looked pretty badass. And being that it was made out of *space-age* material, there had to be other hidden benefits to it as well.

A popping hum of electrical discharge left the heavy stink of burning ozone in the air. Larrs let out a bestial roar. Dropping the alien soldier he stepped back from the corner of the building and cradled his right arm. Smoke rolled from a bloody and charred wound on the back of his right shoulder.

Another V'ril warrior sprinted around the corner and fired in our direction. A crackling ball of light sored by, striking the barrel of Travis's M4. The end of the carbine melted away like hot dripping wax.

Travis threw the ruined rifle at the alien then leveled the barrel of his daddy's old Remington slug gun at the creature's head and fired. The 12 gauge slug struck the creature's forehead with such force that its head snapped backward and slumped to the side in an oddly incorrect way. The alien dropped to its knees, collapsing sideways.

Shag slapped me across the chest and laughed. "Jesus Christ on a cracker, Travis. Ha ha! Did you see that, spook boy? That's how it's done!"

Larrs let out a moaning growl. *"Good riddance,"* the device translated. I knelt down next to the creature's body and rolled its head around where I could inspect the damage from the slug's impact. The body armor, including the helmet and face mask, looked like it was made with some sort of fancy carbon fiber material. The only difference was that there was barely a blemish on the facemask where the round struck. No cracks or dents whatsoever, only a broken neck from the impact of the round.

I looked up at Larrs. "Do these guys have notoriously weak necks or something?" He replied with several grunts.

"Yes, when not fully matured. It is the one flaw of their genetic design."

I shifted and turned the creature's head so Travis could see. Face shape was elongated similar to the snout of a bear or a dog, but with a large chin protrusion. "Headshots are the way to go."

Travis tipped his head side to side, examining the mask. "I'll be damned. And here we thought these guys would be a problem."

Larrs cooed and grunted. *"Do not let these young scouts put your fears at ease. The veteran warriors remaining on the ship will be much more skilled and difficult to dispatch."*

"Gotcha," Travis said. "The privates got stuck doing the shit work while the old guys waited to see what would happen."

"Sounds normal to me," I said. Letting the creature drop to the ground I turned back to Larrs. "Do you think there are any more of them left in the drop shuttle?"

This time his odd noises almost sounded melodic, like a song from some foreign opera. *"Most likely, yes, unless they are short manned. V'ril scouts normally operate in teams of three."*

Larrs reached down and fiddled with something on the back of the helmet that released it and the facemask. He pulled them away from the dead alien's face and tossed them to the side.

"Holy fucking shit, Batman. He looks like a Sleestak on crack."

The Vril's neck was made up of heavily corded muscles that continued into a broad jawline. The damn thing honestly looked like the bastard love child of a rhino and wild boar, with a rough horn on the end of its nose, and several tusk-like protrusions along its chin, all covered with a greenish sharklike skin that was damn near a perfect match to the green of one of those quiet river fishing holes. I looked back to Travis and smiled wide.

"What bat shit crazy idea is forming behind your ugly face, Brax?"

"Larrs, can you still fly that drop shuttle?"

He looked down at his arm, flexed it, rolled his shoulder then nodded, and growled.

"We're about to steal ourselves a spaceship."

"You want to fly in that thing?"

"Yeah, Shag," Travis answered for me. "He wants to fly in that thing."

"Does the shuttle have any external defenses we should know about?"

The hairy alien roared and grunted again. "No, unless it is a modified attack shuttle. That one does not appear to be so."

"Then let's go snag ourselves a new ride."

Larrs retrieved the weapon from the V'ril warrior and several of what I guessed were power packs before we continued around the building. We sprinted across the main road to the parking lot of the old motel and ducked behind several dump trucks parked in the parking lot. The big guy slowed as he approached the nose of the vessel, cautiously making his way to the open hatch on the side.

Before we could reach him, Larrs fired blindly into the opening and then sprinted inside the craft.

With my .45 drawn and aimed I crossed to the opposite side, keeping my sights steady in case Larrs wasn't as quick as he seemed.

I nearly pulled the trigger at the first sign of motion within the ship. Larrs had just gotten straight up stupid lucky. He dropped another of the V'ril soldiers onto the decking of the corridor and let out a barking growl as he stepped to the opening. *"The ship is clear. Once we return to the frigate it will be all or nothing. There will be no return if we do not win. Move swiftly, strike true, and we may yet succeed.*"

"May?" Shag said through panting breaths as he stumbled up alongside of us.

Larrs nodded. *"Yes."*

"I don't know about all that *may* return bullshit, y'all." Shag started backing away. "I think I'm just gonna leave the hero shit to you two. I'll go get on the horn and coordinate relief efforts with the National Guard." He hurried away back across the road and out of sight behind the restaurant.

"Fucking Nonner!" I shouted after Shag, holstered my sidearm, and smacked Travis across the chest. "You ready for this?"

"About as ready as I am to go get a vasectomy."

"That ready, huh?" I laughed and started to step into the ship. "Guess that's about as good as we're gonna get, big guy," I said, looking up at Larrs. "Let's get this show on the road before we change our minds."

Larrs let out a barking chortle. *"Agreed. The sooner this is over, the sooner I may return to my people."* The large alien turned and led us to the cockpit. It was just like something out of Star Wars. A vast array of controls, indicators, and displays covered every possible surface of the cockpit. Not really any different than the cockpit of the F-15 Strike Eagles I'd worked, only there were four independent stations spaced well enough apart to accommodate the wide-shouldered aliens.

Larrs slung the energy rifle across his shoulder and slid into the seat of the forward right station. I dropped into the seat to his left and buckled in, the harness wasn't much different than any of the five-point racing harnesses I'd ever seen in the past. Travis plopped into one of the rear stations and examined the console.

"Wow, that's a crazy layout."

Larrs turned in his seat to look at Travis and let out several barking trills. *"If you would, please do not touch any of the controls. Considering you are sitting at the engineering station, I wouldn't want you to accidentally destabilize the power matrix."*

"Yeah…," I said with a nervous laugh. "Let's not do what he said. Be a good little boy and look with your eyes, not your fingers. What do you say, Trav?"

"Sounds like a plan to me…" Travis settled in and secured his harness. Larrs cycled several controls and pushed what looked like throttles forward on the control console. The sound of the craft changed, from a low-frequency hum to a pulsating throb that resonated throughout the frame of the craft and we lifted off with a sickening lurch.

Larrs let out a chortled cooing. *"Once we are inside, if we are allowed to dock, our only chance is to catch them off guard. Strike fast and strike hard before they have an opportunity to respond."*

I looked back at Travis and he nodded in understanding. "That we can do, big guy," I responded to Larrs. "What can we expect once we're inside?"

The big guy shrugged one of those non-committal shrugs. *"The V'ril are minimalists in a sense. If it doesn't aid in their combat effectiveness, it is an excess. To the V'ril, anything in excess is sacrilegious to them and isn't to be tolerated. Expect dark corridors, a hot and humid atmosphere, and little space to move."*

"So, the worst-case scenario of alien flicks possible is what you're saying," Travis asked, interrupting.

Larrs turned, nodding to Travis before he continued. *"From the launch bay at the rear of the ship, two corridors will branch out and run the length of the vessel, meeting again in the forward section. There will be an upper deck with the command station, officer's quarters, and primary offensive systems. There is also a lower deck composed of cargo bays, holding cells, and rudimentary ship systems that will most likely be empty, but we will still need to clear the area to be sure."*

"Okay. Good to know," Travis said.

I leaned forward as best as I could in the harness and looked at Larrs. "What should we expect weapon-wise? Will they come at us with those ray guns or are we going old-school toe to toe back alley brawling?"

"Several of the officers may have sidearms, but otherwise expect close-quarters fighting with blades from any of the V'ril still aboard. They will fight with a ferocity you have never seen. Beyond any weapons, they still have claws and teeth that will tear flesh with a little effort."

The thought of going toe to toe with a crew of aliens wasn't what I had in mind when I was coming to help my buddy get over the fact that his wife left him for some uppity Yankee banker, but there's no guarantees what life is ever going to throw at any of us at any given time. All we can do is take the situation at hand, run with it, and do the best that we can with what the universe gives us.

It couldn't have been more than five minutes before we were approaching the rear of the V'ril vessel. A small hatch at the back of the ship opened as we approached, allowing us entry. Larrs tapped at the console controls, expertly maneuvering the small craft into the landing bay of the alien frigate alongside other drop shuttles in the bay.

"I'd rather this be a sawed-off," Travis said, gently patting his daddy's shotgun, "but I guess it is what it is."

"It might be better if me and Travis go one way to clear the corridors. We work well together and understand most of each other's hand signals."

Larrs let out a low growl and nodded. *"I am capable of holding my own in most cases. You have a sound strategy."*

"Game on," Travis said, loading fresh rounds into the shotgun.

We sat down in the bay with a light thud, and the engines of the drop shuttle powered down.

"Be on your guard. They will give no quarter. The V'ril have even been known to add unworthy prey to their larders."

"Fuck that noise," Travis blurted out.

"Agreed," I replied, reaching back for a fist bump from Trav.

Larrs stood and quickly looked about the bay through the windscreen, then hurried aft to the hatch. We slipped out of our harnesses and followed behind, weapons drawn.

The bay was as large as a truck garage with several other shuttles parked about. We followed Larrs to a blast door style hatch, sliding to the left side of the doorway while he accessed a control panel on the right. Getting our attention, he made sure to show us what button to hit on the panel before he depressed it. The hatch slid open with a mechanical whir of drive motors.

He turned and let out a low throat rumble. *"Remember, move swiftly, no quarter, and we may yet survive this night."*

The big guy moved as fast as a flash of lightning, sprinting out the door and down the right side of the corridor.

"Lock and load," Travis said, then slipped through the hatch to the left, his shotgun held at the ready.

I followed close behind with my .45 drawn, covering Travis as he advanced into the dark corridor.

It really was like something out of the Alien movies. Dark, barely backlit with a tropical fog that hung heavy in the air. I was already sweating like a stuck pig by the time we'd made it around the first corner. I couldn't imagine how miserable Larrs had to be with his heavy covering of fur.

Travis approached the first hatch on the left of the corridor. He swung wide, stepping to the right of the hatch while I positioned myself on the left, then he pressed the controls to open the doorway.

The door slid open, revealing a small equipment room that I didn't even want to try to understand. I continued down the corridor past Travis and adjusted my aim as I advanced to the next bulkhead hatch. Again we repeated the sequence, making our way through the belly of the ship.

We'd made it through several bulkheads heading forward before coming to a larger set of doors on either side of the corridor. The layout made me think of an equipment passage like I'd seen on a few older naval vessels that had been turned into floating museums.

I nudged Travis and chin nodded at the doors to the right. "Engineering space?"

"Could be the chow hall for all I know," he whispered. "The only thing I know for sure is I want off this boat as quick as we can get this over with. Between the heat and the stink of the place, it's all I can do to not barf."

He wasn't lying. It was worse than the stink of a rancid swamp in the middle of summer and twice as hot. Sweat poured from my pores, soaking through my clothes. It was easily worse than any Louisiana summer I'd endured.

I hurried to the control console and smacked the button. "Then let's get er' done." The door slid open with a grinding, labored moan. The three V'ril in the compartment looked up from their stations with surprise as we rushed in.

"Hey there sweet thang, pucker up for daddy," I shouted as I fired two rounds center mass on the first alien to my right.

"Say hello to my boomstick!" Travis fired several slugs into the V'ril to the left of the door as quickly as the action could cycle.

The third alien fumbled with something on its belt, drawing what looked like some sort of blaster pistol right out of Star Trek. The creature cleared the holster, aimed, and fired in our direction.

Travis let out a blood-curdling scream, dropped his gun, and collapsed to the deck. The heat generated by the beam was insane. It was as intense as any blast furnace I'd ever been around. Heat ripples like you'd see on a blacktop highway in the desert pulsated from the device. My sight blurred and stomach lurched as my knees buckled and I dropped to the floor. The stink of burning hair and scorched ozone invaded my nostrils.

"Travis!"

Three rapid-fire shots from a shotgun rang out in the small space.

"Dammit, Brax! Why couldn't we have just gone for beer and let well enough alone?"

My head throbbed and the world spun like I'd dunked my head in the punch bowl at a squadron party and gulped till it was empty.

"Because we're the good guys."

Travis laughed from somewhere to my left. "That's a big ballsack of bullshit, man. There ain't much good about either of us."

Even though my eyes were starting to clear, they burned something fierce. "Can you see?" Travis laughed. "I can't see shit. What the hell do you think he hit us with?"

I pressed my palms into my eyes and rubbed gently. Colorful swirls exploded in the darkness before my eyesight began to really clear. "If it was sonic, we'd both be deaf and bleeding from the ears. Probably some sort of radiation gun would be my guess."

"Great… So the lizard reject from the black lagoon tried to microwave us like chicken nuggets?"

Finally spotting Travis laying on the floor nearby I nodded in his direction and forced myself up onto one knee. "Yeah, I guess so."

"Let's not do that again."

"Agreed."

"You okay, Brax?"

I pushed myself upright and paused for a moment. "Besides slightly crispy, yeah, I think so. Nothing feels broken or missing. What about you, Travis?"

His chuckle quickly turned into a raspy wet cough. Cautiously I made my way over to his side, barely holding my balance.

"Travis?"

"Yeah, Brax?"

"That really doesn't sound good."

I could tell his shoulders moved up and down in a shrugging motion. "Meh, it's probably nothing. I still can't see a damn thing. I'm sure it ain't nothing a bottle of top shelf whiskey can't fix."

"Uh, hu…" Blinking, I wiped my eyes on my sleeves, trying to clear the haze that still clung there. It took several more moments, but they finally stopped watering enough that I was able to start making out details in the dark compartment. Travis's shirt and face looked like he'd single handedly took on a pissed off flamethrower. The upper half of his body was scorched. Crispy bits of flesh that had cracked and peeled itself back from the extreme exposure glistened from oozing open wounds.

"Well? What's the verdict, doc?"

"Um…"

"Come on, man. I already know it ain't good just by that response."

"Naw, man. It ain't nothing. You'll be up and running in no time. You've seen better days, but.."

"But nothing, Brax. Don't bullshit me. I can't feel anything in my upper body and I can't see a thing. Come on, man. How bad is it, really?"

That's when I noticed his eyes. Two dark voids stared back at me from his mangled visage.

I dryly swallowed, attempting to catch my breath. He didn't look real. More like some animatronic thing from a bad horror flick. I was surprised he could still form words as good as he could considering the amount of meat missing from his lips and cheeks. Blood stained teeth peeked through the holes in his face like some sort of undead thing from a zombie flick.

"I ain't no medic, man."

"For fuck's sake, Braxton. We've seen some shit in our time. Now grow some god damned balls and spit it out already."

"It don't look good, man. You're missing a whole lot of meat and…"

"And?"

"And your eyes are completely gone."

Travis shrugged once more and let out a long sigh. "Meh. Ain't nobody going to miss me anyhow."

He'd be lucky to survive the night, let alone land another hot psycho hose beast like Janice.

In the old self aid buddy care courses they taught us that attitude was everything. Keep their spirits up, keep that hope alive and even the most seriously fucked up grunt could pull through and live another day.

"Bullshit, Travis. I know for a fact you could score with that Kelly chick down in the bottom you talked about. She'd sleep with a dead man for a twinkie."

"No shit, Brax. I know I'm done. I can feel it. And aside from the alimony Janice might try to take me for, there ain't no one going to care one way or the other if I live or die."

"Hell, I'd miss your sorry hide, dumbass. You ever think about that? Doubly so now that you smell like crispy bacon."

That got a chuckle out of Travis.

"Come on man. We got to get you out of here." I knelt down and worked my hands under him to get a grip, then froze. What was left of the shirt was soaked completely through with blood. And greasy gore oozed through the ragged remains of his shirt.

"Braxton, dude. Stop already. I'm not going anywhere anytime soon. Did you forget that we're on an alien ship? Can you fly that shuttle we came here on?"

He was right. Without Larrs to fly the shuttle, there was no way I could get him back to the ground. The only chance Travis had was for us to finish this fight and take the ship.

"Mark it on the fucking calendar," I said sarcastically. "The dumb ass jarhead actually got something right for a change."

Travis let out a tired laugh. "Glad I got to be right at something for once."

I picked up his shotgun and quickly checked it for damage. Other than a little scorching on the wood it looked perfectly serviceable. I racked the action and checked the ammunition. Four rounds that still looked decent. I was glad the plastic shells hadn't melted in the tube or the gun would have been worthless.

"Where's the rest of your ammo, Trav?"

He wheezed then coughed out several bloody chunks that dribbled down his chin, onto his chest. "My right cargo pocket," he managed between straining breaths. "Should be a dozen or so rounds left."

I hurried, gathering the shells and tucking them into the breast pockets of my kutte after fully loading the shotgun.

I could hear commotion from somewhere else on the ship. The discharge of energy weapons and a bestial roar like nothing else I'd ever heard reverberated through the ship's bulkheads.

"Kick some alien ass for me, Brax." Weakly he slapped me across the arm.

"You're damn right I'm gonna. Stay put. I'll be back as soon as this is over and we'll get you off this ship."

Travis coughed through another raspy wet laugh. "Not like I've got a whole lot of choice, bud. Don't worry about me. Just finish the job so we can go get those beers."

Against the protest of my aching muscles, I pushed myself upright and rushed through the hatch we'd come through, activating the next hatch leading forward in the corridor.

Larrs had one of the V'ril Warriors pinned against the wall by the throat. His fingertips dug deep into the alien's flesh, threatening to puncture through the skin under the strain. Smoke roiled from what remained of Larrs's now patchy fur.

The massive walking carpet let out another bloodcurdling roar and ripped the alien's right arm clean from the socket. Tossing the V'ril against the opposite wall, Larrs lunged at the warrior and proceeded to beat it with its own dismembered appendage.

Another V'ril appeared from around the corner at the end of the corridor, aimed, and fired his ray gun at the RohBandī.

I stepped to the left side of the corridor out of his path of fire and brought the shotgun to my shoulder. "Not today, scale face!"

The blast from the shotgun resonated in the tight space, rattling my insides, but the .79 caliber slug slammed home, caving in the right side of the greenskin's face.

Larrs dropped to one knee and leaned against the side of the corridor. He let out several whimpering barks, then pulled himself together, forcing himself back to his feet. In two steps, he brought his size 20 boot down on the Vril's face, caving in what the slug hadn't.

"Remind me to never piss you off, big guy."

He mumbled something that was only echoed with static from the translation device he'd hung on his belt.

"That isn't good, but it isn't going to stop us from doing what we need to do." I nodded down the corridor and brought the shotgun back to ready hoping he understood the gesture. "You lead, I'll follow."

Larrs nodded, picked up the Vril's blaster pistol, and stalked forward toward the corner of the corridor.

The forward equipment compartment looked like it had already been cleared. Two bodies littered the floor, and sparks flew from several of the damaged consoles. Larrs was a one man wrecking crew. If the one V'ril warriors hadn't gotten a shot in when he did, I had no doubt Larrs would have already been on the upper deck wreaking havoc.

The RohBandī didn't waste any time. He leaped onto the hatchway steps leading to the next deck and took three at a time like it was nothing.

Reaching the next level, he disappeared from sight before I was even halfway up the ladder.

Something rock solid slammed into the side of my head as soon as I popped out of the hatchway, sending me sprawling forward across the deck.

The world spun as my head swam. For a split second I could have swore I saw Looney Toons stars circling my head like a Saturday morning cartoon. Whatever just hit me knocked the literal shit out of me, and felt worse than any bar fight I'd ever been in.

Something nearby let out a crocodile-like growl. Forcing myself back to my feet, I shook my head, clearing the cobwebs.

The V'ril was on me and toe to toe in a split second before I could bring the shotgun up. It swatted the barrel aside with its left and delivered another powerful punch to my chest.

I stumbled back, gasping.

The hit knocked the wind clean out of me. I gasped, struggling to get my breath back. If the hit hadn't cracked a few ribs, it was damn close. Cold pain radiated out from the impact point.

The V'ril let out something that sounded like a guttural barking laugh, then advanced again.

"I don't care if fifteen minutes can save me money. Fuck you and your insurance, buddy!"

It charged forward and I rotated the gun around, butt checking his ugly face square between the eyes. The V'ril took a step back, grasping its face in pain.

"Don't feel so good, does it, fuck face?"

The warrior crouched like a linebacker and flexed its massive muscles before letting out an ear-splitting shout. It rushed forward, nose down like the rhino-pig it looked like.

Sidestepping at the last minute I slammed the butt of the gun into the side of its head as it shoulder-checked me, sending me flying into the corridor wall.

The V'ril teetered, striking the opposite wall before it turned, shook its head, and galloped back toward me.

I raised the shotgun enough to fire it from the hip, pulling the trigger as fast as the action would cycle. Three slugs tore into the creature's torso. Black ichor and gore exploded from the creature's back.

Pain radiated across my shoulder and chest from the force of the shots. Maybe there were a few cracked ribs in there after all.

"Fuck, that hurt!"

I rolled my shoulders and pain shot through me. I staggered back and leaned against the corridor wall, still gasping for breath. "Check that. Pretty sure they're broken."

Larrs roared from somewhere deeper on this deck.

"Not sure if that was good or bad," I mumbled to myself as I dug fresh shells from my pocket. I forced a breath past the pain and stood upright, reloading the shotgun.

"This shit ain't gonna finish itself." I hurried in the direction of Larrs's roar, stepping over several more dead and dismembered V'ril.

"Mental note, never piss off a RohBandī." The sound of several energy blasts resounded from ahead. The guttural bellow of another V'ril overshadowed the roar from the RohBandī fugitive. It seriously sounded like Godzilla and King Kong were having one hell of a stand off ahead.

"That really doesn't sound good." Racing forward, I dodged broken equipment and several more bodies littering the corridor that lead to another large bulkhead hatch.

The RohBandī roared from the other side of the hatchway, but this time it sounded different. It wasn't a roar of anger. It sounded more like a wounded moose trying to escape the maw of a grizzly bear than anything else.

I tapped at the controls, and stepped through, shotgun at the ready before the door had fully opened to reveal what I guessed was the ship's bridge. Several stations surrounded what looked like Captain Kirk's chair in the center of the compartment.

Larrs lay back on the deck plating of the alien bridge, propped up on one elbow. A massive V'ril warrior loomed over him firing one of the alien energy pistols.

Smoke spewed forth from his jumpsuit as it smoldered and his flesh burned. Acrid smoke mingled with the stink of burnt ozone, filling the compartment with a bitter choking haze.

"Hey FUCK FACE!"

The V'ril quickly turned his attention to me and smiled. Rows of needle sharp teeth gleamed back at me from its massive maw. It was at least twice the size of any of the other V'ril warriors aboard. Large plates of a bronze like material covered its combat armor.

I had no doubts that this guy was the V'ril commander. None of the others wore anything similar. It snarled then lunged forward, bellowing out a saurian howl.

"Your mom screamed my name louder than that last night!"

Bracing myself, I hip fired the shotgun as fast as the action could cycle. The first three rounds struck the commander across the right side of his chest piece, denting the bronze-like plating.

Pain coursed across my chest and shoulder, drawing my aim to the right. The remaining rounds went wide, ricocheting off the walls of the compartment.

The commander lurched to the side and spun from the impact of the rounds.

Larrs rolled to his side and roared, forcing himself to his knees. He dove toward the V'ril, grappling it in what could only be described as a perfectly executed sleeper hold.

I pulled the shotgun close, stepping to my left and away from the commander as I reloaded another slug into the chamber, racked the action, and loaded the remaining slugs into the tube. Not a full load, but it would have to do.

Larrs roared and barked again. Leaning back, he placed his knee into the V'ril commander's lower back, lifting it off the ground.

The commander flailed helplessly in Larrs's grasp. It strained, massive muscles bulging against the RohBandī's hold.

Larrs barked something incomprehensible at me. I had no doubt what he wanted me to do and darted forward.

"Nighty night, pig boy!" I shoved the end of the shotgun into the Vril's mouth, crouched, and pulled the trigger.

The V'ril jerked violently. Black ichor exploded from the top of its scaly head. I pulled the trigger again, unloading the shotgun into the bastard's skull for good measure.

We as a race might be royally screwing ourselves over with wars and polluting the environment, but fuck anyone who might try to take over and enslave our planet.

The commander's limp body slipped from the RohBandī's grip and slumped to the floor with a hard thud. Larrs, exhausted, collapsed on top of the Vril's corpse.

Larrs was an absolute wreck after the fight. The exposed skin where the V'ril commander's ray gun had burned through was blistered and had begun to slough off in places. The guy must have had an insane level of pain tolerance. There was no way he wasn't in a massive amount of pain, but that didn't stop him from getting back to his feet and back to the job at hand.

The walking carpet had more balls and gumption than I did. After a beating like that, I'd have been curled up in a ball waiting for the reaper to come along and punch my ticket.

After a quick look over the ship's systems, he motioned for me to follow him. Both of us made our way to the next deck, limping, and bracing ourselves against the walls of the corridor.

We found Travis, cold and lifeless, even in the heat of the ship when we returned to the lower deck. It really didn't surprise me that he'd passed away after I left him. He'd taken a direct hit with the same kind of ray gun that had cooked Larrs so badly. At least now I didn't have to worry about him falling back into his depressive funk and drinking himself to death.

Larrs let out a series of soft chortles then lifted Travis over his shoulder with little effort before leading me to a small compartment on the lower deck that looked like something out of a psychopathic butcher's wet dream.

Dozens of bladed, spiked, and otherwise painful-looking tools hung all around the compartment. Dark stains covered the large metal worktable in the middle of the room and the floors surrounding it.

Gently, Larrs laid Travis's body on the table, then made his way to a cylindrical hatch at the back of the compartment. He motioned for me to approach then tapped at the controls for several minutes, cycling through numerous screens of information that looked like hieroglyphic gibberish to me.

The console beeped and the curved hatch slid away, revealing a small chamber. Larrs turned to me, muttering something in his language while pointing at a large green oval on the screen before he stepped into the chamber and nodded at me, motioning toward the control panel.

"You want me to hit the button," I asked, stepping toward the controls. Larrs nodded again and let out an approving growl.

The hatch instantly slid closed. A pale blue glow filled the viewport and the chamber filled with a thick viscous liquid. Pressurized air whistled from the edges of the door as it fully seated and sealed into the frame. Larrs closed his eyes and visibly relaxed, floating freely within the blue glowing fluid.

I watched in amazement through the viewport in the hatch as mechanical arms extended from the walls of the chamber and slowly scanned the RohBandī inch by inch.

Scorched, blistered skin visibly smoothed, then hair slowly sprouted and began to regrow before my eyes. The console beeped and I glanced over to see what looked like a visual readout of the damage Larrs had sustained.

"Well, I'll be damned…"

Several sections of the damage on the display flashed momentarily then highlighted. I stepped closer, leaning in to get a better look through the viewport. Tiny mechanical fingers worked the seriously damaged areas like they were weaving new flesh and bone into place.

A little over an hour passed before the console beeped again. The display now showing the damaged areas in green. Fluid within the chamber began draining, taking little time before the door seals hissed and the hatch slid to the side.

Other than the damage to his jumpsuit, Larrs looked as right as rain when he stepped out of the chamber.

"Damn, man. I hope you feel as good as you look." The large alien smiled and responded with another of his growling chortles. "Even though I can't understand a word you're saying, I'll take that as a yes."

He pointed at me, then stepped aside and pointed at the chamber.

"You want me to get into that thing?" I asked, pointing at the contraption. He nodded and let out a soothing cooing sound.

"I don't know about that man. I never was one for going to the doctor unless something was really busted. Hell, would it even know what to do with a human?"

Larrs poked me in the ribs I'd been cradling since the fight. Pain raced across my chest and shoulder.

"Dude, what the hell was that for?"

He motioned to the chamber once more and repeated the cooing sound.

"Yeah, you aren't wrong. I'm pretty sure I have at least a few cracked and broken ribs at best."

He urged me forward again.

"You sure it ain't going to give me a sex change or add a few extra arms or something weird like that?"

His urging was a little more insistent this time. Kinda like a grandmother at the end of her patience. If my ribs were cracked, it would be at least six weeks if I was lucky before they were healed. Not to mention I still had at least an eight-hour ride back to Georgia when all of this was over. Reluctantly I stepped into the chamber.

"Alright, alright. I get it. But I ain't doing it for you. I'm doing it 'cause I can't ride with busted ribs."

Larrs cooed another chortling phrase then tapped the control console. The hatch slid shut and the chamber filled with pale blue light.

I had no idea how long I'd been in the regeneration chamber, but I felt better than I had in years. Parts that had hurt since my time on the flightline, especially my knees, felt as good as when I was a teenager.

The massive RohBandī smiled wide as I stepped out of the chamber and laughed, then said something in his language. *"Are you feeling better, little brother?"*

"You fixed the translator? How long was I out?"

"Long enough." He laughed again and slapped me on the back of the shoulder. "Help me with your friend."

"But he's dead."

He laughed again. *"Trust me. He's only mostly dead. You'd be surprised what this technology can do."*

After the results I'd seen, it sure as hell wouldn't hurt to try. Worst case, Travis was still dead. Mostly dead was better than all dead any day in my book. So we propped him into the chamber and Larrs activated it once more.

While the machine did its work, I helped Larrs collect the bodies and toss them into the ships' recycling system where the bodies would be broken down and used by various ship systems. He didn't go into the gory details of the process, but all I could think about was the bodies being used in some sort of protein resequencer or replicator-type contraption like you'd see on Star Trek.

Waste not, want not I guess?

By the time we'd finished with the clean up, the regenerator had finished. I expected my buddy to be just as dead as he was when we put him in there, but to my amazement, he yawned and stretched as if he'd just awakened from a long and refreshing nap.

"Travis?"

"Yeah, Brax. What's up?" He started to take a step out of the chamber and began to stumble.

I hurried forward and offered my hand. "How you feeling, man?"

Taking the offered hand he regained his balance and took a slow step out of the chamber. "Good," he said, thinking on the question for a moment as he studied the chamber and his surroundings. "Yeah, good, I think. A little dizzy, but otherwise nothing hurts. Hell, I honestly feel like I could pull off a ten-mile ruck in record time."

I laughed. "Okay, let's not get carried away now."

"What happened?"

"Um…," I started to say something but wasn't sure what to say. Hell, if it were me I'd want to know the truth, so I just rolled with it. "You kinda died, man. One of those scale heads hit you hard with one of their ray guns and cooked you like a microwaved potato."

"You're shitting me, Brax."

"Naw, man. You seriously think this is something I'd shit you about?"

Travis froze, absolute befuddlement showing across his face.

Larrs let our several smooth barks. *"Your friend is correct, Travis. You were not too far gone for the V'ril technology to work. The regeneration machine was able to repair your damaged systems and revive you."* He pointed at the screen readout that showed the damaged areas the unit had repaired and their current status.

"Looks like it even repaired all the damage we did to our livers over the years," I said jokingly, pointing at the bright green spot that indicated the over used organ.

A forlorn look washed over his face. "I guess that's at least something to celebrate."

"Dude, why the long face? You got a second chance at life after we kicked alien ass and saved the world."

Travis shrugged. "Yeah, but what good does that do me when I don't have anything to go back to? Or don't you remember that my wife left me for a no good Yankee banker?"

Larrs let out another series of cooing chortles. *"I must leave soon before your government forces arrive. Several aircraft are enroute to our position. If you have no business to attend here, you are welcome to come along and see what the universe might hold for you out there."*

"Shit, Trav. You could be the next best thing to Captain James T. Kirk to the hot alien chicks out there."

Travis looked at me with confused surprise, then back to Larrs. "You serious?" The big guy nodded and let out another bark.

While Travis considered the offer, Larrs fired up the shuttle and took us back to the ground, landing in the church parking lot just behind my bike.

Hands tucked into his pockets, Travis slowly stepped off the shuttle. "Do you have any problems with pets?" He asked, turning back to the RohBandī.

Larrs cooed in reply. *"What do you mean by… pets?"*

"Like a small domesticated animal companion that you feed and take care of," I replied.

"Oh, yes," the large alien said then laughed. *"There are many creatures throughout the galaxy held in this esteem that you would consider a pet.."*

"Then hold that thought for a minute." Travis ran back toward the boat while we waited. He returned in a fresh change of clothes with a backpack strapped over his shoulders and Butch trailing behind him on a leash.

"Larrs, this is Butch. Butch, this is Larrs." The large hound let out a low growl and hunkered down behind Travis's leg.

"He's a good guy, Butch. Just wait and see."

The beating of helicopter blades in the distance cut our goodbyes short. I leaned back on Jonie's seat and watched the alien craft lift away into the beautiful mountain sunrise with my best friend for what I figured would be one hell of an adventure to tell over drinks the next time I saw him.

The Velvet Hammer

By William Joseph Roberts

First published in Frumious Bandersnatch A Cryptid Horror Anthology– Three Ravens Publishing, October 2025

This story came about after a discussion with artist, Sarah Clemens at the ChattaCon 49 Guest of Honor dinner. That year I was asked to be the Toastmaster and she was the Artist Guest of honor.
Some how or another, we ended up talking about Gardinel's of all things and the evil mind squirrels were off on a run. I had a blast building the backstory to Braxton's friend, Peirce, and giving them a setting fit for any B-rate horror flick.

Whenever I know I'm going to be passing through where an old friend or colleague just happens to be, I'll try to swing in to snag a meal or a beer and maybe, depending on the person I might have a little something for them that I make sure to carry along with me for the trip.

After a dull and boring three-week job out in Arkansas, I'd already planned to swing through Memphis on my way back home to Chickamauga to visit my good friend, Pierce Maggert, who also happened to be a subject matter expert on just about anything strange, rare, or occult related.

We met several years ago while I was information gathering on this particularly nasty possession case, where we were both seeking the same item and it worked out to both of our benefits to work together in order to find the cursed item causing the problem.

Now, I know what you're thinking. Possession is a bunch of bullshit. And normally I tended to agree with that opinion, but to a certain degree, yes, possession is a real and true thing that just doesn't have an explanation yet. I hadn't personally come across any evidence to prove or disprove the existence of angels or demons one way or the other. What I can say for a fact is that there are dark, malicious things that lurk in every corner of our world. Things that thrive on harming others. And those dark things have a varying degree of power and influence over the human mind. Now, some say that this is proof that emotion and energies are imbued into the things around us or the things that we care about or cherish. This is exactly the kind of explanation that Pierce had given me on this particular little music box we were both hunting. The worst of all was trying to figure out why this family had taken turns being the batshit crazy entity that called itself Foster.

Well, once we found the box and neutralized it, things returned to normal for the family. It happens. The father picked it up in the estate sale for his oldest daughter with no idea it was tainted. He just knew he'd gotten a cute little music box that his daughter would love.

Upon that first meeting in Assumption Parish, Louisiana with Pierce many many moons ago, I thought he was Mike Tobacco, the male lead played by Grant Kramer in Killer Klowns from Outer Space. And to this day, he swears it wasn't him, but damn if they don't look an awful lot alike.

Since then, we'd become damned good friends. While I continued working the weird and odd jobs for the government, Pierce had settled down and come into possession of an old mansion in Memphis Tennessee. Originally built by a wealthy wildcatter and homesteader back in the early 1800s before Memphis was incorporated into an official city, the building was renowned for its opulence.

At one point in its sordid past, it had been owned by a very wealthy businessman who abandoned the mansion during the Battle of Memphis in June of 1862, subsequently leading to the occupation of the city by Union forces for the remainder of the Civil War.

Seeing an opportunity amid the chaos of war, a bright and opportunistic young lady, turned the once prestigious mansion into a brothel before Union soldiers could occupy the city. By recruiting girls from other houses and those working independently on the streets, Madam Jobe cornered the market.

Pierce, being the historical nerd that he was, decided to restore the extravagant, four-story structure to its pre-Civil War glory he named the Velvet Hannorah, but most locals just called it the Velvet Hammer.

He turned it into a high-end bed-and-breakfast-style gentleman's club; complete with all manner of vices that you would expect and several that you wouldn't, including several exclusive, off-menu *private* offerings available for those who knew how to properly *order* them. Even though it was technically illegal, I really couldn't care. What two consenting adults did behind closed doors was entirely their business as far as I was concerned and not for me to judge.

Pierce was an Eclectic one, to say the least. Besides being an avid historian, he was also borderline obsessed with the occult and all things odd, strange, disturbing, and weird. And he decorated the place as such. While keeping most of the original furniture remaining from Madam Jobe's time, he added any oddity that he could get his hands on; ancient electric chairs, electroshock units, fully articulated skeletons, pictures of Sideshow freaks, specimen jars, and other macabre oddities.

Anytime I came across something that fit his strange tastes that didn't break the bank I'd try to pick it up for him. Hell, it was the least I could do to show my appreciation for him putting up with all of my stupid questions over the years. It never failed that he'd have some sort of answer that pointed me in the right direction on the really weird jobs. So, getting him a small gift was the least I could do.

I turned off the main street and down the driveway, sliding between the mansion and the modern monstrosity next door. There was only one car in the parking area when I pulled in, but that wasn't a surprise. Most of the regular patrons either parked elsewhere and walked or were dropped off at the front door. Even the girls who didn't live in the Hammer parked elsewhere or called a taxi to take them home at the end of the night.

I knew Pierce was in because the one car in the parking area was unmistakably his. For a man with all of his eccentricities, you'd think he could get more creative and drive something a little more flash and style, like an old Rolls-Royce. I could see him riding around in something like that considering his love for fancy vests and suit jackets. But no… Pierce could not be parted with his beloved *classic*. I called it a god-awful eye sore that needed to be sent to the crusher, but he wouldn't have anything to do with it. No matter how many times I mentioned getting the car restored he refused without a thought otherwise. He argued that he'd lose that *classic* aged look that he cherished in his collected things.

The faded, baby-shit yellow 1973 Oldsmobile Delta 88 sat there, almost seeming to glower at me and the rumble of Valerie, my trusty motorcycle. Valerie wasn't much, but she got me where I needed to be, and she was stupid cheap on gas after I re-jetted the carburetor.

I pulled up next to the god-awful ugly turd of a car, dropped the kickstand, and shut Valerie off. I fished a small package wrapped in simple brown paper from the saddle bags I'd brought for Pierce. It wasn't much, but it was something I'd came across that I knew Pierce would appreciate.

Passing through the heavy wooden gate that separated the parking area from the small sitting Garden, it almost felt like I'd stepped back in time. Originally intended for early morning or a proper high tea for the patrons that followed that sort of thing, *the garden*, had all the vibes of Victorian high society, from the wrought iron furniture to creepy cherub sculptures.

I took the stairs to the veranda and entered through the double doors into the upper parlor, which Pierce tended to keep reserved for special events that required a bit of *extra privacy*.

Almost every surface was covered in something decorative; stained hardwoods, tapestries, beautifully woven rugs, and decorative wallpapers set the mood. It had that Victorian feel mingled with *The Addams Family* vibe thanks to all of the macabre oddities decorating every available surface in the house.

I stepped through the parlor's posh mahogany interior doors to the upper balcony that overlooked the primary parlor and entertainment room. There, in a high-backed chair upholstered in red velvet near a front window, sat Pierce, reading the morning paper with his afternoon tea. Pierce wasn't anything if he wasn't a creature of habit.

"It's good to see that things don't always change."

Pierce glanced up and smiled. That smile right there, could light up a dark room, and I knew for a fact it had gotten him into more trouble than he ever bargained for over the years. He had the look and carried himself like a Baron or Lord from the movies. Pretty boy looks and build, combined with a head full of dark hair that had only recently started showing signs of salt and pepper creeping in at his temples only accentuated his debonaire, lordly charm. That charm sometimes got him into trouble. Pierce was known to woo and swoon nearly about any female he encountered with little effort, but there were several he'd told me about that had nearly cost him his life. He'd just shrugged it off as bad luck.

"Braxton, you dirty old dog!"

Pulling off the black-rim glasses he wore, Pierce sat them on the side table, then stood and straightened his tweed hunting jacket.

Pierce clapped his hands together. "I am so glad you stopped in, Braxton. You've been on my mind of late. And besides, it has been much too long since your last visit, old friend."

"Naw, are you kidding me?" I made my way down the narrow spiral staircase that sat against the outer wall of the house. "It seems like only yesterday we were hunting down that supposed succubus working the streets of Hollywood."

"That was two years ago, Braxton."

"Really? It doesn't seem like it."

"Really."

"Well, sometimes life just gets busy as hell, I guess."

"Maybe for you, Mister Hicks. Time ticks by at an acceptably slow pace for me these days, especially since I left the hunting business to younger, more eager individuals such as yourself."

"That sorta news doesn't hurt my feelings any. It just means more gigs for me."

"Life is never boring for you, is it?"

"Nope, not really."

"Don't you ever take a break?"

"You know, that's a damned good question that you should probably be directing toward the universe instead of me." Pierce gave me one of those confused puppy looks, tilted head and all.

"How So?"

I figured I'd let him in on the inside joke. "It never fails, that any time I try to take a break, shit goes sideways. I stop in to see an old friend, have a few beers, maybe toss in a fishing line or two, and relax a bit. But, oh hell no— that's when swamp ghouls and an undead necromancer decide to pop up out of nowhere to harsh on my calm.

"Wait, are you serious?"

"The universe has this fucked up sense of humor. No matter where I am or who I'm with, it throws me some new curveball to deal with and harshes on my calm." I stopped a pace or two from Pierce. He shook his head like he was at a loss for words. "It's good to see you again, Pierce."

He nodded, snapping back to the conversation, and smiled. "It's great to see you again, old friend." We locked hands, shook, and brought it in for one of those brotherly shoulder hugs. "What's this," he asked, pointing down at the brown paper-wrapped gift I held in my left hand.

"Oh, this…" I said, holding it out to him. "This is a little something I picked up on the side, working an estate job down in Miami. There was this collector who had a few too many dangerous items that I had to confiscate and document. This just happened to get classified as a dangerous item when really it isn't, but as soon as I saw it, I knew it would be something you'd cherish."

Pierce continued to stare at me and blinked several times like his brain had decided to shut down and do a reboot. He shook his head and eagerly accepted the package. Unraveling the rough twine tied around the gift, he ripped away the dull brown paper and exposed a wooden frame.

The small ebony black picture frame, as small as a large index card held what looked like a desiccated piece of rough cured leather suspended and centered in the frame by hair-thin wires.

He rotated the frame ninety degrees at a time, trying to evaluate the item from different angles before flipping it over and examining the item through the rear glass.

Pierce glanced back up at me in total confusion. "What is it?"

"That my friend," I started, "is a one-of-a-kind specimen. You're an intelligent, educated man. What could you deduce that it is?"

"Some sort of cured leather, but no clue as to what." Pierce grabbed his glasses from the side table and looking down the bridge of his nose through the extra eyes like some sort of upscale grandpa, he took a closer look at the gift. "The coloration suggests extreme age, poor preservation techniques, or something I'm just not familiar with."

"What class of creature would you put it into?"

Pierce glanced back up at me, then back to the specimen several times before shaking his head. "I have no idea. By the texture alone, I would guess it was from something like an elephant, hippo, or possibly rhino."

"So, class Mammalia?" He gave me an even longer look of confusion, probably because the dumb biker used a big word meant for brainiacs. He slowly nodded.

"Yeah, mammal," he answered.

"And you'd be completely wrong, Mister Maggert."

He cocked his head to the side again, curiosity painted across his face. "Then what is it?"

"Reptilia." I smiled. He looked back at the specimen, examining it even closer then looked up at me over his glasses. "Do you know the possible genus or family?"

"Sauropod."

His eyes went wide before he stepped closer to the room's large front windows to get a look at the specimen in better light.

"What do you mean sauropod? Is this from some Siberian expedition where they passed off preserved mammoth flesh as something it isn't?"

"Nope," I said smugly, shaking my head. "That my friend, is a piece supposedly acquired by a German explorer hired by the King Leopold II of Belgium and tasked to survey his latest personal acquisition, which just happened to be the Congo Free State at that time."

Pierce started to speak, stuttered, then stopped and composed himself. "King Leopold and the Congo Free State," he mumbled, more asking than stating. His eyes rolled back and forth in their sockets as he thought. "You're talking the mid-1880s."

"1885 to be exact."

Pierce stood straight, taken aback, and smiled. "Well, go on. Don't hold out on me."

"This particular piece, acquired during that expedition into the territory interior and preserved as well as could be in the middle of a tropical jungle, was brought back to Belgium, where it was sold as an oddity to an interested buyer due to its connection to a local legend of the Congo."

Pierce shifted in place, smiled, and let out a nervous laugh. "Okay, and? Listen, you're killing me with this suspense. Just tell me, already."

"From there, it traded hands several more times over the years, finally finding itself in the hands of a rare oddities collector from Providence, Road Island, who eventually moved down to Miami where the collection, including this piece, was passed down to the heir upon the death of the previous collector. This is where I happened to come across the piece and realize just how much this particular thing would mean to you. I figured you'd cherish it well above any of these other trinkets you have decorating this place."

"You do realize, I know karate. I could hurt you in several ways that you wouldn't like."

I waggled my eyebrows at him. "Are you sure about that, big boy?" I smiled.

Pierce glared at me, almost smoldering, then took a step forward.

"Alright, alright." I took several steps backward, both of my hands up in the air, defensively waving him off.

"Supposedly, this is a piece of flesh that was torn away from a Mokele-mbembe that one of the local tribes had trapped by accident, but it managed to escape before the German explorer could lay eyes on the creature itself."

Pierce looked back and forth from me to the specimen several times while he tried to catch his breath and form something resembling a real word.

"Mokele-mbembe? *The* Mokele-mbembe? Are you fucking serious?"

I shook my head and defensively held my arms out to the sides. "I can't guarantee anything, man. I'm just relaying the info I picked up with the piece."

Pierce's smile suddenly faded, and he handed the specimen back to me. "I can't take this."

"Why not? You've got it."

"It's stolen."

"Now…see, that's a seriously grey area there." I pushed the specimen back to him. "Technically no, it isn't stolen. Not only was the previous owner, who, as a side note, never cared about his father's collection in the first place, was handsomely compensated by the federal government for the piece."

Pierce laughed. "What, they paid the guy a few hundred bucks?"

"Pretty much."

"Do you realize how rare this could be if it were real? According to reports from several interviews with villagers in the Likuoala swamp region, the last Mokele-mbembe supposedly died sometime in and around the 1990s."

"Yeah but it only has value to somebody who knows what it is and values it as such," I countered. His smile easily beamed from ear to ear. In all the years I'd known Pierce. I don't think I had seen him this happy before now.

Well…, unless you counted that time in Vegas on New Year's with the Sandusky triplets. Each of them were no less than five foot six with long wavy blonde locks and stacked as thick as a brick shit house.

Triple the pleasure, triple the fun.

Pierce quickly rearranged a few other antiquities on the mantelpiece and made space for the new specimen, then took a step back to admire it. He suddenly sucked in a breath and turned back to me with a snap of his fingers.

"That reminds me. I have something I've been holding onto since I last saw you. Go on ahead into the bar and tell them to pour you a drink on the house."

"That's much appreciated, Pierce. I didn't know you were so generous," I said and smiled.

"Just don't tell the general populace about it. It'll ruin my reputation as a curmudgeon." Pierce hurried up the spiral stairs I'd come down. "It's damn good to see you, Braxton. Make yourself at home. I'll return momentarily."

I turned and slowly made my way into the foyer. The deep rich wood and velvet continued throughout this part of the house. Dark polished wood furniture sat along the walls. Antiquities and late nineteenth-century photographs decorated any available spaces. It looked like something straight out of a movie set depicting a Victorian-era brothel. The room was complete with stained glass lamps, red velvet chairs, and lounging couches. A polished Mahogany bar top and intricately carved back bar complete with what looked like hand-blown mirror panels took up the back wall of the room.

No sooner had I walked in than a half dozen *gentlemen* turned to look at me. The scowls on their faces told me exactly what they thought of a dirty biker walking into their private gentleman's club.

Now, most of the gentlemen's clubs I've ever been in were nowhere near this classy. And generally my attire fit, but not with this bunch. Several of them were wearing high-dollar three-piece suits that probably cost more than a year's pay for me.

For that kinda cost, it was my understanding a patron of the establishment could get everything from cheap wine to expensive top-shelf cognac, fine cigars, and exotic mixtures for the many hookah and water pipes placed around the Lounge. You could even get exclusive extras like a private massage, bath, and laundry services, or a little personal companionship. And if the eye candy scattered around the room was any indication, it was some kinda high-dollar premium package that Pierce was offering.

I smiled and waved at the folks in the room. "How y'all doin'?" I said then sauntered my way up to the bar. "Give me a shot and a beer, preferably something dark and chewy."

Pierce had done well setting this place up for the feel of what it once was. It's like I'd taken a step back in time minus the electric lights and other modern amenities. And of course, Pierce being Pierce, the house had something to do with his collecting habit.

The house had a *history*. Rumor had it the original owner was t an occultist who dabbled in devil worship and things like demon summoning; possibly worshipping the great old ones. Pierce mentioned there were several times throughout the house's history that strange disappearances had happened. He'd rattled off the number to me at one point, but I couldn't remember. He was so excited when he signed the deal for the place.

Lucky for me, I spotted one of my favorite cigar brands sitting in the small humidor of the back bar.

"Hey, buddy, how about one of those sticks too, while you're at it?" I said, pointing at the humidor. "Bottom row second from the left."

The bartender was as stoic and statuesque as a marble carving. From his lack of response, I started to wonder if he wasn't maybe one of the antiquities that Pierce had collected for the place.

"Can I help you, sir?" The bartender asked in a proper British accent, then straightened his round Poindexter glasses and bow tie.

"Yeah, man. I said, give me a shot of whiskey and a beer, preferably something dark and chewy, plus one of those tasty smokey treats in the humidor over there."

This guy had no chances ever in a poker match. His eye roll and body language said everything I needed to know about his attitude. Tired, exasperated, and difficult.

"I am afraid I have to ask you for your proof of membership, sir."

This little shit stain was about to start getting on my nerves. "I don't need a membership. I'm friends with the owner."

The guy scoffed in that pretentious, British way. "I am sorry, sir, but everyone simply must have a membership."

Yup, and there it was. He was dancing on that nerve. "Well, I'll tell you what, buddy. You give it just a few minutes and your boss Mr. Maggart will be back down here. Trust me, you're gonna want to go ahead and pour me that drink, bud."

The doofus reached into his pocket and tapped away on his phone, content with ignoring me.

"So where the hell is Billy Joe?" I asked. "The last time I was here he was running the joint and didn't give me any trouble at all."

The little prick did his little scoff again and smiled at me with one of those knowing glares. "Unfortunately, sir, Billy Joe is no longer employed by the establishment, and has not been for quite some time."

"Well, what happened to him?" I inquired, sliding onto one of the fine leather bar stools.

"I am not honestly sure, Sir. He simply disappeared several weeks ago and has not reappeared, so we do not speak about Billy Joe."

"Was he having lady troubles?"

"Afraid I do not know, Sir. Again, we do not speak about Billy Joe any longer."

"There you are," Pierce said as he hurried into the lounge "Did Nigel have something to suit you on tap?"

I turned to him and shrugged. "I don't know. He won't pour me a drink. Says I need to show my membership credentials first."

Pierce turned back to the bartender and waved at the back bar. "He's a friend, Nigel. Pour him whatever he wants."

Nigel let out one of those disappointed British huffs. "Very well, sir," he said, then turned around to grab a bottle of Jack Daniels.

"Oh, no, no, not that one," Pierce said, waving him off. "Pour three fingers of the Rémy Martin Louis XIII Cognac for each of us, if you would please."

"Straight, no ice," I added.

"As you wish sir," Nigel said reluctantly and moved a step stool to retrieve a beautifully blown glass bottle from the top shelf. He poured three fingers worth of the dark amber liquid into glass tumblers, followed by a draft pour of a dark beer with a foamy head on it.

Pierce picked up his glass and held it up in salute. "To good health and a long life. Cheers."

I picked up my glass and clanked it against his. "Sláinte!" Tipping back the glass, I was thoroughly impressed with the flavor. Better than most bourbons or whiskeys I'd ever had.

"What did you think?"

"That is damned tasty."

Pierce chuckled into his drink. "It better be, for what I paid for that bottle."

That side comment piqued my interest. I turned to him and asked, "So how much did a bottle of this stuff run you?"

"What do you think it cost me?"

"I dunno," I said, shrugging. "Hundred bucks maybe?"

He let out a deep belly laugh and took another drink. "Nope. Not even close, my friend. Do you really want to know?"

"Hell, yeah. You got me all curious now."

"Well, the bottle cost me roughly four thousand dollars, it's a 750ml bottle which is roughly sixteen shots, and a three-finger pour is equal to two shots, so each of these glasses are worth about five hundred dollars each." He smiled and took another drink.

"I'm glad I didn't just slam it back, then," I said and took another drink myself.

I motioned again for one of the cigars, and Nigel was nice enough to oblige me by bringing me two of them. He even cut the tip and lit one for me. The second one I tucked into the breast pocket of my kutte, then puffed on the lit cigar a few times and took another sip of the rich amber liquid. Man was this ever good, but I was glad it was on the house, cause damn if it wasn't too rich for my country blood.

I noticed Pierce nervously fidgeting with his glass.

"What's up, man? You look like something's bothering you."

"I acquired a little something that I think would benefit you more than myself, especially now that I've gotten out of the hunting business."

"Okay," I said around the cigar, taking another puff. "You're just full of surprises today, ain't ya?"

He flashed a wide smile and continued. "It has quite a history, but in your line of work, it could be extremely beneficial." From his right trouser pocket, Pierce produced a silver fob watch on a chain. Beautifully intricate designs of geese and ducks decorated its highly polished surface. The blue crystal glass covering the face of the timepiece gleamed in the dim light of the lounge.

"This is *Saint Aaron's Blessed Timepiece of the Sacrament*," he said as he delicately handed it over to me. "It is said to contain the finger bone of Saint Aaron of Trakai within a vessel of holy water that was blessed by the Pope himself. It is said to protect the wearer from possession and harm from evil."

I glanced down at it and then back to Pierce. "Are you sure you wanna give me something like this? The thing looks like it's made of pure silver."

"It is," he confirmed.

"Then it's gotta be worth a small fortune in scrap value alone."

"Don't ask. You don't want to know."

I tried to hand it back to him but he immediately slid his hands into his pockets. "We saw a lot of weird stuff back in the day. In your line of work, this has a far better chance of protecting you than anything I might do with it. We have been friends for a very long time, and it might just save your ass one day. So, it's yours."

I stared at it for a long minute. The face popped open when I pressed a small button on the side of the timepiece. The gear works were exposed in the back, but in the front, through the blue crystal face, you could see something that resembled a small finger bone suspended in a liquid.

"I don't know, Pierce. This is kind of above and beyond."

"All the times you've helped me, not to mention what you just brought me. It is well worth every penny to me. Consider it a token of our friendship."

"Why is it blue? Almost looks like it's full of glass cleaner or something."

"The facing is a polished piece of sapphire."

"Bullshit. I thought sapphire was a dark blue or purple."

"It is, but it can come in many shades, including greens and reds like any beryl. It just depends on where it comes from. This particular sapphire is thought to have originated in Myanmar."

"Are you sure?" I intently stared back at him.

"Positively."

"Do you think it actually works?"

"Whether it does or not, I don't know, but it wouldn't hurt to have, just in case. Remember, I know how pivotal the right tool can be to give you an extra edge when dealing with the weird and strange."

"Well, thank you, Pierce. I appreciate it much." I tucked the watch into the fob pocket of my kutte and strung the chain over to a buttonhole.

I grabbed the tumbler and held it up for a silent toast. We clanked glasses and took another drink together.

The glassware decorating the back bar suddenly shook and clinked to a rumbling that reverberated throughout the building. I could feel the low vibrations through the soles of my boots.

I turned back to Pierce with a questioning look. "What in the hell just happened? Did we cast some kinda spell or something?"

Pierce let out a gut chuckling chortle. "No, no, nothing like that. The old boiler system down in the basement is acting up again. One of those things I've been meaning to replace but it keeps working, so I haven't."

I took a long drink from the beer, finishing it off in three big gulps. "Well, give me a few minutes and I'll go see what I can figure out on it."

"You know how to work on boilers?"

"I know enough to know how to work on a little bit of everything. Boilers ain't nothing but big water heaters. Fuel, fire, water, exhaust." I shrugged. "I mean, what's the worst that can happen? You'll still have to call someone else out?"

"This is very true," Pierce replied.

"How do I get down to the basement?"

"The stairs are at the back of the kitchen. Here," he said, standing. "Let me show you where it's at."

I followed Pierce through to the back of the house and into the kitchen where he turned a corner and opened what looked like a door to a coat closet, revealing a steep set of narrow stairs. The smell of old motor oil and French fries smacked me in the face as soon as he opened it.

Reaching the bottom, he flicked on the lights that barely did anything to drive back the darkness.

The boiler clicked as if on queue and the blower roared as it tried to ignite the main burner. It suddenly clicked off and the blower spun down. Another click, rumble, and blower running but was left with the click click click of the ignition module. The air was heavy with the stink of motor oil fries now.

"What kind of fuel is this thing running off of?" I asked as I looked over the controls and piping.

"It runs off of waste oil. So it can burn anything from used motor oil to diesel, or whatever we can get our hands on. I managed an agreement with several of the larger chain restaurants around town for their used fryer oil and several of the auto shops for the used motor oil they have to get rid of from oil changes. It's a lot cheaper than buying fuel oil and has worked like a charm for years.

I really couldn't argue with that reasoning. Anything to do with oil was expensive these days.

The unit clicked again as it attempted another ignition sequence. I could easily hear the fuel pump kick in, spraying oil into the combustion chamber. In essence, it wasn't any different than any internal combustion engine. Suck, squeeze, bang, blow. Only in this case, you added fuel and air together, skip the squeeze part, just go straight to burning, and boom, you've got heat.

I turned back to Pierce. "Got a flashlight?"

"Oh yeah. Right here," he said, grabbing one from a shelf near the stairs.

I cut off the main power and opened the control box, exposing an awful tangle of ancient wires and relays with a single fuse in the middle of the mess. Nothing looked out of place. I shook the relays to check them and nothing rattled like they'd broken, so I put it all back together, cut the power back on, and adjusted the temperature to a higher setting so it wouldn't take so long for it to kick back over.

Again, the blower started going and you could hear the fuel pump followed by the ignition sequence, and the click click click of the ignition module was unmistakable.

I peeked into the viewport on the front of the boiler and couldn't see any sort of spark even though the module was clicking. Finding a pipe wrench lying on top of the control panel, I grabbed it and tapped at the side of the control module. For a moment there was a spark and the flurry of ignition. It popped from the excess fuel sitting in the bottom of the combustion chamber.

"Come on, you hunk of shit!" I shouted and kicked the side of the boiler. The boiler roared to life like an angry beast awakened from its millennia of slumber. Flames spilled out from every seam as the casing expanded and rippled. It rumbled with a reverberation that shook the foundation of the building.

"That doesn't look good," Pierce said, backing away.

"Nope, that probably isn't good!"

Before I could back away from what looked like a critical failure, something hooked my ankle, pulling my foot out from under me. I fell backward, landing hard on the cobblestone floor of the basement.

The boiler rumbled, then shifted to the side. The manway on the front end flew open, exposing rows upon rows of razor-sharp teeth. It shifted again to the other side, jerking like it was trying to pull its feet out of thick mud. Telephone line thick tentacles wriggled free from around the concrete footings and shot out in my direction. Hot steam roiled out from what seemed like hundreds of leaks across the boiler beast's shell.

"Pierce! What the hell is that?" I shouted, backpedaling.

"Your guess is as good as mine!"

I turned to run and found that Pierce had already sprinted for the stairs. "You mean you didn't *collect* it?"

"Not this one. The boiler came with the house."

I followed him up the stairs. Droplets of what looked like condensation had started to collect along the floor joists, walls, and ceiling. We both rushed up the stairs and slammed the basement door shut behind us.

"Okay, so if you didn't collect that thing, then what the hell is it?" I asked, and that's when we both heard the screams. Some sounded like honest panic, others like horrific pain and suffering.

We rushed to the front of the house and found the suit-clad patrons, the bartender, and several of the girls gathered, struggling to open the front door. The walls and ceiling began to drip with a viscous yellow liquid. One of the older gentlemen picked up a nearby chair and threw it against the large window alongside the door. It merely bounced off the glass and landed at the man's feet.

Something plopped on the back of my arm. It burned, like battery acid or a bad chemical burn. I hurried to wipe it off on my jeans.

"Pierce," I said, shouting over the panicked complaints of the crowd. "Is it possible that a house could be a cryptid?"

"What?"

"I'm serious. Look at this," I said, motioning around the room at the dripping walls. "It burns like battery acid. What if it was more like stomach acid?"

Pierce snapped his fingers, excitement lighting up his face. "That could explain all of the past disappearances."

"How far apart were the other disappearances?"

"Roughly," he said, mumbling to himself. "About every sixty-seven years or so, give or take."

"Then yeah. I'd bet you're right. It wakes up to feed, then back to being a house again. Ever heard of anything like it before?"

"The only thing that comes to mind is a Gardinel, but I thought they were fiction."

"Apparently not. Now how do we get out of here? Do Gardinel's have any sort of weaknesses?"

"I don't know...," Pierce said, drifting off into thought.

"But, weren't there survivors?"

The grim look on his face told me all that I needed to know. He shook his head slowly and mumbled a dismayed, "No."

I pulled my phone out of my pocket and dialed Mandy, my silent partner in crime as well as the proprietor and sole owner of Karatech, a multi-disciplined business housed in what used to be an old-school Pizza Hut in an outdated shopping center. She handled the heavy research for me when I was on a job.

"Yeah, Brax. What's up? I thought you were on your way back from that gig out west?"

"I am, but I stopped to see an old friend in Memphis. Listen, I don't know how much time we've got. I need to know anything you can find out about a cryptid that is also a house."

"So, like a mimic, but house-sized?"

"You got it. And Mandy, make it quick. Pierce said it might also be called a Gardinel."

Several blood-curdling screams came from one of the upstairs rooms.

"That sounded like Emmy," Pierce said, then sprinted for the stairs.

I followed right behind him, sprinting two steps at a time. "I specifically need to know how to kill one."

"What was screaming and why do you need to know this all of a sudden?"

"Don't worry about that, just get me the info ASAP."

"Keep your pants on," she grunted. "Okay...Oh, that isn't good." She suddenly sounded concerned, which was probably for good reason. "The only thing I'm seeing is mentions in fiction, primarily by Manly Wade Wellman starting in... 1946. On a quick search, the only reference to hurting one of these things is by burning or full-on demolition."

Yeah..., that didn't bode well at all. "Thanks for all the help you give me. I appreciate you and everything you do."

"Um... Okay. Thanks, I think. Brax, what's going on?"

"Nothing you can do anything about. Oh, and Mandy..."

"Yeah."

"I never stopped loving you," I said, then hit the end call button on my phone.

We arrived at the second floor and Pierce hurried to the end of the hall. The corridor flexed and bowed like some distorted thing out of a horror flick. Pierce grabbed the doorknob, then quickly jerked his hand back and wiped it on his pants.

"What happened?"

"It burns," he said, then opened his palm to show me. Sure enough, I'd been burned enough times from pouring concrete or cleaning it with muriatic acid to know what a chemical burn looked like.

Luckily I had tucked my riding gloves in my back pocket. Quickly I slid them on, grabbed the doorknob, and twisted. I pushed, digging my feet in as best as I could on the damp hardwood. I slammed my shoulder into the door several times but it still wouldn't budge.

"Help me," I said over my shoulder to Pierce. On the count of three, we both slammed our shoulders into the door, forcing it open, but at that moment I really wished that we hadn't.

The room was a disaster. Furniture, decorations, and anything that had been in the room looked like it had been tossed into a drink tumbler and mixed thoroughly.

Including the people.

Blood-spattered bones that looked like they had been picked clean were scattered around the room. It stank like the acrid stench of stomach bile after a night of binge-drinking cheap beer and tequila shots.

"We seriously need to get out of this house," I said, then hurried back toward the stairs.

"What are we going to do?" Pierce asked, following close behind.

The guys in the suits had picked up a wooden bench from the foyer, attempting to use it as a battering ram.

"No… not my John and Thomas Seymour bench," Pierce whined.

"Who cares, it's a bench. And I don't know what we're going to do. Got any books that might have something on this thing?"

"Maybe, but it would be back in the library."

"Then let's get to it. We have zero time to waste." I shoved him ahead of me, directing him toward the library while I fished my phone out of my pocket again. I thumbed through the contact list as I walked. Finding Agent Jessie Carter's number, I hit the call button.

Me and Carter went way back. Not quite as far back as me and Mandy, but far enough. She'd been a pain in my ass for years, both in the military and afterward. Damned officers just seemed to have a knack for fucking with a good time. And I had to admit that she was a damn good agent. Probably one of the best friends I ever had, not that she would ever admit to it.

The phone rang and rang and rang. I thought it was about to go to voicemail when it clicked and an exasperated "What" came across the line.

I let out a sigh of relief. "God dammit Jessie, it's good to hear your voice."

"Hicks? Are you drunk or something?"

I barked out a laugh. "By the gods, don't I freaking wish."

"You called me Jessie. You always call me something stupid, like Daisy or Buttercup. What's wrong?" I could hear the concern underlying her bad-girl voice.

"I just wanted to let you know, that I may have given you hell all these years, but that doesn't mean I don't respect you and your skill as an agent. You're damn good at what you do. Don't let any of those corporate-type sniveling asshats tell you otherwise."

"Okay, either you're high or something really bad is going on."

"Just remember what I said and keep up the good work, Carter." I ended the call and muted her number before I continued into the library with Pierce. I grabbed him by the collar of his shirt and dragged him back into the foyer a split second after he opened the library door.

The room dripped and oozed with whatever the hell it was that had burned me earlier. The walls moved and undulated like some sort of muscle spasms.

"How about we not go in there and say we did." I slammed the door shut.

"All right," Pierce said, turning to me. "What do we do now?"

Ya know, it's at times like this that I really wish people didn't put a lot of faith in me, because I wasn't sure what the hell I was supposed to do. I'd always just kind of winged this thing as I got the gigs.

But we were all seriously fucked if I couldn't think of something really quick like. Mandy mentioned burning or demolition. So that meant that these things weren't immortal or impervious. Just seriously tough. Maybe we could start a fire and smoke our way out, but that could just as well suffocate all of us before we could escape.

I hurried back into the lounge and took a quick look around the room. Pierce had all sorts of antiques hanging on walls and sitting on shelves, but hanging over the mantle in the lounge were a pair of axes that looked like something out of a sword and sorcery flick.

"Are those real?" I asked, pointing at the axes. "Or are they just those decorative Bud-K pieces of shit you can get for cheap at the flea market?"

"Oh, they're real all right. And they're about a hundred and fifty years old at least. They were once part of the Danish guard's dress uniform for a short period before they discontinued it in favor of sabers."

"That sounds perfect to me." I reached up and wrenched both the axes off the wall. They were hefty for their size, but solid and looked like something you'd see in a fantasy movie or maybe what a Viking berserker would carry in battle.

"Let's see if we can't blow this popsicle stand," I said and hurried back to the foyer. I reared back and swung the axe in my right hand with all of my might. It struck the heavy wooden front door and dug in deep. Black ichor gushed forth when I wrenched the blade free.

The entire house shuddered and an inhuman aethereal roar echoed throughout the structure

I struck again with the left, pried it free, then again with the right. Dark purplish flesh fell away from the door frame. Ichor oozed down from the wound, pooling on the floor.

The house screamed, sounding like it was in excruciating pain. The walls flexed and undulated, knocking pictures and other decorations to the ground, and then it bucked, striking out. Tentacles emerged from the base of the grand staircase, and a toothy maw opened up where the stair steps were. Rows upon rows of jagged sharp teeth gleamed in that massive ephemeral mouth.

The door struck back before my next swing could land. Everything went suddenly dark. It felt as if I were floating, soaring through the air. Then something struck me hard from behind.

"Braxton." I heard Pierce shouting from somewhere beyond the darkness. "Braxton! Hey! Tell me, you are okay! You aren't allowed to die on me that easy." He shook me, holding me up by the shoulders.

I shifted and flexed, checking myself for any broken bones before I opened my eyes. Blotches of color floated in my vision. I shook my head to clear out the stars.

"This fucking thing is not going to beat me." I shouted, letting out a primal roar. I did not want to give up. And I would fight until my last fucking breath to get us out of the belly of this beast thing. I leapt to my feet and charged at the front door again. The blades flashed in the flickering lights and struck hard.

Screams erupted from behind me. Two of the old dudes were wrapped in the coils of thick purple tentacles. They had little chance of fighting against the Gardinel, and were quickly dragged beneath the stairwell. I hacked and chopped at the door with everything in me, blocking each strike the house took at me.

The light of day finally appeared through a small hole I had carved through the fleshy doors.

Someone shouted something from behind me, but the words didn't translate. I swung again, but the blade of the axe stuck fast into the heavy aged wood of a solid oak door. Bracing my foot against the door I yanked, splintering the aged wood. The door limply swung open on its own, revealing the world outside.

The rumble of the house ceased, replaced by an eerie silence that washed over the room. Panicked whispers and whimpers from behind me found my ears. I turned to see the patrons and employees of the Velvet Hammer, huddled in the middle of the foyer floor. The walls no longer oozed and seeped. The stairwell was once again a stairwell, not the jagged maw of a malformed beast.

I lost count of the bodies that rushed by, escaping the building as I stood there at the open door. One after another fled the scene, among panicked shouts and chaotic ramblings.

"Braxton. You did it. You got us out," Pierce shouted into my ear, shaking my shoulder once again.

I dropped the axes and stepped through the threshold of the front entrance into the dimming evening light. Just to be on the safe side, I headed down the sidewalk, getting myself as far away from the porch as possible. I didn't want to take any chances on this thing waking back up, or catching me off guard because it was playing possum. I sat on the curb and pulled the extra cigar Nigel had given me earlier from the breast pocket of my kutte, then bit off the tip.

Pierce dropped onto the sidewalk sitting next to me and slapped me on the shoulder. He was grinning ear to ear like an idiot.

"Would you have ever guessed that thing was alive?"

I looked at him like he was a crazy man, but he just continued to beam with excitement.

"You're going to keep the place, aren't you?"

He nodded with a shit-eating grin and gave me an affirmative, "Uh huh."

"How are you gonna explain the missing persons? You know I can't do anything to cover that up for you."

"I'll figure something out," Pierce said, smiling back at the house. "If all the old tales hold true, it's fed and good for another sixty-seventy years. I'll just have to make sure that things are…um…prepared for that moment."

He had that gleam in his eye like nothing was ever going to change his mind.

"People think I'm bat shit crazy most of the time, but you really take the cake, Pierce."

"Well, I know what I like." He flashed his best toothy grin before he dialed his lawyer to deal with the insurance company.

I lit the cigar and took a long slow draw, enjoying the flavor of the expensive stick, then turned back to look at the old Victorian mansion. It was beautiful architecture that was beyond reproach, but I don't know that I could ever step foot in the place ever again, especially after the day we'd just had.

My phone vibrated, and I remembered I'd muted it earlier. I pulled the phone out of my pocket and found several dozen texts from Mandy and Carter flooding my inbox. I turned the ringer back on and dialed up Carter.

"Braxton." She yelled into the phone. "What the fuck is going on? Don't you ever cut me off like that again!"

"Aww," I said in as loving a tone as I could. "Agent Carter, I didn't know you cared." She let out one of those shocked, *how dare you* gasps. Before she could get a word in, I continued.

"Daijoubu, Carter."

"What? Speak some sense, Hicks."

"It's all good, baby doll…," I continued. "We're all just golden. Life is shiny and good again, Buttercup. Suppose it's just time for the next gig, is all."

Mooneyed Mandy

By William Joseph Roberts

First published in Wyld Magick– Three Ravens Publishing, November 2025

Oh, the ideas that pop in your head when you're way out in the Alabama back woods. Granted a few of these scene locations were inspired by other places, the primary inspiration for this story and several of the characters came from the herbal and mushroom conference Meg and I attended earlier this year in the spring.

Frogs croaked out their mating tunes in time with the dancing lights of fireflies all around the small lake. A refreshing breeze blew across the water from the south, driving away the stifling heat of an Alabama summer. It seemed like ages since I'd seen so many stars in the sky. Even with the full moon hanging high overhead, I could make out most of the constellations I knew. Some would call it picturesque, but I called it perfect.

A man couldn't ask for a much better evening than this.

I finished baiting my hook and lobbed the chicken liver out into the dark water with all my might, careful not to fling the bait from the hook.

After setting the tension on the reel, I lit a cigar and fished a cold one from my pack. Leaning back against the ancient lakeside oak, I cut the flashlight, popped the top, and took a long swig.

It was easy to get wrapped up in the daily minutiae of life. Even as feral as I was allowed to be, working for the KCG, Krypto, Cults, and Gangs division of the United States Marshal's office. Granted, I wasn't stuck in a cubicle farm like most folks these days, but my work tended to get *freaky weird* quicker than a PTA soccer mom at a furry convention.

"Yup. This right here is the life."

I wiggled, getting comfortable against the tree, and relaxed, taking it all in.

How in the hell did I land this precious bit of downtime? I know, weird, isn't it?

It all started with Mandy signing up for a women's Beltane retreat and herbal conference over in the middle of nowhere, Alabama, at Camp McDowell, deep in the Bankhead National Forest. Since she'd complained so much about the cost of cabin rentals for the event, I suggested we could load up Jonie, my Harley-Davidson Road King Special, and make a weekend of it.

She was reluctant at first—since it was a women-only retreat—but after I told her I'd be spending most of my time down by the lake, out of sight when I wasn't cooking for her, she agreed.

So, we did just that. I loaded everything we'd need for the weekend: grub, fishing gear, a tent for her, a bedroll and tarp for me. It seemed like it had been forever since we'd gone camping and had some downtime to ourselves. Even though we hadn't dated since before I'd enlisted in the Air Force, we were still the best of friends. All good in my book.

Then she showed up at my place this morning with her *luggage* in tow.

I tell you what; it wasn't easy, but I managed to get all of her gear stuffed and strapped into place before we hit the road. You tell me this; how many blankets and pillows does one woman need for a weekend camping trip? Not to mention six extra outfits.

I get that she rides that fine line between girly-girl and bad ass ole' lady, but damn. I'm all for being as minimalist as possible when on the road; camping along the roadside wherever I can find a clear spot when I get too tired to ride. It's simple. I drop my bedroll, tie off the tarp to Jonie to make a quick lean-to, and I can usually have camp set up in fifteen minutes flat.

But it just is what it is. She needed to get away from her command center and her wall of monitors at Kara-Tech as much as I needed a weekend of fishing.

She was anxious before we'd even arrived, worried that she'd miss the special Beltane Fire Ceremony kicking off the weekend. So, while she got herself signed in for the retreat, I set up camp just down the road from the facility. Even in the dark, it wouldn't be hard for her to find it since she set out several of those solar sidewalk lights around our campsite.

The main thing, though, was that this weekend was a chance for both of us to get a break from the daily routine in exchange for some much-needed downtime.

Staring up at the star scape above, I took another swig and slowly puffed on my cigar. "Yup, this is damned good."

The bell at the end of my rod started to jingle, then stopped as suddenly as it had begun. I set the beer aside, placing the cap on top of the bottle to keep the bugs out, and turned on the flashlight, focusing on the fishing pole. It bounced again, barely activating the bell.

"Hell, yeah," I said under my breath as I crept forward. "I'm gonna have me some fried catfish for breakfast. Come on, you son of a bitch. Take it already."

I watched the end of the rod with bated breath. Moments passed as I crouched there, waiting to snag the rod from the stick I'd formed to make a prop. It felt like an eternity, then it hit.

The rod doubled over, and the antique Zebco reel squealed as the fish swam downstream with its prize, fighting against the drag. I snagged the rod and yanked back with all my might, setting the treble hook before reeling in the slack.

Hitting the release, I let the line freewheel for a moment as the fish ran for cover before re-engaging the drag and really setting the hook. The line went taught once again. I leaned back, fighting the fish upstream against the current, reeling in as much of the slack as I could.

The fish fought for several more moments before turning and racing upstream toward me. Reeling like a madman, I took in as much of the line as I could, then the line completely went slack.

"Goddammit, you son of a bitch! I wanted you for breakfast!" I kicked a nearby rock into the lake, and the largest channel cat I'd ever seen exploded from the water, catching me off guard.

The monster catfish gracefully pirouetted through the air in the most beautiful arching backflip I'd ever seen before disappearing into the dark depths of the lake once again. It couldn't have been less than fifty pounds and easily over three and a half feet long from the tip of the snout to the tip of its tail.

The line jerked forward, pulling me off balance. I stumbled, slipping in the thick mud at the water's edge.

"Oh, think you're going to trick me like that? I'll show you, you son of a bitch!"

I yanked back on the rod, then reeled like my life depended on it. I could already taste those fried fillets I'd have in the morning.

We went back and forth; fight, reel, fight, reel, I slowly gained ground. Never giving an inch to the beast.

This was what it was all about: a beautiful night and one hell of a fight for the record books.

After what seemed like an eternal battle of wills, I landed the most beautiful fish I'd ever seen. Its skin glistened in the moonlight as it shimmied across the muddy shore.

Wasting no time, I grabbed my scale and tape measure to record the beast. Sixty-three pounds and almost four feet long. I pulled my phone out of my pocket to snag pictures for evidence, but as soon as I turned on the screen, it beeped twice and shut down.

"Dammit!"

It would be all right, I thought to myself. I could use Mandy's phone to take pictures when she came back from the gathering, or I could charge my phone with one of the booster packs in camp and snag the pics in the morning.

See, problem-solving at its best.

Then, the flashlight suddenly flickered before going out.

"Oh, come on! Really?"

I smacked the flashlight several times. It momentarily flashed to life before going completely dead.

"Dammit to hell. Really?" I glanced around the moonlit bank. It was dark, but not so dark that I couldn't at least fumble my way back to camp.

I gathered my gear and strapped the channel cat to the back of my pack. When I turned toward where I thought the trail had been, I caught the glimmering orange flicker of firelight in the distance at the top of the gradual slope of the hillside. Every now and then, I could hear what sounded like a drumbeat or laughter, but that made pretty good sense. The fire had to be a few hundred yards away at least, and the wind was to my back.

I thought I'd heard voices when I'd made my way down the lakeside path earlier this evening. It must be where Mandy and the others were holding their fire ceremony.

"Shit," I muttered. I didn't know of any other way back to our campsite but the way I'd come. I could go off-trail and forge my own path through the underbrush, but then I'd run an even bigger risk of walking up on a copperhead or timber rattler in the dark. I'd just have to take my chances, being as quiet as possible and pray that my guardian angel hadn't taken the night off, cause there was no way I'd spot a snake along the path, let alone in the thick Alabama underbrush.

Carefully, I made my way along the moonlit walking path, being certain to poke at anything that could be a snake with the tip of my fishing rod. I figured it was better to piss it off than step on it, especially since it was a women's retreat and I wasn't supposed to be here in the first place.

Closing the distance to where I could make out movement around the fire had to have taken over half an hour. Better slow than dead, I thought. By now, I could easily make out the sound of flutes and the rhythmic beat of drums playing out an old-world folk tune of sorts. Laughter, hoots, and hollers resounded from the clearing uphill from me once the music stopped. From this distance, I could tell the fire was more than a simple campfire. Flames licked into the sky from a bonfire any backwoods tailgate party would be proud of.

"Sounds like they're having a grand ol' time," I said, swatting at something chewing at the back of my arm. There was just enough breeze down by the water to keep the skeeters at bay, but as deep as I was into the underbrush, I was an all-you-can-eat buffet to Alabama's state bird.

The fast, heavy beat of drums echoed down the hillside, followed by a warm melodic tune of flutes to what sounded like an Irish jig I'd heard played several times over the years in Irish pubs and at highland festivals.

Humming the happy tune, I continued along the path. I hadn't taken two steps before a blood-curdling scream drowned out the music and laughter of the revelers, stopping me in my tracks.

Sprinting uphill, my feet pounded the ground as I bull-rushed through the underbrush toward the bonfire. Another horrific scream resounded through the forest, followed by a hair-raising cry for help.

This is going to go over like a lead balloon with Mandy, but I couldn't just ignore someone in distress, I thought.

Double-timing it, I reached the edge of the clearing, dropped my gear, and continued across the field amid a cacophony of curses and shouts I was sure were directed toward me. Chaos and confusion ensued as the pack of nude and nearly nude women scattered in all directions, scrambling to cover themselves.

"Braxton!"

"Less beer, more working out," I gasped between panting breaths. "Think fast, be fast. Think fast, be fast."

"Braxton Eugene Hicks!"

Fuck me. I glanced in the direction of her voice and caught a glimpse of the most beautiful sight I'd ever seen in my life. Her tawny skin glowed in the bonfire's light, accentuating every toned and conditioned line of her curvaceous body. Golden amber eyes seemed to glow with an ethereal power. She looked like some sort of goddess emerging onto the mortal plane.

"I swear to God I will cut off your nuts and shove them down your throat, Braxton Hicks!"

Okay, maybe more like a demon emerging from the fiery pits of hell would be a better way to describe her. Either way, she was luscious and sexy as hell.

"Hi, Mandy! Love you!"

"You are a dead man, Hicks!"

Another cry for help drew my attention. I veered toward it, crashing into the underbrush of the hillside on the other side of the clearing.

"Maybe later!"

My legs burned from the exertion as I continued up the light slope. I slowed as grunted words and the sound of a sobbing female caught my ear.

"I'm coming!"

"Help me!"

Something thrashed like an animal in its death throes just ahead of me amid a heavy thicket of underbrush.

"I'm almost there!" Grunting barks that reminded me of a baboon from one of those National Geographic specials answered my reply.

Dumbass!

The one fucking time I left my revolver in my saddlebag *would* be when I'd have to deal with a bear or worse in the middle of the woods.

Crashing through the thicket of bramble vine and privet, I slid to a sudden stop.

I could barely make out the shape of something short and stocky dragging the flailing girl along the ground. The figure's eyes glowed an almost electric blue in the flickering light of the distant bonfire.

The figure hissed and let out a guttural squeal like a sow in heat, then chucked something in my general direction.

I dropped to the leaf-covered ground. Luckily, its aim was for shit.

The girl let out another blood-curdling scream, and the little shit sprinted uphill like some triathlon marathon runner dragging her behind it. Feeling around under the thick leaf litter, I found a stone, stood and aimed the best I could in a dim light before I hurled the improvised weapon in the thing's direction.

The rock hit home with a loud, thud like a Louisville slugger connecting with the back of someone's skull.

If I was lucky, maybe I hit it in the back of the head and not the girl.

Either way, the thing stumbled, letting out a series of guttural grunts, or… something then sprinted away into the night, leaving the scared girl behind.

She flailed and screamed, curling up into a ball.

I hurried ahead, dropping to the ground next to her.

"It's okay, I've got you. That thing is gone," I said as gently as I could, then made a hushing sound as I gently placed my hand on her arm to calm her.

She screamed at my touch, but after hearing my voice she wrapped her arms around my neck with a superhuman death grip like she was holding on for dear life.

Pulling her close, I patted her back and continued making soothing sounds like you would for a frightened kid.

"It's okay, I've got you. You're all right now."

She continued to sob as I picked her up and began carrying her downhill. I was surprised she didn't fight me, but I wasn't a three foot tall troll dragging her out into the forest either.

And man, did I stir up one hell of a shitstorm when I emerged back into the clearing carrying the girl. Dozens of women, wrapped in whatever they could grab, were huddled around the bonfire.

You'd have thought I was the worst piece of shit known to man with the comments and slurs I overheard from the gaggle of cackling hens. No, I take that back. The worst piece of shit known to womankind. I get along with most dudes, and have been told several times over the years that I've never met a stranger, but the moment I stepped foot in that clearing carrying the half-naked young woman in my arms the pack of rabid females surrounded me like jackals on a kill.

If it weren't for Mandy, they probably would have torn me limb from limb, but she rushed over to my side as she saw me and started taking control of the situation like the most protective mamma bear I'd ever seen.

She immediately directed a couple of the girls to tend to the fire and make sure it was out or burned down well enough so it didn't start forest fires and told everyone else to gather back to the main hall as a group for safety's sake.

Grabbing a thin blanket from the ground as we walked, Mandy covered the girl the best she could, tucking it around her so it wouldn't slip off. It was a slow trek in the dark along the long, winding path through the forest back to the main camp building, but everyone was safe.

It took several minutes to get the girl calmed enough that she responded to us with more than whimpering sobs. One of the other ladies brought over a cup of chamomile tea and handed it off to Mandy, who'd sat herself behind the girl and gently rubbed her back, attempting to comfort the girl.

"It's going to be alright. Can you tell me your name?" she asked, offering the girl the steaming cup of tea.

The girl stuttered out a shaky *"Gracie"*, before taking several short sips of the drink.

"You're going to be okay, Gracie," Mandy reassured. "When you're ready, tell us what happened."

Gracie nodded slowly and took another sip of the hot tea before she started to explain.

"I'd gone off into the tree line to tinkle, but before I finished I heard something rustling about in the underbrush nearby. I tried to hurry, but before I could stand, something grabbed me by the hair and yanked me back. I fought against it, swinging blindly behind me and found arms as thick as small trees, then the thing bounced me around like a rag doll. From what I could see in the darkness, its face and beard were ghostly white, and its blue eyes seemed to glow in the dark."

Most of the other women gathered around by this point as Gracie told her story. Low murmurs and whispers passed amongst the crowd.

"Aho," a raspy voice called from the back of the crowd. "Move out of my way. Let me see the girl," barked the wizened voice.

An older woman, maybe in her late sixties, cut her way through the gathered women with a cane as gnarled and twisted as her aged hands. Slightly hunched at the shoulders, she advanced swiftly toward us.

She was dressed in vibrant flowing skirts, with colorful beads adorning her hair and pieces of native jewelry hung about her neck and wrists.

"Say that again," the old lady urged, kneeling down beside Gracie. "Tell *me* what you saw, child."

Gracie repeated herself, a little calmer and more collected this time around.

The old woman pursed her lips and let out a reflective humming sound.

"Did you hear it speak?" The old woman asked.

Gracie nodded slowly, eyes wide but fearful, as if reliving that moment all over again in her head.

"It kept repeating something over and over, but I couldn't understand what it was saying."

"Can you tell me what it sounded like?"

Gracie began silently mouthing the syllables before she spoke again. "It sounded excited and slurred, almost grunting it, but was something like, funny you high."

"Hmmmm." The old crone rocked back on her heels while crouched, more limber than I would have ever expected. She closed her eyes and tilted her head back as if in contemplation.

"Have you heard of something like this before?" I asked. The old woman shushed me in that grandmotherly way. Her numerous bracelets and bangles clinked as she shooed me with a flick of her wrist, never opening her eyes.

Several decisive grunts and nods later, the old crone opened her eyes and turned to look at the girl.

Cupping Gracie's hand in hers, she massaged the back of the girl's hand with her thumbs. "All will be well in time, my child," she said, then glared up at me, extending her hand in my direction.

"You look to be a strong warrior. Be a good boy and help an old lady to her feet."

Helping her up, she gripped my hand so tight it felt as if she could crush mine with little effort, then suddenly pulled me down to whisper in my ear as soon as she was upright again.

"I am in need of your…" she stopped and stepped back, looking me over as if appraising my value. "I need a dog soldier, but you'll have to do. Come with me," she ordered, dragging me along behind her as she pushed through the crowd.

Apparently, it wasn't a request.

Mandy rose to follow us, but the old woman waved her off. "Tend to the girl and make sure she gets back to her cabin safely."

"But…," Mandy started to say before the old woman cut her off.

"Your man will return to you soon enough, little sister." She flashed a conniving grin at Mandy, then continued leading me away toward the back doors of the hall. "I promise you, he will not be too spent for any plans you might have had for tonight." The old woman coughed through a chuckle, her arm draped through the crook of mine as we walked.

We continued out the back of the hall and down the path to one of the nearby cabins. Taking a seat on the porch, she pulled out a corn-cob pipe from an apron pocket and began stuffing it from a small pouch. She puffed, lighting the pipe, and the odd smell of spiced tobacco wafted across the porch.

"Sit, boy," she demanded, pointing toward the rustic chair across from her.

"When in Rome," I muttered, shrugged, and pulled a cigar from the breast pocket of my kutte as I sat. "So you have some idea of what that was?"

"Yes," she mumbled around the pipe between her teeth and nodded, then stared off into the dark forest surrounding us for a long moment.

"And…?"

Her teeth clacked as she bit down on the pipe stem. "Patience, young one. To rush into anything is to spell your doom."

Giving her a moment to collect her thoughts, I lit my cigar, enjoying the smooth, sweet aroma as I lightly puffed it to life.

"I believe what the young lady described was one of the Moon-Eyed people. They were defeated by my ancestors and driven out of the Blue Ridge Mountains hundreds of years ago. For them to appear here is disconcerting at the least."

"Who are you exactly?" I asked, relaxing back in the seat.

The old woman glanced back at me with a look of consternation and let out a light hum. She puffed on her pipe and nodded. "That's right. You aren't part of the women's weekend, are you? Unless you're a woman in disguise."

"No, ma'am, I am not. I was only here to fish the little lake while my friend Mandy did her thing at the gathering with the rest of you ladies."

"My English name is Brenda Lechner," she said matter-of-factly. "But most within these circles," she said, motioning to the camp, "call me Grandmother Lechner."

"Pleased to meet you, Grandmother Leckner," I said, setting up in my seat to bow slightly.

Her eyebrows rose with an inquisitive glance. "And you are?" she asked around the stem of the pipe.

"Braxton Hicks, though most folks just call me Braxton or Brax."

She let out a light giggle-snort, nearly choking on the pipe smoke. She turned back to me with a wide smile after she'd stopped coughing. "In all my years of nursing, I have never met anyone named Braxton Hicks. You do realize what that name means, don't you?"

"Yes, ma'am, unfortunately, I do. But it's the name my mother gave me because she thought it would go along well with Eugene after she heard the nurses mention it in the delivery room."

"Eugene?"

"Yes, ma'am. My father's first name."

"I see." She chuckled. "Please call me Brenda. Ma'am makes me feel old, and I'm only hitting my stride at this point in life," she said, smiling widely.

"So what do we do about these creatures? You said they were called the Moon-Eyed people? Are they people or something more… magical?"

A look of understanding my meaning painted her visage before she continued. "From the stories passed down by my elders, the moon-eyed people weren't much more than savage beasts that lived in the Appalachian Mountains well before my people arrived. There are tales of old that say they enchanted young girls away from their tribes, and that they fed on those defeated in battle."

"Do the tales mention how your ancestors dealt with the moon-eyed people back then?"

She chuckled under her breath between puffs on the pipe and nodded. "The Moon-Eyed people are said to be nocturnal, only coming out at night because they are sensitive to any light. My people tracked them to their underground lairs and drove them out with fire during the day. Supposedly, none were spared."

"Well, ain't that just lovely. What are the chances we're dealing with more than a few individuals?"

She shrugged, letting out a long sigh. "I do not know. Until now, there have been no other sightings that I know of. I suppose it's possible that a few individuals escaped and have existed in seclusion over the centuries."

"If there are any nearby caves, that's most likely where we'll find them?"

Grandmother Lechner nodded. "Yes, according to the tales, but in truth, I have no honest clue. It is only ancient stories passed down from one elder to the next."

"So, run them to ground, like a fox, and we'll find where they've been hiding." I sat there, puffing my cigar for a long moment in thought, staring off into the night. If they were a feral race, then it means they're a possible threat to anyone in the area. But then, if they hadn't been seen for hundreds of years, could they be a lost race of humans or fae that have skirted the edges of modern life by hiding in the shadows of the world like Bigfoot and other cryptids across North America? By right and writ, I had all the power of the federal government backing me to remove them from the national park, but for whatever reason, that just felt wrong, like a repeat of the Trail of Tears.

I'd have to figure out what to do with them one way or the other, because they did pose a threat to the locals. But what could I do, short of busting in and double-tapping each and every one of them I found? If… and it was a big if… If I could find where they were holed up at. For all I knew, this one was by itself and maybe even the last of its kind.

I'd have to talk to the facilities manager in the morning about caverns in the and where their entrances were. But for now, it was probably time to turn in for the night. I had a feeling tomorrow was going to be busy.

I bid Grandmother Lechner a good night and headed back to our campsite.

Mandy was already back at camp by the time I returned. I'd taken care of pitching Mandy's tent as well as setting up my roadside lean-to and bedroll under Jonie, my Harley-Davidson Road King, while Mandy was off doing girl things with the rest of the women's group. It's much easier to set things up in the daylight instead of fumbling in the dark when you don't have to.

She'd set up several of her LED lanterns around the site and was pacing back and forth in front of the tent, frantically fighting with her phone as I walked up. She smacked at her arms and legs, then let out a frustrated screech and kicked at a large root by the fire pit.

"Why won't you connect?" She scratched frantically at the back of her arm and then stuck her nose into her phone again.

Mandy, being the electronics genius that she was, must have been trying to get any signal she could on her phone. I could only imagine how the lack of signal was like an alcoholic fiending for their next drink. And when her *"drug of choice"* was the World Wide Web, the lack of connection had to be excruciating for her.

The only problem was that she wasn't likely to get any signal at all. The entirety of Camp McDowell sat at the bottom of a geographical bowl where cell signals were nonexistent at best.

"That isn't going to work," I said calmly as I approached the firepit.

"Finally, you're back. So why is that, Mister Wizard?"

"Geography."

She flashed a scowl in my direction, rage burning behind her golden amber eyes. "What the hell does geography have to do with anything?"

I shrugged and started stacking the twigs and small branches I'd collected earlier in the day to start a campfire. "Geography has everything to do with the lack of signal here. Camp McDowell is geographically about a hundred feet or so lower in elevation than the surrounding ridgelines. Without a nearby tower that covers the area, we're effectively cut off from the outside world without a hardline."

"Shit…" She kicked at the root again.

"Beautiful, isn't it?"

"What?"

"The silence."

She didn't respond, but her scowl had turned into one of the sternest angry glares she'd ever given me.

I smiled wide and went back to building the fire. "Nothing but us, the wind, and the critters of the forest. Kinda nice for a change."

"Braxton!"

The growl growing in her voice was all I needed to know she was nearly at her breaking point. Mandy being totally pissed off at me for the rest of the weekend was not on the top of any list, especially with the attack that happened tonight. I sat back on my heels and turned to her. "Okay, okay. What are you trying to look up?"

She crossed her arms, and her head tilted to the side with a look I knew all too well. Yup, she was really getting pissed.

"What?"

"What the hell do you think I was trying to look up? It's not like we had anything weird happen tonight."

"Like a pack of half-naked women dancing around a bonfire wasn't weird to start with," slipped out of my mouth before I could catch myself.

Mandy roared with frustration and kicked the root again before flopping herself on the ground in front of the tent.

"How am *I* supposed to do my job, so *you* can do your job if I can't access the tools that I use? Do you not understand how frustrating this is? That girl could have been hurt or, God forbid, killed, and I'm helpless to do anything that might help stop that creature."

"What makes you think it's some kind of creature?"

Her head did that weird angry tilt to the side thing again that I hated so much.

"Braxton!"

I held my hands up defensively. "No worries. It's all good," I said before turning back to starting a fire. "I've got it all under control."

"Bullshit."

"No shit." I looked up at her and flashed her my best smiling wink.

"Dammit, Braxton," she screeched and then threw a rock in my direction that went way too high and wide to count.

"You still throw like a girl."

"And maybe if you paid more attention, you'd realize *I* was one." She pulled her knees up close, wrapped her arms around them, and tucked her head before she began to sob.

Ouch, that kinda hurt.

"Listen…"

"No, you listen, Braxton Hicks," she shouted, cutting me off. "There is something out there in the woods that has the potential to hurt innocent people, and you're treating it like a joke!" She stood up, grabbed her jacket out of the tent, and started marching away from camp.

"Mandy! Where the hell are you going?"

"To find a signal and figure out what this thing is so you can kill it!"

"Mandy, stop. Please come back."

She turned and growled, then threw another rock at me. "Why, Braxton? Why should I? You keep acting like this is nothing but a joke."

"Because I know what *they* are."

"Wait? How?"

"You know that old lady I went off with?"

"Yeah…" She thought for a moment. "Grandmother Lechner. She's a Cherokee medicine woman. What did she tell you?" The tone in her voice shifted from anger to excitement.

I stood and slowly started walking towards her. "She said what the girl described sounded similar to the Cherokee tales of the Moon-Eyed people. Her ancestors drove them out of the Appalachian Mountains hundreds of years ago."

"Wait? That name sounds familiar," she said excitedly, turning back to her phone. Several taps on the screen later, she let out another frustrated growl. "Dammit! I know I've seen mention of them before, but I can't remember what it was. I think it was something about a lost tribe of

Welshmen that even predated the Vikings and the Vinland Sagas, but I can't confirm it because my phone is useless here in podunk, nothing, Alabama!"

"Don't worry about it, then," I said with a shrug, then went back to lighting the fire.

"Don't worry about it?" Mandy laughed with that sarcastic undertone I knew so well. "And how exactly am I supposed to *not* worry about it?"

I shrugged again, and then lightly blew on the infant flame. Slowly it grew, then quickly spread through the pine straw I'd lined the small pile of twigs with. "You just don't."

"Arrr! Why are you so damned incorrigible, Braxton?"

I sat back on the ground next and continued feeding the small fire larger bits of wood as it grew.

"Awww, I love you too, Mandy." I smiled up at her. She kicked another rock in my direction.

I stayed silent and leaned over to grab my backpack from Jonie. Mandy impatiently tapped her foot while I fished out a can of scum weenies, aka Vienna sausages, and popped the top.

"What exactly do you plan to do, Mister Know-it-all?"

"I think I might go for a walk in the morning." I skewered one of the gelatin-covered meat sticks with my pocket knife and popped the scum weenie into my mouth, smiling up at her as I chewed.

For the most part, Mandy was a diehard camper. It didn't matter where we went or how bad the weather got. She was usually even good with camping on the side of the road during some of these cross-country treks we'd done over the years.

Hell, for someone who looked like a glamorous girly girl, she was about as country and tough as they came. She chalked it up to all the time she'd spent hanging out with her Vietnam-era Marine grandfather.

I chalked it up to pure stubbornness.

But for whatever reason, this Moon-Eyed thing really had her spooked. Maybe it was because after all of these years of helping me with case after case, it was her first time knee-deep in the shit, so to speak.

So, to ease her paranoia, I stayed on fire watch all night, catnapping fifteen minutes here and there by the fire.

The night passed slower than a snail in molasses, and about the only thing keeping me sane was keeping the small campfire stoked so it cast enough light around the clearing to drive back the shadows.

By the time Mandy woke, the coffee was ready and breakfast was cooking. One of those 'life is good' moments, when the smell of breakfast mingled with that early morning dew and blooming honeysuckle scents.

She surprised the hell out of me with how fast she scarfed down her breakfast. I questioned if she'd even breathed while she shoveled the bacon and eggs down her gullet, then chased it with a piping hot cup o' joe, eager to get on the move to talk with the camp director.

Now, I'm one of the first people to go on about getting your ass in gear and getting shit done. But when it comes to a morning coffee and cigar, that's something that's almost sacrilegious to rush, especially considering the beautiful setting surrounding us.

It was one thing for the universe to screw with each and every vacation I'd tried to enjoy, but a man's morning coffee was as sacred as a man's bike or Ole Lady.

You just don't fuck with it.

No sooner had I downed the last swig of coffee in my tin, she was off like a shot heading up the hill toward the camp's main hall.

Luckily, we didn't have to wait long. We caught the camp director, Doug Collins, in the main hall, just sitting down with his breakfast.

He was a nice sorta dude, even though he had that odd creeper vibe about him. I never could bring myself to trust someone who wore one of those creepy smiles that you knew hid more than they let the public see, like a televangelist or used car salesman.

But, he was nice enough to oblige us and talked while he ate.

He said he'd grown up on the property, taking over the running of the camp after his parents, the previous camp directors, had retired, passing down the responsibility to him. He estimated he'd explored at least ninety percent of the property, if not more, during his lifetime, even making maps of the area in his younger years.

He went on for a while describing the ruins of old homesteads, abandoned logging equipment, and even the remains of an old whiskey still gouged full of holes from the local sheriff's axe deep in the forest. When we brought up that we were interested in any caves in the area, he described a small holler near the northeast corner of the property where a natural spring on a hill rise fed a waterfall, forming one of the nearby streams. And behind that waterfall was the entrance to a pretty extensive cave system.

He never explored the caves, but knew of other people who had over the years, mapping the subterranean corridors leading into the underworld.

The man had barely gotten the information out of his mouth when Mandy was tugging at my arm, ready to go. We thanked him, then grabbed another cup of coffee on the way out before heading back toward camp.

Mandy hurried ahead and turned to face me, trotting backwards as I walked. I'd say she looked excited, but that would have been an understatement. She beamed with excitement.

"What's your plan, Brax? How are we going to take care of this Moon-eyed person?"

"Whoa," I said, chuckling. "Hold up, now."

Her eyes narrowed, and she pursed her lips before I had gotten the words out of my mouth.

"*We,*" I emphasized, "aren't going to take care of this Moon-eyed person. I'm going to track it down and deal with it when I find it. You, on the other hand, are going to go back to enjoying your Women's Conference. Maybe you'll make a few friends for a change instead of sitting in front of those damned computers for weeks on end."

She stopped dead in her tracks, crossed her arms, and gave me that tilted-head glare again.

"What?"

"What? What do you mean, what?"

"I mean exactly that. I'm operating on almost no information. I have no idea what this creature is capable of, and *you* have absolutely zero field experience. You're an amazing researcher, Mandy. But you don't know the first thing about tracking down a critter, let alone a possibly magical critter out here in the wild."

"But, Braxton..." she started to argue.

"But nothing." I continued on down the road towards our campsite. "You have no idea about some of the things I've dealt with. Yeah, I've told you some of the stories about these gigs, but you don't *really* know the shit that I've dealt with out there."

"Braxton *Eugene* Hicks."

Fuck me. I felt bad for future youngins *if* she ever had kids, because that was one hell of a *mom voice,* and she used my middle name.

"Nope, no way in hell you're going with me." I side-stepped her and continued toward the campsite. I'd barely taken a step past her when she *sucker-punched* me with a roundhouse kick between the shoulder blades. I stumbled forward, bracing myself on my knees, and fought to catch my breath.

"What the hell was that for?" I squeaked, gasping.

"What do you think? Did you forget that I run a martial arts studio, among other things?"

"So?"

"You know, it's really annoying when your Captain Obvious brain shows up. I can handle myself, Brax. My grandfather taught me everything he knows."

I straightened, stretching the angry muscles in my back. "What the hell are you talking about?"

"My grandfather…" She let out a frustrated growl. "The Marine Recon Vi-et-nam veteran grandfather who spent five tours in-country as a tunnel rat and more?"

"You can't just kick the shit out of a ghost or any of the other supernatural critters out there. It just doesn't work like that. Hell, you of all people should know that. You're the one who feeds me all of the info on these things."

"And right now I can't feed you anything, but if you think for one second you're going to keep me from coming along, someone will have to feed you through a straw!" She shoved her finger in my face, digging the tip of a manicured fingernail into the tip of my nose. "Do not argue with me. You almost always need backup, and right now, I'm all you've got." She turned on her heel and marched away toward camp.

Dammit to hell if that woman wasn't pigheaded stubborn. But she did have a point. Having backup for no other reason than someone who could get word back to my handlers if something went sideways would be better than nothing. The gods know how many scrapes I'd been in when I didn't know if I'd come out alive or not.

"Mandy, wait!"

She stopped in her tracks, turned on her heel again, and stomped back toward me. "I don't want to hear it, Braxton," she shouted, jabbing me in the chest with her manicured acrylic nail.

"Ouch, that freaking hurts."

"Good! It'll be even worse if you don't shut your trap and get moving. We're burning daylight, dammit."

I let out a reluctant sigh and rubbed at what I assumed was a puncture wound on my chest. Those damned nails were as sharp as a bobcat's claws.

"Fine."

"Fine, what?" she growled.

"You can come. But don't do anything stupid that'll get both of us unalived."

She let out a barking laugh. "Me? You're one to talk…"

Oh, yeah. This was already turning out to be a great idea…

Before heading out, we stopped in to visit with Grandmother Lechner, and ask her a few more questions about the Moon-Eyed people.

Legend says that they like music, and especially drumming, singing, and dancing. The Cherokee legend says, *Sometimes their drums are heard in lonely places in the mountains, but it is not safe to follow it, for they do not like to be disturbed at home.*

And of course, after several hours of trekking through the backwoods of the camp into the national park, the forest rang with birdsong in time to the beat of a distant drum.

Mandy froze at the first beat she heard and turned to me, her eyes wide with surprise.

"What the hell is that?"

I shrugged and continued walking. "Sounds like drums. Nice solid beat, too. It kind of reminds me of some of the older AC/DC tracks I listened to on the ride here."

"Didn't Grandmother say that was one of the signs of the Moon-Eyed people?"

"Yup."

"Okay, so what do we do?"

"We keep trekking"

Mandy let out a frustrated growl.

"What?" I stopped and turned to look at her. "Don't growl at me."

"Shouldn't we be reporting this to someone or recording it or something?"

I just glared at her and then continued up the trail.

"Braxton."

"Exactly who are we going to report to? We have no cell signal, remember? And why would we record anything? I can barely hear it."

"To document the encounter."

"I hate to break it to you, but so far there is no encounter. At best, we probably have a couple of hippies getting high, dancing naked around a campfire, and playing drums in the backwoods."

"But what if it isn't?"

"If it isn't, then it isn't, and maybe we get to find the Moon-Eyed people."

"But if it is, we should be documenting everything we can for posterity's sake."

I let out a frustrated breath of my own and rubbed my face. "Listen. If I stopped to document every little bang, creak, or other sort of noise, I'd never get the job done. I'd be too damn busy documenting every little thing that didn't matter, and then probably get my ass jumped and eaten alive by whatever critter was waiting on me just around the bend."

"Okay, then, Mister professional. How do you normally deal with things like this?"

"I find it and deal with it," I said, shrugging before I continued on.

"Oh my god, Braxton! What the hell? You can't just wing it. You have to have a plan, dumbass."

"Dammit, Mandy. We need to find that waterfall and see if that's where they are *before dark*, mind you, and I'm willing to bet that's where the drums will lead us. If it is just a bunch of naked hippies, we might get lucky and there will be beer and tits. Simple as that. This ain't my first rodeo, Mandy. I go with my gut, and my gut tells me to go this way. I'll deal with whatever it is when I get there. If you don't like the plan, the path back to camp is right behind you," I said, pointing back down the trail, continuing up the trail.

I knew I would pay hell later if I survived, but at this point, she was just slowing me down.

It wasn't long before I heard her growl from down the trail, so I stopped to let her catch up.

Cautiously, we continued along the trail. I wasn't too worried about one of them jumping out at us since the sun was still up, but you never know. Myth and legends are just that or complete bullshit and should be taken with a grain of salt in most cases.

The drumming continued, getting louder the farther we trekked, with the path eventually leading us to a small gorge with a waterfall running down a cliffside.

It was absolutely gorgeous, like something out of a fantasy flick. The cool mist from the waterfall drifted eerily in the air and felt amazing compared to the muggy Alabama summer heat.

The hair on the back of my neck suddenly stood on end when I realized this was the perfect place for an ambush. I half expected pixies, fairies, or something else malicious to pop out of nowhere and start harassing the shit out of me like usual.

I stopped and scanned the area, looking for any movement or sign of anything unusual. Luckily, my apprehension was nothing more than good old-fashioned paranoia, so I pressed on.

We quietly crept into the gorge, careful not to disturb any rocks that would fall into the water as we made our way towards the waterfall and the drumming.

It was rhythmic, resonating among the crumbling stone walls of the gorge and down the valley along the water's surface.

I leapt from one boulder to the next, making my way towards the wide stone ledge at the base of the waterfall.

"Braxton," Mandy shouted in a whisper. I could barely make out the sound of her voice over the roar of the falling water, but I still turned and motioned to her to be quiet, placing my index finger against my lips.

"What are we doing?"

I motioned to myself, pointing towards my eyes, then towards the waterfall. She nodded in understanding and slowly followed behind me. Taking the low route, she waded through the chilly mountain stream instead of bouncing from boulder to boulder like I had done.

Carefully, I crept up along the edge of the falls and slipped through the ice-cold sheet of water.

Sure enough, just like in any good adventure flick, there was a cavern entrance behind the falling water. The gaping maw of the opening was easily twice as tall as a man and at least forty feet wide, hidden by a stand of limestone that blocked the entrance from view.

Cold air flowing out from the opening mixed with a heavy mist was enough to drop the temperature enough that I started to involuntarily shiver.

Kneeling, I dropped my pack and rummaged through it for the pair of flashlights I'd tossed in there before leaving camp.

Mandy let out a short scream as she passed through the cold water and immediately began gasping for breath. I cupped my hand over her mouth with one hand, and the back of her head with the other.

Glaring at her was all it took, no words, nothing else. She nodded in understanding, and I handed her a flashlight, then slung the pack back over my shoulders and continued.

That's when I noticed the drumming had stopped.

Shit, I thought to myself. There went any element of surprise that we might have had.

I looked back at Mandy and let out a low growl of my own before I continued over the slick rocks into the cavern.

It quickly descended, dropping at a steep angle into the dark abyss below. The flashlights only illuminated about thirty or forty feet ahead of us.

That was the last time I bought cheap flashlights from the big-box store. Cheap Chinese crap, man.

Boulders and loose rubble littered the bottom of the cavern. Footing absolutely sucked, so I went slow, making sure I could catch Mandy if she slipped.

You could tell somebody had been through here recently just by the scuff marks on the rocks and the disturbance of sediment along the path.

A hundred yards down the slope, the path began to narrow and level out. Small rivulets of water trickled down the walls, collecting along the edges of the cavern before flowing deeper into the earth as two tiny underground streams. I panned the light upward, discovering a massive cathedral of rock formations above us. Light glistened on the damp limestone and calcite surfaces.

"That is so beautiful," Mandy mumbled, stopping beside me.

I nodded in agreement and leaned over to whisper in her ear. "You still like cave diving?"

She stepped back and nodded.

"Then we might have to come back here to explore a bit after we square away these Moon-Eyed shenanigans."

Mandy smiled up at me and leaned in for a side hug. "Deal." The sweet smell of her perfume filled my nostrils and assaulted my senses, fueling a flurry of memories that pulled me away from reality.

It had been years since we'd officially dated, and you'd think that any sign of affection would be nothing since we were still best friends, but I'll be damned if this woman didn't have some sort of demonic hold on my heart and soul. There were times I missed waking up beside her, but the scales of balance always turned things against me.

I reciprocated the lean and wrapped an arm around her, pulling her in close.

The sound of a tumbling stone echoed through the cavern, breaking the silence and ruining the moment.

Mandy froze and sucked in a short breath of surprise. Every muscle in her body seemed to tense as hard as stone.

I panned my light down the path and spotted a movement of light. Two blazing red orbs wavered about in the distance, reflecting like the eyes of a deer in the headlights and then quickly disappeared deeper into the darkness.

Mandy's breathing suddenly sounded shaky, shallow, and forced as she tried to form words. "W…w…what was that?"

She had a fair question, and I honestly wasn't sure. The fact that they reflected the light from our flashlights meant there was a good chance the thing was a living thing, but it wasn't necessarily an indicator of anything supernatural.

What that living thing was, was anyone's guess. It could have been anything from a cougar, bear, wild dog, maybe even one of the moon-eyed people or a wild forest elf, even. Been there, done that already.

The fact that it's most likely something living, means if it comes down to it, I can make it bleed and it can die.

Reaching behind my back, I drew my Smith & Wesson .357 Magnum, and continued ahead. There wasn't any way I'd have left it behind this time, knowing I was hunting something unknown.

It didn't take us long before we started seeing signs of habitation. Whoever had been living here had been here a long time and seemed to be a bit of a pack rat. Scattered bits of clothing, tools, kids' toys, ect., ranging from modern to antique, littered the space.

We continued into a large open chamber. Something skittered ahead of us on the wet stone, then let out a yelp as it sounded like someone had fallen into a pile of junk.

Before I could spot what was moving, something let out a throaty growl and then slammed into me, biting down hard on my left leg.

Off balance and struggling to stay upright, I backhanded the thing with the butt of the revolver. The blow landed, and whatever it was felt hairy and solid. Fat lotta good it did me, because *it* doubled down on its bite; throwing itself into the act like a starving dependapotamus on rib night at the Chuck and Shuck outside of Seymour Johnson Air Force Base.

Grabbing a handful of hair on the back of the thing's head, I pulled it away from my leg.

"Sorry, sweetheart, I'm not into furries," I said, then let out my own roaring growl.

Frantically, I pistol-whipped the creature over and over again on what you'd assume was the side of its head before kicking it away.

It winced, growled, then scrambled away, back into the darkness. I rapidly fired several shots in the direction I heard it run off, hoping I'd at least slow whatever it was down.

Mandy screamed, dropping to the floor. The .357 magnum slugs ricocheted several times off the walls of the chamber, sending sparks into the air before plinking into a pool of water somewhere near the back of the space.

I picked up my flashlight and turned its beam in the direction the thing had fled. There among the abandoned refuse was a small figure in ratty, filth-caked rags. It let out a growling hiss, covering its eyes with its hands when the light hit it.

"Mandy, are you okay?" I asked, keeping my attention on the grubby little cave troll.

"Do you think I'm fucking okay?"

"Are you hurt?"

"No," she excitedly replied, panting.

The individual was short, maybe four feet tall at best, and as broad across the shoulders as I was. He sported a long white beard and hair that was matted in several places, but was otherwise a wild mess. He honestly looked like the homeless, bat-shit crazy uncle of the dwarves from The Lord of the Rings.

Pasty white skin shone through where the grime had been smeared and knocked away by my blows; small red rivulets trickled down the side of the guy's face.

Apparently, I had done some damage after all.

The little man let out a keening wail, then scrambled to get behind the remains of a rotten canvas tarp that hung from the cave wall, mumbling something under his breath.

"Keep your light on him and don't take your eyes off," I said over my shoulder to Mandy as I panned the light around the chamber. The last thing I needed was to get ambushed by another one of these crusty dudes hiding in a dark corner.

Nothing else moved in the cavern; only the sound of the dwarf's whimpering and the slow trickling echo of water filled the space.

I panned the light down to check out the damage to my leg. The force of the bite still hurt, but luckily my jeans hadn't torn and there weren't any bloodstains to be found. Other than a little bit of pain, and what I expected to be one hell of a bruise in the morning, I was no worse for wear.

The dwarf repeatedly mumbled something under his breath that I couldn't make out.

Mandy sucked in a sharp breath and took a step forward. "Brax…"

I looked up and turned my flashlight back at the dwarf. It was still more or less hidden behind the tarp, so I turned the light toward Mandy and quickly scanned her for injuries.

"What's wrong? Are you hit?"

"No…," she said softly, kneeling on the damp stone floor.

"Then what is it?"

She crept closer, staying low on her knees.

"What he's saying, sounds familiar. Unalii," she said in a gentle tone, but loud enough to be heard over his mumbling.

"Unalii?" the dwarf parroted and slowly, ever so cautiously, peeked around the edge of the tarp, shielding his eyes from the light.

I moved the beam lower towards the floor so we could still see him, but hopefully he wouldn't be as blinded.

Mandy nodded and smiled at him. "Unalii." Taking off her pack, she rummaged around for a moment before producing a bright yellow banana she'd stolen from the camp chow hall for a trail snack.

"Unalii," she said again, holding the banana out to him.

Concern, fear, and indecision painted his face all at once before he stepped out from behind the tarp and forward toward Mandy.

Instinct kicked in, and I raised the revolver, aiming for center mass.

"Braxton Hicks," Mandy hissed. "Put it down. Can't you see he's just hungry and scared?"

I shifted my footing, looked down at her and then back up at the dwarf. "What was it you said to him? Unalii? What does that mean?"

She turned back and looked up at me, smiling-wide, like she'd just cracked some sort of high-level security code.

"It's Cherokee for friend." Sliding forward, she handed the dwarf the banana and then took several steps back.

He sniffed it like a hound on the trail, muttered something I couldn't even begin to comprehend and devoured the banana, peel and all.

"So you can talk to him?"

"No, not really."

"Then how did you know it was Cherokee?"

"I sorta took classes for a few years when I was running around up at Red Clay. One of the grandmothers took an interest in teaching me and helped me to learn as much as I could in the short time we had before she passed away."

"But you don't know enough to understand everything he's saying?"

Mandy let out a giggle. "Not even close. It's similar enough that I can understand, and speak some that he understands, but I think he's using an older dialect."

"Then how do we tell him to move on and leave the girls alone?"

"We need Grandmother Lechner's help. She speaks Cherokee fluently, so there's a better chance she can understand him."

"Sounds like as good a plan as any," I said, dropping my pack to the ground.

"What are you doing?"

Rummaging around in my pack, I pulled out what snacks I had with me, along with a bottle of sweet tea, and sat them out in front of the dwarf, keeping a few strips of jerky for myself before handing the grub over to him.

I held up a piece of jerky, then bit into it, motioning toward the bag I'd tossed in his direction.

Eagerly, he dug into the dried meat and indulged himself.

"Go back to camp and find Grandmother. Do whatever it takes to bring her here. I have a feeling we will never get him out of this cave to meet her, so she has to come to him."

"What are you going to do in the meantime?"

I retrieved a cigar from the breast pocket of my kutte, and struck a light. The dwarf flinched and stared at the lighter flame.

"I'm going to make a new friend."

Dance with a Daemon in the Pale Moonlight

By William Joseph Roberts

First published in It Came From the Trailer Park Volume 5– Three Ravens Publishing, October 2025

By the point I started working on this story, we'd already dove several seasons into the TV series, Supernatural. Without a doubt, the show had an influence on the way I saw how Braxton should do business, as well as story layout.

"I don't think tonight could have been more wonderful, Thomas." The young blonde stopped suddenly, glancing around the dimly lit path. The quiet of the Lullwater Conservation Garden was almost serene; an oasis of natural beauty amid the gilded opulence of Druid Hills.

"What is it, Marianna?" Thomas asked, turning to face his companion.

"I…," she began, then shyfully looked away.

Gently, he caressed her delicate cheek with the back of his index finger, then directed her gaze upward. Tears glistened in the corners of her eyes as indecision twisted her angelic face. He gazed deep into those emerald-green eyes.

"I love you, Marianna."

Her lips pursed, biting back the emotion that threatened to explode forth. Forcing a smile, she took a shuddering breath.

"I love you too, Thomas." Tears escaped, trickling down her pale cheeks in thin rivulets. "But, how could I ever leave Richard? He has given me everything I've ever wanted."

"Except love," Thomas replied. "You said it yourself, Marianna. He may provide for your every physical desire, but he's cold, disconnected, and unemotional."

"But…," she began to say, then sucked in a short breath. "What was that?"

"What was what, dear?"

"I thought I heard someone whispering from the bushes."

Thomas stood rigid, listening intently for anything above the ambient hum of the Atlanta suburb surrounding this tiny slice of paradise. "I don't hear anything, Marianna. Perhaps you heard something that carried on the wind?"

"He loves you…," caught Thomas' attention, whispered from somewhere behind him, followed by soft, childlike laughter.

"Who's there?" Marianna tucked herself close against Thomas' chest.

"Wish you knew… Wish you knew… Hehehehehe," the soft voice whispered from the shadows.

Thomas wrapped his arms protectively about her, pulling her tightly against him. "Show yourself. I have a weapon I am not afraid to use!" His voice cracked and quavered.

"Hehehehehe," came again from the dark underbrush, but from the opposite side of the walking path.

Thomas stepped between Marianna and the voice as he retrieved his phone from his trouser pocket and dialed 911. "Whoever you are, you need to leave us alone. I'm calling the police."

"911, what is the nature of your emergency?"

"Too late, too late, too late," the voice whispered, then let out a cackling screech.

"Thomas!"

"That bitch screamed at us like we'd killed her favorite hen," said the old timer. He retrieved a pouch of Ol' Red tobacco chew from the chest pocket of his overalls and stuffed a chaw into his cheek. He chewed a moment, arranging the wad before he spit a viscous stream of brown liquid on the ground between us. "Wasn't our fault *she* didn't secure the cargo," he said around the large chaw of chewing tobacco. "Old Widow Russel wouldn't even let us touch the load in the first place."

"Yeah," added the other old timer in the worn straw hat. "She was so proud and paranoid about that batch, she'd insisted on loading everything herself." He cocked his head to the side and looked at me with one of those questioning, *are you an undercover fed* sorta looks. "What'd you say your name was, boy?"

"Braxton. Braxton Hicks, sir."

He nodded, then spit off to the side. "Ain't from around here, are ya?"

"No sir, just passing through, and saw that beauty when I stopped to fill up," I said, nodding toward the classic muscle car he leaned against.

"How'd she expect you to unload it?" I asked, getting the conversation going again.

"She didn't," continued the first old timer, who adjusted his chew like a cow chewing cud. "She expected the customer to unload their own hooch."

"What she didn't count on was Sherif Willy Barnes having a full-blown trap waiting for us where Verner Mill Road crossed the Chauga River. He had two of his deputies on our ass and running us hard to box us in. Wasn't no way they'd have ever kept up with the 428 Cobra Jet under the hood in a flat-out run. Them damned Pinkos had to go and cheat to even stand a chance of catching us."

"We never did find out who tipped off Little Willy," added the old timer in the hat. "Might have had to pay a visit out to old man McElroy's pig farm if we had."

I crossed my arms and sucked in a long, contemplative breath. "So how did you get out of the trap?"

"Jumped the river." The first old timer smiled wide and chuckled. His teeth glimmered from a greasy brown coating of tobacco juice.

Stepping back, I took in the proportions of the 1969 Mustang Mach I fastback. She was more nose than body and easily front-heavy, especially with a big block V8 under the hood. "No way in hell you jumped this old girl and not crashed the shit out of her. She's too nose-heavy."

"You calling us liars, boy?" The old timer with the hat pulled back the side of his untucked shirt, revealing the wooden grip of an old revolver tucked in the side of his pants.

The first old timer placed a hand on his buddy's shoulder and laughed. "She isn't nose-heavy with the beefed-up rear suspension and two dozen cases of product tucked in the trunk and back seat. We made damn sure she was as balanced as could be."

"Ain't no way you jumped her and didn't come to a screeching halt. I'm sorry boys," I said, tossing my hands up defensively as I started to back away. "This car jumping a river is just a bit too far-fetched to me."

"Wasn't nothing like you'd see them Duke boys pull off, but we sure as shit did. Straight sailed over that little bit of river, bounced on the edge of the bank, and kept right on going once the tires really grabbed."

"Didn't even break a single leaf spring," the one with the hat said matter-of-factly. His fingers tapped at the worn wooden grip like he was itching for a fight.

"So you made your delivery?"

"Sure as shit did," the first old timer proudly stated. "We had enough of a head start on the pigs; we made it to the drop off, locked the car in the barn, and took off in the truck the widow had arranged for us to leave in. And don't forget the best part of that night," he said, tapping the other across the back.

A wide grin crossed straw hat's face as he drifted away for a moment in memory. "Oh, yeah… Hard to forget the Verner twins."

"They promised us a little *celebration* that evening after we finished our run," the first one added. "Too bad the load didn't make it after that jump." He shrugged.

"Didn't make no matter to the twins that evening." Straw hat let out a chuckle like a donkey choking on a possum.

I stepped back and took another look at the old Mustang. Not my normal cup of tea when it came to classic muscle cars since I preferred Chevys, but the lines of a Mach I fastback was a completely different beast; sleek, mean, and meant to run hard.

"You thinking awful hard about her, ain't you, son?" The first one asked. "She might not look like much, but she'll still outrun any of those foreign jobs out there on the road."

Letting out a long breath, I took another glance under the hood and checked the straightness of the body panels.

There wasn't any kind of obligation for me to pick up this ride. I just happened to stop for fuel at a backwoods gas station before I left South Carolina, and she was sitting there with a for sale sign on the windshield. These boys were first cousins to the gas station owner, who called them up as soon as they'd seen me looking her over.

But she was in damn good shape for a car her age. Minor surface rust where you'd expect it, all of the trim was there, and the interior was mostly intact. It wouldn't be anything to restore her and turn her around for a quick dime.

She wasn't anything I'd want to keep long term since she was a Ford, but she was still pretty.

"What are you wanting for her?"

"Twenty-two thousand," the first old timer said, not missing a beat, and I choked on my own breath.

"Twenty-two? You gotta be bat shit crazy to think she's worth that. Six or seven, maybe. But twenty-two?"

Straw hat stepped forward and started to slide the revolver out of his waistband. "Boy, you'd best watch your mouth in the presence of a lady."

I started to reach for my own revolver, but forced my hand to my side instead.

"Hold on, Beauford. Apparently this youngin' don't know her true value. She's an all-original parts matching muscle car, minus the suspension mods we made back in the day. Hard to find something in this good a shape with matching numbers."

"Does she run?"

"Well, no," the first old timer answered. Motor locked up nearly thirty years ago. That's why we parked her."

"So you want twenty-two K for a boat anchor that might or might not be rebuildable, and a running gear that ain't really moved in thirty years?"

"Boat anchor?" Straw hat shouted incredulously.

"Calm down, Beauford. The boy ain't from around here." The first old timer returned to me with a serious look. "You interested or not, boy? The day's a wasting and we got shit to do."

"Naw," I replied. Best to end things as gracefully as possible before hat man pulled his steel. "I think I'll pass, but I appreciate y'all coming out. Sorry to waste y'all's time."

"Didn't I tell you this was gonna be a waste of time, Donnie?" Straw hat stormed back to the ratty pickup they'd arrived in.

"Suit yourself, son. But I guarantee you won't find another vehicle like it in the tri-state area for less." The first old timer followed his friend and had barely climbed into the passenger side of the pickup before they were slinging gravel, pulling out of the parking lot.

At least the stopover wasn't going to be a total loss, I thought to myself. Those two yahoos aren't the only ones that can hook up with twins. I met a pair of drop-dead gorgeous redheads at the bar last night down the road from the Shady Oaks motel I was staying at, and had a raincheck for tonight.

The best part: they easily classified as fun size. Five foot nothing, maybe one hundred ten pounds each if they were dripping wet. Easy to toss them around for a few hours if my luck held out.

I sat down on the seat of Jonie, my Harley-Davidson Road King, and fished around in the saddlebag for a snack before I got back on the road. Supposed to be some nice scenery around here, and I wasn't meeting the twins until later this evening.

I figured I'd take a little scoot, check things out, and just relax for a little bit. I would have let them take me home with them last night, but they were both a little too far gone into their drinks for me to try to take advantage of them.

And needless to say, the motel wasn't exactly the best digs, either. It was a cheap and dry place to rest, but that was about as good as it got.

I bit down on a chunk of peppered jerky and ripped off a tolerable piece just as my phone rang. Pulling it from my pocket, I glanced down at the screen.

"Fucking Freeman."

My handler. I let out a contemplative breath. At least I wasn't already cruising some choice roads or on the water with lines in somewhere. I tapped at the button to answer the call.

"How's it hanging, G-man? You doing alright?"

"None of your business, and not too bad, Brax. What podunk town are you hiding in, and what is her name?"

The man was nothing if not all business and to the point. "What makes you think I'm hiding in a podunk town?"

"Because you hate anything to do with a respectable city, or city girls."

I had to admit, he wasn't wrong at all there. But if he was calling, it meant one thing. It wasn't a social call; he had a new gig for me.

In all the years I'd been working under Freeman for the KCG, Krypto, Cults and Gangs unit, attached to the US Marshals office, we'd never really became friends, but that was more on his end than mine. Freeman was the all work and no play type: clean cut, proper, and wound so tight no one would ever pry that corn cob out of his ass.

Hell, the man wouldn't even have a beer with me the few times we'd met up out on the road while on a case.

Now, the six-million-dollar question at the moment was, did I really want a new gig right away, or was it worth taking a few days off to toss in a line on the Saluda River? After Candy and Mandy, the twin redheads I'd met at the bar last night, invited me out to their daddy's fishing lodge for cold beer and "one hell of a good time", that was a damned hard choice.

"I don't know, Freeman. I kinda had *something* going on the next few days, if you know what I mean." I chuckled.

Freeman grunted.

"What if I told you that the investigation involves several murders in Druid Hills, and basically down the street from your friend Drew Aston's home?"

Fuck, me. I stood and mounted Jonie, getting her ready to hit the highway. I'd have to call the twins later and take a rain check on that *good time.*

"Say no more, Freeman. Text me the details, and I'll haul ass to Atlanta, but give me the quick skinny so I can start thinking on it."

"You might have a serial killer on your hands, Braxton. Neither the locals nor the feds have put two and two together, but something's not adding up. The odd part is that the few eyewitness accounts mentioned a sad clown.

Why did it have to be clowns?

"On it. Shoot me the details and I'll let you know when I have something."

When I stopped for gas, I called ahead to my buddy, Drew, who lived in Druid Hills, to see if I could crash at his place and have a base of operations. He was cool with it. Been a long while since we'd hung out and had a few beers.

Once upon a time, Drew was a programmer who'd come up with some software for the military machine and made a killing at it. Stuff like he worked on was way above my pay grade, but I couldn't knock a guy for bettering himself by his own means.

I'd gotten to know Drew through Mandy, who'd been dating him at one point, shortly after I'd gotten out of the military. It didn't take long before me and him started talking fishing, cars, craft beers, and Mandy claiming I'd stolen her boyfriend.

What did suck was that she dumped him out of spite, because we were getting along so well. Honestly, I was just trying to be sociable. Turned out I made a new friend. Wasn't the first time she'd claimed I'd never met a stranger. It was just who I was, ya know.

The number of disdainful looks and noses stuck up in the air from uppity rich bitches as I made my way into Druid Hills was almost hurtful.

Almost.

You'd think none of them had ever seen a dude on a Harley before. I'd almost guarantee there were tons of Harleys in the neighborhoods around here, but I seriously doubted they came out of the garage more than once every year or two. Status symbols and garage queens. Kinda sad if you ask me, but not everyone enjoys riding like I do.

Probably my one and only highlight of the ride into town was a group of kids on crotch rockets, all decked out in color-coded suits and helmets to match their bikes. They'd come up behind me at a red light. When I saw them, I turned and gave em a rider salute—two fingers pointed at the ground—just showing respect for being ballsy enough to ride around in city traffic. You'd have thought I told them Santa Claus was real or something. The guy in the lead of their little group rolled up next to me for a fist bump, excited beyond anything I ever expected. The whole group acted like they'd never had a guy on a Harley show them any sort of respect.

I don't care who you are or what you ride, two wheels is two wheels. They might have been a bunch of nonner rich kids for all I knew, but at the end of the day, they were riding. And when you're on two wheels, you have to ride like everyone is out to kill you, cause most of the time, they are. We're out here dodging the impatient cage drivers who are too busy playing on their cell phones to pay attention to the road or the others around them. And god forbid you inconvenience any of them, but that's a whole other rant I don't want to get into.

At least the last bit of the ride was pretty, if slow. It was one of the upper end neighborhoods around Atlanta where *the money* lived, complete with manicured lawns, electric vehicle charging stations and dog water fountains.

Not my preferred surroundings, but an interesting change none the less. Drew's place was one hell of a joint. A turn-of-the-century brick with Victorian wood trim details, five or six thousand square feet, hardwood floors throughout, an in-ground pool, and sat back on the hillside like the domineering thing it was. And as far as I knew, it was just Drew unless he'd gotten married since the last time we'd really talked, but he never mentioned it over the last few years.

I pulled up the steep driveway that led behind the house to a series of garages and a wide parking area.

Drew, smiling ear to ear, stepped through the back door as soon as I'd dropped the kickstand and shut Jonie off.

"I thought that had to be you coming down the street," he said as he approached. He shoved a hand in my direction before I could get my gloves off, but he humored me. I dropped the gloves into my helmet and dismounted, taking his hand in a firm shake.

"Good to see you, old man."

"I might be old, but that doesn't stop the fun." He barked a laugh and smiled wide, chuckling under his breath. "I'm sorry you're stuck working a case while you're here. It would be nice to catch up and play a few hands if we have time. It's been entirely too long, Braxton."

"Oh, I wholeheartedly agree. This new gig has had me busier than a one-legged man in an ass kicking contest. I thought I was going to get a few days off before the call for this case came in."

Drew let out a long sigh, shaking his head. "All work and no play doesn't do anyone any good."

"You aren't lying," I said.

"What sort of case are you working… if you can tell me anything," he said, his eyes going wide when he shifted gears. "I'm sorry. I shouldn't pry. If there is anything I can do to help, or resources I can supply, I would be more than happy to acquiesce."

I thought for a moment, but as long as I didn't give him anything the public didn't know, I'd be alright.

"You know the murders that have been happening in the area?"

Drew sucked in an anxious breath. "Yes, unfortunately, I do. I knew of several of the victims. Nothing more than a passing knowledge of each other at best, but in the end, we were still neighbors."

"Well, that's what I was called in to work. The Feds still don't have any idea of who the killer is, and considering the high-profile clients and the weird reports, they fast-tracked the case to me."

"I take it that's good?"

"Yes and no, but it won't matter if I can't track down the killer."

"Well, just know that I and my resources are at your disposal should you need them."

"I appreciate that, Drew. Just letting me crash here while I'm on the case is plenty enough. I can chip in on room and board, too. Don't think I'm trying to freeload. The Feds give me a decent stipend, so I'm not staying in lice-infested motels."

"Nonsense. The way I see it, you're doing this community a public service, and I'm happy to pitch in however I can."

"That's appreciated, Drew."

"Don't mention it. You thirsty? I stopped by a local microbrewery and picked up a little of everything they had that was *dark and chewy*." He let out a laugh, more than pleased with himself.

"That sounds absolutely wonderful."

The unmistakably distorted baseline and power chords of Type-O Negative echoed along the street, followed by the sound of a very powerful engine racing up Drew's steep driveway.

"Oh, Morgana is home." Drew turned and again smiled wide, almost giddy.

"Morgana?"

"Yes, Morgana. My roommate and personal assistant."

That's when the shag wagon of death barreled around the corner of the house toward the garage like it was making an appearance in a Marilyn Manson music video. The Cadillac hearse slid to a stop just feet from slamming into me, Jonie, and Drew. Drew never so much as flinched.

Even though she was one hell of a land barge, someone had done the hearse up right. She had to be a 1959 or 1960, since she looked similar to Ecto-1 from the Ghostbusters. Her lines were clean and solid for a vehicle of that age. The roof had been chopped, and the suspension lowered, giving it an angry and aggressive stance. It was painted a solid, vivid black, including the massive grill and bumper without an ounce of chrome to be seen, and heavily tinted windows.

She was one sexy beast.

What I assumed was a General Motors big block roared once more, then came to a growling halt before the driver's door smoothly popped open and one drop-dead gorgeous hippie goth chick stepped out. She wore a lacy black long-sleeve shoulder jacket over a flowing tie-dyed patch skirt that accented her thin curves.

She'd rounded out the hippie goth chick look with a head of short and unkempt hair, dyed raven black over silver, and several piercings in her ears, eyebrows, nose, and lips. Multiple necklaces, bangles, and bracelets clinked when she shifted to close the heavy Cadillac door, then suddenly stopped and looked from me to Jonie, admiring the Harley's sleek blacked-out lines. A very small smile crossed her face before she turned back to me.

"Nice bike. Newer Milwaukee 8? 114 cubic inches?"

"Thanks, and yes, but I upgraded her to a 131 stage four with Cat and baffle delete. She growls when needed, but purrs above a hundred and twenty miles an hour. Her name is Jonie."

Morgana sucked in a long, sensual breath at that and let out an approving hum.

"That's a nice dead sled you've got yourself. 1959 or 60?"

Morgana's eyes lit up, and she smiled wide at my question.

"59," she replied, almost purring in a sultry tone. "I fully rebuilt her from the frame up and upgraded the powerplant with a General Motors 500 cubic inch big block from a 1976 Cadillac Eldorado."

She closed the driver's door and gently caressed the body lines, leaning her hip against the side of the car.

"I call her Ophelia." She pushed herself up and sat on the fender, letting her feet dangle over the side, then flashed me one of those interested but not interested shy smiles.

"Morgana, this is Braxton. Braxton, Morgana," Drew said, breaking into the conversation. "Braxton will be staying with us for several days while he investigates his latest assignment."

That brought out one hell of a smile and a look of excitement.

"Oh, really? What sort of investigation? Would it have something to do with the Druid Hills Butcher?"

"That depends," I said, tucking my thumbs into my pockets. "Will I need to slap cuffs on you after my investigation?"

"No," she said coyly. She glanced away, blushing. "But I wouldn't complain if you did *before* the investigation." Her shy demeanor quickly shifted when she glanced back at me. Her smile widened, revealing a set of sharp, vampire-style fangs, and she suddenly looked like a predator about to pounce on its prey when she slid from the Cadillac and took a slow step in my direction. Her split tongue licked across each of her pointed fangs.

"What do you two think about take out for dinner?" Drew asked, interrupting our exchange.

"Works for me," I replied.

Morgana stopped, lost in thought for a moment. "I don't know, Drew. I could really go for nice, fat sausage right now." She flashed a wry smile in my direction over her shoulder before she continued into the house.

"Ooo, that does sound good," Drew added, motioning me into the house. "I know this little Ukrainian place down around Five Points that delivers with the most amazing sausage plate, and their pierogies are absolutely to die for."

"Yeah… Sounds good, Drew." Poor dude might have been a genius, but he had to be one of the densest people I knew.

Ya know, considering I was starting to feel like I might need an adult, staying here might not have been the best of ideas in hindsight. But then again, it was a big house. This was going to be an interesting stay.

Between the innuendo and Morgana spending most of dinner playing footsie with my neither regions, that had to be the most uncomfortable meal I have ever had, by a long shot. Normally, I'd have been returning every bit of it tit for tat, but it was Drew's house, and Drew's *assistant*. I wasn't about to assume they had a completely professional relationship and potentially screw up a great friendship.

Could be she was just the cock teasing type and more interested in having a little fun teasing me than actually *having a little fun*, so as soon as I'd finished my dinner, I excused myself quickly to start digging through the information Freeman had forwarded to me.

There had been seven murders in the past three weeks. Two of them were somewhat witnessed by locals walking along the street near the park, and one who spotted a clown in the neighborhood. Not the fluffy, happy, bright-colored type either, but one described as an opera-style sad clown from the turn of the century with the ruffled collar and little tiny hat.

There was nothing in the area that Mandy could find that was out of the ordinary. No strange deaths or violent murders, ruling out an angry or vengeful spirit.

This whole case could just be a John Wayne Gacy wannabe instead of something supernatural, for all we knew. The other disconcerting part of this case was that the victims all seemed completely random. Other than they were residents of Druid Hills, the victims had no other connection between them that I could find whatsoever.

They worked at different businesses, were from different social statuses; some living well beyond their means, others living the high life because they could, but nothing connected them.

The next best thing I could do was to put boots on the ground. Get out to the park, do a little inspecting myself, and see if anything showed up. Worst case, I could speak with the victims' families and the witnesses who were willing to talk.

So, I pocketed everything I thought I needed and headed toward the park. The entrance was only three houses down from Drew's place, a hop, skip, and a jump away, which really didn't make me feel good.

Before I left, I warned Drew and Morgana to stay inside and not come out after dark, since that's when all the murders had happened up to this point.

Besides making sure I had my trusty Smith and Wesson revolver on me, I packed several knives, a little bit of holy water in a cross embossed flask passed on to me by my great grandfather before he passed, salt, a small stainless crucifix that doubled as a punching dagger, and an EMF receiver into my pockets from the hidden compartments in the bottom of my saddle bags. Nothing really crazy, but maybe just enough to get me out of a jam if something *were* to happen.

The park was actually quite nice and relaxing to be hiding in the middle of suburbia. It had been meticulously manicured, seasonal flowers planted along the paths to accentuate the natural foliage, and the grounds were beautifully kept.

The only real disturbance that stood out from this little slice of paradise was the sounds of civilization beyond the wooded park.

Probably the most disconcerting thing to me was the sound of electric vehicles driving by on the surrounding streets. That weird electric hum just didn't sit well with me.

There's something just totally wrong about an electric vehicle, and don't get me started about the electric motorcycles. They are blasphemous on so many levels.

The other surprising thing that I found about the park was a lack of evidence.

No police tape, no flags, nothing.

It was as if the seven murders in the last three weeks hadn't even occurred. I guessed the groundskeepers were under strict orders to restore the park back to its original pristine condition as quickly as possible.

Couldn't bother disturbing the locals, now could we?

Luckily, the EMF meter did pick up some residual energy in each of the areas, with the highest concentration being right across from Drew's house, and that really didn't leave me with the warm and fuzzies. So I set off down the street about a block and a half away to the first victim's house.

Where I come from, every house in this neighborhood would have been considered a mansion. Not many people lived in places this big unless they were some stupid rich doctor or lawyer. Most folks I knew in northwest Georgia grew up in little thousand-square-foot mobile homes, not something that was well over six times that size. Luckily, the house I grew up in was a little bit larger. It was an old manor house built back in the late 1800s on the backside of Chickamauga. Yeah, it was run down in spots, needed a little work here and there, but mama did as good as she could, raising us two boys all on her own since my father had booked it out of dodge pretty quickly.

The big upside was that it had been paid off nearly a century ago, built by my great-great-great-grandfather way back when, and passed down in the family since. At some point in the future, me or my brother would inherit it, but since returning from military service, I picked up my own little trailer for cheap that mom let me set up on the back of the property.

It might not be much, but it was mine, and it kept me from living under Mama's roof. No rules, no bitching at me. I was free to do whatever I wanted, when I wanted, how I wanted.

And even better, I didn't have to worry about paying rent. I managed to trade an old GM square body I had parked in the back for the tiny 1960s-era trailer. Hell, Drew's kitchen alone was the size of some people's houses, including my trailer, and that kind of space difference can be almost mind-boggling when you aren't used to it.

The first victim's house was right on par with all the others in the neighborhood; a massive brick building, with decorative carved wood accents, like something you'd see in a movie.

I made my way up to the front door, gave a knock, rang the doorbell, and waited.

And waited.

Knocked again…waited a little longer, but nothing.

I knew there were people home because I could hear them moving around inside, and I could see a few of them through the side windows of the door.

The next three homes were the same result. I knew people were home, but no one was answering the door. After visiting the last victim's home, I was really starting to get frustrated. It wasn't like I was some sort of door-to-door salesman; I was trying to do my job here, people.

That's when I noticed the camera. It was one of those tiny doorbell deals that you could watch from any device. I was sure the other houses had something similar, and to be honest, it didn't surprise me.

I really couldn't blame them, either. I'm sure most of these folks had worked hard to get where they were, and a little paranoia kept them from losing everything they had. So, I quietly moved on to visit the first witness's house, going back up the street, four doors past Drew's house.

At this point, I wasn't expecting much. Again, I knocked and rang the doorbell. To my surprise, I heard someone from inside yell, "Coming!".

The female voice shouted again.

"I'll be there in a moment."

Cautious not to scare whoever was coming to the door, I took an extra step or two back, just to give them a little extra room. A few moments later, I could hear rattling and clanking as several latches were undone before the door slowly cracked open, and a small pair of blue eyes stared up at me from inside.

"Hello, is your mommy or daddy at home?"

Her pigtails swayed as her little cherub face nodded. She couldn't have been more than seven or eight at the most.

"Could you go get one of them for me, please?"

A quick smile crossed her face, then she nodded again and closed the door, latches and locks securing behind her before I heard the distinctive sound of small feet tramping away deeper into the house.

Again, I patiently waited, taking in the manicured lawn and flower beds. A few minutes later, latches and locks clattered, and the door opened once again. This time, it was a young woman standing behind the pig-tailed girl, maybe in her late 20s, a petite little blonde, cute if a little on the skinny side.

"See, I told you, mommy. There was a biker at the door."

"Howdy," I said.

A look of concerned bewilderment crossed the mother's face, and she started to stammer. "Can I help you?" She gently pushed the little girl back behind her, looking like she was about to slam the door in my face.

"Yes, ma'am, I hope so. I'm investigating the…" I looked down at the little girl and then back up at the mother. "The incidents in the park across the street."

She started to slowly nod her head in understanding with a concerned smile. "Sure you are."

She started to back away and close the door. I held my hands out defensively.

"I'm going to reach for my badge. It's just inside my pocket here," I said, pointing. I slowly reached into the inside pocket of my cut, pulled out my badge wallet, and flipped it open to show her my ID and my badge.

"The locals and the feds aren't having any luck figuring this case out, so they called me in to take a look at it."

"KCG," she read, squinting. "What does that stand for?"

"Krypto, Cults, and Gangs, ma'am. I'm a specialist that gets called in on the tough or weird cases."

"All right, Mister…" She leaned in and looked at my badge a little closer, then let out a giggle. "Braxton Hicks?"

"Yes, unfortunately, that's what my mother named me."

"All right, Mister Hicks, how can I help you?" She flipped her hair back, trying to hide a smile and not fighting back a laugh.

I cleared my throat and got back on track. "According to the police report, you witnessed something in connection with the case?"

"Yes." She turned and crouched down to talk with the little girl. "Aubrey, can you go inside and finish your coloring? I'll be there in a minute."

"But Mommy," the girl whined. "I wanted to talk to the big bad biker."

"Aubrey, now."

"Aww." The little girl huffed, crossing her arms, pigtails swinging as she stomped away. The young woman stepped out onto the porch and pulled the door closed behind her. She wrapped her arms about herself, rubbing the back of them as if trying to calm herself.

"Earlier this week, we were sitting on the porch, enjoying the evening, watching the fireflies, when someone dressed as a clown stepped out of the bushes from the park onto the road before they skipped away, heading that way," she said, pointing down the street towards Drew's house.

That made me feel even less good about this whole situation. I had to figure out what this was, and fast, if for no other reason than to protect the little one that's living right across from this thing.

"Did you see anything else?" She shook her head, eyes darting back and forth in thought.

"No, it was a clown dressed in all white, like a big baggy jumpsuit with a lacy, fluffy collar and a tiny bowler hat. Nothing like a circus clown. More like an old opera clown."

"Other than that…Did you see where it might have went?"

"No." She shook her head again. "It just skipped away down the street, happy as could be, whistling a little tune behind it." Her eyes suddenly brightened. "I recognized the tune, but I just can't place it. It's one of those that they used in old cartoons." She hummed several bars of the tune.

"The Camptown Ladies," I answered, recognizing the tune immediately from Blazing Saddles.

"Thank you, ma'am. I appreciate your time. You and the little one have a good evening and stay safe."

"What do you suppose is going on? Is there a serial killer running loose like they are saying?"

"I don't know yet, ma'am. All I know for sure is no one's been able to figure it out. But that's why they call me." I started to back away and stopped. "And ma'am, just to be on the safe side, you and your family stay inside in the evenings. Nothing seems to happen during the day, only after dark."

She nodded and went back inside.

Since she pointed right where she saw the thing come through the woods, I made my way down the street and found a small game trail. The EMF was going off, but nothing major. It could just be background noise from a buried power line or a transmitter of some sort in the area. Still, it sure as shit wouldn't hurt to take a look.

I checked the time and looked up at the sky. It was going to be dark soon. Maybe I'd get lucky and catch this thing in the act. So I pushed my way through the brush and down the game trail.

The thick foliage from the edge cleared up pretty quickly, turning to basic scrub and weeds that grow well in the dim light beneath the canopy.

Stepping into this place was almost like being transported to another world. One minute, you're in suburbia, next you're in the backwoods. The hike along the trail was an easy hoof, mostly level and little in the way of briar or bramble vines.

It didn't take long before the small game trail opened up to the paved walking path of the park. Streetlights had already started coming on. Their Victorian lantern look left a little bit to be desired, considering the circumstances. It left me feeling like I was walking in some London park expecting Jack the Ripper to jump out of the shadows at any moment.

Still nothing substantial on the EMF, just a low-grade background hum. I still couldn't discount it, but I couldn't trust it either. Hell, you never know. Somebody might have a satellite dish wired up the wrong way and pointing in this direction, causing it. I'd seen weirder shit over the years, so who knows.

I continued south until I came upon a set of benches facing a small statue in a small flower garden off to the side. I decided to sit a spell to see what I might could see.

It didn't take long before the hair on the back of my neck stood up. I could hear the muffled sound of a child's giggle from down the path, but it had an ethereal tone to it.

The EMF in my pocket started buzzing.

"Well, all right then. At least I know I'm not dealing with a serial killer, or at least not one from this life," I mumbled to myself. Retrieving the EMF, I glanced at it and turned it off before tucking it back into my pocket. Only a three or four on the scale, but that means it's probably getting closer at least.

Casually, I retrieved the flask of holy water from another inside pocket of my kutte, and unscrewed the top, getting ready for whatever might come.

"You're next, you're next, you're next," the childlike voice whispered, seeming to move around, circling me. Eerie giggling from the underbrush caused me to flinch and turn, looking behind myself.

"Whatever you are, I don't want any trouble," I said out loud. "I just want to figure out why you're here."

"You're mine now," the voice whispered, sounding like it was standing right next to me.

I swung with the hand holding the flask, dousing the area next to me in holy water. My forearm started to burn. I looked down at the protection sigil tattooed on my left forearm, and it was beginning to glow a deep, dark electric blue. Tendrils of pain crept out from the sigil, causing my entire arm to ache and throb.

Quickly, I pocketed the flask and drew my revolver. Dumping the hollow points from the drum, I dropped in a speed loader of .38 special birdshot rounds packed with rock salt and slammed the drum in place.

"Come out, come out wherever you are."

"You're next, you're next, you're next," it repeated, the sound of its voice bouncing all over the place, closer, farther, closer, farther. The thing was toying with me like it was trying to get me to run or scream.

"Show yourself, if you've got the balls. I'm here for the long haul, buddy."

A branch snapped overhead and fell. I dove to the side, the large branch from a pine tree narrowly missing me. Hurrying to my feet, I quickly scanned my surroundings, looking for any sign of the thing.

"Your mind, your mind, your mind," echoed along the pathway.

The statue began to tremble slowly, then more violently, its mounts shaking free from the base.

Backing up several steps, I suddenly bumped into something soft but solid. I turned, regretting that I ever took on this case.

"Fucking clowns…"

Just like the woman had said, there stood the clown in all white, sad face makeup and a tiny bowler hat topping its head.

Not taking the time to aim, I fired before it could say another thing, and it vanished in a puff of misty smoke.

"Freeze! Atlanta PD," someone shouted from behind me. I started to turn but froze and slowly put my hands in the air.

This is turning out to be a great little adventure, isn't it?

At least three individuals tackled me to the ground, forcing my hands behind my back and my face into the pebblestone walkway.

It took several hours stuck in a hole before I was able to convince the local PD that I was actually an undercover federal agent investigating the killings and that they needed to call my handler, Ronald Freeman.

They'd never heard of the KCG, because honestly, most people aren't supposed to know. It's undercover for a reason. After contacting the Federal Marshal's office, they finally confirmed what I was telling them, and in minutes, Freeman was blowing up their phone lines.

He convinced them to release me, return all my gear, undamaged, and to ignore any other calls about me wandering the area.

They really got their panties in a wad when the head cheese of the Atlanta office showed up to rattle their cages about obstructing a federal investigation. Apparently, Freeman pulled out all the stops.

Needless to say, the rest of my evening was quite the adventure, and so late that by the time I was able to call a cab, it was already after midnight, and I was starving. So I had the cabbie drop me at the nearest bar that served grub this late, nearest to Drew's place.

While I waited on my order, I gave Mandy a call.

"Braxton! What the hell do you want? It's one in the morning."

"Had a little problem."

"You, nooo, never. What problem could you ever have?"

"I just got out of jail."

"Really? They might have been better off keeping you in there."

Considering my line of work, I really couldn't argue with her on that point. I did tend to get into some shit from time to time, but that was beside the fact that I had a job to do.

"Can this not wait till morning?"

"It probably could, but I'm wide the fuck awake waiting on my dinner, and something's just bugging me about this case."

"Okay, so what is it?"

I proceeded to fill her in on the night's events, from wandering the neighborhood to meeting the local spook in question, and of course, Atlanta PD's finest.

"Okay, so it's some kind of haunting. What about it, Brax?"

"I couldn't find any cases of serial killers in that area, especially with this kind of MO, ever."

"So what could it be?"

The waitress placed a decent looking cheeseburger, fries, and another beer in front of me and smiled. I mouthed thank you before returning to the conversation.

"Beats me, Mandy."

"You know how this works, Brax. There's a hundred different things that could cause a wandering spirit like this. Something that was disturbed, something got moved, remains spilled, or any other number of possibilities. Just get some sleep and call me in the morning, Braxton."

"Are you sure you're not up for this tonight?"

"Yes, Brax. I'm sure. I want to sleep. I've been up late the last three nights trying to get this other server update done, and I'm not getting anywhere fast because their software sucks, their hardware sucks, and their VPN access sucks. So, needless to say, it's been one problem after another. You adding to that problem count does not help my attitude or my blood pressure any. So, if you would *please*, finish your meal, go to bed, and call me tomorrow."

"All right, Mandy, all right. I'll call you later."

The next morning was a little rough. I didn't roll in till well after last call, and couldn't get to sleep to save my life. I grabbed a cigar from my kutte and stumbled my way to the kitchen. Luckily, there was already coffee brewed. I poured myself a cup of coffee and wandered into the living room looking for Drew and Morgana. The warm glow of a massive salt water fish tank spilled into the kitchen, giving the doorway a feel like some sort of side quest waited just on the other side. Several colorful fish and sea horses floated about aimlessly on the weak current of the filter.

When I turned the corner into the large open living room, the protection sigil on the inside of my forearm immediately began to burn. I quickly scanned the room and there on the shelf just above the mantel sat a small porcelain head clown doll, that looked exactly like the creature I'd seen the night before, staring down at me from its perch. That painted face just as creepy as the real thing.

I froze and stood there for several moments, staring at it in disbelief. I honestly expected the clown to jump from the shelf and take off running.

"What in the ever-loving hell," I mumbled to myself. "Fuck me. Sidequest acquired, I guess." I sipped at my coffee and stepped closer to examine the doll. It sat atop an aged wooden box bound with iron and an antique padlock like you'd use a skeleton key on. Several other odds and ends sat on top of the box, surrounding the clown doll.

Then I heard Drew's voice and laughter coming from the doors leading from the living room to the pool. I hurried through the beautiful French doors to find Drew and Morgana stretched out on pool lounges, sipping mimosas and chattering.

"Ahhh. The prodigal son is awake. Good morning, Braxton."

"Morning, Drew. Morning, Morgana," I replied, hurried. "What can you tell me about that small clown figure in the living room?"

Drew looked absolutely perplexed for a moment, then a look of pure excitement washed over him.

"Oh, that. I found that in the attic a few weeks ago. We were cleaning out the nooks and crannies so to speak, and found several things from the previous owners tucked away in the back of the attic."

I wiped a hand over my face, pretty sure I'd found the source of the murders. "Do tell... How many owners has this house had?"

"Oh, four or five, I believe. It sat empty for the longest time because people said it was haunted after the death of a young woman and her daughter, who were the first owners of the home."

"When did that happen?"

"Round about 1918 or so, if I'm remembering correctly."

"Anything suspicious about the deaths?"

"Not that I know of," Drew answered. Morgana at this point had turned in her seat toward me. A look of interested curiosity painted her face as she sipped at her mimosa.

"No idea other than there were people living here, people died, the house was empty, then it sold, and it sold again, and a few more times before I came along and lucked into this place at a very, very reasonable price. I even paid cash for it," he said excitedly.

"I'm sure you did, Drew. What condition was the clown in when you found it?"

"Oh, it was locked away in that box it's sitting on. It took me a little while, but I managed to hammer the lock loose and take the chains off of it. Then lo and behold, inside was that little clown doll with some other doodads and things I'd put on top of it just because it looked pretty cool and vintage. It makes for a wonderful discussion piece when we have people over."

"Right…," I said, letting out an exasperated sigh. "Thank you, Drew. You have been more than helpful."

"Would you like to come sit with us for a bit? We were just discussing the current political landscape."

"No, not right now. I might have a lead on the case and need to make a phone call."

"Really?" Drew turned and stood up from his seat. Morgana leaned in closer, paying attention to my every word at this point

"Is it some sicko perv or pranksters turned rogue," Morgana asked.

"No, unfortunately not. That would be too easy to fix. I hate to chat and run, but I've got to make that phone call for some more information before the day gets away from me. I'll catch you two later."

"Let us know what you find out?" Drew's look of excitement about the case almost made me feel sad for him, but I could count dozens of folks who'd rather have his life than their own day to day struggle.

I already knew it was going to have to be something with that doll. It was too coincidental. He'd opened the box several weeks ago, which just happened to be when the killings started, and it looked exactly like the thing I saw last night. It had to be the answer.

Whatever it was that was attached to that fucking doll, Drew had unknowingly let it loose when he opened that box. I turned and hurried back into the living room, getting a closer look at the box and clown without touching a damn thing.

Sigils that reminded me of Voodoo markings I'd seen in New Orleans were branded into the wood of the box. Wrought Iron banding and latches this thing was made of looked a lot like the older ward boxes my buddy Caleb had stashed in the necropolis on his property. I've taken several things to him over the years for safe keeping because they were too dangerous to let the government get their hands on.

Pulling my phone from my pocket, I hurried out to Joanie, sat on the seat, lit up my cigar, and dialed Mandy back.

My coffee had gotten lukewarm by this point, but I didn't care. I still needed the caffeine to keep the evil headaches away.

The phone clicked as she picked up and answered.

"Good morning, my beautiful morning dove."

"Dammit, Brax, it's still early."

"Yeah, but I've got a lead."

Mandy's research turned up some interesting details once I relayed what Drew had told me.

The house was originally owned by Joshua Roberts, a wealthy businessman who had built the house for his wife Candice back in 1910. Their oldest daughter, Guinevere, died at the age of seven during the Spanish flu epidemic in the winter of 1919.

Distraught, the mother had become a recluse according to family journals found online and became obsessed with everything dealing with death and illness. It was amazing what historical societies will tuck away and put on display for everyone to see, but seeing as the family line had all but died out, there wasn't anyone left to complain.

The records showed that the mother had committed suicide by hanging herself in the attic in the spring of 1922, after her husband was found brutally murdered. The newspaper of the time reported he'd been stabbed over three dozen times and left floating in the pool the month prior.

Most of the dirt Mandy was able to dig up pointed at Candice as the primary suspect in the murder of her husband, but her confession that it was the devil earned her ridicule and a fall from social grace.

Their surviving daughter, Elizabeth, who had been six at the time of the suicide was found cowering in her closet. Elizabeth became a ward of the state, passed from one home to another for the mentally ill. Leaving the estate empty for over a decade until Elizabeth came of age, and was put into the care of a distant aunt who took charge of the estate and property.

She had apparently recovered enough from the incident to live a somewhat normal life, eventually settling down in the home to raise a family of her own, but died by suicide in 1946. The last living member of that family, Elizabeth's only child, Emmeline Higdon, currently resided nearby at Twilight Acres, a retirement and hospice community.

"Were there any other incidents over the years?" I asked.

"Um… Huh. Well that's interesting."

"What?"

"It looks like the family might have gotten a bad rap for being a family of black widows," Mandy said, surprised. "The men in their family kept dying, it seems like. Shot, stabbed, hung, accidental fall down the stairs, but nothing was ever found to be conclusive of who had done it, their alibis were solid and the women were found to be innocent time and time again."

"Okay, and you said the surviving granddaughter was in an old folks home?"

"Yeah, I'll send you the address."

"What are the odds that she's actually of sound mind?" I asked, not expecting much out of the woman, but any lead was better than none.

"No idea, but it sure doesn't hurt to take a ride over."

"No, it doesn't."

The ride over to Twilight Acres was actually enjoyable. Very little traffic and the traffic lights seemed to be on my side for a change. It didn't take long before I rolled into the parking lot of one upscale complex. Private golf course, tennis courts, pool and sauna, the facilities were a bit on the higher end compared to some of the rat holes I'd been to when visiting older family members over the years.

When I asked to see Mrs. Higdon, the nurses lit up with excitement and were more than happy to show me to her apartment. Apparently the widow Higdon hadn't had any visitors in years other than the other residents of the facility, which didn't surprise me. She'd become reclusive herself, rarely leaving her apartment, and her paranoia was exacerbated by that fact. From what Mandy was able to dig up, Mrs Higdon had no other surviving relatives. It didn't even seem to matter that I wasn't a relative to the nurses. They were hoping that she'd come out of her shell just a bit because I was there.

Probably the worst part in my opinion was that she never had any children of her own, so her estate would land in the lap of some distant relative that never knew she existed or the state would take every penny they could get hold of.

Kinda sad really, to wither away alone.

The head nurse led me to Mrs. Higdon's room, where she was sitting by the large bay window, sipping tea and enjoying the humming birds flitting about the feeders hung outside her window.

"Mrs. Higdon," the nurse said softly with a light knock to the open door. "Mrs. Higdon, you have a visitor."

"Oh, really?" She turned, placing her cup gently on the delicate saucer. "Come in, come in." She started to stand and the nurse rushed over to her side.

"Mrs. Higdon, be careful. We don't need you falling again."

"No," she grumped. "Don't bother yourself, dearie. I am more than capable of standing on my own."

The nurse flashed me a look of annoyed humor. "I know you can Mrs. Higdon, but I'd rather be safe than sorry, ma'am, but there's no need to trouble yourself. This nice young man wanted to speak with you for a moment."

"Oh, wonderful. I'd be happy to. Please, sit. Would you like a cup of tea?"

"I'd love a cup, ma'am," I answered, pulling out the other chair from the small cafe table.

Mrs. Higdon started reaching for one of the neatly organized tea cups on the window sill and the nurse rushed around, grabbing the cup up quickly before she poured tea for both of us. Mrs. Higdon huffed, giving the nurse a perturbed side-eyed glare.

"Mister Hicks is part of the U.S. Marshal's office."

"Oh?" Mrs. Higdon looked back to me, her eyes wide with surprise that almost instantly turned to a look of stern tenacity. "I told the officers then, Charlie didn't do it. Those government men that kept harrassing us staged everything."

I blinked, confused about what she was talking about.

"I'm not even sure who Charlie is, Mrs. Higdon. I'm currently in the middle of an investigation. I'd like to ask you a few questions about your family if that's alright."

"Oh, yes. That is perfectly fine, young man, though I couldn't imagine what the US Marshals would want to know about my family."

The nurse tapped her on the arm. "I'll leave you two to it. Just holler if you need anything."

"Thank you, Meridith," Mrs. Higdon replied as the nurse turned and walked out of the room.

"Now, what is it that you would like to know, Mister Hicks?"

"I'd like you to tell me what you know about your grandmother and what happened at the family home on Lullwater road."

She froze in mid-sip and placed her cup back on the saucer with a shakey hand.

"Why would you want to know a thing like that?"

"Because I have interest in your family's history, ma'am. Specifically about the circumstances before each of their suicides."

Mrs. Higdon stared at me with a look of frightful concern. Her eyes reddened and began to glisten from the tears threatening to well up.

"Oh, I don't know why you'd want to talk about that. That horribile incident was so long ago, and I'd prefer to forget about it entierly." She picked up her lace edged napkin and dabbed at the corners of her eyes.

"Ma'am," I continued in the most calming, professional voice I could mister, "people's lives may depend on what you can tell me."

"I'd really rather not talk about that," she said matter-of-factly and sat back in her seat, crossing her arms.

It wasn't the first time I'd gone into something blind, but the more I knew, the better chance I had of dealing with this thing.

It could be anything from a ghost, imp, or even some sort of trickster god running amok and having fun. If she wouldn't talk, it was what it was.

Considering she looked like the most stubborn two year old, scrunched up with her arms wrapped around herself, I figured it was worth a shot in the dark to show her the clown.

Pulling out my phone I brought up the clearest picture I'd taken of the clown sitting on the box and showed it to her.

"Do you recognize this clown, ma'am?"

Her lower lip began to quiver, and almost immediately, several tears escaped, running down her cheeks.

"Oh, please, no. Please, put it away," she sobbed.

"Do you know what this is, ma'am?" I shut off the screen and tucked the phone back into my pocket.

If the old woman could have backpedaled out of her seat, I bet she would have. She was beyond scared. Something about that clown doll had her absolutely terrified.

"Ma'am," I said, leaning forward, placing my hand on her arm. "I think this clown doll might have something to do with the current murders going on around Druid Hills."

That's when the dam burst and tears poured down her cheeks.

"Mrs. Higdon, if you can tell me anything at all," I pleaded.

Covered her mouth, she nodded through a muted sobbing wail.

Slowly she pulled herself together, taking slower and slower breaths.

"Yes…" she reluctantly let out, fighting back another bout of sobs.

"That was my great aunt's doll."

"Your great aunt?"

"Guinevere, my grandmother's sister."

"Did Guinevere die during the Spanish flu epidemic?"

Mrs. Higdon nodded, then reached out for her cup of tea and slammed the drink down in one gulp before she stood and shuffled towards the nearby cupboard.

"I believe I need something a little bit stronger," she mumbled to herself and retrieved an ornate crystal decanter full of a thick, ruby red liquid.

Returning to her seat, she poured her cup full and slammed it back as fast as any practiced bar fly I'd ever met.

"Would you care for a snoot full?" she asked before pouring herself another cup full.

I was starting to get the feeling the old broad had lived a wilder life than the woman of privilege she was.

"I'm not normally the drinking type," she continued, her voice hoarse and raspy from crying, "but on occasion it is warranted. And at the moment, I need something to calm the nerves a bit."

"Normally I would, ma'am, but considering I'm on duty at the moment…"

"Oh, poppycock. Act like you have a pair, son." She tossed my cup of tea out the open window, poured the cup full from the decanter and tapped her cup against mine.

"I've drank bigger men than you under the table. Drink up, sonny." She turned the cup up once more, draining it dry.

Reluctantly I picked up the cup, saluted her and downed the contents. The sickly sweet burst of cherry reminded me of cough syrup as the thick viscous liquid coated my throat. The vapors stole my breath, burning my sinuses. I coughed, fighting back the urge to spit out the strong liqueur.

"Good, isn't it?" The old woman closed her eyes and smiled wide as if bathed in a flood of memories. "It's like a velvety cherry kiss. Oh, how I miss my days abroad in Copenhagen." Quietly she chuckled and let out a self-soothing hum.

Catching my breath, I set down the cup that she promptly refilled, wiped my eyes, and tried to get us back on topic.

"Anything you could tell me would be of great importance, Mrs. Higdon."

"As I said before, that doll belonged to my great aunt, and those events happened well before I was born. All I can really tell you about the doll is what was told to me by my mother before she took her own life. My own experience was very very brief," she said with a shuddered breath, "and I fear I may have been the cause of her death." The old woman wrung her hands, fighting with the long abandoned memories flooding back.

"That's alright, ma'am. Any information is better than what I have right now."

Taking a deep breath, Mrs. Higdon visibly braced her resolve and continued. "My aunt Guinevere became ill and passed away shortly after. Grief stricken, my grandmother reached out to soothsayers, mystics, and clairvoyants of the time, hoping to contact my sister."

She paused a moment, taking a light sip of the cherry liquor before continuing.

"Now, mind you, my grandmother was a good Christian woman who wouldn't have had anything to do with the occult otherwise. My family has always been good Christians, but she was desperate, you see." She took another long sip, fortifying her nerves.

"At some point, my grandmother had begun hosting seances with these people, at my grandfather's protest, of course. And sometime after that began, my grandfather was found murdered.

"Now, mind you, I wasn't even a glimmer in my mother's eye at this point. I wasn't born until several years later.

"When I was very young, I loved to explore," she said with a joyful laugh. "To a small child, that house was immense, and the adventures I could have with my dolls were endless. But after I found that doll..." she said, pointing toward the phone in my pocket, the look on her face had suddenly shifted to a dead cold serious glare.

"My mother told me what she'd seen, after I found that damned doll... and things began happening." Mrs. Higdon started to dryly swallow, then took another sip before continuing.

"Mother was supposed to have been in bed, but instead she had snuck downstairs and hid away outside the parlor so she could watch the adults. She said she'd never seen my grandmother's special guest before. Said the woman looked like a gypsy. That night they held a seance to summon the spirit of my aunt, but instead they freed something else entirely."

She took a moment to breath and stare out the window, discomfort of something showing on her face.

"They had used my aunt's doll as a point of reference, something that she'd loved to connect her to this plane. At first, the voice sounded soft and child-like, then things started happening. Other voices, dark voices began shouting, things flew about the room and my mother swore that she saw the clown doll stand on its own and walk around the table, speaking to each person present.

"She didn't know what they had summoned, but it was not the spirit of my Aunt Guinevere. It was something else entirely. Something dark. Something evil."

The old woman paused again, blankly staring off into the distance.

"Mrs. Higdon?"

Slowly, she turned her attention back to me, her eyes red and puffy.

"Eventually, servants and others began to turn up missing. After my grandfather's death, my grandmother summoned the gypsy woman who had carried out the seance to bind the doll and seal it away."

She turned away once again. Gooseflesh prickled across her arms. "On one of my adventures about the grounds, I found the box they'd used to seal away the doll. I should have known better than to go snooping where I shouldn't, but it seemed to call to me. Begged me… Even tucked away as it was, that *thing* still held great power."

"Where was the box kept?" I softly asked. She let out a nervous chuckle.

"It was locked away in a large steamer chest, hidden in a dark corner of the attic. But to a resourceful young explorer," she said, emphasizing the word with a finger in the air, "it wasn't hard to find the key to the treasure." She cocked her head to the side and flashed a knowing smile, then poured another cupful for both of us.

"What happened when you found the box?"

"It showed up."

"It?"

"The clown. Not the doll mind you, but a clown the size of a full grown man. It began haunting my nightmares. Eventually my mother sent me away to a facility to help me *deal* with my, *condition*, but I already knew what I was seeing was real."

At this point, it really sounded like a deamon or demon had slipped through during the seance and possessed the doll. Without knowing for sure which it was or how to destroy it, my best bet was to contain and store the damned thing so the public was safe and I could properly dispose of it.

"I'm sorry to hear that, Mrs. Higdon. How long were you in there?"

"Only a few months. It wasn't terribly horrible. The food was horrid, but otherwise it was just another life experience. Shortly afterward, my mother took her own life."

Before the day got away from me and the sun set, I really needed to get back to Drew's to lock down that doll. In a perfect world, I could toss the clown doll into the box and call it a day, but the fates liked to laugh at me way too much to let it be that easy. The more time I had, the better.

"I believe I know what I need to do now. Thank you. I really appreciate you taking the time to speak with me, ma'am." I finished my drink then stood.

Not the smartest of ideas. I didn't know what the ABV of the cherry liqueur was, but it must have been equal to racing fuel. My head started to spin as soon as I'd moved. I might have to sit in the parking lot for a little while before leaving, but I'd at least be out of her hair. I extended my hand to shake hers.

She gave me a questionable nod, but still took my hand. "You're very welcome, Mister Hicks. You're more than welcome to come visit me anytime you like," she said, batting her eyes at me.

Apparently, it had kicked in for her, too. Her face glowed a nice shade of rosey pink.

"I might just do that, ma'am." I smiled and hurried out of the room. I was not opposed to a good time, but GMILF level of fun was not on my list.

And all in all, it was kind of a useless visit, but she at least managed to confirm what I was thinking. On my way out the door, I called Mandy to give her a heads up to confirm my plan. Sure enough, without the aid of a priest, my best bet was to try and re-contain the doll and transport it to Caleb's farm for storage.

By the time I made it across town through the wonder that was Atlanta traffic, the sun had already begun dipping below the treeline.

"Drew! Morgana," I shouted as I entered through the back door into the kitchen. No one answered.

"It might be a good thing if they aren't here," I mumbled under my breath, continuing into the living room. "Anyone home?" Muffled screams answered me from above.

Quickly turning I looked up to find both Drew and Morgana suspended by rope from one of the large wood beam rafters above, both of them bound and gaged with a duct tape job any flightline maintainer would be proud of.

"What the hell?"

Motion at the edge of my vision caught my attention. Something small was hiding at the end of the couch. By the time I'd turned, it was gone.

"Please tell me you guys have a cat," I said over my shoulder, drawing my revolver from the holster at the pit of my back.

I scanned the room, gun at the ready, risking a quick glance toward the fireplace. The doll was gone.

"Fuck me."

Drew and Morgana simultaneously let out muffled screams, then I caught the blur of something small and white moving out of the corner of my eye. Jumping to the side I brought my revolver around and fired.

Ceramic shards from a table lamp exploded.

"Sorry! I'll pay for that."

Again, at the edge of my vision, the blur scuttled to my left across the hearth of the fireplace with an evil, child-like giggle. I spun and fired again, the round ricocheting off the stone fireplace.

"Stand your Bozo ass still!"

"Fast as fast can be," it said, laughing.

Again, it darted behind a large antique hutch in the far corner of the room. Slowly, I made my way toward the hutch, keeping my weapon aimed. The hutch sat all the way back against the wall and had a piece of bottom trim all the way around. There wasn't any physical way the doll could have gotten under or behind it. But then again, this thing wasn't exactly normal either.

"Come out, come out, wherever you are," I sang, then tapped the corner of the hutch with the toe of my boot. "Come on out, little guy. I promise I won't hurt you…much," I said under my breath. Carefully reaching for the handle on one of the doors, a hot panting breath suddenly raced down the back of my neck.

Before I could spin on my heels I suddenly felt the literal weight of the world lift away as I soared across the room, crashing into a set of shelves on the opposite side of the room that immediately sent an avalanche of books falling on my head.

"You're mine…you're mine…you're mine," it whispered from all around me in that creepy, evil voice.

A high-pitched screech buffeted my eardrums. Pain, unlike anything I'd ever felt, seared through my mind. My eyeballs felt like they were trying to vibrate themselves out of their sockets.

Dropping my gun, I covered my ears to block the sound, hurrying back to my feet, ready to retreat and regroup.

The moment the sound stopped, I opened my eyes… that was a fucking mistake.

The demon clown loomed over me in the high ceiling room, viscous dark drool oozing from it's twisted maw. Sharp, fang-like teeth protruding from its cracked, leathery lips. The low light glow of the massive salt water tank making the thing look even more demonic and evil.

I let out a loud barking chuckle as an idea struck me, and pulled my flask of holy water from the inside pocket of my kutte.

"Ya know, if it's green and drippy, you should really go see a doctor. They have meds for that sort of thing."

Quickly, I unscrewed the flask and dropped it into the top of the tank. Standing on tiptoes, I dipped my fingers in, then quietly recited the evangelical version of the Lord's Prayer.

"The Lord bless you and keep you; the Lord make his face shine upon you and be gracious to you; the Lord turn his face toward you and give you peace."

The demon clown roared, lunging at me.

I tucked and rolled to the side, grabbing my revolver, narrowly missing the clown's grotesquely disfigured and clawed hands. Rolling to my feet I dropped to a knee and aimed for the tank.

"Surfs up, ya damn dirty clown!"

I emptied the remaining .357 hollow point rounds from the revolver into the side of the fish tank. The thick laminated glass spiderwebbed and instantaneously shattered in an explosion of glass and colorful sealife. The ensuing wave of salt water engulfed the clown, forcing it to the ground.

Instantly, I grabbed the stainless crucifix from my pocket and leapt over the couch, landing on top of the thing. I planted the crucifix into the back of the demon clown's head and began reciting the Lord's Prayer again.

It went rigid under me, like its entire body had seized, and I'm not one to look a gift horse in the mouth. Drawing my belt knife, I cut open the clown costume and began carving my grandmother's protection sigil into the skin at the top of its shoulders while it was still paralyzed.

The blessed silver coated Old Timer cut like a hot knife though butter, its enchantment searing the demons flesh in the process.

Crying out in pain, it gasped, its muscles rippling uncontrollably like I'd just hit it with a taser. Wind roared through the room from out of no where, lights flickered out and a darkness engulfed the room. The demon's cries became a frantic cacophony amid the roaring chorus of voices.

Then nothing.

Ringing tinnitus suddenly filled my ears in the eerie silence, and the lights about the room flickered back to life.

Looking down, I found the clown doll lying on the floor beneath me, face down, the back of its costume cut open and exposed dirty brown stuffing threatened to escape. Gingerly I picked up the doll like a sick kitten and made my way over to the fireplace, where I placed the doll and the other items back into the box, secured the chain as best as I could for now and quickly carved the protection sigil into the aged wood.

"Hopefully, that'll do for now. I'm sure Drew has a lock I can borrow." I froze. "Shit, Drew." Turning, I looked up to find both Drew and Morgana still attached, hanging high above, both frantically struggling against their bonds.

Considering how high up they were hanging, I wasn't sure how I'd get them down, but they were alive and unharmed…mostly. Nothing about this gig was easy to handle mentally, and I was sure they'd both probably need a bit of therapy after this. But first, I needed to get them down and probably get a stiff drink into them.

Moving so both of them could see me, I crossed my arms and smiled. "Ya know, I'm going to have to come visit more often, Drew. It's great just *hanging around* with y'all." I don't think he liked that so much, considering the muffled curses coming from his duct-taped mouth.

"Um…You don't happen to have a ladder, do you?"

The End.

We hope that you enjoyed this title and look forward to many more to come. Please, leave us a review! Reviews matter to all of our authors.

And don't forget to check out the latest edition of **Car Wars**

http://www.sjgames.com/car-wars/

Or the other amazing titles from
Steve Jackson Games

http://www.sjgames.com

…or the latest in the Car Warriors: Autoduel Chronicle fiction series.
https://threeravenspublishing.com/car-warriors-autoduel-chronicles/

Take a look at some of our other award-winning series at
https://threeravenspublishing.com/series-universes/

Visit us at https://www.threeravenspublishing.com and sign up for our
newsletter for the latest and greatest news on upcoming titles and events.

Other series and titles you might enjoy.

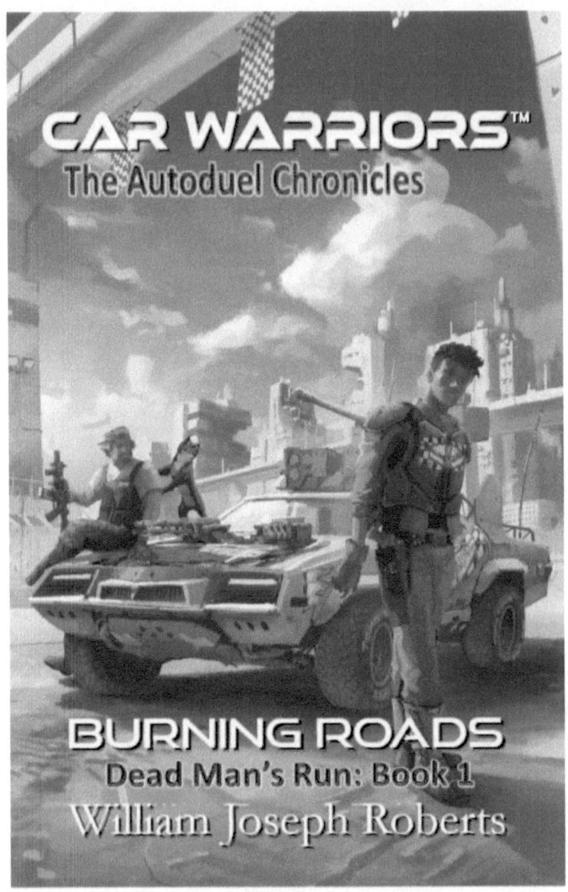

AVAILABLE ON AMAZON
JOINT TASK FORCE
13
HOLDING THE LINE
BETWEEN HEAVEN AND HELL

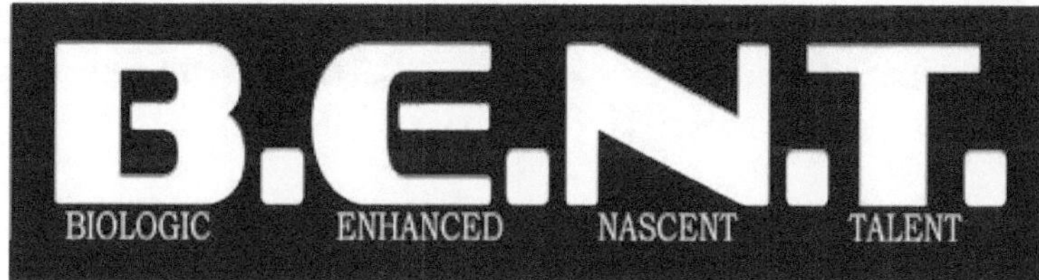

B.E.N.T.
BIOLOGIC   ENHANCED   NASCENT   TALENT

STARFLIGHT

IT CAME FROM THE
TRAILER PARK

You can also keep up to date with our latest release announcements on Scifi.radio and get some of the best fandom programing on the planet.

Scifi for your Wifi

And don't forget to check out our other Sponsors and Affiliates

Revolution X is a testament to the power of collaboration, blending four unique styles into a cohesive, revolutionary sound. When these four individuals unite, the result is nothing short of musical Revolution!

Would you like to learn how to write and market your own titles? The following affiliates links might be helpful.

A southern Appalachian jewel for craft beer lovers, Buck Bald Brewing offers something for everyone. With delicious, locally brewed beverages from across the spectrum, Buck Bald Brewing offers craft brews that are consistently amazing.

From the dark and smooth Shesquatch Scottish ale, to the intense hops of Hippibilly IPA, to the puckering sour of the blackberry and cinnamon in Berry My Heart at the Trailer Park, and more than 60+ rotating brews, you'll find what you're looking for and more.

With smiling faces behind the bar ready to help you find your next favorite brew, a constantly rotating selection of delicious craft beverages, toe-tapping tunes always playing, and the biggest games on TV, you can kick your feet up in either Copperhill, Tennessee or Murphy, North Carolina and immerse yourself in the Buck Bald Brewing experience. So, come out, fill a pint, fill a growler, and fill your mind at your new favorite family-owned craft brewery.

To discover more visit us at buckbaldbrewing.com or follow us on Facebook @buckbaldbrewing and @buckbaldbrewingmurphy.

Vesper Wren's
TRAILER PARK
PIXIE
PUNCH
· A PEACH STRAWBERRY SELTZER ·
BUCK BALD BREWING

BRAXTON HICKS
MIDNIGHT MOCHA MILK
STOUT
BUCK BALD BREWING

Peanut Butter Paws
Peanut Butter
CHOCOLATE
STOUT
BUCK BALD BREWING
BUCK BALD BREWING